a BRIDGE *unbroken*

A MILLER'S CREEK NOVEL

Book Five

CATHY BRYANT

East Baton Rouge Parish Library
Baton Rouge, Louisiana

WordVessel Press

Books by Cathy Bryant

MILLER'S CREEK NOVELS
Texas Roads
A Path Less Traveled
The Way of Grace
Pilgrimage of Promise
A Bridge Unbroken

❖ ❖ ❖

A Bridge Unbroken
© Cathy Bryant, 2014

 Published by WordVessel Press
Santa Fe, New Mexico

All rights reserved.
This novel is a work of fiction. Names, characters, places, and incidents are either the product of the author's imagination or are used fictitiously.
ISBN: 0-9844311-8-7
ISBN-13: 978-0-9844311-8-2

What Readers Are Saying

TEXAS ROADS

"Very good story with great characters and plot. A good lesson in following the path that you were meant to follow. I look forward to reading more of the Miller's Creek series." ~Amazon Reviewer

"Uplifting book, easy to read, engaging. Cathy Bryant is an excellent author. Her love and faith in God is evident in every word she writes." ~Amazon Reviewer

A PATH LESS TRAVELED

"I 'stumbled' across this book for free in the e-book section. I know I 'found' it for a reason. If anyone is looking for the path to God, this is a very important book. I found it very profound in exactly what I need at this time. Trust in God. That's all you need. I can't describe the way I feel about finding this book at this time in my life. What I really enjoyed is that it is a work of fiction, not someone telling me how to do what I need to do." ~Amazon Reviewer

"How often we miss God's perfect plan by following our own. Well written and so refreshing to read a great novel showing God's amazing grace and faithfulness." ~Amazon Reviewer

THE WAY OF GRACE

"This is the first Cathy Bryant book I've read, and I was caught up in it from start to finish.... Cathy Bryant is a fine Christian writer, and I can't wait to read her other books." ~Amazon Reviewer

"The Way Of Grace is a beautiful story of showing mercy and grace as Christ did. A few unexpected turns and keeps you wanting to read on. I Love this series of novels. Can't wait for the next one." ~Amazon Reviewer

"Cathy has done it again! Her books just keep getting better. With an air of mystery, this book grabs and holds the reader's attention from the start. Rather than just a 'predictable' book, the story takes some unexpected twists and turns. It's not just a 'happily ever after' book; instead, the reader encounters a story of danger, courage, life-changing choices, love, and the amazing grace of God." ~Amazon Reviewer

PILGRIMAGE OF PROMISE

"Though I have not read the earlier books in the series it did not take away at all from the story, which was engaging, humorous at times, and impeccably well done. Bryant has some really great talent and knowledge, something that is very obvious in her writing and characters. It was really hard to quit reading!" ~Amazon Reviewer

"For me, Pilgrimage of Promise was Karen Kingsbury meets Nicholas Sparks." ~Amazon Reviewer

"Another great read! I just cannot put these books down once I start them. The blessing of a great story in combination with being reminded of a spiritual truth is time well spent." ~Amazon Reviewer

To my lovely daughter-in-law, Megan.
You are the daughter of my prayers. Thank you for being
a wonderful wife to my son, a loving mother to my
grandchildren,
and an amazing addition to our family. But more
importantly,
thank you for living your life for the Lord.

*Be kind to one another, tender-hearted,
forgiving each other,
just as God in Christ also has forgiven you.*
~Ephesians 4:32

Special Thanks

Every author will tell you that birthing a book is not a solitary effort, but the effort of many to make the story all that it can be. I couldn't agree more. Here are just a few examples, since there could never be enough space to personally thank everyone.

To my readers: You all will never know how much your encouragement means to me. Whether on the Facebook author page or the Miller's Creek Reader's group or in a personal e-mail, you push away my insecurities and doubts with your kind words. Please know that I pray for you often!

To the Miller's Creek Main Street Team and beta readers/editors: Only God could have ordained these two groups. He knew how much I would need your help. I couldn't dream of a better team of people as my support group. A mere word of thanks seems woefully inadequate.

To my family: How did this country gal get so blessed in the family department? Your love and support give me wings. Thank you all, and thank the Lord for the unparalleled blessings you bring to my life.

To my baby sister, Tessie Mayo, for her keen eye in the photography department. Her talent provided the perfect cover for this story on forgiveness, best demonstrated in the bridge God built for all of us through Christ. Love you, sis!

Last, yet first, I give praise, thanksgiving, honor, and glory to my Lord and Savior Jesus Christ. His forgiveness makes life possible. Oh, Lord, may I be quick to forgive others the way You've forgiven me!

Chapter One

Heart thumping wildly, Dakota peered out the peephole at the figure of a man obscured by the semi-darkness of early morning.

"Just peachy." She kept her voice to a hushed whisper in the small and dingy apartment she'd called home for the past few months. What now? No longer secure, her downtown San Antonio getaway had obviously been compromised. But calling the cops wouldn't work--a lesson she'd learned the hard way with scars as evidence. No, Kane had friends in high places.

Lord, help me. She inhaled sharply and backed away from the flimsy front door, willing her heart to slow its frantic pace. *Calm down, Dakota. You've prepared for this scenario.* Emergency backpack? Check. In its usual place by the window that led to the fire escape. Now to gather her bedding, meager food rations, and laptop. At least she was already dressed. Another lesson she'd learned in a life on the run.

A sharp knock sounded.

"Sorry, buster. I'm not falling for that trick." Especially at this hour of the morning. Her neighbors partied until 3 a.m. and slept until noon. Whoever banged on her door at this ungodly hour wasn't a neighbor or friend.

She sped to her bed in one corner of the room and rolled up her bedding. Less than a minute later she returned to the escape window, her computer bag slung over one shoulder. With nimble fingers, Dakota snapped the sleeping bag onto the backpack latches and strapped the drawstring trash bag that housed her food to a dangling carabiner clip.

The polite knock on the door now erupted into a persistent pounding.

Her pounding pulse responded in kind. Dakota struggled to lift the old window, finally able to raise it high enough to crawl through the narrow opening. A shiver rattled her body at the cold blast of autumn wind whistling between the tall brick buildings. She yanked her overstuffed backpack through the opening and hoisted it to her back. The weight almost pulled her backwards. Why hadn't she thought to practice her escape with the heavy backpack in tow? She pushed against the outside of the window with every ounce of her strength. It screeched its objection, but finally clattered into place. Hopefully the closed window would buy extra time.

A hefty body thudded against the front door. With that kind of force it wouldn't hold long.

She froze, her breathing shallow. Another thud against the door. *Move it, Dakota!* She flew down the rusty stairs, aware of the clanging sound of her boots against the metal, but powerless to soften her steps. At the first floor landing, she stopped abruptly and yanked on the ladder to access the alley. Frozen in place by rust and years of disuse, it didn't budge. She pushed again with a guttural grunt. Nothing.

"Great." Her brain sped into overdrive. What good was a fire escape if you couldn't escape? Lips clenched, she searched the area for any reason to hope. To the left of the landing a gutter pipe inched to the ground, but would it hold her weight?

A screech raised her eyes to the apartment window five floors above, and she flattened herself against the cold brick of the building. A hooded head peered out, barely visible in the pre-dawn light, then a stocky figure climbed from the opening.

"Busted." Her heart tapped out a ferocious dance against her ribs. This guy meant business.

Praying the gutter would do the trick, Dakota scrambled over the rail and grabbed hold of the ice-cold pipe. The metal strap holding the gutter in place pulled precariously away from the grimy brick wall, exposing rusty nails.

"Don't you dare let go," she commanded under her breath. Determined, she clamped her bottom lip between her teeth, her gaze on the strap as she shimmied to the ground. Once her boots hit the asphalt alleyway, she raced toward her pickup, the sound of heavy steps pounding the fire escape behind her.

Lungs exploding, Dakota neared the truck, unbuckled clips, and yanked off her pack. She glanced back just long enough to see the quickly-approaching figure, then tossed the backpack to the far side of the pickup's cab and jumped in. The man drew closer--close enough to note the black hoodie he wore, but not enough to make out the shadowy face beneath. Definitely not Kane--too short and too stocky--but most likely one of his many hired goons.

Overwhelming panic erupted in her gut, blazing a fiery trail to her stomach. With fumbling fingers, she inserted the key in the ignition. *Please start.* The pickup roared to life on the first try. Just as the man reached her bumper, she threw the truck into gear and shot out into the street. In the rearview mirror, the guy slowed his steps and stared after her a brief moment before he turned and ran in the opposite direction. Probably going after his vehicle.

Her spirit deflated, whooshing air from her puffed-out cheeks. This chase wasn't over. Not by a long shot.

Dakota pressed the accelerator. "Well, Miller's Creek it is." The decision made for her. With San Antonio no longer a safe option, her deceased grandparent's farmhouse made the most sense. J. C.'s late call last night couldn't have come at a more opportune time, God's guiding hand once more on her shoulder.

Only when she merged into the thickening morning commute traffic on Interstate 35 a few minutes later did Dakota semi-relax. She twisted her neck from side to side to release tension from her neck and shoulders, still trying to wrap her brain around returning to Miller's Creek. The only problem with Mawmaw and Pawpaw's farm was the possibility of facing Chance again. Could she withstand the magnetic pull he'd always exerted over her heart? Even more importantly, could she handle the guilt and blame he'd most certainly place on her?

An ache landed in her chest. If only things had turned out differently between them. Dakota gave her red curls a shake to dislodge unwanted thoughts and emotions from her system. "Didn't you suffer enough the first time, Dakota?" She checked her rearview mirror as a black car moved in behind her. "Nope. I'm through with all men, including Chance Johnson." Her palms pounded the steering wheel to punctuate the self-serving promise. J. C. hadn't mentioned his grandson. Hopefully Chance had moved on somewhere else.

Dakota flipped on her blinker and changed lanes. The black car followed, right on her bumper. A frown pulled her forehead tight. The guy could at least stay far enough back for her to see his license plate.

Uneasiness skittered down her spine. Had the guy in the black hoodie caught up to her? Even in all this traffic?

"Chase back on." She floored the gas pedal and swerved around the car in front, the black car tailing her every move. Dakota drove as fast as she dared down the interstate's thick traffic through San Marcos and New Braunfels, the black car never far behind. Finally, out of desperation, she decided to detour around downtown Austin, through a suburban neighborhood, and then down a little farm-to-market road. She checked the mirror. A tiny black speck topped the hill behind her and grew steadily closer.

Not again. "Kane must be paying you a hefty sum, Mister."

Once more Dakota punched the accelerator. "C'mon, old truck. You can do this." Her clunker's motor sputtered for a moment and then shot forward. She squinted her eyes against the brightening Texas day. It wouldn't do any good to get away from this guy if she got stopped for speeding, nor would it help if he tailed her all the way to Miller's Creek.

For the rest of the day she zigzagged across central Texas, doing her best to give no rhyme or reason to her travel pattern, only stopping when she needed gas.

A little after nine p.m., the car's bright headlights disappeared behind a lengthy train at a crossing in some small nameless town that looked like all the others. Finally she'd caught a break. Rather than continue her trek, Dakota whipped the pickup into a dark parking lot of a towing company. Her jalopy fit right in with the other wrecked and disabled cars. The chain-link fence and tall stacks of tires provided further camouflage.

She waited well over an hour and used part of the time to call J.C. to let him know she was on her way. Then convinced she'd finally lost her pursuer, Dakota resumed the trip to Miller's Creek, suddenly eager to start her new life in the one place that had always felt like home.

The repetitive beep of the alarm clock roused Chance to a sitting position. His fingers danced around the top of the bedside table until they landed on the alarm clock and brought a halt to the beeps. After a few blinks, his eyes adjusted to the darkness, but not to the lack of sleep. Would his body ever get used to the work schedule at the hospital? Not that he was complaining. For the first time in forever, he was finally moving forward and leaving the painful past behind.

Chance drug a hand across his stubbly chin and rolled out of bed with a groan. Who had called Grampa's house at such a late hour last night and disturbed his precious sleep? Whoever it was needed a few lessons on appropriate times to make a phone call.

He stumbled to the hall bathroom and washed his face, then headed to the kitchen to start a pot of coffee. Normally he didn't drink the stuff, but since starting work at Miller's Creek new hospital, his body craved it like his lungs craved air. Once the caffeine kicked in, he'd read his Bible, grab a quick workout, check on his grandfather, and eat a piece of fruit on the way to work, the familiar routine somehow comforting.

The coffee pot had barely started its cacophony of gurgles and hisses when the wooden floors creaked behind him. He glanced over his shoulder to see his grandfather, his IV pole in tow. "You're up awful early."

Grampa's gentle smile lit the eyes so much like his own. "Only 'cause of all that racket you're making." Then without warning, Grampa's smile faded, and he reached for the old chrome and yellow dining table.

In two steps Chance was at his grandfather's side and helped him sit. "You okay?"

The old man nodded weakly. "Yep. Just one of those dizzy spells."

Chance's chest tightened. If only the nursing skills he'd acquired over the past few years could reverse the aging progress and his grandfather's quickly-failing health. He placed a hand on Grampa's back and gazed down at him. "Sure you're okay? Need anything?"

Grampa waved a hand in front of his face as though swatting a pesky fly. "Aaah, nothing a few hours of sleep won't cure. Sleep I'll get as soon as you quit making such a ruckus."

Chance chuckled and moved to the cabinets. "Wanna cup?"

"Sure."

He poured two cups of the dark, fragrant liquid and made his way to the table, a steaming cup in each hand. "Who called so late last night?"

An ornery look crossed Grampa's features, but he said nothing. Instead he pursed his lips and blew on the coffee, then brought the cup to his lips.

Chance took a seat across from him. "You got a lady friend you're hiding from me?"

"Hmph." His grandfather followed the grunt with a snort. "Never had any plan on replacing your sweet Grandma. The only woman I ever loved."

Longing swirled around his heart and pulled tight. Would he ever experience that kind of love again?

"Besides," his grandfather's voice softened, "you're the one who needs a lady friend."

Chance lowered his head, took a quick sip, and sat his cup down with a little more force than intended. "Don't have time."

"Then make time."

Really? Were they going to have this discussion again? "C'mon, Grampa, cut it out. With a face like this no girl my age is interested in anything other than friendship."

"Hogwash." His grandfather's typical smile disappeared. "You just need to quit feeling sorry for yourself and get out there and start living."

"And just when do you suggest I do that, huh? I work twelve-hour shifts, and then come home to help you." As soon as the words flew from his lips, he wished them back in his mouth. Chance shook his head. "Sorry. Shouldn't have said that."

Grampa's shoulders slumped. "It's the truth. Sorry to be such a bother. If you want me to hire somebo—"

"No way." When he moved here for nursing school, his plan had been to take care of Grampa, pay off student loans, and hopefully one day re-open the family drugstore. He was right on track, even though the hours were long and hard at the moment. Chance looked his grandfather straight in the eye. "I'm here because I want to be. One day I'll have the opportunity to get out there and start living, as you put it. But right now, I'm doing exactly what I'm supposed to do, and wouldn't have it any other way."

Grampa turned his head away quickly, but not quick enough to hide the tears welling in his eyes. A sniffle sounded. "I need you to do me a favor."

"Not a problem."

"And I need you to do it before you go to work."

Chance eyed the old kitchen clock, which sported a knife, spoon, and fork for hands. Just now 5:30 a.m. He should still have time to follow his routine, shower, and have enough time to run a quick errand before his shift started at seven. "Also not a problem. What is it?"

"I want you to run out to Levi's farm."

"What on earth for?"

"Just wanna make sure the place is secure. With the weather turning cooler, we might have some unsavory characters trying to camp out there over the winter." Grampa's jaw clamped in a stubborn pose.

"And why can't I do it after work?"

"Dagnab it, boy. Will you just do what I ask?"

Chance's eyebrows jumped up his scalp. Never had he seen his grandfather so testy. Was he really so bothered by possible vagrants, or was something else at play? "Okay."

His grandfather stood in one liquid motion, and almost knocked his chair over in the process. He swiveled around and tottered from the room, mumbling under his breath. What aliens had abducted his kind and gentle grandfather? And what crotchety old grump had they left in his place?

At 6 a.m. on the dot, Chance hurriedly backed his Ford 150 out of the driveway and headed toward the late Levi Kelly's farm. Frustration headed the list of a myriad of emotions colliding within. To fulfill his grandfather's strange request, he'd showered without reading his Bible or his workout, without taking the time to finish his one lousy cup of coffee. In addition, there was no fruit in the house, which meant Grampa had finished off the bananas and forgotten to write them down on the grocery list.

He rubbed the nape of his neck. But the one thing that bothered him most, like a hidden undercurrent beneath it all, was a crippling fear. Fear that being on the farm would resurrect memories he'd worked long and hard to forget.

The sky took on pale purple hues as he headed south on the farm-to-market road which led to the dirt road where the old farmhouse stood. As much as he tried to put Amy out of his mind on this foggy fall morning, he could not. Instead, thoughts of her elbowed their way to the forefront of his memory--her perfect smile, curly blond hair, infectious laugh, and flirtatious emerald eyes. Why were the memories as vivid as though they'd happened only yesterday?

He gritted his teeth and gunned the motor as familiar questions returned. Why had she left so suddenly? He played over the events of their last night together. How the evening ended was her fault, not his. But the resulting heartache was due to his own poor judgment. That's what he got for falling for a girl of questionable character.

Chance reached the turn-off and slowed his speed to make the turn onto the seldom-traveled bumpy dirt road. As expected, the washboard-like road rattled his new truck and threw up a cloud of chalk-white dust behind him.

Great. Add washing the truck to his grievance list.

A few minutes later he pulled onto the private road that stretched over rolling hills until it came to rest behind a grove of pecan trees. Right beyond the pecan orchard sat the two-story farmhouse, secluded enough that only those who knew it existed could find it. And a mile past that the creek and old bridge where...

He rounded the final corner, so over grown it no longer seemed familiar, and his jaw dropped. The old house, once a beautiful yellow among a forest of green, was sorely in need of a paint job, raw wood exposed, bleached gray by the hot Texas sun. No lights shone from the windows, but a rusty old jalopy of a truck sat out front. Grampa had been right after all.

Chance pulled his pickup as close as he dared and killed the engine, his eyes trained on the house for even a flicker of movement.

Nothing.

Gravel crunched beneath his boots, the only sound in the mostly dark morning. He made his way all the way around the house to look for any sign of the intruder. Quietly, he climbed the steps to the front porch, weathered wood sagging beneath his weight. Add new decking to the much-needed paint job for the old house. Chance paused at the front door, his ears strained for any sound within the old house.

Suddenly from behind, the distinctive sound of a shotgun being pumped reached his ears, made louder by the quiet of the countryside.

Heart in throat, he instinctively raised his hands. But before he could speak, a female voice sounded, a voice he never expected to hear again.

"I don't know who you are, Mister, but you're about two seconds shy of getting your backside loaded with buckshot."

Chapter Two

Dakota's pulse roared in her ears. Really? Her first twenty-four hours back at the farm, and already she had a gun pulled on an intruder. But whatever she had to do to get him off the property and keep him off. She took a step back, the shotgun still trained in the general direction. It had been pure luck when she'd located Pawpaw's shotgun in his secret hiding place after all these years. Hopefully the intruder wouldn't figure out she'd never shot a gun before, and that she didn't even have ammo.

Her writer's imagination took over and imagined all sorts of terrible outcomes while she did all she could to keep from shaking—partly from the cold, partly from fear. Okay, it didn't help that she was barefoot in below-freezing weather.

The man raised both hands up and slowly turned around. "It's me, Amy."

Her mouth went dry. Now the trembling began in earnest, her worst fear realized. She'd known when she decided to come to Miller's Creek that she might run into him, she just didn't count on it being this soon. Dakota focused her attention on keeping her tone even and steady. "Hello, Chance."

"Mind pointing that shotgun elsewhere?" His face masked by darkness, his voice was flat and dry.

"Oh, sorry." Was he dressed in scrubs? She brought the gun to her side, careful to aim it away from her bare feet. How did one un-cock a shotgun? "I guess J.C. told you I was here?"

"You dyed your hair."

Actually she'd let it return to its natural color in keeping with her decision to run away from Kane, but that information didn't concern Chance. "There's no need to check up on me, especially at this hour. I'm fine."

"It's six o'clock in the morning. As I recall, you used to be an early riser."

True, but that was when she went to bed with the chickens during her summer stays, not after she'd spent fourteen hours in an old truck trying to evade Black Hoodie Man. Besides, without electricity it wasn't like she had anything else to do but sleep. Her teeth chattered in her head, and her tummy rumbled. "Well, I was up a little later than normal. Now if you'll be so kind as to leave, I'll go back to bed."

"Are you barefooted?"

Even in the dark she could imagine the scolding look on his face. He obviously still had the objectionable quality of judging others by his own high standards. Too bad those high standards applied to everyone else besides him.

"You are, aren't you?" He stepped closer, peering down at the ground. The lily-white skin of her feet glowed in the dark. "It's gotta be in the twenties out here. You'll get frostbite." Before she had time to react, he scooped her up in his arms. "Front door unlocked?"

"There isn't a working lock on the front door anymore." Which was why she'd moved every stick of furniture she could find to put behind it. "But it's—uh, blocked." Now if she could only put a block over her out-of-control thoughts and emotions.

Chance headed to the back door, soon gasping for air. "You've gained weight."

It was all she could do to bite her tongue. He'd learned a long time ago how to get under her skin, but she couldn't afford to let him get her riled. That was the surest way to start a raging wildfire with her Irish tongue, one where she blasted him for the way he'd treated her and told him exactly what his judgmental attitude had done to her. But the last thing she wanted or needed right now was for him to learn the truth.

They reached the back door of the old farmhouse, and he set her down on the bottom step. "Mind if I come in for a minute? I'd like to talk."

Something deep within her welcomed the idea, but she'd learned this lesson over and over again when it came to men. Other than Pawpaw and J.C., men just weren't trustworthy, and she wouldn't open herself up for any more heartbreak in her life, especially after she'd worked so hard to turn over a new leaf. "There's nothing to talk about. Thank you for your kindness in carrying me to the back door, but I'm a big girl now. What's in the past will stay there. Do I make myself clear?"

"Perfectly." Sarcasm oozed from his voice. "I see you still haven't forgiven me for whatever imagined wrong I committed against you."

Imagined!? "Forgiveness is a two-way street, Chance, but obviously you still haven't figured that out. Please leave."

"But I'll have a better day knowing you're safe out here all by yourself."

It was still too dark to see his face, but the tone of his voice painted a clear picture of his curled lip and accusing eyes. "I'm not afraid."

"Which explains why you pulled a shotgun on me."

Touché. "Really, Chance, go home." She turned to make her way up the rickety back steps. Without warning, one cracked and gave way and sent her spiraling toward the ground. The shotgun hit the ground right before she did and went off, the noisy blast echoing through the cold fall morning. It was loaded?

"Amy, are you all right?" Chance's voice held panic.

"I—I think so."

Strong arms wrapped around her and lifted her into the air before she could protest. Carefully, Chance made the step from the ground to the back door without putting a foot on the back steps. Once inside, he set her down on the dusty kitchen floor. "Where are the lights?"

"No lights without electricity." The leg that went through the wooden steps began to sting as though she had ants in her pants. Was she bleeding?

"What?" Now his voice held an angry edge. "You mean to tell me you're staying out here without electricity or heat?"

"I built a small fire in the wood stove."

"Oh, that's brilliant. Did it ever occur to you that the chimney might need to be cleaned before you built a fire? What if you died from carbon monoxide poisoning?"

The thought sobered her. She clearly hadn't thought things through. But staying in an old farmhouse was surely safer than spending the night at the side of the road.

"Stay here. I'll be right back." Chance left, slamming the back door behind him.

Dakota gingerly felt of her sore leg, her fingers immediately sticky. This wasn't good.

Chance returned with a flashlight and black bag and beamed the light on her bare feet and bloody leg. "Why didn't you tell me you were bleeding?"

"I didn't know for sure until I just felt it while you were gone. I'm sure it's just a scratch."

"Sit down and let me take a closer look at it."

No way would that happen. "Look, it's not that big a deal. Besides, you're an architect, not a doctor."

"Actually I'm a nurse."

"Yeah, right. Since when?"

"As a matter of fact, since May."

Well, that explained the scrubs. "But I thought—"

"People change, Amy. I've changed, as I'm certain you have. I made the call to become a nurse shortly after you left Miller's Creek." Fatigue lined his words. "Now sit down and let me look at that leg, or I'll make you sit down."

Anger flared, but she managed to keep it in check. She sat on the kitchen floor, amidst the dust and no telling what kind of insects and critters, and stuck her leg in front of the light. A large gash snaked down the inside of her lower calf, oozing blood. The sight made her woozy, so she leaned back against both hands and struggled to stop her spinning head. "Am I gonna need stitches?"

"Don't think so. I'll put a Steri-strip on it after I clean it up. That should do." His whole demeanor carried professional authority. "You had a tetanus shot in the last ten years?"

Had she? "Yes." What he didn't know wouldn't hurt him, and the sooner she got him out of here the better.

"Got any water?"

"Bottled."

An exasperated sigh escaped from him. "You *are* a crazy lady. Sometime you're gonna have to explain to me why you decided to stay out here without electricity or running water."

Maybe, and then again, maybe not. She opted not to respond.

"Where's the water?"

"Living room."

"I'll be right back." His footsteps echoed in the empty house. A few seconds later he returned. "You're sleeping on the cold, hard floor."

A statement, not a question. "The sleeping bag softens the blow."

"Not much." Chance knelt and poured water on the wound, then reached around for his bag. He opened it and withdrew a white bottle.

"Oh, no, you don't." She yanked her leg away from him.

"Amy, give me your leg."

"No alcohol."

"I have to make sure the wound is disinfected."

"Good grief, it's just a little scratch."

"A little scratch in a very dirty house. Now stick your leg back over here."

She ignored his command.

"Okay, two can play this game." He lowered himself to a sitting position, crossed his ankles, and drew his knees up under crossed arms. "I'll just stay here until you decide to follow my instructions."

Of all the obstinate, pig-headed people! "Oh, all right!" She extended her injured leg back his direction, intentionally kicking him in the process.

"Ow! Cut it out, Amy!" He groused the words as he opened the bottle. "Maybe you haven't changed as much I thought. Still have that Irish temper, I see." Chance drizzled alcohol on her leg.

"Ay-yi-yi!" She immediately lowered her head down and huffed out short bursts of air. Once the burning stopped, she peered up at him through narrowed eyes. "You actually enjoyed that, didn't you?"

"More than I expected." He followed the sarcastic words with a laugh.

She punched his arm with all the force she could muster. The flashlight clattered to the floor and spun around a few times before the beam landed on his face.

Her throat grew thick and lumpy, and a gasp fell from her opened mouth. Red spidery scars crisscrossed the left side of his face. "What happened?" Her entire being flooded with compassion, and she reached tentative fingers toward his face.

He flinched, his bluish-gray eyes surprisingly dark in spite of the light shining on his face, but said not a word. A muscle pulsed in his jaw. As her fingers made contact with his face, he grabbed her wrist and forced her hand away, his eyes searching hers. An agonizing groan growled from his throat and he jumped to his feet. Now his voice came in short, angry bursts. "I told you people change, Amy." He pointed to his face. "This is one way of many that I've changed since you decided to skip out on me." Without another word, he grabbed his bag and stomped out the back door, accentuating his angry words with a door slam.

Chance sped down the dirt road, not caring that the truck bounced all over the road because of the ruts, or that his once-shiny black pickup was now covered with powdery white dust. All he cared about was getting away from Amy as fast as he could. Obviously she'd been in contact with his grandfather, because she'd questioned whether J.C. had told him she was in town. His eyes narrowed, and his teeth clenched. The ghastly scenario that had just taken place had interfering-old-grandfather written all over it.

Chance pounded the steering wheel with his fist then immediately let off the gas pedal and tried to make sense of the gamut of emotions surging throughout his body. Why was he so angry? Was it because she'd seen his scars? Or was it the sympathy in her tone? Or could it be a sense of betrayal from his grandfather, who of all people should understand his desire to find someone to love him for who he was, not because they felt sorry for him?

The sky, now bathed in the myriad colors of dawn, captured his attention. He braked to a sudden stop in the middle of the road, immediately aware of the presence of God.

Oh, Lord, I thought I was over her. Help me know what to do. Help me get past all these painful feelings.

Forgive as you've been forgiven.

Forgive? But he'd already done that years ago. He'd picked up the pieces and moved on with his life. Hadn't he? Chance tried to answer the question in his heart and head, but the more he mulled it over, the more confused he felt. Obviously he needed some godly counsel, and someone different than his grandfather. Grampa was just too close to the situation. He loved Amy, too.

One glance at the clock let him know he at least had time to stop by Mama Beth's house on his way to work.

Five minutes later he pulled into the gravel driveway beside the pristine white picket fence. Once he moved to Miller's Creek fulltime to attend nursing school in Morganville, it hadn't taken long to discover the wisdom of the mother figure of the community. Though Mama Beth had lost her husband to cancer back in the spring, she was still a listening ear, a shoulder to cry on, and the dispenser of godly medicine. She'd surely be able to confirm his belief that he'd forgiven Amy a long time ago.

He hurried across the cobblestone walkway, up the immaculate steps and porch of the two-story Victorian house, and rapped on the screen door.

From inside, he could make out her shuffling footsteps and heard her call out: "Coming!" A second later the door opened, and her round face lit up like downtown Miller's Creek at Christmas. "Well, my goodness, you're the last person I expected to see this early in the morning, but I'm glad you're here. Come in, come in. How's J.C.?"

"He's been better. Dizzy spells are getting worse, so please keep him in your prayers."

"Always."

Chance smiled. In addition to be the wise lady everyone in town turned to for advice, she was known about town as a prayer warrior. "Hope I'm not disturbing you, Mama Beth. Only have a few minutes before I have to be at work, but I could use some of your wisdom this morning." The smell of bacon, eggs, and homemade biscuits drifted to his nose, setting off rumbles in his stomach.

"Well, it's not exactly my wisdom. Any smidgen I have comes from God, but I'm always happy to help however I can." She bustled toward the kitchen, motioning for him to follow. "I just finished fixing breakfast for me and Steve, but he called to say he's taking Dani and Elizabeth out for breakfast. I have extra. Want some?"

"I thought you'd never ask. Please."

Within a couple of minutes, they both sat at the country farm table with full plates. Mama Beth took his hand. "I'll ask the blessing." She lowered her head. "Dear Lord, thank You for this food you've provided and for the one You've given to share it with. Grant me wisdom and guide my words that I might help him clearly see Your answer to his questions. Amen."

A frown crossed his forehead. He already knew what God wanted, and he'd done it. Chance grabbed his fork and stuffed in a mouthful of fluffy scrambled eggs.

"So how can I help you?" Mama Beth peered at him with her piercing clear blue eyes.

"Well, there's this girl."

Mama Beth's lips tried to wiggle into a smile. She held them in check momentarily before they blossomed into a full-blown grin. "There usually is, but that's my favorite kind of problem." Her cackling laugh followed.

Heat climbed up his back and landed in the tips of his ears. "It's not like that. At least, not anymore."

She swallowed her bite of food and chased it with a sip of coffee. "Ah, a girl from the past. Intriguing. So what's the problem with this girl from the past?"

He shifted uncomfortably, searching for words. "Well, at one time I thought I loved her."

"You *thought* you loved her? In my experience, love's something you either do or you don't do."

"Okay. I loved her."

Mama Beth nodded her approval, as if to encourage him to state the facts accurately. "Does she live in the area?"

"Well, I wouldn't say that exactly. To be honest, I don't really know." Why hadn't he thought to ask Amy if she was just in town for a while or moving here permanently? "She's staying on her grandfather's farm. You might have known him. Levi Kelly?"

She nodded. "I knew him well. A wonderful man, and one of your Grampa's best friends." Mama Beth's eyes took on a distant look. "I met one of Levi's granddaughters last spring, right before Bo passed. She came over with Trish and had an unusual name as I recall."

"Amy."

Mama Beth shook her head. "No, must be a different granddaughter. This girl had long red curly hair and the prettiest green eyes I've ever seen."

"That's her, all right." Why had she dyed her hair red when she looked gorgeous as a blond? And why had she used a different name? "Anyway, we became close during the summer after our senior year in high school. We both spent that summer with our grandparents, and we worked with Levi in his construction business."

Mama Beth nodded encouragingly as she loaded one of the steamy biscuits with some of her homemade plum jelly. "Go on."

Chance inhaled a deep breath and released it slowly. How much should he tell her? He chewed the inside of his jaw as he considered the question, and in the end decided to keep it simple. "Like I said, we were really, really close."

The older woman's eyes narrowed perceptively. "I think I know what you mean."

The heat in his ears worked its way to his face. His scars were probably flaming red. "S-something happened that shouldn't have, and I think we both had problems dealing with it. She eventually left town, and I haven't seen her since, until a few minutes ago."

"Do you still love her?"

He shook his head. "That's not the issue."

"Then what is?"

"I was really angry when I left the farm. I stopped to watch the sunrise and pray, and I sensed God telling me to forgive her."

"That's usually a good place to start."

"But I've already forgiven her years ago. I had to forgive her so I could move on with my life."

Mama Beth's face took on compassion. "Forgiveness can be difficult because we get all tangled up in our emotions. Truthfully, forgiveness is an act of the will that comes out in our actions. Sometimes we think we've forgiven people when we really haven't. What we do instead is stuff our angry feelings in our souls and lock the door, assuming we've done our part. Trust me, I know what I'm talking about here. I've lived it."

Something inside him hardened, like clay in the fire. "Maybe that's true for you, but not me."

Her eyebrows rose. She lowered her head a minute and stared into her coffee. "Perhaps." Mama Beth raised her steady gaze to his. "But you'd be wise to do a heart check. Especially if you have any hopes of restoring your relationship with this woman."

Was that what he wanted? Why should he take her back in his life, after the way she'd waltzed out on him as if the whole scenario were his fault?

"I can see your wheels turning there, Chance. Don't forget it takes two to tango. She's probably had to do her own share of forgiving." She paused momentarily. "The biggest hurdle is spiritual pride. That only leads to judgmental attitudes and more pain for everyone involved."

Chance nodded, but didn't answer. He couldn't. Instead, he munched on a crunchy piece of bacon and finished off his coffee. Obviously, Mama Beth was wrong in this case. She hadn't been there, hadn't walked in his shoes. He *had* forgiven Amy—or whatever her name was now—and had moved on. And after thinking it through, there was no way he intended on letting her back in his life, when all she'd do was break his heart and run away just like she'd done the last time.

Chapter Three

Dakota carried the white paper sacks of food up the front porch of J.C.'s craftsman bungalow, praying the entire time that Chance wasn't at home. She'd come close to losing her resolve about keeping her distance from him earlier that morning when the flashlight revealed his scarred face. It hurt to know he'd been so badly injured, but apparently her compassion had sent him into a rage.

Though she'd done all she could to convince herself to not let her soft side loose, it would always be a part of who she was. She'd proved it time and time again with the same old results. Meet a guy. Feel sorry for him. Let him get too close. Get burned. Well, not this time, and not ever again.

She rang the doorbell, suddenly eager to see J.C. How she'd missed him. Shuffling steps and something being rolled or scooted across the creaky floors sounded from within. The door squeaked open slowly. His shoulders bent a little lower, and his hair was thinner and whiter than when she'd seen him at Pawpaw's funeral. J.C. peered at her from the same wise blue-gray eyes she remembered so vividly—eyes that reminded her so much of Chance.

"Can I help you, miss?" The same kind voice, the same humble smile.

She lowered her head as a heavy breath escaped. Only a small measure of the tension which stiffened her shoulders receded. He obviously didn't recognize her. Dakota lifted her head and smiled. "You don't remember me, J.C.?"

His eyes widened, and his mouth fell open. "Amy? Is that you?"

Hearing her old name still affected her in strange ways. Did that person even exist anymore? "Yes sir." She held up the bags of food. "I brought lunch like I promised. Mind if I come in?"

"Not at all." The door swung open. "Come on in this house and give me a hug."

As she entered the room, he engulfed her in a tight embrace. Even through his heavy duty flannel jacket she felt his bones. J.C. had grown old and frail in her absence.

He pulled away, eyes full of unshed tears, gripping an IV stand with one hand.

She quickly shifted her eyes away and sucked in a deep breath. Seeing him so feeble was something she hadn't prepared for. Unable to look at his face for fear of crying along with him, or at the bag hanging from the aluminum pole on wheels, Dakota opted instead to stare at her feet.

"When you didn't stick around after Levi's funeral, I wasn't sure I'd ever see you again." J.C. shuffle-stepped to a green recliner and slowly eased down into it. "Please have a seat anywhere." He waved a bony hand toward the same orangey-brown plaid sofa she remembered from the time she'd spent here years ago.

Dakota quickly moved to the couch and took a seat, finally able to look him in the face. "I'm sorry you're not doing well, J.C." She couldn't stop the tears that pooled in her eyes.

"Aaah." Again he waved a hand. "Just part of growing old." A light sprung to his eyes. "Won't be long 'til I go home to see Jesus, Sarah, Levi, Bo, and a whole host of others I've been longing to see for a while now."

She gritted her back teeth to bring an end to the tears, a trick she'd learned from her years with Kane. Whatever she could do to take her mind off the resulting emotional pain.

He cleared his throat. "If you don't mind me asking, why'd you leave so quick after the funeral? You didn't even stay for the graveside."

Where did she start? Her aching heart over losing her beloved Pawpaw? The fear of facing Chance? The terrible way her sister continued to humiliate her? "Lots of reasons, actually. I guess I couldn't deal with facing certain people."

"Let me guess. All of them?"

She nodded.

"I don't mean to hurt you more than you've already been hurt, Amy, but someday you gotta lay down that load of bitterness, resentment, and hurt feelings."

Tears returned and dripped down her cheek. This wasn't like her to cry at the drop of a hat. Must be the fatigue from yesterday. That and the kind and caring way J.C. had of putting his finger directly on the pulse of the problem. "I know. It just takes a while to get over some things."

"You've had a few years now. Maybe you're trying to do it in your own strength instead of letting the Lord help you."

The words lodged in her brain and trickled down to her heart. There was truth in his comment. "Thank you, J.C. I'll certainly give it prayer and thought."

He leaned forward and patted her arm. "Didn't mean to make you cry. Just want to see you move past all the pain from your childhood. Carrying it around just weighs you down and keeps you at a distance from others."

The lump in her throat made it impossible to speak, so she nodded instead.

"Chance loved you, you know."

His softly-spoken words slid like fiery ice down to her stomach, her muscles now frozen in place. The air grew thin. Dakota opened her mouth to gulp in a breath. Finally her words found voice. "I loved him, too." She inhaled another deep breath and released it. "But sometimes love just isn't enough."

J.C.'s expression revealed he didn't believe a word of what she'd just said, but thankfully, he changed the subject. "You staying at the farmhouse?"

Again she nodded, still working at regaining her composure.

A slow smile crept to his face. "Figured you were."

Dakota lowered her head and looked at him sideways through narrowed eyes. The sly old codger. He'd sent Chase out there to check on her. "So you're the one who told Chase to come check on me at the crack of dawn."

Now he laughed out loud. "Guess I did put a bug in his ear." His face sobered. "You need to borrow some money to get the electricity turned on and put propane in the tank?"

She clamped her lips together and shook her head vigorously. Only here a few minutes and already he was offering handouts. "No. I'll take care of that on my own."

"Don't mind you living there. You're welcome to live there as long as you like, free of charge."

Dakota frowned and puzzled over the statement. "But I thoug—"

"—that the farm belonged to you?"

"Or at least belonged partially to me."

"Levi's will left it to you with a few stipulations."

She swallowed. "Such as?"

"You had to be present at the reading of the will."

Her heart plummeted, her dreams of a reclusive life ripped to shreds with a few words. And she had nothing to say in return. There was no excuse. It was her own fault.

J.C.'s kind eyes held understanding. "I tried to find you, but when you left town, you did a good job of covering your tracks. Your sister gave me a few snippets of information, but nothing that helped me locate you. She sent me your phone number just last week."

Her insides froze and took her lips along for the ride. Well, it wasn't too hard to figure out what those 'snippets' Angie had given him might be.

J. C. shifted in his seat, a grimace on his face, as though trying to find a comfortable position. "He left the furniture and money to Angie, but not the farm. Said it belonged to you when you got your life in order. Until that time it's under my jurisdiction."

Dakota's shoulders heaved upward, and the tightness in her shoulders multiplied.

"So do you have it in order now?"

Her gaze met J.C.'s. Though his eyes still held kindness, there was also a certain reproach to his words that knifed through her.

"Yes sir, I think I do."

He studied her for a long minute, and then leaned his head back against the recliner, his eyes closed in obvious pain. "Based on our earlier conversation, I'm not sure you do. But stick around, live at the farm, and come see this old geezer from time to time. Once I'm satisfied you have what it takes to stay in one place for any length of time, the farm will be yours. In other words, no running away, no matter how hard it gets."

Dakota allowed the words to sink in. If Kane or one of his thugs showed up, she'd have no choice, but that was the least of her worries at the minute. The farm was far more important. She raised her eyes to his, pleading. "J.C., I don't think you know what that farm means to me." Her very life could depend on it.

"Oh, but I think I do. You just need to realize how hard your grandparents worked for that place. I won't give it to you for you to up and leave anytime you get hurt and angry." His voice remained kind and steady.

"But what happens to the property if you don't give it to me?"

"I have the option of doing with it whatever I choose."

At just that moment the front door swung open and Chance entered, his eyes trained on her.

One look at his face and she knew he'd heard every word.

"Home to check on me?" J.C. directed the question to Chance.

He nodded, but then returned his blue-gray gaze to hers.

Was that a look of triumph she saw in his eyes? No matter how kind and wise J.C. was, if it came down to deciding between her and his grandson, Chance would surely win. The thought left her cold.

J.C. stood. "Well, you needn't have bothered. I'm fine." He tottered toward the hallway. "But I am feeling a bit tired. Think I'll take a nap. You two enjoy your lunch."

Neither one of them spoke for what seemed like an eternity to Dakota. She for one couldn't find words. And she couldn't look at him either. The scars on his face prevented it. She was too afraid of giving in to her soft side and letting her guard down. And she certainly didn't want to set him off the way she had early that morning.

Finally Chance broke the silence. "I'll leave if you want."

Something in his voice sliced into her heart. Loneliness? Coming from Chance Johnson, who'd always been the life of the party and loaded with friends? Maybe it was time to start making some of the changes J.C. suggested. She shook her head and motioned for him to have a seat. "It's not necessary for you to leave. We're adults now."

His eyebrows shot upward. "Well, I sure didn't see that one coming." He took a seat while she opened the bag, but she could feel his eyes studying her.

"Didn't anyone ever tell you it's impolite to stare?"

"Just trying to figure you out."

"Surely I'm not that complicated." Dakota tore apart a chicken leg and nibbled around the bone. She'd always been simple. On the other hand, he was Mr. Complicated and had been as long as she'd known him.

Chance begged to differ, though he kept his opinion to himself as he nabbed a chicken wing and took a bite. He'd never met someone so complicated, so buried beneath layers and behind walls she'd built one lonely brick at a time. Based on what he'd overheard in her conversation with Grampa it was time to get some answers, but he'd have to possess surgical precision to extract them without sending her back into her hole. For now she at least seemed open to sharing lunch with him. Was it because of the farm? Or because she felt sorry for him? "Mind me asking why you changed your hair?"

Her green-eyed gaze pierced through him. "Why is my hair color so important to you?"

Good question. Why did it matter? "I asked first."

"So what? I asked second."

He released an exasperated sigh through his nose. Amy obviously wasn't going to make this easy on him. "Just thought it was pretty when it was blond."

Her face hardened. "So you think it's ugly just because it's red?"

"Quit putting words in my mouth." Chance tried to nonchalantly eat his chicken wing to put her at ease. Right now she looked like a balking mule, ready to kick him in the shins. He eyed the clock. The new hospital administrator, who already had a reputation for being hard on nurses, had been kind enough to let him take his lunch break at home. It certainly wouldn't be wise to abuse the privilege, but he also needed answers. "Wanted to make sure you weren't trying to go incognito because of some hidden danger."

He meant the words as a joke, but Amy's hands immediately grew restless, like she wasn't sure what to do with them, and she avoided all eye contact. She didn't respond to his comment, but picked up her soft drink, yanked off the plastic lid and straw, and took a big gulp. Obviously, he'd hit the nail on its proverbial head, but exactly what danger was she in?

When she finally looked at him again, her eyes, loaded with compassion, went straight to the scars. More proof that his scars only elicited sympathy from available women. "What happened to your face?"

Now it was his turn to squirm uncomfortably. How like her to move the focus to him when she felt vulnerable. As far as the scars, well, he didn't want to go into all the details at this point. That was information best kept to himself for the purpose of guarding his heart. But at the same time, if he opened up a little bit, perhaps it would encourage her to do the same. "Car accident soon after you left. Honestly don't know how I escaped alive."

Amy's green eyes darkened to the color of emeralds, full of angst and compassion. "I'm so sorry, Chance, but I'm glad the Lord protected you."

Her tender words touched him in a way he hadn't expected, and he struggled to keep his composure. The fact that she'd mentioned the Lord in such a personal way gave him hope. Maybe she belonged to God after all, something he'd questioned on more than one occasion over the past few years. Something he'd prayed for her specifically when she came to mind. Finally he found his voice. "And He's used it for good in my life since then."

She nodded. "I think we naturally shy away from difficulties, but God uses them to grow us closer to Him and help us depend on Him."

His eyebrows floated to the middle of his forehead. One thing he'd never expected to hear from a woman with a bad reputation was godly wisdom. Curse words perhaps, but not this. Maybe he'd stumbled across a new common ground between them. But what suffering had she endured to grow so wise? The thought gnawed at his insides. "Went to see Mama Beth this morning after I left the farm. She said something similar."

"Mama Beth?"

"Our local wise woman. Been through a lot. Lost her husband last year."

"Oh, yeah, I met her. Trish's step-mom."

The way she grimaced let him know she was sorry she'd made the comment. But why? "She mentioned she'd met you. Said she remembered you having an uncommon name."

She grew dead-dog still, her gaze lowered, her lips pinched, lost in thought. At last she heaved a sigh and looked at him directly. "I do go by a different name now, Chance, but I won't explain why."

The implication of her words socked him in the gut. First of all, it was obvious she was on the run from someone. Why else did someone change their name? But the second part delivered the blow. She didn't trust him. No wonder she kept herself hidden away behind all those walls and layers. That's why she'd asked him to leave when he showed up at her doorstep this morning. "I understand."

Amy studied him a minute longer, as though searching for meaning behind his words. "In fact, I meant to say something to J.C. as well. I'd appreciate it if you would both call me Dakota from now on. Dakota Kelly."

Chance contemplated her request. Changed hair. Changed name. Changed person. What—or who—was she running from? He couldn't help her unless he knew the answer, and she'd never tell him as long as she didn't trust him. And she'd never trust him until she could forgive him for whatever sent her running away in the first place. He placed his chicken bones with the stack he'd acquired during their conversation, rested his elbows on his knees, and looked her directly in the eye. "I'd like to help you, Dakota." The name sounded so foreign on his tongue, but it somehow perfectly fit this familiar-but-unfamiliar woman who sat in front of him. "But I can't unless I know what's going on."

She said nothing.

"I know you don't trust me, probably for the same reason you won't forgive me."

Deep sorrow filled her eyes, so deep it threatened to suck him in. Surely she realized that what had happened between them was just as much, if not more, her fault, as it was his. If she hadn't been so quick to run away, they eventually could've fixed things. "I want to do whatever I can to re-establish that trus—"

"Stop! Just stop!" Now her Irish eyes flashed with anger. "What I said this morning still stands. What happened in the past stays in the past, and there won't be a do-over. If you're hoping we can pick up where we left off, you are sadly mistaken!" She scrambled to her feet and headed for the door.

At just that moment, Grampa hurriedly shuffled into the room, his face awash with concern. "What's going on?" Dakota whirled around, her face livid. Grampa directed his gaze to Chance. "What'd you say to upset her like this?"

"Me? I didn't say anyth—" He didn't get a chance to finish his defense.

Grampa's face turned gray. Then he crumpled to the floor.

Chapter Four

Dakota froze in horror, unsure of what to do, her fingers plastered to her face.

Chance jumped from the sofa and knelt beside J.C.'s still form. He glared at her, his face contorted, his blue-gray eyes swimming with tears. "Don't just stand there. Come help me!"

She hurried over to them. "What can I do?"

Chance checked his grandfather's pulse, then bent his head close to the older man's chest. "Call for an ambulance. You have your cell phone?"

Cell phone. No, it was out in her truck in its regular place in her always-packed backpack. She shook her head, her heart rising in her throat.

He reached to his waist, unsnapped the holder, and tossed her his cell phone. "Use mine."

All she could do was stare at the fancy phone, while Chase unbuttoned his grandfather's shirt. Her cell phones had always been the cheapest thing she could find at Wal-Mart, the ones where she could pay as she needed, the ones that were supposedly harder to trace and not so connected. This one had all the bells and whistles, and she had absolutely no idea how to use it. "Um, I don't know how this phone works." The excuse sounded puny even to her.

"You know CPR?"

She twisted her head from side to side.

Chance snatched the phone from her hand. "Guess I'll have to do both." He laid the phone on the wood floors, rapidly punched three times, and then put the phone on speaker, one hand monitoring his grandfather's pulse.

"911. Is this an emergency?"

"Yes, this is Chance Johnson. I'm an RN, and in Miller's Creek at 215 Pecan Street. Need an ambulance for my grandfather, aged 79." In spite of the tears in his eyes, his voice remained calm and cool. At least with the 911 operator.

"And what's his condition?"

"Collapsed a few minutes ago, now unresponsive. Pale, and pulse is weak and erratic."

"Is he breathing?"

A muscle pulsed in Chance's jaw right below a particularly jagged scar. "Yes, but it's shallow. My best guess is myocardial infarction. I'll administer CPR until the ambulance arrives."

"I'm dispatching an ambulance, and then I'll stay on the line with you until they arrive."

Chance placed both hands on J.C.'s frail chest and pushed repeatedly. He glanced up at her. "It would be helpful if you'd go outside to direct the ambulance to the right place."

"Oh. Okay." In a split second she was out the door, her breath coming in short gasps as she peered up and down the street for any sign of an ambulance. In the distance a siren sounded. *Lord Jesus, please help J.C. make it. Give Chance and the other medical professionals wisdom and skill. Help me know what to do and how I can help.* Feelings of unworthiness and guilt poured over her. Why couldn't she be smart enough to figure things out, especially something like a stupid cell phone?

The ambulance rounded the corner down the street, siren blowing full force. The vehicle driver screeched to a stop and jumped from the vehicle.

"They're inside. Please hurry."

Two guys hurried inside, black bags in hand, while the driver, a guy about her age, approached. "Hi, ma'am. Can you tell me what happened?"

Dakota repeated what she'd heard Chance relay to the 911 operator. The man listened intently and interjected questions from time to time, which she answered as best as she could.

"Are you related to Mr. Watson?"

"No. I'm just a friend."

He smiled kindly and patted her shoulder. "Don't worry. Your friend's in good hands. I know Chance from the ER. He's a good guy and knows his stuff."

All she could do was nod, but tears brimmed unexpectedly. Good guy? Really?

"I'm sure Chance will want to ride in the ambulance with us. Normally we don't allow it, but since he's a medical professional, we will. Can you drive a vehicle to the hospital for him to take home later?"

"Yes." Dakota followed the man into the house. J.C. was already on a gurney, and they prepared to wheel him out the door. Chance seemed more in control of his emotions now, though his face was pale and drawn and bathed in concern. Dakota peered over to the coffee table where she'd seen him lay his truck keys. Good. They were still there.

Without a word to her, he followed the gurney out the door, climbed into the back of the ambulance, and sped away.

What now? Dakota prayed for wisdom while she locked the house and followed after the ambulance in Chance's dust-covered pick-up. She arrived right behind the ambulance, parked in emergency parking, and scurried to the Emergency Room doors.

The back of the ambulance burst open, with people shouting directions and rushing the gurney toward the Emergency Room. The only words she heard were "Code Blue." Chance's face held sheer terror.

He chased after the gurney, but whirled about right in front of the swinging stainless steel doors and pointed directly at her, his voice rising above the hubbub. "This is all your fault." With the words ringing in her ears, he stiff-armed the doors and disappeared behind them.

The waiting area grew immediately quiet, with all eyes trained on her, and the faces of the nurses and doctors behind the desk held cold contempt.

Dakota lowered her head and moved to a dark corner of the waiting area where she could hide away, pray, and lick her wounds. *Heavenly Father, please be with J.C. I know he's ready to go home, but please give Chance more time with him, according to Your will.* Prayer always brought such comfort. God was always in control.

She ran her fingers through her curls to brush out at least some of the tangles, her brain rehashing the tension of the past half hour. Chance's tone and attitude had sliced through her more times today than she cared to remember. Yes, it was because he was scared and worried—kind of a 'kick the dog' mentality—but that didn't make his actions and words any less painful.

She closed her eyes and laid her head back against the wall, willing herself to breathe deep. It was a coping mechanism she'd learned years ago and practiced innumerable times since, and it would help her push the hurt into the darkness so she didn't have to deal with it.

A half hour later, Chance exited the double doors with a smile on his face. He didn't look her direction, didn't even check to see if she was anywhere around. Instead he sauntered behind the nurse's station, where pretty young nurses lined up to hug him. Then he once more disappeared behind the doors.

Had he forgotten she was even here? Apparently J.C. was okay, or Chance's disposition would've been very different. But what should she do now? Dakota gathered her courage, rose to her feet, and approached the desk.

A young woman looked up at her with cold eyes. "Can I help you?"

"Yes. I'm a friend of J.C. Watson, who was brought in a few minutes ago. Can you tell me his condition?"

"Are you a family member?"

"No, just a friend."

The other woman shook her head. "Then I'm not allowed to give you any information because of medical privacy laws." Her gaze didn't waver.

"Okay, thanks." She pulled Chance's keys from her coat pocket and slid them across the laminate countertop. "Would you please give these to Chance Johnson?"

The woman nodded. "Sure."

"Thanks." Dakota hurried outside. No use sticking around. Chance obviously had no need for her. As she traversed the black asphalt of the hospital parking lot, she shivered and pulled her jacket close. The day had started off fairly warm, but judging by the hovering dark clouds and increased winds, a cold front would soon be pushing through, most likely bringing thunderstorms along with it.

She'd barely made it across the highway on her trek to J.C.'s house to get her truck, when rain and small pieces of hail pelted from the sky. She half-walked, half-ran through the ongoing icy rain. By the time she reached her rusty old rattletrap, she was soaked to the bone. Not even in Miller's Creek a whole day yet, and already she'd pulled a shot gun on Chance, gashed her leg open, caused an old man's heart attack, and managed to get drenched in the process. So much for the simple country life she'd longed for.

Weary beyond words, Chance stared down at the patient paperwork trying to make the words come in focus. The new hospital administrator--or Ivan the Terrible, as he liked to refer to him--had insisted he make up the time by adding hours to his already long twelve-hour-days. Here it was Friday afternoon, and he still hadn't found the time to get out to the farm to see Dakota.

He scribbled a note on the paperwork and clicked the ballpoint to closed position. Thankfully, Grampa was better, though he was a long way from being out of the woods or the hospital, with his heart only pumping at thirty percent capacity. Not good.

His gaze traveled to the clock. Only a few more minutes and then he'd be free to go check on his grandfather. Once Grampa was tucked in for the night, he'd take the time to go see Dakota.

Guilt stabbed holes in his conscience as he thought about the way he'd treated her. In his concern for his grandfather, his unleashed tongue had made her responsible for something that was no one's fault. Even after the way he'd accused her, she made sure he had a vehicle to get home in, responding with grace and forgiveness.

Chelsea, one of his fellow nurses and a single woman about his age, hurried into the nurse's station. "You're still here?"

"For just a few more minutes, thanks to Ivan the Terrible."

"Sorry he has it in for you." She laid a hand on his upper arm.

"So I'm not the only one who's noticed."

"Don't take it personally. I hear he treats all the male nurses that way."

Well, that tidbit was news to his ears. "Really?"

"Yep. From what I've been able to gather, he's pretty old school that way." Chelsea opened a file cabinet and shoved in a file, then slammed the drawer. "He thinks only women make good nurses."

"That's the most prejudicial thing I've ever heard." His tongue came unglued again. "Well, I have a piece of advice for Ivan. He needs to join the twenty-first century."

Chelsea's face paled and her brown eyes latched on someone over his left shoulder before she turned a chagrined expression his way.

Chance's stomach fell to his toes. "He's behind me, isn't he?"

She nodded, then scooted out of the nurse's station.

"Yes, and I heard every word, Mr. Johnson. If you think I'm Ivan the Terrible now, wait until you hear my next piece of good news."

He faced Jeremy Gains. "Look, I was out of line. Please accept my apology."

"Apology accepted." His lips were so tight, creases shot out in every direction. "But that doesn't change the news. One of the other nurses asked for emergency leave next week to visit her ailing mother. I'm dividing her shifts among you and two other nurses."

"But my grandfather is ill as well."

"Yes, and he's receiving expert care. Don't mind if you check on him during your breaks, as long as we don't have a repeat of the other day."

Chance nodded obediently though everything in him wanted to protest. As he filed the paperwork, a thought came to mind. He closed the cabinet and leaned against it. "Just as a matter of curiosity, who are the other two nurses I'm splitting shifts with?"

Gains didn't even look up from the clipboard he held in his hands. "Mike and Jimmy. Why do you ask?"

There was no way to answer his boss without blowing his top. At just that moment, the minute hand moved to eight p.m. Finally. He stalked out of the station and to the elevator. A minute later he stood outside Grampa's room. Familiar laughter and voices sounded from behind the cracked door.

"Sorry to drop in on you so late." The voice was Mama Beth's. "I was waiting on my ride."

"As was I," added Trish Tyler dryly.

"And I'm the guilty party." He'd recognize Andy Tyler's laid-back voice anywhere. "Everyone thinks lawyers have an easy life. Sheesh."

"Have a seat." Grampa's voice held weakness that hadn't been there last week. The heart attack had definitely take its toll. "Thank y'all for stopping by. Andy, I'm actually glad you're here. Sorry to add to your work load, but I've been meaning to get a hold of you for a while now."

"No problem. Something you want to discuss now?"

"Naaah. I won't bore the ladies. Just drop by some time when it's convenient."

"Chance ate breakfast with me Tuesday morning." Mama Beth joined the conversation.

"He did?"

"Yep, wanted some advice about Levi Kelly's granddaughter."

"Amy?"

Chance shifted positions so he could see Mama Beth's face. She twisted her lips to one side. "I don't remember that being her name. Trish, you brought her over to my house earlier in the year. Pretty red head with big green eyes."

Trish nodded. "Dakota."

"That's it!" hollered Mama Beth. "She was your best friend in high school?"

"No, the youngest sister of my best friend. I saw Angie when Mr. Kelly passed away. Angie's really changed. And not in a good way." Trish's words trailed off, and she seemed to check out of the conversation for some place unknown.

"Amy changed her name? Does anyone know why?"

Exactly what he'd like to know. No one answered.

"Well, just so you can be prepared, Andy, I want to visit with you about my will."

Andy pulled a pen and small note pad from his suit jacket pocket and jotted down a note. "I'll bring all the pertinent info when I come. I know tomorrow's Saturday, but I have another client visit in town. Would it be okay if I drop by then?"

"That'll work." Grampa laid his head back on the pillow. He was fading fast. Time to make an entrance.

Chance pushed open the door and entered the room. "Hey, everyone." He hugged Trish and Mama Beth and shook hands with Andy before moving to the head of the hospital bed. "How you feeling, Grampa?"

Grampa looked up. "Okay. Just ready to go home." His words held underlying significance.

An ache rose in his heart. How could he let him go? Chance patted his grandfather's arm. "I know. I'll try to find out from the doctors when that'll be."

The talk soon turned to the latest chatter scuttling about Miller's Creek, so Chance begged off with a comment about being tired, and hurried out to his pickup. Already it was later than he'd hoped. The last thing he wanted was Dakota pulling a loaded shotgun on him again, but he might as well get this over with.

Fifteen minutes later, he pulled up outside the farmhouse, surprised to see lights shining from the windows. He exited the truck and made his way through the dark, calling out loud. "It's Chance, Dakota. Just here to see how you're doing and to apologize."

Her silhouette appeared in the open doorway. "It's a good thing you added that last part, or I wouldn't have even bothered to open the door."

He moved up the steps with a laugh. "I deserve that and more." Dressed in a denim shirt un-tucked from the waistband of her blue jeans, she was once more shoeless. "Sorry about how I treated you Tuesday afternoon. There's no excuse for my behavior other than to say I was really scared. But even that's not good enough."

She gave one brief nod. "I know you were scared, Chance. It's okay."

"And thanks for leaving my truck at the hospital." A stray thought struck suddenly. "How'd you get back to Grampa's house?"

Dakota lifted a foot in the air. "The original form of transportation. In the storm. With hail and rain soaking me to the bone."

Chance swallowed against the wad of guilt in his throat. "I'm so sorry. How can I make it up to you?"

"Well, now that you mention it, I could use some manpower on a little project." Her eyes held a teasing gleam.

"Such as?"

"Rebuilding the barn."

Chance snorted. "I thought you said little."

"Size is relative, right? Trust me. I have several projects that are much bigger."

He glanced down at her bare feet. More than anything he wanted to spend more time with her, to work on the trust issues between them. But was the timing right, especially with Grampa's condition?

"Would you like to come in?"

Chance entered the open door, and his mouth fell open. It was almost like walking into Levi Kelly's house several years prior, only updated nicely. "Wow, this place sure looks different. You've been busy."

She shrugged. "It's amazing what a little elbow grease and paint will do."

"I'll say. And you have electricity." And heat. She'd turned down money from Grampa, so she must have some financial resources.

"How's J.C.?"

"Still weak and tired."

A look of concern clouded her face. "That's how he was when I saw him earlier this morning."

"You've been to see him?" Why? To pressure him into leaving the farm to her?

"Every day." Dakota moved toward the kitchen. "Can I get you some water?"

He shook his head. "No, thanks. Why'd you go see him?"

She faced him, her head cocked to one side. "Because I'm concerned about him. It's okay if I go to see him, isn't it?"

It should be, but it wasn't. He just didn't trust her motives at this point. But he couldn't exactly come right out and say it without the risk of offending her.

Dakota released a scornful laugh. "You're a piece of work, Chance Johnson. You think I'm going to see him because of the farm, don't you?"

He cleared his throat as he scrambled for words. "Don't mean to offend you, but—"

She turned her back. "You just did." Dakota yanked a water bottle from the carton on the kitchen counter with more force than necessary.

Time to change the subject. "So how long do you think our work on the barn will take?"

Rather than answer, Dakota pushed past him and stopped when she reached the front door. "Don't worry about it. Maybe your time would be better spent figuring out how to get your hands on my farm." With that, she opened the front door, gave a pseudo bow, and held out her left arm, indicating her desire for him to leave.

His anger catapulted to volcanic levels, but reasoning with her would only lead to more hurtful words. Instead, he stepped outside. "Good night."

Her response was a slamming door and the click of the lock.

Chapter Five

Well, one thing was for sure. With or without Chance, the barn wasn't going to re-build itself. And without a barn--and the animals to go with it--she'd never be able to sustain herself on the farm.

Dakota shrugged on her ratty jacket and headed out the front door. Why had she let her anger get the best of her last night? Even as pig-headed, egotistical, and downright infuriating as Chance could be, having some help was better than none.

She stepped inside the open entrance of the barn and surveyed the problem. Not good. The posts supporting the weight of the roof had rotted away on the bottom, and caused the whole structure to lean to the left. Maybe if she could find a way to shore up the outside rafter with the new lumber she'd picked up the other day, she could remove the rotten post and replace it with a new one.

She moved to the dark recesses of the barn and hoisted a four-by-four post. A long splinter on the side shoved its way under the tender flesh of her palm. "Ouch!" The heavy post thudded to the ground as she used her chewed-to-the-quick nails to remove the splinter. All but one tiny piece came out, but the one tiny piece was buried deep. It would just have to wait.

Once more she grabbed the offending post, lugged it to the front left corner, and set it in place. Though she pounded as hard as she could, it refused to budge. Frustrated, she reared back to give the post the hardest blow she could muster, but the hammer slipped and landed on her left thumb.

Unintelligible words fell from her lips through gritted teeth. She released the four-by-four and the hammer to grab her throbbing and bleeding thumb. It didn't help that she'd been up until the wee hours of the morning for the past several nights trying to finish up the lousy first draft of her next novel. No new books meant no money to live on or to make the much-needed renovations to this place.

Outside a car door slammed. Dakota hurried from the barn, still clutching her injured thumb. Dressed in blue jeans and boots, Chance looked like she remembered him from their teenage years. Dangerously handsome. He waved and sauntered her direction. As he drew closer, the smirk he wore became apparent--an I-told-you-so smirk.

She clenched her jaw to keep her Irish tongue curtailed, but everything in her screamed to send him packing. A luxury she just couldn't afford at the moment.

He stopped just a few inches away and pushed up the brim of his cowboy hat to survey the leaning barn. "You ready to concede defeat and let me help you?" His gaze traveled to the blood dripping from her injured thumb. In one fluid movement he snatched up her hand and studied it more closely. "Man, you must've been swinging pretty hard to do that kind of damage."

"Thank you, Captain Obvious. Now would you help me get it bandaged so we can get this barn fixed?"

A laugh sounded from his throat and his blue-gray eyes twinkled.

Dakota yanked her hand away and strode to the house, Chance right behind. Fine, she'd doctor it herself.

"Anyone ever tell you you're pretty when you're mad?"

She ignored his comment and quickened her pace.

"Anger goes well with that carrot-colored hair of yours."

Carrot-colored? She'd give him carrots, all right. Up his nose. She stomped up the wooden steps and across the porch.

"Not everyone can carry that look off as well as you do."

Her blood boiled at blow torch levels. Dakota halted, fists clenched. That. Was. It. She whirled around and landed a blow to Chance's mid-section.

He groaned and doubled over, while she shook the hand that delivered the blow to make sure it still worked.

Chance straightened slowly, a devilish grin curling his lips. "Guess I had that coming."

Understatement of the millennium. She wiggled her fingers to see if anything was broken. "What are you made of anyway? Steel?"

He patted the abs of steel. "Everyone knows boys are made of snips and snails and puppy dog tails, while girls are made of—"

"—sugar and spice and everything nice." She finished the rhyme for him, nose in the air and hands on her hips.

Though he didn't respond, Chance perused her childish pose, a bemused expression on his face, then strode around her to open the front door. "Yeah well, someone left out your sugar and nice."

A slow smile formed on her lips. Sugar wasn't good for you anyway, and nice wasn't all it was cracked up to be. Of the three, she'd settle for spice, and plenty of it. Maybe Mr. Abs-of-Steel would think twice before baiting her again.

He stopped in the open doorway and turned his head. "Let me guess. You don't have any bandages?"

"Nope."

"Be back in a sec." Chance squeezed past her, sauntered to the passenger side of his pickup, and returned a minute later, carrying the familiar black bag. He let it drop to the porch floor. "This is the second time in a week I've had to doctor your wounds. You accident-prone or something?"

She peered at him sideways through narrowed eyes.

Chance held up both hands in mock defeat. "No offense intended, so keep your shotgun and your fist to yourself. By the way, where'd you learn to punch like that?"

Dakota shifted her weight, ignoring the question. Better that he didn't know at this point.

"You know we've gotta disinfect this, right?"

She huffed out a sigh and looked heavenward. "Of course."

He doused the thumb with alcohol, his gaze locked on her face.

Ouchiewawa! Not even the hammer hurt this bad. But no way would she let him know it. Instead, she clamped her lips tighter than Ft. Knox.

His eyebrows arched. "Good girl." A few seconds later he finished and laughed at the bulbous white gauze on her thumb. "Hey, you look like Little Jack Horner and his plum."

"Whatever. The only plumb I'm interested in at the moment is the barn walls, thank you. Now, before we get to work, would you mind getting this splinter out of my hand?"

Chance made a face as he examined the wound. "Man, that thing is in there deep. I can get it out, but it's gonna hurt." He stooped and shuffled through his black bag of tricks.

"Whatever it takes."

"Okay, but I want you to thank me now, 'cause you won't be thankful afterwards." His lips curved into a Howdy Doody grin. "I'm waiting."

"Thank you." She mumbled the words reluctantly.

"What? I can't hear you." He sing-songed the last four words as he bent over her hand with a pair of tweezers and some sort of digging tool.

"Thank you!" She bellowed the words as loud as possible.

He grimaced and yanked on his left ear lobe. "Thanks for making my ears bleed."

"You're very wel-- Ow!"

Chance held up the removed splinter, the Howdy Doody grin back on his face, a grin her right palm itched to remove. That is, if it didn't already hurt so much.

His cell phone buzzed. He frowned as he read the screen, then punched a few buttons and put the device to his ear. "Hey, Chels. What's up?" The color drained from his face as he took off at a lope toward his pickup. "Be right there."

Fear raked her insides. J.C.? Dakota chased after him. "What is it?"

Chance didn't slow his pace or turn to face her, but headed for the driver's side door. "Grampa isn't doing well. I gotta get to the hospital."

Her mind swirling with concern and prayer, Dakota sped to the passenger side and crawled in just as he started the engine and put the truck in gear. "I'm coming, too."

"Hold on." Deathly claws raked at his heart, and a metallic taste coated his tongue. *Hurry, hurry*, the word pounded against his skull. Every muscle in his body coiled for action, Chance whipped the steering wheel around and floored the gas pedal. The truck bounced down the road, spewing dust into the downed windows.

Dakota coughed and gripped the arm rest with one bandaged hand while she attempted to buckle her seatbelt with the other. Her face, chalk white, made her green eyes stand out more than usual.

He focused his attention back on the task at hand. The speedometer climbed. Forty. Fifty. Were they already too late? *No!* He couldn't go there. Not yet. They just had to get there in time. In time to tell Grampa at least one more time how much he loved him.

"The next curve is pretty sharp, and there's lots of loose gravel." Dakota yelled the words over the road and engine noise.

Chance slowed his speed to make the curve.

"It's pretty much a straight shot from here to the farm-to-market road, so you can go as fast as you want." Dakota reached across her body to grip the arm rest with both hands.

The pavement approached, but Chance slowed only enough to insure there was no oncoming traffic and to make the turn.

"Another straight shot until you get to the right-angle turn at the edge of to—"

"I know, Dakota." He ground the words out between clenched teeth and stomped his foot to the floor. The speedometer needle moved to sixty, then seventy. It wasn't like he hadn't been down this road a million times, and she, of all people, should know it.

She stared straight ahead, her lips pinched between her teeth, still gripping the armrest as though her life depended on it.

A siren sounded, and red and blue lights flashed from the top of the black and white car in the rearview mirror. "I'm not stopping."

Surprisingly, Dakota didn't argue. Instead she nervously worked her mouth as though chewing the inside of her jaw.

The police car flashed its headlights and pulled closer. Chance released an exasperated sigh and yanked his foot from the accelerator. No need in killing them all. He carefully steered the truck to the grass at the side of the road.

"What're you doing?" Now her eyes held--what? Fear?

"I have to stop, Dakota. I think it's Ernie. He'll understand." Chance stopped the truck abruptly, threw the gearshift into park, and yanked open the door just as Ernie approached. "Hey, Ernie. Just got a call from the hospital. Grampa has taken a turn for the worse. I need to get there as soon as possible."

The town cop with the thick graying moustache nodded and sprinted back to his car. "I'll lead the way."

Chance had barely put the truck in gear when Ernie passed, sirens blaring. He tore out behind the policeman and both pulled up outside the hospital a few minutes later. The two men entered the hospital together, Dakota just a few steps behind, and hurried toward Grampa's room.

As they reached the door, Jeremy Gains exited. Chance made a move to go around his boss, but the man latched on with both arms, then peered past him at Ernie and Dakota. "Sorry, but there's not room for you in there right now. The doctors and nurses are working to resuscitate him. You'll have to stay in the waiting area for now."

Chance shot the man a withering glance to let him know exactly how he felt. But beside him, Ernie and Dakota both grabbed hold of his elbows.

"C'mon, Chance, it'll be okay." Dakota's voice was low and soothing.

Chance yanked his arms from their grasp and stalked off down the narrow hallway, both hands on his head. This couldn't be happening. Not yet.

Once in the waiting room, Dakota faced him. "We need to pray."

Numb from shock, both from the scenario playing out down the hall and from her request to pray, Chance could only nod. Yes, prayer. That would help.

She took both his hands in her own. "Father, we lift J.C. up to you. Preserve his life, so Chance can talk to his Grampa again. Give the doctors and nurses special skill and wisdom. Surround Chance with Your peace and comfort. In Jesus' name, Amen."

He inhaled a deep breath, his rapid pulse immediately slowing. He smiled his thanks as Ernie's eagle-eyed gaze honed in on Dakota. "Pardon me for staring, ma'am, but you look mighty familiar."

Gains appeared from around the corner. "Chance, you can go in now. You won't have long."

Heart heavy, Chance nodded and held out a hand to Dakota. *God, give us strength.* Together they hurried down the corridor and into the room devoid of noise except for the erratic beep of the heart monitor.

Grampa lay in the hospital bed, small and frail, his skin a pasty white. His eyes fluttered open as they approached, and he smiled wanly. "So glad to see the two of you together." He weakly lifted a hand and placed it on theirs. "Thank You, Lord." Grampa's hand rested on theirs a moment longer, his eyes shut. Praying, but for what?

"Grampa." Tears flowed, unstoppable, the words seeping through his brain woefully inadequate. "I want you to know how much I love you. How much I appreciate all you've done for me." Chance used his shirt sleeve to wipe away the blur in front of his eyes. "I only hope I can be half the man you are."

Love shone from his grandfather's eyes. "I love you, too, Chance." He moved his gaze to Dakota. "And you, too, Amy."

Tears spilled from her eyes and down her pale cheeks. "And I love you, J.C."

Grampa nodded weakly, and once more closed his eyes. They fluttered back open. "About the farm..." His words drifted away, his gaze trained on some distant spot on the ceiling. A radiant smile erupted on his face, and then he was gone.

The stabbing pain in his chest knocked Chance to his knees as a groan erupted from somewhere deep inside. Now he had no one left. In a split second Dakota was on her knees beside him, taking him in her arms.

All he could do was cling to her and cry, her tears mingling with his.

Chapter Six

A throbbing ache squeezed Dakota's heart as she took one last look out her old bedroom window at the place which had always been so special to her. The one place that felt safer than all others. Could her heart survive leaving the farm again? She made her way out of the room and descended the stairs. There should be just enough time for a quick trip to the old bridge she and Chance had helped Pawpaw build. She released a heavy breath. Then it would be time to drive to Miller's Creek for the meeting at Tyler and Tyler Law Firm. Already her meager belongings were packed in her backpack and loaded in the pickup. Just in case.

Why Andy even wanted her there for the reading of the will was beyond her ability to comprehend. J.C. had been hospitalized shortly after her conversation with him about the farm, leaving no time for him to make necessary changes. Besides, there was no chance he'd choose her over his own grandson anyway. Perhaps he'd left her some little trinket, some memento to remember him by. As if she needed a trinket to remember J.C. Never would she forget him and his kindness toward her.

Dakota exited the farmhouse and headed through the overgrown pasture toward the old bridge. Of all places, it held the ability to resurrect painful memories and was the one place she'd not yet allowed herself to visit. As she approached, she could almost hear laughter ringing, could almost see a younger and blond-headed version of herself running from Chance in an impromptu game of tag, could almost hear Pawpaw's forced gruffness as he told them to quit horsing around and get busy.

The cool autumn breeze caressed her cheek and whispered through the tall browning grass. Dakota halted and closed her eyes, willing the happy memories to continue. It had been so long since she'd felt such joy and peace, and now it was all about to come to an abrupt end.

Profound sorrow trickled through every ounce of her being as she opened her eyes and resumed her walk. It was for the best that things were turning out the way they were, a fact she'd known since Chance had held her close and mourned his grandfather's passing. Living in such close proximity to him would never work. It would always be a temptation to let her heart go where she'd sworn to never go again. And worse yet, there was always the chance she would inadvertently reference her life's greatest heartache, one for which Chance would never forgive her. One she couldn't even forgive herself.

The old bridge came into full view. The structure had held up better than expected, though nails, rusty with age, had popped their heads up from the surface of the worn and weathered boards. A sudden desire, swift and unrelenting, washed over her, and she brought a hand to her cheek at the recognition. Part of her had hoped and dreamed of repairing the bridge once more. And an even deeper part of her had wished for Chance to help, as though the bridge had somehow become a metaphor for their fractured relationship. Was she falling in love with him again after such a short time? Or had she ever truly stopped loving him?

An exasperated groan escaped as she stared at the cloudy sky. Hopefully her current confusion was all bound up in her heartache over losing J.C. A lone tear inched down her cheek. She closed her eyes and sent more tears cascading down her face, too world-weary to even wipe them away.

When she opened her eyes a few minutes later, she'd at last reached that familiar place of numbness, where nothing mattered. Least of all herself.

Time to face the inevitable. Dakota retraced her steps to the farmhouse, climbed in her a pickup, and made the familiar trek to Miller's Creek. Fifteen minutes later, she arrived at the posh Tyler & Tyler Law Firm and headed indoors.

Every limb heavy, she approached the receptionist's desk. "Hi. I'm Dakota Kelly. I'm supposed to meet with Andy Tyler."

The woman nodded. "Let me tell them you're here."

Dakota waited while the receptionist punched a button on the fancy phone system.

"Yes?" Andy Tyler's familiar voice sounded through the speaker.

"Miss Kelly has arrived."

"Okay. I'll be right there."

Dakota stepped away from the counter and prayed silently. *Lord, help me get through this graciously, no matter the outcome.*

A second later Andy stuck his head through the swinging door which separated the waiting area from the private offices. "Hey, Dakota, come on back. Chance is already here."

Her heart somersaulted at the mention of his name. She'd kept her distance since J.C.'s passing, not just to give him grieving time, but to protect her shredded heart from further damage. Dakota followed Andy and his immaculate black suit to a well-decorated conference room where Chance sat talking to a beautiful Hispanic woman.

Andy held out a hand toward the petite woman dressed in stylish business clothes. "Dakota, I'd like you to meet my sister-in-law and partner, Grace Tyler."

The woman stood with great effort and stretched a hand toward Dakota, a kind smile on her face. "Hi, Dakota. Nice to meet you."

Dakota smiled back. "You, too." She cast an anxious glance at Andy and approached the long table, unsure of proper protocol. It was all she could to avoid Chance's direct gaze, which burned a hole in the right side of her head.

"Please have a seat." Andy plopped to a leather chair and opened an extra-thick blue file folder. He looked up, alternating his gaze between her and Chance as he spoke. "Let me once more express my condolences. J.C. meant a lot to this town and to me personally. I know he also meant a great deal to both of you."

Dakota fought unexpected tears while Chance voiced his gratitude. Why weren't her emotions following her orders today? She finally found her numb place and once more looked Andy in the face.

"I met with J.C. at the hospital the morning he passed."

Hope quickened her pulse. Was there a chance J.C. might've actually left the farm to her?

Andy continued. "He requested a codicil to his will concerning the farm Dakota's grandfather willed to him. Under his current condition, J.C. also requested that we draw up the paperwork right then and there so it could be signed, witnessed, and notarized." He paused, a sad smile on his handsome face. "He sensed the end of his earthly life was near." Andy slid the document across the table to Chance. "I think you'll find everything in order."

Chance studied the pages for just a second, then nodded and passed them back to Andy.

Just as quickly as hope arrived, it departed and took another piece of her heart with it. J.C. had probably just added special instructions to his will to insure that Chance legally received the farm. They'd simply brought her here to make sure she understood the will, so she wouldn't cause any problems down the road.

Andy looked directly at Chance. "Chance, your grandfather left you the farm."

Shards of glass, thin and fatal, pricked her heart. Dakota's eyes closed at the ensuing pain, but she quickly re-opened them to salvage what self-respect she had left. It was for the best. God would take care of her wherever she landed. She stole a forbidden look at Chance.

He at least had the decency to appear shocked. "But—"

Andy held up both hands. "Let me finish, please."

Dakota lowered her head, wishing she were anywhere else. *Lord, hurry up and get me out of here.*

"Dakota, J.C. also left the farm to you."

She jerked her head up, eyes wide. Surely she hadn't heard him correctly. "But I don't understand."

Beside her, Chance shifted uncomfortably, shook his head from side to side, and chuckled uneasily. "This is never gonna work."

Andy ignored the comment for the moment and focused his attention on her. "It was J.C.'s desire for you to inherit the farm with Chance, with each of you owning an equal share."

Chance was right. Not only would this not work, it was much too dangerous to be in such close proximity to him on a regular basis. "I'll forfeit my half and give it to Chance."

His mouth agape, Chance yanked his head her direction. "You would do that?"

She didn't make eye contact, but nodded. Yes, she would do that. For him. And for her confused and bruised heart. Under the conditions of the will, it was the best alternative.

Andy exchanged a knowing glance with Grace, then leaned back in his chair. "J.C. thought that might be your response."

A bucket of shame rained down on Dakota's head. The kind old man had known her better than she knew herself. He'd known her tendency to run when her heart was at stake, and had guessed she'd make a run for it again. What was it he'd said during their almost-lunch together? Something about not giving her the farm until he was satisfied she wouldn't run away.

She looked into Andy's ocean-colored eyes. To her right, Chance's intense gaze continued to bore a hole in her. At least Grace Tyler had the graciousness to look down at the table to spare her further embarrassment.

Andy sent a reassuring smile. "He made a contingency in the will that if either of you opted to forfeit your portion of the farm..." He shifted his gaze to Chance. "...or the financial responsibility that goes along with it, the property would immediately be auctioned off to the highest bidder."

The blood drained from her face, then resurged to a furious boil. "Over my dead body."

Andy laughed out loud, his dimples pronounced. "J.C. called that one, too." He lifted his face to the ceiling. "Atta boy, J.C." He chuckled again and then returned to lawyer mode with a straightening of his tie--and his smirk. "Anyway, where were we?"

"I think we just co-inherited a dilapidated farmhouse and overgrown farm." Chance's tone was devoid of inflection. "A money pit if there ever was one."

"Money shouldn't be an issue." Confidence flowed from Andy. Your grandfather left plenty for the work on the farm. If you're frugal, you might even have some left. Chance, in addition he left you some extra money and a letter, which we'll discuss after Dakota leaves."

Chance leaned forward, eyes bulging from their sockets. "Let me get this straight. I inherit money I could use to pay off my student loans and get the family drugstore up and running again, and I have to spend it on a farm I don't even want?"

Andy cleared his throat and swallowed. "That pretty much sums it up. Of course, Dakota will be expected to contribute as well, as she can afford to, that is."

The room grew both quiet and chilly. If it weren't for the cold glares Chance lobbed her way, Dakota was sure her cheeks would've been flaming red. "I'll do what I can."

Chance pounded a fist on the table, effectively drawing her attention. His face contorted with anger. "You don't even have a job!" Each word grew louder and louder, until she actually heard the exclamation point.

She flinched at the blast of hot air that hit her face, then stared him down. "You don't know anything about me." Had never really tried to know her actually, especially since the night that forced them apart. He'd formed his opinion, right or wrong, and adhered to it religiously. Like a Pharisee.

His eyes searched hers with such intensity she felt she would melt, but at last he blinked and backed down.

"As I was saying, you'll both contribute as much time, effort, and resources as you can. At the end of all this, one of you can purchase the house from the other if you so choose. And the sooner the house is marketable, the sooner you can go your separate ways." His voice trailed off momentarily and then he chuckled outright. "That is, if you don't kill each other first."

Even the very self-controlled Grace Tyler bit her lips to keep from smiling, but Dakota wasn't amused even the least little bit. Based on his closed off body language, neither was Chance.

Andy brought his dimpled grin under control and pulled another paper from the light blue file folder. "Hmm, anyway, here's the title. If you're both in agreement with the contents of the codicil, you need to sign the back of the title to transfer ownership to yourselves."

Chance signed first, an angry scratch that barely resembled his name, then pounded the pen to the table.

Andy slid the document and pen to Dakota.

She sat back for a moment, still troubled by Chance's response to all this. Even in spite of how he'd hurt her, she didn't want to make a decision that was wrong for him. "If I sign now, can I still change my mind later?'

"Only if you're willing for the farm to be put up for auction."

Dakota cast a glance at Chance, who glared into thin air, his chin at rest on his right fist. Then she looked back at Andy and Grace. Both sent encouraging smiles. She picked up the pen with shaky fingers and located her place to sign.

Andy stretched a hand out over the paper at the last minute. "Oh yeah, almost forgot. You'll need to sign your legal name since this is a legal document."

Now the pen began to shake in earnest, but Dakota focused all her effort on signing the name of a person she no longer knew or resembled. A person she had hoped to leave behind. A person who had somehow followed her back to Miller's Creek where she now owned a farm with the man who, unlike Kane, had not left scars on her body, but on her heart.

Chapter Seven

Chance placed the heavy barbell back on the braces, his muscles pumped to the limit, then stood and pulled a sweatshirt over his tank top. A Saturday afternoon jog was just what he needed right now, the perfect cure for what ailed him--in this case, a green-eyed redhead with a hot temper, a checkered past, and a tendency to run away whenever the urge struck. But the prognosis for his recovery was slim to none, especially if he decided to honor Grampa's final wishes.

In spite of her past, there was something about Dakota he couldn't quite define. Something that drew him in. One corner of his mouth lifted wryly. Drew him like a moth to a scorching flame.

He stepped out onto the concrete porch of the stone house that now belonged to him, immediately struck by the fragility of life. Just one week ago today, Grampa had passed to the next life. He soaked in the thought and jogged down the steps into his neighborhood near downtown Miller's Creek.

The fall day was picture perfect, not cold, but with a crisp coolness that typified the fall season in central Texas. The Bradford pear trees, maples, and red oaks had all begun their annual display to see which could outdo the other for the accolades of those who lived in the area. Across the street, one of the twin sisters who owned and operated Granny's Kitchen burned pecan leaves in her front yard, while the other stooped to pick up pecans which she dropped in a plastic ice cream bucket. Both waved as he passed.

"Sorry about your grandfather," one yelled.

"J.C. was a great man," called out the other.

Chance smiled and waved, but continued his jog. He wound his way through the neighborhood, travelling his normal route, but when he reached Creekside Park he veered from his regular routine, the beautiful afternoon begging him to linger longer. To catch his breath, he slowed to a walk, tramping toward the gurgling creek across the Bermuda grass of the city park, already browned from cold nights. Tufts of green winter ryegrass dotted the ground in a few places.

He reached the creek. Though it held some water, it ran much lower than normal because of the recent drought. It always fascinated him how one year the creek would flood and the next be dry as a bone, but that was the weather in this particular part of the world--beautiful, but unpredictable.

Just like Dakota. He released a sigh and lowered his head with a shake. What was he going to do about her? If he went forward with this whole farm deal, how would he ever have enough time to help her with his crazy work schedule?

He puzzled over the situation for several moments, then as bewildered as ever, broke into a full sprint and headed toward the picturesque downtown area of Miller's Creek. He passed Granny's Kitchen, full of old men shooting the bull over an afternoon cup of coffee. Passed the peaceful town square with its gazebo and park benches. Passed City Hall where Steve Miller still presided as mayor.

Chance didn't stop his full-out run until he reached the century-old building which once housed the family drugstore. He peered up at the beige and brown two-story. Barely visible above the doorway from the paint that had peeled away, he could still make out the words, Watson's

Drugstore. It had long been a dream of his to add the drugstore to the long list of renovated buildings and thriving businesses in Miller's Creek. The downtown area had become a mecca for city dwellers longing for a simpler life, and the local chamber of commerce had done a great job of organizing events which pulled people and their much-needed business into the little country town year-round.

Stories from his grandfather's childhood floated to his memory, like the bar lined with happy teenagers as they sipped away at their cokes and root beer floats. The town needed this place. Anyone with a prescription had to travel all the way to Morganville to get it filled. What a great way to use the inherited money and honor Grampa's memory at the same time.

An elderly man tottered up. Chance immediately recognized him as Otis Thatcher, known throughout town for his caustic tongue and argumentative grouchiness.

"Aren't you J.C.'s grandson?"

"Yes sir." He extended his right hand. "And you're one of his old geezer buddies. Mr. Thatcher, right?"

The man stayed true to his reputation. "Hmphf! Always hated that name, old geezers." He shook a bony finger inches from Chance's nose. "Mighty disrespectful if you ask me."

"I meant no disresp—"

"Oh, I know the whole town calls us that."

Yeah. That and town grouch. Did he know about the less-than-flattering reputation?

"Whatcha doin' just standing here looking up at this old building?" Otis scrunched up his nose, his chin in tow, to peer at Chance through the bottom of his bifocals.

"Well, I'm actually considering renovating the building and re-opening Watson's Drugstore."

"Ha! That's the best idea I've heard in years. Tried to talk J.C. into many times."

"Really?"

"Yup, but he wouldn't hear of it." Otis' head shook, his sagging jaws and under bite reminiscent of a bull dog. "Said there were better ways to spend the money."

A frown puckered Chance's forehead as phrases of Grampa's last letter trickled through his brain. "Did he happen to mention any of those better ways by any chance?"

Otis shook his head, his lower lip jutted out. "Nah. Just wanted to spend it on himself, I guess. Well, I'm glad you got to see me. Best be gettin' on before the wife gets her feathers all ruffled." Without another word, he tottered off down the street and climbed in the old 70's model Cadillac he'd probably driven since the day he drove it off the showroom floor.

Chance took one last look at the old building, then scratched his head and took off for the house in jog mode. The only way to solve this quandary was to get the advice of friends. But other than Mama Beth, all the others had families, with weekends rightfully reserved for family activities.

A few minutes later he reached the craftsman-style stone house. Might as well give Mama Beth a call. If he was lucky, she might just invite him over for a home-cooked meal.

He stepped in the front door just as the phone rang. Chance hurried to answer it. "Hello?"

"Well, it's about time. I've been trying to reach you all afternoon." Mama Beth's voice scolded.

"Hey, Mama Beth. Sorry. Just got back from a jog. I was actually about to call you."

"Whatever for?"

"To invite myself over for dinner."

She laughed heartily. "And I'm calling to invite you to dinner."

Now it was his turn to laugh. "Great minds think alike."

"A lot of great minds actually."

"Huh?"

"The whole crew is coming over—Steve and Dani, Andy and Trish, Matt and Gracie."

A smile pulled his cheeks tight. Good. The timing of this impromptu evening with friends couldn't be more perfect. Now he'd have the opportunity to share his thoughts and receive the loving and helpful advice his friends always provided. "I'd love to. Can't think of a better way to spend the evening."

"And why don't you bring Dakota while you're at it. I'd like to get to know her better."

At the mention of Dakota, he sobered. "Er—that's not really gonna work for me at the moment."

"Oh. Okay." There was a long silence on the other end. "Well, dinner's at six-thirty, and I think everyone else will be here around six. See you then."

Lights shone from every window of Mama Beth's two-story charmer when Chance arrived later that evening, very much reminding him of a family holiday gathering. He breathed in deep of the cool night air as he swung open the picket fence gate and sauntered toward the wraparound porch.

The front door stood open, and lively chatter emanated from the kitchen and dining room. Just like Mama Beth to leave the door open for him to make him feel welcome and like part of the family. He tiptoed noiselessly across the living room floors to surprise them. Instead, their conversation brought him to a mortified halt.

"What do you mean he wouldn't bring her?" Dani's soft Southern drawl bespoke her genteel upbringing.

"He said something about it not working for him at the moment," Mama Beth explained. "And for the life of me I couldn't think of a thing to say in response."

"I think that's about the rudest thing I've ever heard." Trish sounded indignant.

Steve's face appeared in the doorway. "Thought I heard someone." He smiled at Chance and held out his hand. "Good to see you, buddy. Hey, everyone, Chance is here."

Chance pasted a grin on his face, hugged necks, and exchanged handshakes. The last person in line was Matt. Chance landed a gentle pat on his best friend's back. "Hey, Matt."

"Hey, yourself. Doing okay?"

"Not as good as I thought. Was it my imagination or was my name being taken in vain right before I stepped into the room?"

Matt chuckled. "You'd be right on that one, but don't let it bother you."

Easier said than done. Chance shoved his fingertips into his jean pockets to appear unbothered. "Doesn't bother me at all." His friends hadn't spent as much time with Dakota and didn't know her past. If they'd been on the receiving end of her blistering tongue or taken a punch in the gut as he had, they'd be singing a different tune.

A few minutes later, Mama Beth announced time for dinner. They all held hands around the farmhouse table while Steve said the blessing. The chatter then resumed, combined with the clinking of silverware and dishes as the awesome-smelling food was passed and loaded onto plates.

"Chance, Andy tells me you and Dakota are going to be renovating the old Kelly farmhouse." Trish pinned him to the wall with her brown-eyed gaze as she passed the French fries to Gracie.

"It's one option."

Her eyes narrowed. "Option?"

"I haven't yet made the final call."

Gracie passed the fries on to Matt, and made brief eye contact with Chance. Though she spoke not a word, the expression on her face was one of disappointment.

Matt stuffed a fry in his mouth. "It's definitely a big decision."

Finally someone saw his side. Good old Matt. Chance smiled his appreciation, took the bowl from his friend, and raked some of the steaming fries on his plate between the hush puppies and fried catfish. His mouth watered. "Supper looks and smells delicious, Mama Beth."

"Thanks. Little Bo caught the fish out of the big tank at the ranch." She lowered her head for a moment then looked directly at him, those wise blue eyes of hers lasering a hole straight through him. "Do you mind me asking why you would go against J.C.'s wishes for Levi's farm?"

Chance eyed the bite of flaky fish on the end of his fork, then sighed and laid down his fork. "It's not that I want to go against his wishes, Mama Beth. I'm just not convinced it's a wise idea financially." Or personally.

She nodded, apparently satisfied with his answer.

He breathed a sigh of relief and reached for his fork.

"So the decision for you is strictly financial?" Dani, who normally wore a cheery grin, sat ramrod straight, her gaze as direct and unrelenting as her mother's.

Chance laid down his fork again, choosing his words carefully. The women had taken Dakota's side in the matter simply because of her gender. "Not strictly, no."

"If you're worried about having the right skills, there are plenty of people in the area—"

"It's not that at all," inserted Chance. "Dakota and I worked for her grandfather several years ago. He taught us both a lot about the construction business."

"Then what are the other factors?" Quiet Gracie, who normally only spoke when spoken to, delivered the comment as though he were on the witness stand under cross-examination.

Chance cleared his throat and looked to Matt for help.

His friend just stuffed a forkful of food in his mouth and shrugged with a boyish 'you're-on-your-own' grin.

He turned his gaze back to Gracie. "I know it must be hard for y'all to understand, but you don't know Dakota like I do."

"I beg to differ," said Trish. "Her sister and I were best friends during our freshman year of high school."

"Then you know Dakota ran away from home on multiple occasions and even got into trouble with the law?" Frustration resonated from his words. He had to get his point across somehow, if the women would give him a chance.

Trish didn't move a muscle. "So? That doesn't necessarily reflect on who she is now. Besides, she may have had a very good reason to leave."

Not according to what he'd been told by Dakota's sister herself. "Maybe. Maybe not." No way would he back down. "She's still on the run. That's why Levi left the farm to . Isn't that right, Andy?"

Andy's clouded expression revealed his displeasure at being brought into the fray. He nodded. "In a roundabout way, yes, though it was more about the fact that she wasn't there for the reading of her grandfather's will."

Triumph shone from Trish's eyes. She clearly claimed Andy's remark as a score for her side.

"Well, I know for sure it's why Grampa didn't just out and out give the farm to her. I heard him say it."

Steve leaned back in his chair, a studious look on his face. "Chance, why do you suppose J.C. didn't just leave the farm to you?"

He considered the question. Why indeed? The answer popped into his head and out his mouth. "Because he was an interfering old man who wanted to find a woman for his only grandchild."

The comment at least elicited smiles and laughter from the others.

The mayor of Miller's Creek grinned. "Sounds just like him." He looked over at the pretty blond woman he'd married. "In fact, I'm certain he was one of the biggest matchmakers involved in getting me and Dani together." His face sobered as he peered back toward Chance. "J.C. was very wise and very kind, wouldn't you agree?"

"The best. They don't come any better."

Andy and Steve exchanged glances, a sort of silent communication that set Chase on edge. Andy leaned forward. "And in my estimation, there was no better judge of character than J.C."

Chance nodded. Very true.

"He believed in me when no one else did." Dani's big blue eyes misted over.

"And he loved you very much." Mama Beth directed the comment at Chance. "I don't remember many conversations with him where you weren't mentioned. He was so proud of you and wanted nothing but the best for you."

"I'm very blessed."

In the end it was Gracie, kind and quiet and sweet, the one most like his grandfather, who circled in for the kill. "Let me get this straight. Your grandfather was kind and wise, a great judge of character, who saw potential in people and brought out their best. On top of that he loved you and wanted nothing but the best for you. Yet you're willing to toss his dying wish aside because of your personal prejudices and greed?"

A march of angry ants stomped up his spine and onto his neck, bringing lava-hot heat with them. The room grew deathly quiet, all female eyes trained on him like hungry lionesses on the prey. All the guys at least had the decency to stare at their plates.

Chance squirmed in his seat, swallowed hard, and scratched in the vicinity of the ants.

Matt came to the rescue and pushed his chair away from the table. "Well, that was a delicious and delightful meal. Great company and semi-great conversation."

Andy chuckled from the other side of the table and was soundly punched by his wife.

Chance puffed out his cheeks and released a breath. At least he was out of the hot seat. For the time being anyway.

Others stood and moved away from the table with their empty plates. Chance stared down at his now-cold food, his stomach growling. Not one bite had made it into his mouth. Oh well, a cold home-cooked meal was better than none. He made a move for his fork.

"Here, let me take that for you, Chance." Trish scooped up his plate and added it to her own without even looking at him.

He didn't dare object.

As friendly banter resumed, Chance stood made a beeline for Matt. "Thanks for saving my neck."

His friend laughed. "Just glad it was you and not me." Matt's smile faded, and his eyes took on a compassionate gleam. "Listen, why don't we have lunch one day next week? I know you're worried about working with Dakota on this house renovation thing, but you might be able to really help her. She sounds like a very troubled young woman."

Had the words come from anyone else, Chance would've immediately objected, but the comment raised two questions in his mind. First, was Dakota helpable? Was there a chance she could truly change? And second, could he survive? "Sounds good to me. The only problem is my boss. Might have to be an after-work snack instead."

Once the kitchen was cleaned, the clan began their good-byes. Even the lionesses included Chance in their farewells, and on his way out the door, Andy pulled him off to one side of the massive front porch.

"I didn't want to say anything in front of the others, but there have been a couple of inquiries at the office about the farm."

Chance shoved his fingers into his pockets. "Really? Anyone I know?"

"I don't think so. One guy was really kind of creepy in a weird sort of way. I'd run a background check before doing business with him. The other inquiry was from a land mining company."

"Land mining company?"

"Yeah, they make their money by buying up land for bottom dollar, then they mine it for landscape rock, paving materials, minerals, and oil if they find it. They also sell all the hardwoods off to the highest-bidding lumber companies. It totally destroys the land, but they make their money back with a hefty profit to boot." Andy appeared especially interested in his response.

"And the house?"

Andy shrugged. "Dunno. Guess they'll bulldoze it."

Chance took in a deep breath along with the information. And just what would happen to Dakota?

Chapter Eight

Dakota slipped in the back door of Miller's Creek Community Church, intentionally late to avoid being seen in her raggedy blue jeans and denim shirt. More than anything, she needed answers, even if she did look like a hayseed.

An usher greeted her with a friendly smile and order of service, seemingly not taken aback by her lack of traditional church dress. "Morning. Can I help you find a place to sit?" He stretched out a hand. "Steve Miller."

"No, thanks." Dakota shook his hand and took the offered slip of paper. "Nice to meet you."

The man opened one of the large wooden doors, and Dakota stepped through. Music played while members of the congregation milled about greeting one another and handing out hugs. Dakota procured a seat about halfway down the aisle.

Several rows ahead, Chance sat with a whole row of people, including Andy Tyler and his sister-in-law, Grace. The familiar yearning for friends gripped her heart. Those kinds of friends only came from roots in one place, a luxury life had yet to offer her.

As the worship began, Dakota focused on the words on the screen and sang along. Like a desert in need of rain, her thirsty spirit soaked up the peace and comfort that rained down, and her heart cried out in silent gratitude to God. A few minutes later, the pastor stepped to the podium and gave the scripture reference for the sermon. Dakota opened her well-worn Bible, eager for the message to begin. God never failed to speak to her in some way or another, faithful to meet her needs.

The pastor raised his Bible to chest level and lowered his head to read. *"'Everything is permissible for me'—but not everything is beneficial. 'Everything is permissible for me'—but I will not be mastered by anything."*

Another nearby passage was referenced, and all across the hushed sanctuary pages whispered. *"Therefore, if what I eat causes my brother to fall into sin, I will never eat meat again, so that I will not cause him to fall."*

Dakota's eyes honed in on the verses once more. *Lord, what do You want me to learn today?*

She closed her eyes and waited, at last finding a place of peace. God was with her no matter where she went. He'd never failed to provide for her. This time would be no different.

The pastor moved from one side of the pulpit to the other. "As God's church, our decisions affect each other. They also affect a watching world who needs to know Jesus. So we must make decisions based on what Christ wants. He sets us free from slavery to sin, making us free indeed. But our lives are not our own. We've been bought at a price."

Dakota quickly grabbed a pen from her pocket and scribbled a few notes on the back of the order of service.

"Some decisions in life are pretty straight forward, or appear to be at first glance." He smiled from the pulpit. "But just because something is permissible doesn't mean it's beneficial. So the first question we need to ask ourselves when making decisions: Is this helpful?"

Dakota turned the question over in her mind. It would be helpful to have a place to live and a working farm, a dream come true in every sense of the word. What an answer to prayer to stop running and put down permanent roots. To have the friends she so desperately needed. But would it be helpful for Chance as well? She rubbed her forehead. That's where this got difficult. Only he could make that call.

The pastor continued. "Look at the second part of 1 Corinthians 6:12 again. *'Everything is permissible for me'—but I will not be mastered by anything.* Some things look so good. They seem beneficial. But once we let them in our lives, we find that they take on a life of their own. And rather than us owning them, they own us and bring us under their control rather than the Spirit's control. So our second question in making decisions is this: Will it bring me under its power?"

Hmm. A little harder to answer. She skewed her lips to one side. Past addictions proved that anything had the potential to enslave. In this case, the work to the farmhouse and even Chance could possibly consume her. If she stayed, it would mean a constant heart check to make sure she stayed in step with God's Spirit.

"Our third question is: Does it hurt others and cause them to stumble, or does it demonstrate an attitude of love and concern for my fellow man?"

Another reminder that her decision also affected Chance. Dakota frowned. He hadn't been happy about the prospect of working with her on the farm. He'd made that more than clear in Andy Tyler's office. She couldn't arbitrarily make the decision to stay, knowing it would cost him time, money and effort, all things he might not ever recoup.

"All we do should bring glory to God. So this last point is really a combination of questions. Will this choice bring glory to God? Or, will it bring Him dishonor and hinder my walk?" He looked up briefly. "One more thing I need to mention is the enemy. When we try to align ourselves with what God wants, Satan will fight back. One way he fights is with a weapon called fear. We cannot base our decisions on fear rather than faith."

The words ricocheted in her brain. How many of her decisions had been prompted by fear? At some point she had to stop being so afraid. And whether staying in Miller's Creek or setting out for someplace new, her choice needed to be one of faith.

The pastor closed his Bible and moved down the steps to stand in front of the pulpit as soft music sounded from a guitar. "Really all decisions--whether big or small--boil down to this one thing." He held up one finger to emphasize his point. "Are we going to go our own way or follow Him?"

Heart overflowing, Dakota's chin dropped to her chest. *Oh, Lord Jesus, thank You that I don't have to make this decision alone. Thank You for being there to guide me. Help me make decisions that are godly and helpful and won't lead to slavery. Help me make choices that take others into consideration and bring You the honor and glory You so richly deserve. Amen.*

Dakota breathed easier than she had in several days. Yes, she still hadn't reached a final decision, but at least she knew what she needed to do next. When the service ended a few minutes later, she didn't hurry out like she'd originally planned. Instead, she shook hands with those who stopped her and even shared her name. She'd just finished speaking with the lady who called herself Mama Beth, when Grace Tyler stepped forward, a man in baggy jeans and a brightly-colored t-shirt at her side. He looked very much like Andy Tyler, only more laid back.

"Hey, Dakota. So glad to see you. This is my husband Matt."

Matt's hearty grin and handshake immediately melted away all Dakota's timidity. "Nice to meet you."

"You, too. Your brother's an attorney. Your wife's an attorney. Are y—?"

Infectious laughter fell from his mouth. "Hardly." He motioned to his clothes. "Do I look like one of those uptight lawyer types?"

Grace elbowed him. "Watch it."

Dakota giggled. "Not even close."

"Whew!" Matt wiped pretend sweat from his brow. "Had me scared there for a second." He reached in his pants pocket and handed her a business card, slightly wrinkled and bent at the corners. "Actually, I'm a counselor here at the church. If you ever need anything, Gracie and I are here to help."

Dakota felt an immediate connection to the couple. Would she get the opportunity for those roots to push through the ground into full-blown friendship?

Chance sauntered up to join them. He made eye contact with her for the first time in forever, and a soft smile curved his lips.

Matt patted her arm, then pointed to the card and latched onto his wife's hand. "You have my number if you need it." Both he and Gracie waved as they moved on down the aisle.

She turned her attention to Chance. "Hi."

He shifted uncomfortably from foot to foot for a moment. "Listen, about the other day. I was a real jerk. I'm sorry."

His words affected her in a way she couldn't explain. Apologizing was hard for anyone, but for someone with Chance's personality, it must be doubly hard. His judgmental pride had been part of the force that drove her away in the first place. "No worries. I know you had lots on your mind."

He shook his head, his lips firm. "That doesn't excuse my behavior. Would you like to go to lunch with me? It might help to talk through things, especially after that sermon, on decision-making." His eyes softened.

"I know. Me too."

"So you'll have lunch with me?" He seemed surprised.

Dakota nodded. "I'd love to." Then she immediately launched into another silent prayer for the wisdom and courage they needed to reach a decision. *And please, Lord, protect my heart.*

Chance hadn't quite believed his eyes when he'd looked up at the conclusion of the church service and seen Dakota in front of him in the center aisle chatting with Matt and Gracie. Of all people, she was the last person he'd expected to see at church. But the still, small voice inside him had prompted, so he'd asked her to lunch for the purpose of making a serious decision. A decision that would impact both of them.

Now she sat quietly, red ringlets framing her face, still clutching the armrest like she did last week on their trip to the hospital.

"I promise not to speed this time."

A faint smile touched her lips. "Good."

"So you can let go of the armrest."

"Oh." She glanced down at her white knuckles and peeled them from the door. "Habit, I guess."

Yeah, definitely a habit for her to be ready to bolt, like a jackrabbit on constant high alert. "You don't have to be afraid, Dakota."

She faced him, frowning and eyes troubled. "I'm working on it."

"What makes you afraid?"

Now she turned away. "Nothing I can be specific about."

Okay. Guess that topic was off-limits.

"I miss J.C. so much." The words fell from her gently parted lips, her gaze trained somewhere in the distance. "I miss his friendship and his wisdom. He could always help me figure things out. Now I have this huge decision to make, and he's not here."

Her forlorn words tugged hard at his heartstrings. How many times over the past week had he felt the same way? But as his friends had not-so-delicately pointed out last night, his wise old grandfather had a reason for what he'd done. Perhaps that was the answer. "I feel the same. Don't know how to say this other than to just come right out and say it. For whatever reason, Grampa thought fixing up the farmhouse and farm was important for both of us."

Her head snapped his direction, eyes wide. "I hadn't really thought of it in that light."

"Please don't jump to conclusions or read anything into it. I'm not trying to sway us to one side or the other."

She frowned and nodded, then immediately worked her cheek and lips, most likely gnawing away at the inside of her cheek like she always did when deep in thought. Finally she spoke. "I think J.C. was concerned for me and wanted to make sure I was taken care of."

"Agreed." And he'd wanted Chance to consider the possibility of a deeper relationship with Dakota. But could he make it past--well, her past?

People change.

The words of the still, small voice within were similar to what Trish had said last night. "Do you mind me asking about your relationship with God?" The question popped out rather abruptly.

Dakota's mouth fell open, and her eyes grew round and large.

"Not trying to pry or anything, but you prayed in the waiting room last weekend, and then you were at church today."

"I'm a believer, Chance. I gave my life to Christ a few years ago." Her green eyes pierced his soul. "Do you find it impossible that a bad girl with a reputation could possibly be a Christian?"

"No." After all, Christ had forgiven Mary Magdalene and others like her, changing their lives for the better. Chance sighed through his nose. But he did have a hard time understanding why Dakota was still on the run unless she had something to hide. Or was it someone to hide from? And how could he voice his questions without setting her off?

Her lips clenched for a moment. "Just so you know, I had no intention of going to church this morning. But I felt like I was supposed to, like God wanted me to hear the message on making decisions. I believe He meant for us to eat lunch together today to make this decision. Neither of us can make it on our own, because it affects both of us."

He nodded. Well, at least they were on the same page, a thought that both scared and shocked him. They reached the parking lot of the Montana steakhouse. Chance located an empty space, pulled in, and killed the engine. "Ready for some lunch?"

She stared at the restaurant sign. "I've never eaten here before. Is it, uh, expensive?"

"Not too bad." He climbed from the driver's side and moved to the front of the pickup to wait for her. She joined him a second later, and he used the remote to lock the truck.

Once inside and seated with menus and water, Dakota scoured the choices.

Chance sipped his water. "Made up your mind yet?"

Dakota shook her head. "Nope. I have a really hard time deciding."

"Well, everything's good."

"But not necessarily beneficial."

A laugh erupted from his throat, joining with the dining room chatter. "Well, someone listened to the sermon this morning." He glanced around the dining room while Dakota perused the menu. A big burly guy at a table not too far away had his beady eyes latched onto Dakota's every move. Chance was just about to get the guy's attention when the waitress appeared and blocked his view. "Hi, y'all. You ready to order?"

"Dakota, you go first."

"No, you. I still haven't decided."

"I'll just have water to drink, but for my meal I'd like the rib-eye, cooked medium, with a garden salad, honey mustard dressing. And instead of a baked potato, could I substitute the grilled vegetable medley?"

The waitress smiled flirtatiously. "You betcha. A man who knows what he wants. I like that."

Across the table from him, Dakota rolled her eyes in disgust.

"And you, Hon? What would you like?"

"First, I'd like a separate ticket."

Chance almost choked on his water. "That's not necessary."

"I insist." Dakota gazed directly at the waitress. "Can I still order from the breakfast menu?"

The woman nodded.

"Okay, then I'll take an order of biscuits and gravy."

Biscuits and gravy? A heart attack on a plate? Then reality sank in. Her order was probably the cheapest thing on the menu. For the first time he noticed her clothes, one of two outfits she'd worn every time he'd seen her. She was more financially destitute than he'd realized.

"And to drink?"

"Just water."

The waitress gathered the menus and headed to the computer to enter their order.

Chance struggled to find a way to ask the question burning in his mind. "Please don't think I'm trying to pry or anything, but I have to ask some questions in order to know how to reach this decision."

She rolled her bottom lip under for a moment. "I understand. But know that for reasons I can't explain, I might not be able to answer all your questions. Whatever happens, I trust that the decision you reach will be good for both of us."

He frowned. She made it sound like he'd be making the decision for both of them. "Mind if I say a quick prayer for us?"

"Not at all." She bowed her head.

"Dear Lord, thank You for this beautiful day and the inspiring message from Your Word. Please bless the food to the nourishment of our bodies so we might be better servants for You. And help us reach the decision that most honors and glorifies You. Amen."

Dakota glanced up, but she must've seen something or someone else, for she kept looking furtively to her right. Then she half-hid behind her left arm as she rearranged her red curls and looked away, nibbling on her upper lip.

Chance glanced in the direction of the big guy. Yep, he was still ogling her. "Would you like me to say something to him, Dakota?"

"No. It's okay." The words machine-gunned from her mouth.

He studied her. Visibly shaken, nervous, and uncomfortable, and doing everything in her power to hide it.

"What questions did you want to ask?" She picked up her water glass and sipped, her face still partially hidden from view behind her left hand.

"Uh, yeah. The other day at Andy's office you indicated that you have a job?"

She nodded and sat her glass on the table. "Yes, I'm a writer."

His eyebrows scurried up his forehead. Wow, he hadn't seen that one coming. But it certainly made sense. Even back during their summer together, she'd been an avid reader, always entertaining him with snippets from the books she read. "What kind?"

"A little of everything, actually. I pick up whatever freelance jobs I can find on the internet, but my real love is fiction."

"Published?"

"Yes, but independently."

"Meaning?"

"Meaning I'm also my own publisher." She scratched her neck so hard she left red marks. "I'm my own everything actually. I design my own covers, do my own formatting, marketing, publicity, etc."

"And you can make a living?"

She hesitated. "As long as I'm frugal. That's actually one of the things that concerns me most about restoring the farmhouse. I don't know how I'll have time to write. But without the writing, I don't know how I can help pay for the renovation."

Something he could easily relate to. "I have the same issues. I work twelve-hour shifts and come home exhausted. Not sure how I could pull off a renovation on top of my job."

"At least you have money." She immediately scrunched up her nose and lowered her head, as though regretting the words.

He'd suspected as much, but since she opened that can of worms. "And you don't?"

She leveled her honest gaze at him once more. "I have a little saved, but it won't go far."

The waitress brought their food and set in front of them. "Can I get y'all anything else?"

"No thanks." Fingers of guilt lowered his head to view his loaded plate, then raised it to her measly meal of bread and gravy. No wonder she was so thin. Somehow he'd find a way to pay her ticket without her knowing it. A plan hatched in his mind. "You have any other concerns besides needing time to write?"

Dakota didn't look up. "Not really. Like I said before, I trust your judgment."

Irritation erupted inside him, and his fork and knife clattered to the plate. "Don't do this, Dakota."

She glanced up, eyes wide. "Do what?"

"Don't shove this all off on me, so you don't have to deal with it or take responsibility later."

Sparks flashed in her eyes, but to her credit she said nothing. Her shoulders sagged, taking her head with them. "Honestly, Chance, I'm not trying to do either. I'm just at a stalemate where this whole thing is concerned. I look at the whole thing and see an even mix of positives and negatives, most of which I can't discuss." He opened his mouth to speak, but she cut him short. "Don't ask why, Chance. I just can't." She inhaled deeply and released the breath through pursed lips. "That's why I want you to choose. The Lord will take care of me either way, and I know He'll do the same for you."

Something twisted inside him. Hearing such words of faith spoken from a sincere heart, coming from the beautiful woman in front of him touched him in a way he hadn't anticipated. He carved off a piece of the juicy steak and stuffed it in his mouth. *Lord, what do you want me to do?* Immediately an idea popped into his head. Her response to news he was about to deliver would give the answer he needed. He finished the bite and leaned forward.

She looked up from her almost-empty plate. "There's something on that brain of yours, Chance Johnson. Spit it out."

A smile reached his lips in spite of his attempt to keep it from happening. She'd always had the uncanny knack of reading him like one of her books. "I just remembered something Andy mentioned last night. Apparently, there have been a couple of inquiries on the property."

"Possible buyers?"

He nodded. "Andy said one guy was pretty rough-looking." Chance turned his head to look across the crowded room to the guy he'd spotted earlier. Gone, thank goodness. "And the other is a company that buys up farmland for the purpose of harvesting natural resources."

Dakota laid her fork on the plate, her forehead creased. "Meaning?"

"Meaning they harvest the land for lumber, rocks, minerals, paving materials, whatever they can find that will make them money. Oh, and they'll probably do the same with the farmhouse."

Her face went more pale than its normal creamy-white, and turned her eyes into emerald-colored orbs, large and dark.

All the answer he needed.

Chance laid the cloth napkin on the empty plate and leaned back while the waitress removed their dishes and scurried off toward the kitchen. "I think I know what we're supposed to do."

She swallowed, pressed her lips together, and looked at him intently, waiting, but not speaking.

"Don't know how it's ever gonna work, but I think we'll renovate a farmhouse."

The next thing he knew she was at his side, hugging the stuffing out of him.

CHAPTER NINE

A buzz sounded at the door, immediately followed by a camera shot on Krater's computer screen. Foley. He'd been in contact off and on since Sunday night late after locating Amy in a restaurant with a guy named Chance Johnson. After following them back to a church parking lot in Miller's Creek, Foley had tailed her all the way out to the secluded farm where she now lived.

A smile curled his lips. Amy Stephens. Dakota Kelly. A.K. Aston. No matter what name she tried to hide under, he knew them all. Had found her. Just like he always did.

Valmoor purred at his feet. Krater picked him up, and then stepped to the control panel to punch in the code.

"Trick or treat." Foley, his pot belly protruding like a ripe watermelon, wheezed into a snicker, obviously very much amused by the comment.

A non-amused laugh sounded from Krater's throat. "Fresh out of treats, Foley, but are you sure you really want a trick?"

Foley's smile faded, and he rapidly shook his head from side to side, his fleshy jowls flopping.

Poor idiot. One he'd endure only until his services were no longer required. Krater stepped back and motioned Foley in, Valmoor tucked contentedly in the crook of his arm. "I expected you yesterday." He held out his hand for the large envelope containing the maps of the area and layout of the farmhouse.

The man handed them over as he waddled in. "Well, I wanted to make sure things were going down the way I thought they were. You'll be glad I waited." Foley's face was covered with several days' worth of growth, which only served to highlight his double chin and yellowed teeth.

"New information?"

"Not exactly."

Careful not to disturb Valmoor, Krater swiftly landed a punch to Foley's more-than-ample body.

The man crashed into the closed door, then brought the back of his sleeve to wipe the trickle of blood oozing from his mouth.

"I don't take kindly to my employees taking advantage of me. You should know that by now." He didn't raise his voice. There was no need.

Foley whimpered in response, but nodded, his eel-like tongue licking at his busted lip.

"Now, the explanation of why you're late."

"I went back to that guy's law firm."

"Andy Tyler?"

"Yeah. I wanted to verify that the property wasn't going up for sale. That our little chickadee planned on staying put."

The wheels in Krater's head began to spin. "And?"

"Not on the market at the moment is what the guy said, like he still wasn't convinced things would work out."

Interesting. "Did he say why?"

"Something about only by prayer and the grace of God, or something like that."

His eyes narrowed. There was much more to this story than what he knew. Information he'd have to know in order for his plan work. "And you didn't ask what he meant?"

Foley shifted the weight of his bulging belly from one foot to the other, his beady eyes restless. "He didn't give me a chance. Had a court date to get to. I woulda stayed longer, but you told me to get here ASAP and make sure I wasn't followed." The slovenly man's words erupted into a slimy barrage of word vomit, and he twisted his hands in front of him.

Krater turned away and moved across the room to allow his thoughts to process. For now at least, Amy was holed up at a secluded farm not too far from here, which meant it shouldn't be too difficult to get to her without causing a scene. Chance Johnson could be problematic, but he had other ways to get him out of the picture.

The contents of the grandfather's will had left the farm to the both of them with the contingency that they work together to restore it. But apparently the two weren't completely sold on the idea based on the attorney's reply to Foley.

Hmmm. With a well-manicured finger he lifted the chin of the purring black cat and peered into its golden eyes. "What should we do, Valmoor? Do we wait until Amy decides to run again, or do we make our move sooner?" So many variables at play, but none insurmountable. The main thing was to be patient. The last thing he needed to do was make a costly mistake, especially when he was this close to achieving his goal. He faced Foley, who worked his lips back and forth, his lips itching to speak. "What is it, Foley? You have something to say, so say it."

"It's just that, I—I was wondering if I could get an advance to tide me over to the next pay day."

"Already spent it all on booze and cigarettes, eh?" He clicked his tongue.

Foley didn't answer, but his eyes bulged.

So easy to anger, this one, which would make him all the more disposable later. "Let me make you a deal you can't refuse."

The overweight man's face brightened. "Okay."

"You bring back every piece of information you can get on Mr. Chance Johnson and his relationship to Amy. Be thorough. Then, and only then, will I consider giving you your requested advance."

"But that means going back to Miller's Creek."

Krater crossed the room again, headed straight toward Foley.

"Which I don't mind doing at all." Foley flinched and moved out of the way to let him pass.

Krater punched in the code and opened the door. "I thought you might see it my way." He gently closed the door behind Foley, then moved to his desk at command central. Time for a planning session.

Chapter Ten

Sheer panic careened through Dakota's insides, bouncing off her bones. She squatted to the ground, focused on the fresh cigarette butt, her mind littered with questions she couldn't answer. Who had been here? Were they still around? What were they doing? What did they want?

She shivered. Her. They had always wanted her and would stop at nothing. But how had they found her way out here in the middle of nowhere?

Dakota stood, examining the cigarette butt in her hand and noticing teeth marks in the filter's thin paper. An image of Kane flashed to mind, with his cigarette dangling from his lips as he screamed at her.

Fireworks of fear exploded, her breaths coming in short, open-mouthed spurts. *Breathe, Dakota. Think!*

She scanned the vicinity, searching for the slightest movement, ears strained to pick up the faintest sound. Nothing but the gentle coos of the dove and the wind rattling the tall field grass. A minute or two later, she finally slowed her breath and racing heart, comforted by one thought. If Kane had been here, he would've let her know. His raging ego and temper would've played out immediately.

Dakota tossed the cigarette to the ground. Maybe in addition to making her to-do list, she should also check the area for further signs of a visitor. Although Kane might not have been here, someone had.

The sound of an engine drew her gaze toward the main road. Chance. The cloud of white dust beyond the tree line confirmed it.

She glanced at her list, evenly divided into two columns. One held the work she could do alone, the other what she needed his help with. While he was at work she hammered away at her side of the list--mostly trim work, painting, caulking, cleaning, and flooring. Then every evening when Chance arrived, they'd grabbed a quick bite to eat and tackled the bigger projects. They worked until nine-thirty or ten, at which point Chance left to get sleep before the next day of nursing, while she headed to her old bedroom and makeshift desk to put in four or five hours of writing. Make that attempted writing.

Chance's pickup came into view, as she thought through her measly writing efforts over the past week. It could be summed up in three words. Major writer's block. With too much hanging over her head and not enough time to do it, every activity seemed to take extra effort and thought, both of which were in short supply due to decreased sleep.

He parked the pickup and climbed from the cab, leather work gloves in hand.

All week she'd waited for Friday and Saturday to arrive so they could make real progress on the projects she couldn't handle alone, projects that required extra hands and muscle, like the Beast in the downstairs bathroom.

He approached with his usual quick-paced stride, but minus a smile.

Oh, boy, this should be a fun day. "Hi." She smiled and tried to infuse her voice with a gaiety she didn't particularly feel. "You okay?"

"Tired." Suddenly he frowned, his gaze drawn to the ground, and scuffed at the dirt with the toe of his boot. His lips tightened perceptibly, then he focused stormy gray eyes on her. "You smoke?"

"No."

An exasperated whoosh of air fell from his mouth, and he stooped to pick up the cigarette butt she'd thrown down a few minutes earlier. "Don't lie, Dakota. Here's the proof." He held it up inches from her nose, his eyes daring her to deny it.

She chafed at his attitude and tone. How dare he assume the cigarette belonged to her. Just more of his jumping to conclusions to prove to himself that she wasn't good enough for him. No way would she speak even one word in defense. If he wanted to be a horse's rear-end, let him, but she had work to do. With her mouth clamped nail-in-a-coffin tight, she stomped past him toward the house.

He caught up and latched on to her arm. "If it doesn't belong to you, then whose is it?"

Dakota wriggled free from his grasp and continued her march toward the farmhouse, taking the new porch steps two at a time.

Chance raced around her and blocked her entrance to the house. "Quit running away and answer me!"

Her hurt burst into full-blown rage. "Quit being a bully and I might. For your information, I saw it right before you did. I don't know who it belongs to."

His eyes narrowed. "You're telling the truth?"

Her eyes roved to the bead board of the porch ceiling as she released a sigh. "No, I'm telling you a big fat hairy lie!" She moved around him, into the house, and slammed the door behind her.

A sledge hammer rested against the newel at the base of the staircase. She grabbed it as she passed to give the old cast iron tub another try. The bathroom was a wreck. Literally. She'd spent a large portion of the week demolishing the space. Everything, including the fixtures and sheetrock, had been removed, leaving only the stud walls and a built-in bathtub she'd nicknamed the Beast.

The grungy tub had earned its moniker. Built of cast iron, it was way too heavy to move. The only solution was to hammer it into smaller, more manageable pieces. She'd tried several times during the week, but to no avail.

Now, fueled by her anger, she hoisted the sledge hammer overhead and gave the tub the biggest whack she could muster. To her surprise, a large chunk gave way in one corner.

"Here, let me have that before you break something." Chance entered and reached for the sledge hammer.

She pulled it from his grasp. "No way. Besides, breaking something is the whole idea. I've been hammering on this thing off and on all week. As it turns out, all I needed to get the job done was you here to make false accusations and irritate me. Now get outta my way before I use this thing on you."

Hands up in the air in surrender, Chance backed out of the room.

Once more she raised the sledge hammer above her head and let it fall. The head clanged against the side of the tub with such force her bones and teeth vibrated. But instead of cracking off another piece of the Beast, the sledge hammer's handle busted.

Chance leaned against the door frame, arms and legs crossed, the familiar 'I-told-you-so' smirk back on his face.

Her anger elevated to maximum boiling point. She couldn't even run away, because Chance stood between her and freedom. Instead, Dakota slumped to the floor and tossed her end of the broken sledge hammer to the ground. Her back against a bare stud, she pulled her knees to her chest and lowered her head to crossed arms.

Why had she been so excited when Chance made the call to go ahead with J.C.'s plan? The answer came immediately. Hope. It had given her hope of a permanent place to live and write and be happy. It was her own fault. She should've realized life just didn't work that way. How stupid she'd been to think it was even possible. Several more minutes ticked away with neither of them making a sound. Finally she lifted her head.

Chance stood in the same location with the same stance. But his face was different. Cold, hard anger had replaced the prior smirk.

"I'm not sure this is gonna work, Chance."

His upper lip curled into a sneer. "Like I didn't see that coming. When things get rough, you run away."

The words hit a little too close to home. She turned her gaze toward the double-paned window they'd installed earlier in the week. Light cascaded through the window, spilling a rectangular pool of bright sunshine at her feet. Yes, she did have a tendency to run away, but so far that had proved to be the best way of dealing with the hand life dealt her. It's how she'd escaped the lecherous clutches of her mother's boyfriends. How she'd managed to survive her father's verbal attacks. Even how she'd avoided further emotional pain from Chance's exalted opinion of himself and low opinion of her.

"You're right, it is how I deal with things, but it works for me."

"Well, not this time, sister." He moved in like a man on a mission and fell to a seated position beside her. "Trust me, I wanna quit just as badly as you do. This takes up my time, my money, and my effort."

"Your time and your money and your effort? It's always about you, isn't it?"

The words obviously caught him off guard. His mouth fell open, and wounded eyes searched hers. Finally he spoke. "Sorry if it comes across that way sometimes."

"If?" Dakota faced the patch of blue sky just beyond the window. If only she were a bird. "Sometimes?"

No sound came from the lips that in the past had justified his sin while loudly proclaiming hers.

"What? No excuses? No reasons why I'm responsible for not only my bad choices, but yours as well?"

His gray eyes clouded under thunderous dark brows.

"What's wrong, Chance? You finally noticing the beams in your eyes after all these years of trying to remove the specks in mine?"

Again, no response.

A sigh escaped. "We don't have time for this, Chance. Let's talk and get this worked out, or move on."

"You want this to work out?" Low and soft, his words knifed to her core. "I kind of got that impression at lunch the other day. Now I'm not so sure."

She thought through his question and comment, not at all happy about her conclusion. "I do want this to work out, but we're gonna have to come to a few understandings first."

"Agreed. First rule. No running away."

A cynical laugh burst from her mouth. "There you go again with those rules of yours. But, hey, at least you're voicing them instead of having them in your head and expecting me to live up to them."

His frown grew even darker, his scars more pronounced. "Is that really how you see me? A self-righteous know-it-all with rules?"

"Yep. That pretty much sums it up."

"Why didn't you say something years ago?"

Why indeed? Maybe because it felt too much like taking on his harsh attitude when all she longed for was peace and harmony. "I hate confrontation, Chance. I hate it when people criticize me, so I don't criticize others. No matter how founded my complaints are."

"Which explains your tendency to run away, if not physically, then in every other sense of the word." His tone held boy-like fascination, and his expression softened like he'd finally reached a place of understanding.

"Bingo!" She bonked the tip of his nose with one finger.

To her surprise, he laughed.

To her even bigger surprise, her mouth turned traitor and smiled. Smiled! When all she wanted to do was stay mad at him for the rest of her life.

"You should really do that more often, you know." Chance nudged her with his left elbow.

"What?"

"Smile. Yours is particularly gorgeous."

Uh oh. Drawbridge up, alligators released to the moat. She much preferred her anger to vulnerability. She'd even take his false accusations and self-righteous attitude over this softer, more appealing, Chance Johnson. A Chance Johnson who made her want to once more believe he could be trusted.

He turned his head slightly, studying her from his peripheral vision. "What just happened? It's like a wall went up when I admired your smile."

Ramrod straight, she sat up, her eyes trained on the Beast. Finally, she faced him again. "Did I mention that I absolutely hate confrontation?"

Chance chuckled and thumped his chest with one palm. "Let me have it. I can take it." Apparently he thought better of his words, because just as quickly, he raised both hands in a defensive posture. "But not with your fist. Just words."

"Chicken."

"Bwock. Bwock." He stuck his fingertips beneath his arms and flapped imaginary wings.

"Wimp."

"Oh, c'mon. Is that the best you can do?" His smirky grin was back.

"Okay." She scooted along the floor until she faced him, knee-to-knee. "Ask and ye shall receive."

His dark brows climbed up his forehead, but he said nothing.

Dakota carefully chose her words. They came halting and stilted, much like her writing here of late. "Because, of, uh, some things that have happened in the past, my brain interprets comments like the one you just ma—"

"The one about your smile?"

"Yes."

"Okay. Just wanted to make sure I was following."

She mentally tried to re-gather lost words which scattered like a herd of deer the minute he uttered a sound. "As I was saying, those kind of comments make me put my guard up."

"Why? I was just paying you a compliment."

Dakota skewed her lips to one side, searching for an answer. "In my experience, comments like that always come attached to expectations."

"Like I'm hitting on you?"

Good. It was out in the open. "Yes. Which brings up the second rule to keep things between us on nothing more than a platonic level."

"Now look who's coming up with rules."

"Okay, so maybe 'rule' wasn't the right word."

"Semantics." He yawned. "Let's just cut to the chase, shall we? So far, we've decided no running away and no compliments. Agreed?"

She nodded out of habit.

"Aha!" He held up an index finger. "There's another thing we need to discuss."

"What?"

"Your tendency to be agreeable."

What was wrong with being agreeable? It was just plain old polite. "There's nothing wrong with being agreeable."

"Yes there is. You do it to be polite, but I interpret it as your willingness to agree, then you get mad at me for things you've already agreed to, and I'm left standing there wondering what just happened."

She blinked. "Whoa, dude. You seriously need help with those run-on sentences."

He twisted his head to one side, lips pressed together. "Quit changing the subject, Dakota. I'm serious. Did my run-on sentence make even a little bit of sense?"

"I think I understand what you were trying to say, if that's what you mean." Good grief. Now her words sounded as confusing as his.

"Good. A perfect example is this. I don't think you're opposed to compliments. I think you're actually opposed to anything that might infer that I want something other than friendship from you."

A tiny light dawned. Was he asking for more clarity in her communication with him? Well, why didn't he just say so in the first place? Oy. This communication thing was gonna be far more complicated than she'd first thought. She brought fingers to massage the growing pain behind her eyes. "Okay, let me see if I have this straight. Rule number one: no running away. Rule number two:

Compliments are okay, but only with the stipulation that nothing other than friendship is inferred. Rule number three: Communicate clearly."

He listened intently, then beamed. "That's it!" Relief crossed his features. "Boy, am I glad that's over." He made a move to stand.

"Not so fast, Buck-o." She grabbed a handful of his pants leg and tugged him back to a sitting position.

"There's more?" he asked weakly.

"Oh, yeah." She'd barely scratched the surface. "Rule four: No accusing tone or acting as though you're better than me in any shape, form, or fashion."

"Okay. Rule five." Chance held up a hand, fingers splayed. "When either one of us feels angry at the other, we take time to sort through things."

She nodded. "Rule six. Don't say things that hurt the other person's feelings."

He made a face. "That's such a girl rule." His face crumpled as though sobbing, and he brought both fists to his eyes to wipe pretend tears. "Wa-ah. You hurt my feelings." The words came out whiny and high-pitched.

She knuckle-punched his arm and glared.

"Oh, all right, we'll keep the girly rule. Rule seven: no carrying grudges or keeping score."

A short snort sounded through her nose. "I'm not the one who does that. That would be you."

The air grew thick. Chance, more quiet than she'd ever known him, searched her eyes for several minutes, his own dark and foreboding. "Then tell me why you left all those years ago, even after I apologized." The softly-spoken words were edged with hurt.

The mention of the past carried ancient power, bringing with it a host of vivid memories. Dakota ducked her head. How could she explain that it wasn't a grudge that had sent her packing, but knowing he would never again see her in the same light? Never again treat her the same? "It was more the way you apologized, Chance. It wasn't that I was harboring a grudge."

"What do you mean, the way I apologized? An apology is an apology."

There it was again, that same old condescending tone. The tone that revealed his true opinion of her. "Listen to yourself. It's like what I was trying to tell you earlier, which by the way, you completely ignored."

"What are you talking about?"

"Earlier when I mentioned your tendency to look at the speck in my eyes while ignoring the beam in yours."

Just as before, he didn't comment.

"Ever since that night, you treat me like I'm the only one to blame, like you were completely innocent." She hesitated, praying for an explanation. Should she continue, or was it really worth it to dredge up these painful memories? He'd already broken their newly-made rule four. If she continued down this path of conversation, she'd be communicating all right, but words with a potential for hurt. She pressed her lips together and shook her head. Back at square one. Being confrontational just wasn't her style.

"Let's just go ahead and tackle the elephant in the room. I don't think either of us really wants to go there, but if we don't, we'll continue to skirt the issue." He licked his lips, as though considering his words. "The way I remember it, you *were* the one at fault."

Chapter Eleven

No doubt about it. He was in the dog house with Dakota big time. Chance scratched his head and climbed from the pickup at church the following Sunday morning. Naming the problem was part of the solution, right? That's what he'd always heard, but it sure didn't seem to fit this scenario. A big part of him wanted to back out of the whole deal, but he couldn't exactly do that after making the rule of no running away. But something had to be done. They'd worked all day yesterday with her hardly saying a word. What else could he do to get back in her good graces? Especially since he was right. How could he convince her she was the one at fault?

He waved to Mama Beth as she scurried into another building. The memory of that night had replayed in his mind at least a million times. She was the one who had instigated everything by how she dressed and acted. Like she'd intentionally set out to trap him. Well, trap him she had, and he'd given in to temptation at her hands.

A heavy sigh escaped, the perfect expression of how he felt on the inside. Burdened. Bogged down. *I've forgiven her, right Lord?*

He searched the cloudy sky as he walked toward small group session and listened for the still small voice. Silence. As though the clouds served as some sort of barrier between him and God. Resolute, he entered the door to the small group study led every Sunday morning by Matt. Maybe his time at church could point him in the right direction.

People congregated in small groups, munching on donuts or fruit, steaming cups of coffee in hand. Chance made his way to where Matt stood talking to a new friend of theirs who'd recently joined the Miller's Creek police force.

"Hey, Carter. Matt." Chance shook both their hands.

Matt chuckled. "Don't mean to be the bearer of bad news, my friend, but based on the luggage under your eyes, you might want to check into taking a vacation."

Chance tried to smile, but the only thing he could muster was one corner of his mouth. "Thanks for stating the obvious, buddy."

"You okay?" Carter Jennings, who towered over both he and Matt, sipped his coffee, his eyebrows raised, his eyes trained on Chance.

"Honestly, I've been better." He turned toward the nearby table and snatched a donut.

Matt frowned. "Mr. Health Nut eating a donut? Something really is eating you."

Chance stopped in mid-chew and eyed the donut. Good way to clog an artery or two. He took another bite, not caring at the moment.

"Wanna talk about it?" His best friend often wore his counselor hat, generous, but sometimes to the point of being nosy.

He shook his head. "Maybe later. Gotta wrap my brain around it first."

"Sometimes talking through it speeds up that process."

Chance eyed the clock. Good. Almost time to start. "Not now."

Matt nodded, his eyes clouded with concern, then backed away toward the front of the room. "Later it is.

Okay, everyone, find a seat. Today we're talking about forgiveness. What it is and what it isn't."

Chance's jaw clenched at the mention of forgiveness. Maybe he should've slept in this morning. Had Matt somehow sensed his struggle and decided to preach at him during small group time? He took a seat close to Carter.

After a word of prayer, Matt moved to the dry erase board. Red marker oozed words. Repentance. Apology. Reconciliation. Pardon. Forgiveness. Forgetting. Judgmental attitudes.

Ouch. The very thing Dakota had accused him of.

His friend continued to write as bits of muted conversation and laughter sounded around the room. Hurt. Anger. Bitterness. Resentment. Blame. Holding a grudge. Justice. Mercy. Grace. Revenge. Retaliation. Failure. Guilt. Acknowledging wrong. Excusing. Restoring trust.

"Sure we have enough time for this topic, Matt?" Carter drawled out the words, and laughter erupted.

Matt turned, his good-natured grin in place. "That depends on y'all, not me. We'll stay until you learn how to forgive." Laughter and conversation erupted once more. He turned back to the board and continued writing. Love. Hate. Punishment. Sorrow. Regret. Confession. Distance. Isolation. Withdrawal.

Okay, now he was describing Dakota to a T. Behind him the door creaked open and quietly closed, followed by light footsteps and the squeak of a metal chair as someone put their weight down.

Matt wrote with rapid staccato strokes, and the board grew more red than white. Forgiving others. Forgiving yourself. Forgiving God. His friend faced the group, who had grown strangely quiet. "As you can see, a whole host of things are tied up in our concept of forgiveness. Before we start this discussion, let me say we're not talking about small grievances here. Those are things we can easily let go of and chalk up to differences of personality. Instead, we're going to talk about those life experiences that send us reeling. Those events that are personal, unjust, and deep. Those wounds we can't explain away or find purpose in." Matt's eyes took on distance, as though reminded of his own deep wounds. "So with that in mind, what is forgiveness? And what is it not?"

"It's not excusing the behavior of the other person."

"Or smoothing it over as if it didn't mean anything."

"It's something we do out of obedience to God."

"We forgive because we've been forgiven," came another voice.

Matt smiled and nodded. "Y'all make it sound so easy."

The room quieted again. No, forgiveness was one of the hardest things any believer ever had to do.

"It's letting it go." The voice was Dakota's, and it came from the back of the room, timid and soft.

His stomach churned, and Chance had to force himself not to turn around and glare at her. What was she doing here anyway? This made two weeks in a row, but, hey, based on the past couple of days, she could use a lesson in forgiveness.

Matt pointed her way. "That's the perfect definition of forgiveness. We're commanded to forgive as we've been forgiven, but that's so much easier said than done. Right?"

Heads nodded, and low murmurs of assent skipped across the room.

"True forgiveness isn't natural to us. What do we crave instead?"

"We want revenge and retaliation and retribution. We want the other person to hurt like us, and we want them to pay. We want justice." Chance spoke the words, hating them and recognizing their truth at the same time.

Matt nodded. "But as Dakota just pointed out, true forgiveness occurs when we're able to release both the offense and the offender. When we let it go. Now how do we do that? Everyone turn to Genesis 45. We all know the story of Joseph, the favorite son of his father. Joseph had dreams that put him on a higher level than the rest of his family. Then he made the mistake of telling his brothers. To make matter worse, Joseph's father gave him a special gift, which made the brothers hate him even more." Matt pointed to the word 'hate' on the board. "So what did they do? They threw him in a well and talked about killing him. Finally they sold him into slavery and told their dad he'd been killed by wild animals. Later in his life, Joseph was falsely accused by his master's wife and landed in prison. He had every reason to hold a grudge against his brothers and maybe even against God." Matt circled 'grudge' and 'forgiving God.' "Years pass, and old Joe gets a promotion to the second highest position in the country. His brothers come in search of food. When they realize who he is, they're understandably upset. This brother they wronged many times over now has the power to destroy them. Someone read verses five through eight of chapter 45."

Dani Miller began to read, and Chance followed along in his Bible. *"And now, do not be distressed and do not be angry with yourselves for selling me here, because it was to save lives that God sent me ahead of you. For two years now there has been famine in the land, and for the next five years there will not be plowing and reaping. But God sent me ahead of you to preserve for you a remnant on earth and to save your lives by a great deliverance. So then, it was not you who sent me here, but God."*

Matt rubbed his chin and paced across the front of the room, his Bible in one hand. "Joseph could speak these words of forgiveness to the people who'd ruined his life because he kept his focus on God and realized God's hand at work. What's the lesson here for us, especially in light of letting things go?"

"By letting offenses go and releasing the one who hurt us, we turn it over to God, recognizing He has a higher purpose, the ability to judge the situation accurately, and deal with it as He sees fit." Andy spoke the words with conviction.

Matt's eyes narrowed as though deep in thought. "Is turning an offense over to God something we do one time and then forget it?"

This time people shook their heads.

"Why?"

"Because we have trouble forgetting, and we want to keep dredging things up." Chance's eyes widened. Had those words come from his mouth?

"Exactly." Matt smiled. "We've all heard the expression 'forgive and forget,' but I think we'd all agree that's not even humanly possible." His friend scanned the room. "The more we try to focus on forgetting, the more we're focused on the things we're trying to forget. Does God forget?"

"He chooses not to remember." Again, Dakota's voice sounded.

"Wow." Matt's face held reverential awe.

Tears pricked at the back of Chance's eyes at a love so strong. God had chosen to forget his faults and weaknesses. His sin.

"Next question. Does the offender have to repent in order for us to forgive?"

Conflicting answers came from all directions.

Matt let it continue momentarily then raised a hand to silence the group. "Interesting. We seem to be pretty evenly divided over this one. Okay, let's start with a definition of what repentance is. Anyone?"

"It means being sincerely sorry for what you've done, confessing it, and apologizing." Trish Tyler answered.

Andy shook his head. "Sorry, honey, but I don't believe that. First of all, how do we know someone's sincere in their apology? Just because they look or act a certain way? And I don't think confession, apology, and regret are the same as repentance."

"Why not?" Matt had a way of forcing people to get to the heart of a matter without ruffling feathers or making someone feel put on the spot. "Anyone remember our earlier discussion about what confession is?"

Carter spoke up. "Agreeing with God about our sin."

"Yep." Matt nodded. "Did God forgive us before or after we agreed with Him about our sin? Before or after we confessed?"

"He forgave us while were still sinners."

Confusion spiraled through Chance. Every time Dakota spoke, wisdom and truth flowed from her lips. She definitely wasn't the same person he'd known before.

"Yes, He did." Matt's voice softened, and his eyes took on a radiant gleam. "God's forgiveness is based on His never-ending love, mercy, and grace. When we say the Lord's Prayer and get to the part that says 'Forgive us our trespasses as we forgive those who trespass against us,' have you ever stopped to think of what you're saying? Have you ever considered that you're asking God to forgive you in the same way you forgive others?"

A sacred hush descended, so quiet and still even the tick of the clock sounded deafening. Chance's chest tightened with each jump of the second hand. *Oh, God, I'm so sorry. Help me to forgive as You've forgiven me.* He looked up to see other heads around the room bowed in silent prayer.

Tears swam in Matt's eyes. "I don't know about y'all, but when I think of how much God has forgiven me, it makes me want to be more forgiving. Maybe that's what Jesus tried to teach His disciples, and us. We learn to forgive by remembering and understanding just how much God has forgiven us."

He paused a moment to wipe his eyes. "Okay, let's head back to repentance. Here's a mental snapshot." Matt stepped toward one side of the room and pointed ahead. "I'm heading toward sin, doing what I want to do when I want to do it, ignoring God." Suddenly he stopped. "Then I realize it." He pivoted and started in the opposite direction. "I turn away from my sin, and in the process I head back to God. That's repentance. Now, based on all we've just discussed, is repentance of the offender necessary for us to forgive them?"

"No, but it sure helps." Carter's deadpan tone brought on more laughs.

Matt's hearty chuckle joined the rest. "It might make it easier for us to forgive, but it's not a requirement. Same can be said of apologies, contrition, regret. We may want to see those things in a person who's hurt us, but nowhere in the Bible are those things mentioned as things that have to take place before we forgive." Matt moved to the whiteboard and circled the word 'apology.' He faced the group with a smile on his face and his right hand raised. "As kids, how many of you ever had to say you were sorry to someone for something you did?"

Hands raised around the room as laughter and comments broke out.

"And how many of you apologized without meaning one word?"

The laughter increased.

Matt lowered his hand. "Let's talk about apology a sec. We've already seen it's not necessary for forgiveness, but let's talk about why." He walked over to where Chance sat. "If I wrong Chance and go to him and say 'Man, I'm really sorry for what I did,' does that require any sort of response from him?"

Heads shook from side to side.

"But what if I say, 'Man, I'm really sorry for what I did. Will you forgive me?' Now that demands a response on his part. How does that change things?"

"It puts both you and the offender one step closer to reconciliation." The same familiar voice from the same back corner of the room.

"Now there's another concept all tied up with forgiveness. Will we always experience reconciliation when we forgive?" Matt shook his head, the corners of his mouth turned down. "That's the ideal, but it doesn't always work. Both parties have to be on board with reconciliation for that to ever happen. What about trust? Is it always restored when we forgive others?" He eyed the clock on the back wall. "One more thing before we go. How do we know when we've truly forgiven someone?"

No one answered.

"Pray and think about that question this week. Let's pray, and then we'll be dismissed."

Chance's head swam with thoughts as he stood with the rest of the class to be dismissed in prayer. All this time he'd confused the issues of forgiveness, repentance, confession, reconciliation, and the restoration of trust. He rubbed a hand across his mouth. Enough to give anyone a headache. At some point, he had to come to grips with the fact that even if he and Dakota forgave each other, they might never reach reconciliation and restored trust. Those two things would have to be mutually agreed upon. Did he even want reconciliation? Did he actually believe they could trust each other after all that had happened between them? His shoulders slumped. *Oh, Lord, help us both. This thing is too big for us to handle on our own.*

Chapter Twelve

Dakota breathed in deeply. The scent of musty earth rose from the base of the old oak near the church, the shade cool and inviting, a place to hide away from Chance while she waited for Matt and Grace Tyler. On a whim last night, after a very long and trying day of working with Chance, she'd pulled out Matt's counseling card and given him a call.

She wiped sweaty palms against her jeans. At this particular moment it seemed like an incredibly stupid move, but she was at her wit's end about how to handle the situation with Chance.

With a step backward, she leaned against the rough bark of the tree, her eyes trained on the people descending the church steps. The farmhouse renovation just had to work. Yes, to honor her grandparents and J.C., but more than anything, she longed for some place safe and permanent.

But how much more hurt could she endure from Chance? This morning's lesson on forgiveness had been both thought-provoking and inspiring. Just what she needed to hear. And Chance too, for that matter, if he'd listened with the idea of applying what he learned to himself. Letting hurts go was something she'd worked on for years, but having Chance as a constant accuser had re-opened old scabs and scars, like a piece of rough grit sandpaper against her heart.

Matt and Grace appeared in front of her out of nowhere. "There you are." Matt held his wife's hand, a friendly grin in place. "We almost didn't see you in the shadow of this old live oak."

"I meant to keep an eye on the front door so I could step out when I saw you. Guess I got distracted."

"Okay if we eat lunch at our house? Thought we might have more privacy there." Matt searched her face, as though waiting not only for an answer, but also digging deeper for non-verbal clues.

She lowered her head. "Sure. That sounds great."

"You can follow us to the house. I'll get lunch together while you two talk." Grace spoke the words kindly, but also matter-of-factly. One of those get-straight-to-business types.

A few minutes later Dakota followed behind the Tyler's brand new SUV in her rusty old tank of a pickup. A slow burn moved to her cheeks, and she brought fingertips to rub it away. What had she been thinking? Yes, she needed someone to talk to. Desperately. But Matt and Grace were way out of her league.

By the time they arrived at the beautiful two-story house a minute later, she'd almost decided to call the whole thing off. The Tyler's pulled into the long driveway, then waited by the concrete steps leading to the front porch, both with welcoming smiles.

"Your house is beautiful." Dakota approached slowly, peering up at the architectural detail of the early twentieth-century house.

"Thank you." Grace started up the steps, Matt at her side.

Dakota bit her lip and tried to think of an excuse to leave. Nothing.

Inside, the home was surprisingly modern and up-to-date, with clean-line furnishings and a contemporary color palette which fit the couple. "Very nicely done." Dakota gazed through the open-living concept space, past the gargantuan stair case, living room and dining room, and into the expansive kitchen.

"Why don't you two sit in here by the fire to chat while I get lunch together?" Grace clicked a remote to turn on the gas log fireplace.

Nice.

Matt held out a hand toward a comfortable-looking chair while his wife's shoes clipped unevenly against the hardwood floors, revealing her pronounced limp. Hadn't Chance mentioned something about a bad accident which had paralyzed Grace for a while?

"Glad you called last night, Dakota. Gracie and I've been hoping to get to know you better." Matt removed his jacket and laid it across the back of the sofa before taking a seat.

Spanish music sounded from the kitchen, and Gracie sang along softly.

"If the music bothers you, we'll turn it off. We're both music lovers."

"Gracie has a beautiful voice, and it doesn't bother me at all." In fact, she preferred it. Maybe it would keep Grace from hearing her conversation with Matt. The last thing she needed was for someone she admired so much to think less of her.

"We enjoyed having you in small group this morning, too. You had great answers. I can tell you're a fellow believer."

Her cheeks flushed. "Thank you." Dakota lowered her gaze, searching for words. Maybe she just needed to spurt it out before she completely lost her nerve. "The topic of forgiveness is actually the reason I called."

"Oh?" Matt crossed an ankle over his knee and rested one arm along the back of the couch.

"Yeah. there's someone I thought I'd forgiven, but being around this person seems to dredge up old issues and hurts, making me wonder if I've forgiven them at all."

"I take it we're talking about Chance."

A breath lodged in her throat. She hadn't wanted to make this person-specific, but who else could it be? Her hands grew restless in her lap, and her knees began their own little dance.

"What do you think causes those old hurts to resurface?"

How did she say this without sounding accusatory? "I guess because he blames me for something that happened a long time ago and treats me accordingly."

"And how is that?"

Like trash. "Like an inferior." She paused. "I know I'm to blame for part of what happened between us, but I don't bear full responsibility. When he treats me like it's my fault, it hurts. I know I have to forgive him. I don't struggle with that so much as why I should continue to allow him to hurt me."

"You shouldn't." Matt's lips clamped in a thin line. "You don't do anyone a favor when you allow them to treat you poorly. Like we said this morning in class, forgiveness doesn't mean excusing what the other person does, but it also doesn't mean you become a doormat."

Just what she'd done with Kane--become his doormat--and she had the shoeprints on her back to prove it. "That's a problem. I have to work with Chance. I can't figure out how to be around him without being in constant emotional pain."

He rubbed a hand across his mouth, then propped his chin on his hand, an index finger at rest directly below his nose. "I can see where that would be a problem. Have you tried explaining how you feel?"

Had she? "I've tried to tell him how he's acting." But sharing her feelings wasn't something she did easily.

Matt cocked his head to one side, his gaze directly on her, his eyes sincere. "That could be part of the issue. Most people don't like their shortcomings pointed out."

Dakota nibbled at the inside corner of her mouth. Come to think of it, neither did she.

"Maybe you should just explain to him how his behavior and comments make you feel. Instead of starting a sentence with the word 'you,' try rephrasing it with the words 'I feel.'"

"I can do that." Wow. Matt had given her really useful advice in just a few minutes time. Now if she could just figure out how to accurately describe her feelings to Chance without turning into a weepy mess.

"But something about it bothers you."

Very perceptive man. Dakota sucked in a deep breath. "I'm not good at focusing on my feelings. At least not with another person."

Matt nodded. "That's common, Dakota. Nothing to be embarrassed about. In fact, sometimes people who are the most vulnerable are often the one's who struggle with it the most."

Vulnerable? Did she really come across as vulnerable?

"That bothers you, too."

"I don't like to think of myself as vulnerable. I've survived a lot more than most people my age. I think I'm strong and able to handle just about anything."

"Vulnerability doesn't supersede personal strength. It takes a lot of strength to be vulnerable with someone."

Dakota thought through the statement. Yes, but did she have that kind of strength?

Matt's expression underwent a subtle change, like an unwanted guest had knocked on the door of his heart. "Sounds like you might've had a childhood similar to mine."

She sat up straighter. Matt Tyler had a bad childhood? And he'd turned out so well. The thought somehow offered hope. "What do you mean?"

"My mother abandoned Andy and me shortly after I was born. Dad never got over it, and preferred the company of alcohol over his sons. Andy became the head of the house at the ripe old age of five. I handled it differently, with long hair, tattoos, and a rebellious streak."

Compassion flooded her heart and leaked out her eyes without warning. She swiped at tears. "Kids have to live through so much sometimes."

His forehead wrinkled, and he nodded. "You mind me asking what you had to deal with?"

Every muscle in her body tensed. Not a topic she particularly wanted to discuss, but since she was already here. "My dad had an affair when I was a little girl. Mom couldn't forgive him, and they divorced. My mother and older sister always hit it off. I was a Daddy's girl. After he left, I had no one." Tears flowed down her cheeks, unstoppable. "After that, I had trouble in school and trouble with Mom's boyfriends. I ran away several times, which also put me in trouble with the law. I ended up in juvy, then got tossed around from place to place until I ended up at my grandfather's farm at the end of my senior year." The words spilled out, as though long pent up behind a stone-hard dam.

"Your story's pretty common, unfortunately. You mentioned your mom's boyfriends." His light brown eyes held questions.

Dakota released a shaky breath, her gaze back at rest on her trembling hands. "Yeah. Imagine the worst, and that would pretty much explain it."

"Did you tell your mom?"

She nodded. Not that it had done any good.

"And how did she react?"

A slow tremble rumbled through her body, and she stared toward the sunlight streaming in the glass plate window, made blurry by a wash of tears. "She didn't believe me. Said I was lying to keep her from being happy."

Matt handed her a tissue. "So sorry, Dakota." His voice was soft and thick with emotion.

The room grew painfully quiet while she wiped her face and blew her nose. Finally she raised her gaze to his, one shoulder lifted in a half shrug. "I just wanted to be loved. Wanted it so bad, I would've done just about anything to have it."

"Especially love from a man?"

Her throat thickened. That's why she'd acted the way she did towards Chance. She'd loved him and wanted to prove it. Wanted him to love her in return. "I know I didn't handle things well. I wish I could go back for a do-over."

Matt patted her arm. "Your story's the same as millions of women around the world, Dakota. Yeah, it might not should've happened, but it did. The only thing to do now is learn to deal with it and move forward."

She sniffed and swatted at her nose with the soggy Kleenex. "I know. But being around Chance makes it hard to get past it and move forward. I don't understand why, but this seems to be where God has dumped me. At least for now."

He leaned forward, elbows on knees, his kind eyes latched on hers. "Think about what you just said, Dakota. God did indeed place you here, which means He has a reason. You just have to trust that He knows what He's doing. He took my mess and turned it into a message. He can do the same for you."

The words brought instant peace. Her heart's prayer. Yes, God was the answer and always had been. The love she'd sought not just from Chance and Kane had been fully met in Christ. He accepted her as she was, scars and flaws included, the perfect picture of true forgiveness. Dakota managed a grateful smile. "Thank you, Matt."

He shrugged. "All I did was listen. Sounds like you've been holding that in a while."

She nodded. "I've never told anyone what I just told you."

"That's not healthy. You always have someone to talk to here." His eyes left hers and landed on his wife, still in the kitchen. "Not just me, but Gracie, for that matter. She's quiet, which a lot of people interpret as aloof and indifferent. Nothing could be further from the truth. I can see the two of you being really good friends."

An immediate rush of joy, followed by panic, churned through her system in a matter of seconds. Never had she experienced that kind of relationship with any of the women in her life. How would she know how to act or what to say?

"Just be yourself, Dakota. That's all any of us can do well." He paused a second. "Don't mean to stick my nose where it's not wanted, but what happened after you left Miller's Creek the first time? Why the name change?"

Familiar bricks of the familiar wall she'd built years ago for protection, instantly re-stacked themselves, despite her effort to keep it from happening. She couldn't tell him everything, but she could share a little bit. "I found another man, of course, but this one wasn't so nice."

Matt grimaced. "Abusive?"

Abusive might not be a strong enough word, but there wasn't just one word to describe Kane. Add to it controlling, manipulative, derogatory, stifling, dangerous, the list could go on and on.

"Is that why you changed your name? Are you hiding from him?"

She nodded. At least his guess was partially correct. Best not to elaborate too much, for his safety as well as hers.

"What about the police? Have you tried a restraining order?"

"Yeah, but he has friends in high places. The police found me the first time I left and took me straight back to him." The night he'd almost killed her. "This time around I've avoided the police altogether."

A heavy sigh sounded from Matt's throat. He lowered his head and shoulders toward the floor, his head wagging from side to side. For several seconds he stayed that way, then finally lifted his head. "You'll be safe here, Dakota. I won't say anything to anyone, but I highly suggest going to the local police with your story. They're good guys."

Not an option. Thankfully the doorbell rang to save her further explanation.

"Wonder who that is?" Matt stood and strode to the door. "Hey, buddy."

"Hey."

A voice she'd know anywhere. Chance.

"Come on in. We're just about to eat."

Her frayed nerves just couldn't take a dose of him right now. Dakota hurriedly wiped her eyes and gathered her purse. She rose to her feet just as he entered. Her gaze automatically went to his face, and she swallowed hard.

His blue-gray eyes almost disappeared beneath a dark scowl. He didn't speak.

Matt's eyes flitted back and forth between the two of them. "Um, Dakota's having lunch with us, too."

The perfect segue, which she jumped on. "Actually, I need to get back to the farm."

Her new-found friend and confidant grew very still, but he nodded, understanding in his features. "Maybe some other time then. I'll give you a call later. And maybe you and Gracie could have lunch one day next week."

Grace stepped in from the kitchen to stand beside him. "I'd like that very much." Her dark eyes held nothing but kindness.

"Me, too." Dakota moved to give them both a hug, and then stepped past Chance to let herself out the front door.

Chapter Thirteen

The wind gusted, stirring up dust from the road and blasting against Chance's bare arms late Tuesday afternoon. He rubbed away the sting and sudden chill bumps, then glanced at the quickly darkening skies and knocked on the door again. "Dakota?" Daisy sat beside him obediently, but looked up with questioning eyes.

The door opened. In one hand Dakota held a can of bean dip and in the other a bag of Fritos. She didn't move from the doorway or invite him in, and her chin jutted out defensively. Uh oh. With her in that kind of mood, this peace offering thing might not go as planned.

"You know how bad that junk is for you?"

Her eyes disappeared momentarily behind closed eyelids. At last her eyes reappeared, though they held uncustomary coldness. "*Au contraire.*" Dakota held up both items. "Beans and corn. Also known as veggies, which are supposedly good for you." She swirled around and waltzed away from the door. Maybe not the friendliest of invitations, but at least she hadn't slammed the door in his face.

Chance followed and closed the door behind him, a tight grip on the leash of his apology gift. Hopefully his little surprise would heal the rift between them.

Dakota plopped down on her thrift store couch. Only then did her eyes latch onto the German Shepherd. The upper part of her face wrinkled and her mouth fell open. "What is that?"

"A dog."

She glowered and cocked her head to one side. "Duh. You think? I know it's a dog. But when did you get it, and why did you bring it out here?" Distaste colored her expression as she eyed the dog.

A slight whimper sounded from Daisy, and she sat back on her haunches.

"You're scaring her with that scowl on your face."

"Good. A little healthy fear is a good thing as far as I'm concerned. Did you forget that I hate dogs?"

His eyebrows scuttled up his forehead. Uh...she hated dogs?

Dakota raised her gaze to the ceiling and shook her head. "Why am I not surprised? Don't you remember that house we were working on with PawPaw? The one with the Chihuahua who deliberately tried to intimidate me?"

An image of Dakota scaling a tree to get away from the pint-sized dog and his especially ferocious bark entered his mind, and he laughed out loud. One look at her un-amused face was enough for him to rapidly bring his laughter under control. He lowered his head to conceal the grin he couldn't whisk away. "I'd forgotten all about it. He knew you were afraid of him. If you let dogs know you're the boss, they can be really great companions."

Dakota turned her head, her lips clamped as though containing some sarcastic comment. Outside the wind howled mercilessly.

"Come here, Daisy." The dog followed him to the metal folding chair beside the couch, tail a-wag. Chance sat on the edge of the chair and pointed to the hardwood floors that now shone with a fresh coat of polyurethane. "Sit, Daisy."

The dog just smiled and continued to wag her tail. Only now it was more like the tail wagging the dog.

Chance snapped his fingers and pointed to the floor again, the way Carter had showed him. Daisy jumped up and nipped at his fingers with her ultra sharp teeth. "Ow!" Okay, so maybe he'd mixed up the signals somehow. He yanked his hand away and examined it for puncture marks.

Dakota laughed as a clap of thunder rumbled. "Hey, I might like this dog after all." She eyed the dog with a hint of trepidation. "Come here, girl."

Chance released the leash. The dog trotted to the couch, sat obediently without being told, and laid her head on Dakota's knee, her big brown eyes looking up adoringly. Traitor.

"I think she likes me." A gorgeous smile broke out on her face. She gingerly brought her hand to the dog's head. Daisy sighed through her nose, bringing forth a delightful laugh from Dakota.

His heart stopped beating momentarily, and then resumed, but with uncustomary flips. He brought a hand to his chest. Okay, this whole missing her thing that had gone on all week was wreaking havoc on his physical well-being.

Dakota continued to stroke the dog, but her head turned toward him. "I'm a little surprised to see you since you went MIA on me."

He leaned back quickly, eyes wide. It wasn't like her to be so confrontational, and this from someone who insisted she didn't like confrontation. "I got the impression you didn't want me out here."

"Yes and no." She relaxed her knees and stretched out her legs. "I was upset at you for a comment you made, but I also need your help on this house."

Her words were distinct and to the point, with no beating around the bush or hem-hawing around like she usually did. "What comment?"

She leaned forward, rolled up the bag of Fritos, and re-lidded the bean dip. "About what happened between us being my fault."

"Well, it was. I can't change the truth."

Without explanation, she jumped to her feet and ran from the room. Daisy followed with a whine. The bathroom door slammed behind her.

Not a good sign. As though taking a cue from what had just happened, the bottom of the sky gave way as a torrent of rain unleashed, unbearably loud against the tin roof of the farmhouse. Now what was he supposed to do? Apologize for telling the truth?

Daisy's whimpering continued from the hallway.

An exasperated sigh exploded from his lips. He rose to his feet, stomped to the bathroom door, and pounded on it, raising his voice to be heard above the storm's din. "Sorry, Dakota. I didn't mean to upset you." Sniffles sounded from beyond the closed door. She was crying? Never in all his spats with her had he ever seen her cry.

"Go away." The words were muffled, as though her mouth was covered with a wad of tissues.

This was so not going according to plan. He stomped back to the metal chair and let his weight fall to the chair. It gave way and crashed to the floor. Chance groaned, and rolled over to one side. That's what he got for not controlling his temper.

In a flash, Dakota was back in the room, hovering over him. "Are you okay?" She stared at the broken chair, then turned her green-eyed glare on him. "You broke my chair."

He sat up and rubbed his side, checking for a cracked rib. "I may have broken more than that."

"Good. You deserve it." Tears glistened on her cheeks.

Something inside him melted. Went all gooey, like ice cream on an August day. Chance pulled himself off up the floor and gazed at her apologetically. "I didn't mean to make you cry."

Her teary eyes searched his face momentarily, then released him. She moved to the quilt-covered couch and plopped down again, Daisy right on her heels. "I want you to know how badly your accusations hurt me, Chance."

The knife in his gut twisted, slicing through more tissue. He hadn't intended on hurting her. Had he? He'd merely been trying to be honest, right? Or had he subconsciously punished her for the way she'd hurt him? "I never meant to hurt you. Or at least I don't think I did."

A bewildered expression appeared on her face.

Thoughts multiplied in his head, swirling around. Had he projected the bulk of his own guilt onto her small shoulders? The truth hit him between the eyes. His mouth gaped wide without permission, and he brought the back of his hand to his forehead. "You're right. I'm just as much to blame as you."

Eyes large, lips apart, she took a step back and stared at him in disbelief. "Well, I'll be a monkey's uncle. I never expected to hear those words outta that mouth. Matt was right."

Matt? Chance bristled. They'd discussed him? He marched over to where Dakota sat, hands fisted. "You mean to tell me that you talked to Matt about me? About us?"

She shrunk back a little. "Yeah. Isn't that why you showed up at his house on Sunday?"

"Matt Tyler is my best friend." He ground the words out between clenched teeth. "What exactly did you tell him?"

Her face paled considerably. "I didn't give him all the intimate details, if that's what you mean."

Chance did a palm plant on his forehead and stared up at the ceiling. How embarrassing! He half-sat, half-fell, to a crossed-leg sitting position on the floor, his head in his hands, Daisy immediately in his lap, licking his face. Except for the pounding rain and the slurping dog, the room grew deathly quiet. After a few minutes of chasing away his anger and humiliation, Chance looked up.

Dakota's eyes were large and round. Fearful. She said nothing, obviously waiting for him to initiate the inevitable.

"Would you mind explaining why in the world you decided to air a very personal problem to my best friend?" He gave himself a mental pat on the back. Somehow he'd managed to speak rather than shout.

She swallowed, her lips taut. "I didn't know he was your best friend, Chance. I just knew he offered free counseling."

A pounding headache built in intensity behind his skull. He closed his eyes and massaged his forehead. "You'd talk with a total stranger rather than talk to me?"

"First of all, I tried talking to you. But trying to get through that thick skull of yours is like trying to nail Jell-O to a tree." Her green eyes now shot sparks. Finally the Dakota he was used to had showed up. "In spite of my attempts to talk things out, you were determined to accuse me for something that was every bit as much your fault as it was mine. I didn't go to their house to specifically talk about what happened between us. I went to get some insight on how to work with someone bent on destroying me." Tears spilled on to her cheeks, and she buried her face in her hands. Her shoulders shook with heart-breaking sobs.

"Hey." He scooted to the couch, moved to a sitting position beside her, and placed a hand on her back. Every fiber of his being longed to cradle her in his arms, but he couldn't. Not without losing himself. "Please don't cry. It's okay."

A long minute passed, but finally she controlled her tears and looked up at him. "I didn't mean to make you angry. I just needed someone to talk to." Her wistful tone and mournful look just about did him in.

Poor thing. She had no one. "You couldn't have made a better choice than Matt. He'll keep what you said in confidence."

The words seemed to bring relief, but she didn't speak. Then her face contorted in horror, her gaze fixed over his left shoulder. "Oh no, you don't, Daisy, stop!"

He jerked his head around. Daisy stood in the corner of the room, back legs splayed, a steady stream splashing against the newly-varnished floors.

Pressure built inside Dakota and threatened to explode all over the place. She'd just redone those floors, and now one corner was coated with dog urine. Past time for both Chance and the dog to go. One for obvious reasons, the other because she couldn't trust the crazy way her heart was responding to Chance's unexpected kindness. Yes, Matt's suggestion had worked, but she hadn't been at all prepared for the way it would affect her.

"Sorry, Dakota. I'll clean it up. You have any paper towels?"

She shook her head in disgust, her gaze on the yellow puddle. "No, but I've got some old rags." Dakota hurried to the kitchen, snatched up a couple of old t-shirt rags she'd brought at a thrift store, and grabbed the trash can on her way back. "Tell me again why you brought that mutt out here."

"Daisy's not a mutt. She's a full-blooded German Shepherd and trained by a friend. By nature, Shepherds are very protective. I'll feel better knowing you're not out here alone."

Oh, so now he was concerned about her safety. "This coming from the man who hasn't been here in days."

Chance took the rag from her outstretched hand and sopped up the mess.

"And if you think you're leaving that dog out here with me, you are sadly mistaken."

He didn't respond, but deposited the soiled rag in the trash can she held out at arm's length. "I need to wash my hands."

"You'll have to use the bathroom sink. The kitchen's all torn up."

The sound of his boots clomped down the hallway, then picked up speed and volume as his footsteps grew closer again. His head appeared in the doorway. "You finished the bathroom."

Why did he look so surprised? Had he expected her to sit back on her hands, bemoaning the fact that she didn't have a man to help her? "Yeah well, the work must go on, with or without you."

"How'd you get the old bathtub out?"

"One lousy piece at a time."

"And the new one in?"

"The guys who delivered it put it in place, and then I called the plumber."

His expression darkened. "You hired a plumber?"

A sigh burst from her lungs. "I didn't feel comfortable doing the plumbing work. It made more sense to hire that work out."

"And how much did that cost me?"

Oh, yay. The accusing tone was back. "Not a penny, thank you. I paid for it myself."

His face took on the same hang-dog look she'd seen a few minutes earlier.

Her heart quickened its pace. Hmm, maybe it was better if she had the accusing Chance back, instead of this unfamiliar guy with apology in his clear blue-gray eyes.

"I'll pay you back, Dakota. How much do I owe you?" His tone was respectful and sincere.

She waved a hand and turned away, bothered by her body's Benedict-Arnold-response to this new and improved Chance. "Nothing. Now would you go wash your hands? The thought of you standing there with dog pee on them is grossing me out."

Chance laughed and disappeared. A few minutes later he returned, hands held in the air for her inspection "All clean." He continued his trek until he towered over her, something unfamiliar in his eyes.

Admiration?

"You do good work, Dakota Kelly. That bathroom looks like a million bucks."

A warm glow spread throughout her, like a flower warmed by the summer sun. "Thanks. I'm ecstatic about how it turned out. The tile that's behind the vanity was on sale. Doesn't it look great?"

He nodded. "Better than great. And the floors look amazing, too. That laminate you installed in the bathroom perfectly matches the wood floors. Mind if I take a look at the kitchen?"

"Be my guest." Dakota stood and followed him.

"Whoa." Chance spun in a slow circle, his eyes taking in the demolition. "When you said all torn up, you meant it."

The walls and ceilings were down to bare studs, and she'd ripped out the old linoleum to reveal the subfloor. All accomplished through her raging fury, spurred on by Chance's absence.

Now his gaze focused on her, his voice soft and low. "Between finishing the bathroom and tearing out the old kitchen, you've been one busy lady. Had time for writing?"

"A little." Little was the perfect word. Mark Twain would be proud. It was as though someone had stuffed all her words in a bottle and corked it tight. At some point, she had to find her muse and drag her back, kicking and screaming, if need be. Then she had to find some way to buy Chance's half of the house once this project was over. If not she'd be forced to sell and use her half of the proceeds to start over somewhere else. Based on her confused emotions at the moment, that might be a better idea anyway.

Chance peered around the room once more. "Well, I have some groceries in the truck, just in case you were amenable to me fixing you dinner, but I guess that's out of the question now." He turned his head to stare into her eyes. "You can't live on Fritos and bean dip. Want to join me at my house for dinner?"

Mesmerized by the lights dancing within those bottomless pools of his, one word tumbled from her lips. "Sure." What? How had that happened?

A small smile lifted the corners of his mouth. "Good. Daisy and I'll wait in the living room while you get your shoes on."

All the way up the stairs, Dakota gave herself several internal kicks and punches. What had possessed her to say yes to his offer? It certainly wasn't the food, because right now her stomach turned somersaults, leaving a queasy, uneasy feeling in its wake. A few minutes later, her resolve reinforced to keep an emotional distance between them, she returned to the room.

Chance stood by the bookshelf she'd fabricated from a few old pieces of lumber and some cinder blocks. He held one of her books in his hands, but looked up as she entered. "I see you like A.K. Aston's books, too. Great writer."

The warm feeling returned, spreading through her insides like a Texas wildfire. How about that? Chance Johnson liked her books.

Krater watched the two for several more minutes as they engaged in their childish horseplay. Their laughter quadrupled as a chase ensued and ended with shrieks of laughter. The lanky nurse slipped in the mud, and their game of tag came to a halt. Amy doubled over in laughter, then made her way to his side, a hand extended. A second later, her slight scream sounded as she fell to the muddy ground beside him.

A sudden movement caught Krater's attention. From the direction of the house a German Shepherd bounded, barking, growling, teeth bared. Chance brought an arm up to protect his face, while Amy bolted to her feet, yelling at the top of her lungs. "No, Daisy. Stop!" She yanked hard on the dog's collar, which allowed Chance the opportunity to stand. Hmm, fear in her voice, which proved she cared for Chance a little too much for his liking.

"Well, at least I know she does what she's supposed to do." Chance still sat in the mud, his knees drawn to his chest.

Amy continued to scold. "Bad dog, Daisy, bad dog."

"Don't get onto her. She thought I was hurting you. It's her job to protect you." Now the man rose to his feet.

Amy petted the dog, who sat obediently at her feet. "I made sure to push the storm door shut all the way when we left the house. How did she get out?"

The tall Texan strode to the end of his pickup and looked toward the house. "Uh, you're not gonna like this too much."

The comment forced Amy to a run. She slowed as she surveyed the damage. "Just great. Now we need to replace the screen door, too." She placed both hands on her hips.

Oh, she was going to be so much fun once he claimed her as is. Krater brought the binoculars down slowly, his lips puckered in thoughtful pose, his eyes narrowed, his

CHAPTER FOURTEEN

Krater climbed into the deer stand and took his position beside the high-range directional microphone. His new toy easily picked up sounds across the pasture. Surrounded by the cedar, live oak, and wild fruit trees which bordered this part of the creek, the stand was practically invisible. Even if it weren't, no one in this part of the country would question an average-looking man dressed in camouflage clothing climbing into a deer stand.

He brought binoculars to his eyes and adjusted the depth until he focused in on Amy. A contented smile settled on his thick lips. With her hair back to its original red color, she barely resembled the woman in online photos and the pictures he'd snapped without her knowledge. It really mattered very little whether her hair was blond or red. All he cared about was putting the plan into action that would finally make her his.

Laughter rang out from across the field that separated them. He quickly shifted the binoculars, his smile replaced by steel-cold anger. So her friend was back again today, was he? Krater mentally checked off the facts he'd acquired about Chance Johnson. A nurse with a reputation for helping people in distress and medical emergencies, his face had been severely scarred by an accident which claimed the lives of his parents. After that, he'd lived with his ailing grandfather until he passed, currently working at the hospital and spending every spare minute out at the farm with Amy. He pinched his lips together. Well, he'd do whatever he had to do to keep the man otherwise occupied.

left hand cupping his now-scraggly chin. Somewhere in the tangle of miscellaneous facts he knew about Chance Johnson lay at least one piece of information he could use against them both. It was just a matter of finding it. At some point in the past, Amy had to have known Chance Johnson for his grandfather to put such an odd inclusion in his will. Maybe that was his answer. Now to come up with a plan to dispose of the dog.

Krater climbed from the deer stand, careful not to slip in the heavy rubber galoshes he'd worn, and slogged his way back toward the hideaway. This unusually wet weather could be a problem, especially if more rain came. Already the creek that lay between his location and Amy was swollen and flooded. Impassable, thanks to the almost washed-out bridge. In addition, the low-lying pasture land on either side of the creek was muddy, slick, and difficult to traverse. With every step, his boots gathered more mud. By the time he reached his place, the boots weighed considerably more than they had when he'd left a half hour earlier.

He sat on a rock near the entrance and removed the boots, doing all he could to avoid a layer of mud beneath his recently-manicured nails. Leaving the boots near the front entrance, but hidden behind a tree, Krater carefully followed his regular protocol and checked the door. Good. No signs of tampering with his lead wires. No one had inadvertently--or purposefully, for that matter--stumbled upon his lair while he was away.

He scanned the overgrown and forested area, taking pleasure in this perfect hideaway. A slow smile curled his lips. Knowing Amy would soon be his made the years of waiting well-worth the wait.

Chapter Fifteen

Something wet and floppy hit Dakota in the face, eliciting a sleepy groan. Was she dreaming? She rolled over in bed and squinted at the clock. 6:30 a.m.? Ugh. Thanks to her late writing night trying to catch up from all the time she'd spent with Chance, she'd managed to snatch a whole two hours of sleep. Two hours!

The wet, soggy something hit her again. Groggily she moved to swat it away, her hand now covered with a translucent and slimy, glue-like substance. Eeewww! Shuddering, Dakota sprung to a sitting position and used the bed sheet to wipe dog slobber from her face and hands.

The guilty culprit sat obediently at the side of the bed-- looking at her in eager expectation--a doggy grin plastered across her black snoot.

"You are in so much trouble, you stupid dog." At least, she would be as soon as the room stopped spinning. Dakota collapsed back onto the bed.

The headache exploding inside her skull coursed down to her toenails, which then picked up the pulsing throb, her whole body in mutiny. She closed her eyes as her muscles relaxed against the soft mattress Chance had picked up and set up over the weekend. Sleep. Just a few more minutes of...

...whining dog. Daisy was back on all fours, her long pink drippy tongue coming perilously close. She whined. She whimpered. She danced. She pranced, her toenails clicking out a staccato rhythm against the wood floors like a vaudeville tap-dancer.

Dakota yawned, willing her body to wake up. Whining dog at six-thirty a.m. meant only one thing--a dog who needed to go to the bathroom. And Daisy had already proved she wasn't afraid to do her business indoors if warnings went unheeded.

"Oh, all right." Dakota threw back the covers and swung her legs over the side of the bed, searching with her toes to find the warmth of her slippers. Squish! She looked down with a grimace, her right house shoe shredded and soggy. "Dai-syyyy." The low guttural growl she released hit its target.

At least Daisy had the brains to know she was in trouble. She sat and laid her ears back, her big brown eyes avoiding Dakota's grumpy glare. But in the next second, she was back on her feet as if to say, "I really have to go."

Dakota did a rapid tiptoe to the closet across ice-cold floors, stuck the front of her feet in her tennies, and shrugged on her housecoat. "All right, all right, I'm coming."

But once outside, Daisy acted as though nothing were wrong. Not only did she not go to the bathroom, but she sat down and peered out toward the creek as though enjoying the morning breeze and fresh air. A cold breeze blasted beneath Dakota's bathrobe setting off her own dance. "You lied to me, you dumb dog."

Now her head felt as though someone had taken an ice-pick to her skull. Coffee. That would help. She lugged Daisy back inside, nabbed the coffee can from the makeshift shelf in the dining room, and gave it a shake.

"No. Please, no." With quick fingers she pried off the plastic lid. Empty. Chance had used up in two days what would've lasted her another week. She raised shaky fingers to her throbbing temples. Well, she'd just have to get ready and run errands this morning. That way she could nab a cup of coffee at B&B, pick up the joint compound and tape she needed to finish up some drywall work in the kitchen, and stop by the grocery store for coffee and headache medicine. And while she was at it, she'd grab some groceries for her and Chance to let him know she could cook. The thought momentarily froze her in her tracks as she climbed the stairs. Wait, no. This couldn't be happening.

A full-blown battle ensued inside her achy head as she made her way down the upstairs' hallway. How had she allowed herself back into this position of falling for him again? True, she and Chance had done so well together over the past few days. They'd laughed and actually had fun. Whether working on the house or playing in the mud, it was as though their relationship had turned the corner to a brighter horizon. Into a beautiful spring day. With birds singing and the fragrance of flowers wafting on the breeze. And Disney princesses swirling about.

"Just stop it right now, Dakota!" She growled the words into the bathroom mirror, much the same as she'd growled at Daisy earlier. Beside her, the dog sagged to the floor, groaning like a bored teenager, as though to protest that she hadn't done anything wrong.

"I'm talking to myself, not you." The words groused out of her mouth, and her thoughts returned to the situation with Chance. Good grief. What was worse--fighting with him constantly over his judgmental attitudes, or this new and improved Chance, who treated her better than she'd ever been treated her entire life?

Dakota piled her disobedient red curls on top of her head, and quickly secured them with a scrunchee. Her recent time with Chance had been full of lively chatter and laughter, like two old friends trying to catch up after years apart. Every problem uncovered in the demo of the house had been solved equitably and mutually. He'd even picked her up for small group and worship on Sunday, by her side the entire time.

Even with her head bonging, she planted her forehead into her palm with a disgruntled grunt. What was she doing? This was getting her nowhere, and fast. Not to mention that it broke a very important vow she'd made to herself the day she left Kane's clutches for good. Never. Again. Nope. Nada. End of discussion.

She moved to the bedroom and changed clothes. A few minutes later, with her newfound snippet of questionable determination in tow, she grabbed her small back pack from the sofa, her grocery list from the table, and headed out the door, making sure it closed well behind her so Daisy wouldn't escape.

Dakota hadn't been on the road long when her traitorous thoughts shifted back to Chance. She immediately rebuked herself and continued all the way to Miller's Creek, speaking out loud, hoping that actually hearing the word 'no' would get through her pounding, thick skull. "This just won't work. You've got to keep your wits about you before you do something really stupid." Really stupid, like telling him the truth.

The thought slammed into the inside of her head with hurricane force, unleashing fears and doubts and old hurts. She entered the outskirts of town, her shoulders sagging. There was no use in even having an ounce of hope for her and Chance. Even if they were to continue with the same sort of camaraderie throughout the renovation, once he knew the complete truth there would be no forgiveness or effort to get past the hurt, grudges, and bitterness.

Tears welled in her eyes, but she blinked them away with years of practice and parked the truck in front of B&B Hardware/Convenience Store. A musty odor reached her nose, and the old wooden floors creaked as she entered the door, the bell overhead announcing her entrance.

First things first. She headed straight for the group of men crowded around the coffee pot near the counter. In unison they shuffled off to one side to let her pass, then shuffled back into position as she carried the steaming hot liquid to the counter.

"You Levi's granddaughter?" The elderly man behind the counter held a wad of chewing tobacco in his cheek, which leaked what appeared to be beetle juice onto his teeth.

She tried not to stare at the man's mouth, especially since her stomach had decided to join forces with her head. "Yeah."

"So you're the one Chance is always griping about?" He grinned over at his men friends, revealing more bug juice. "I bet with that red hair of yours you can hold your own."

Now the smell from his mouth toyed with her pounding head and nauseous stomach. Part of her wanted to blast him through the plate glass window with a piece of her pounding mind, but the other part needed food. Why hadn't she at least thought to grab a granola bar on the way out of the house? "I'm sorry, but I'm not feeling well. Is there a place I could sit? Maybe a cracker or cookie or something?"

The men all jumped to action at once. One procured a folding chair from a table behind the counter, another grabbed a sleeve of crackers from the shelf, and a third whipped out his cell phone.

Cell phone? Why on earth did he need his cell phone?

He rapidly punched buttons, proof that this guy was a closet gamer. "Hello. Can I speak to Chance? It's an emergency."

She tried to shake her head, but the room began to spin.

Another man she didn't know--this one with a pot belly that would put any State Fair champion pig to shame--handed her a wet cloth, his ample belly bookended on either side with neon orange suspenders that teased her rumbling tummy. "You're lookin' mighty pale there, young lady." He trumpeted the words like the people five counties over needed to hear.

Okay, had he spoken in a normal voice, she would've made it just fine. Instead the effect was the same as using a gigantic gong to pound her over the head.

Meanwhile Mr. Cell Phone Guy continued to reveal his diagnostic prowess. "Yeah, Chance. That Dakota lady you've been telling us about?"

Oh, Chance was gonna pay big time for his little gossip sessions with the guys from Hee-Haw.

"Yeah, well, she's sittin' in the store lookin' three sheets to the wind."

Drunk? He thought she was drunk? She opened her mouth to protest, but one of the other guys popped open a can of ginger ale and stuck it in front of her face.

"Yeah, we won't let 'er leave 'til you git here." He pocketed the phone and stared at her.

Come to think of it, all of them were staring. And quiet. "I'm feeling better. Thank you, gentlemen. Now if you'll let me pick up some joint compound and tape and pay for my things, I'll be out of your hair." Not that they had much.

"Sorry, little lady," bellowed the big guy, his thumbs hooked beneath the neon strips of orange, "but we can't let you go anywhere in your condition."

Her jaw slackened. In her condition? They really *did* think she was drunk. She groaned. Man, this would be all over the county before she had a chance to even spit on the sidewalk.

Big man opened his equally big mouth again. This time Dakota prepared herself for the blast. "Your grandpa and J.C. were my two best buddies, and I think it's mighty nice what y'all are doin' to fix up the farm and house. I'd like to bring you a present, something to express my appreciation."

Well, she couldn't exactly refuse when he put it that way. Images of the stereotypical country doctor handed a freshly-plucked chicken for his services skittered into her thoughts. She somehow managed to make her lips behave.

The bell above the door clanged out an arrival. Dakota glanced up to see Chance striding toward her, his face awash with concern. He knelt in front of her, one hand going to her forehead, the other to her wrist. "You okay?"

"I'm not drunk, if that's what you mean." She whispered the words between pinched lips.

He peered up at the guys encircling them and nodded, a knowing look on his face that screamed 'she's-drunk-as-a-skunk.'

"Why you, dirty devil!" All of Miller's Creek would be talking, their tongues wagging faster than Daisy's tail first thing in the morning. She planted the toe of her boot in his thigh.

Immediately his hands left her and landed on his newly-acquired injury. "Ouch!"

"That's what you get for making them think something that is absolutely not true."

Now Chance rested back on his heels, a bemused smirk at play on his face. "Cured."

"What?"

"I pronounce you cured of whatever ailed you." Almost as if he suspected she was play-acting the whole time.

The elderly codgers fencing them in snickered and giggled, whispering to each other behind wrinkled and calloused hands.

She tried to focus all the pain in her head into a laser beam to shoot out her eyes for the purpose of obliterating Chance Johnson from the face of the planet, but over her left shoulder she heard the comments of two men.

"Boy, he's got it bad, don't he?"

"Yep, he's a goner."

A plan clicked in her brain, bringing a sense of mischievous delight. Dakota leaned forward, lips pooched out, and patted Chance on the head. "Sugar booger, thank you for coming after me, and I'm so sorry for giving you an owie on your leg." She used her syrup-iest baby voice on the last four words for added emphasis.

The snickers turned to barely-controlled bursts of laughter and snorts.

"Huh?" Chance's jaw gaped open, eyes horrified and his face flushed.

"Do you forgive me, honey bunny?"

There was no stopping the laughter now, no holding back the old codgers' guffaws. They held their sides, their faces purple, moisture seeping from their eyes, all while Chance scowled.

Dakota stood, moved around him to the hardware aisle, procured her joint compound and tape, snagged a package of powdered-sugar donuts on her way back to the counter, and sat it all down with a thump.

The laughter had abated somewhat, now interspersed with gasps and 'whew-ee's.' Bug Juice Man rang up the items with an unabashed grin, the evidence of his vice all over his teeth. "That'll be twelve-fifteen."

She collected her items and used her head to gesture over her left shoulder toward Chance. "Put it on his bill."

With chin held high, Dakota stomped out of the old building and to the truck, pretty sure that by now Chance had sworn all the men to a vow of silence.

It was mid-afternoon by the time Dakota made it back to the farmhouse. There had only been one checker at the grocery store and three little old ladies in front of her, all intent on carrying on a conversation among themselves. Then she'd been stuck behind a huge flat-bed trailer, loaded down with three over-sized round bales of hay. That guy had finally turned off, only to reveal a trailer full of cattle.

She had barely pulled into the driveway, gathered her things, and unlocked the door when another pickup pulled up.

His bright suspenders identified him before he'd even crawled all the way out of the tiny pick-up cab. He waddled toward her, hand outstretched. "I didn't get to properly introduce myself earlier. My name's Coot." His fleshy hand swallowed hers. He hiked up his pants, then gestured behind him with one sausage thumb. "I got your present in the back of the truck. Whatcha want me to do with it?"

"You can bring it up on the porch, I guess." Probably some last-minute crops from his garden before freezing weather hit. On the other side of the partially-opened front door, Daisy whimpered and scratched against the newly-refinished floors. "Just a little while longer, Daisy, I promise." Dakota tightly held to the door knob and stuck one leg in the door to keep Daisy from escaping through the crack. She turned just as Coot clomped up the wooden steps with a large cardboard box.

"That's a big box." Dakota stopped herself just shy of adding 'of vegetables.'

"Well, they need a bit of room to roam around."

Roaming vegetables?

"'Course they've probably pooped all over the place by now."

She swallowed. "Eh, what's in the box?"

"Why, chickens of course. That's what I do for a living. I raise chickens."

Her mouth opened, but words wouldn't form. What was with every mad man in the county bringing her animals? Did they think she didn't have enough to do? Yes, she wanted chickens eventually, but not until she knew for sure if she'd be staying.

Before she could respectfully decline, Daisy charged out the door, heading straight for the bright-orange suspenders, the protruding belly, and box full of chickens.

In a matter of seconds, Coot dropped the box and semi-flattened himself against the outer wall of the house.

The air seemed to instantly mass-produce white feathers, as a blur of flapping, flopping, squawking chickens scattered, chased by a nipping, growling, barking blur of tan and black.

Dakota squeezed her eyes shut, fearful of what might come next.

Thankfully, Chance's pickup pulled around the bend in the driveway. As if by magic, Daisy left off chasing the chickens and calmly trotted toward him, her nonchalant manner proclaiming that the strange white critters had made the mess and not her.

A half hour later--with Coot gone, Daisy in the house, and all the chickens accounted for and closed in the barn--Dakota strolled beside Chance toward the house to clean what appeared to be exploded pillows off the front porch. "You got off work early today."

"All the overtime from last week. Plus it was a really slow day, and my boss is out of town." A small grin appeared on his lips. "One emergency call kind of messed up my day."

She backhanded him. "Cut it out. I can't believe you let the town geezers persist in their belief that I was tipsy."

Chance laughed out loud. "Sorry, couldn't resist." He cast a sideways glance her direction. "Besides, you managed to get me back pretty good. No telling what those guys are telling their wives right about now."

Her head snapped around to face him. "You didn't swear them to secrecy?"

"Why would I be bothered that I was your honey-bunny? Even though sugar booger took it a little far." Chance suddenly came to an abrupt halt, his frowning gaze trained down the curving driveway.

Dakota stopped as well, and followed the direction of his stare.

He put a protective arm around her shoulder. "You know who this is coming toward us?"

She gave her head a slight shake. "No."

Chance resumed walking. "Let me do the talking, okay?"

No complaints there.

The other guy--rather nondescript and average-looking--strode closer, smiled, and stretched out a hand toward Chance. "Hello there."

Chance returned the smile and handshake. "Hi. Can I help you?"

The man, bundled up in a typical man's coat, leaned his head to the left. "Live on the next piece of land over and decided to stop by and introduce myself." He paused a second as he toward the creek. "Would've come that way, but the bridge is just about washed out."

Dakota's forehead wrinkled. "Really? We haven't even been down to the creek since it rained so hard the other night."

Now the man held out his hand toward her, nothing particularly frightening in his demeanor, but somehow unsettling just the same. "Vincent Hopkins."

She took his hand, but for some odd reason the hair on the back of her neck stood at attention. "Dakota."

His eyebrows twitched ever so slightly, then he turned his attention to Chance. Within a matter of minutes the two were talking deer hunting like they'd hunted together for years.

Dakota pretended to distract herself and picked up pieces of old wire from the ground, all the while eavesdropping and trying to figure out what bothered her about this man.

Later, when her new neighbor was out of earshot on his way back down the driveway, Dakota faced Chance. "I don't trust him."

Chance half-laughed. "That guy?" His lips turned down at the corners in an expression of doubt. "I don't think you have anything to worry about. Seemed friendly enough."

Maybe. But as they walked toward the house, each lost in their own thoughts, her troubled mind suddenly found the answer it sought. What kind of guy who lived on a farm, would go by Vincent rather than Vince or Vinny? And why would a backwoods Texan have a voice and manner of speaking laced with culture and hands so incredibly well-groomed?

Chapter Sixteen

*L*ord, *please help this to be a fun evening for both of us.* Chance crawled from the pickup cab and started toward the farmhouse. He peered up at the autumn sky, the stars so big it seemed like he could reach out and pluck one from the sky. He released a breath, and a puff of vapor rose into the cool night air.

Tonight could literally go either way.

His heart pounded like a junior high kid on a first date as he climbed the steps and stepped across the porch to Dakota's front door, as though this were a school dance rather than the hospital's Thanksgiving Fundraiser Ball. He raised his fist, and rapped on the door.

From inside, her steps sounded--not the usual sock feet padding on the floor--but the dainty click of a lady's shoe.

The door swung open, Dakota silhouetted against the room's light behind her. "Come in." Her voice sounded shy and strained.

Chance stepped inside, his attention riveted on the dress which perfectly matched her green eyes. Her hair was swept up onto her head, except for a few red curls that refused to be tamed, creamy shoulders exposed beneath the thin straps of her dress.

She seemed to wither beneath his perusal, her hands flighty and her eyes nervous as her teeth gently tugged at her lower lip. "Sorry about the dress. It's the only thing I could find at a consignment shop Dani told me about." Dakota fidgeted with the neckline as though trying to make sure she was adequately covered.

The knowledge that she'd purchased a used dress tugged at his heart. "You look beautiful." His voice took on an unusually husky-toned growl.

"Th-thank you." Her cheeks flushed and she lowered her head.

Definitely not the same girl he'd known so many years ago. Amy and Dakota were as different as night and day. Or were they? He shoved the thought aside for another time. "You ready?"

She nodded.

"You might want to get a coat. It's nippy out there."

A grimace spread the corners of her mouth tight, exposing her teeth. "I didn't think about looking for a nice shawl to wear. All I have is my work coat."

Chance frowned. A coat with paint splatters and a rip in the sleeve just wouldn't do. He hastily removed his tux jacket. "Here. Wear this for now. I have shirt sleeves. You don't."

"Thank you, Chance." A relieved smile covered her face as she made eye contact.

Unexpected warmth spread through him, and he lowered his head to clear his thoughts. *Easy, Chance.* With a hand in the small of her back, he led her to the passenger side of the pickup and helped her in. A few minutes later they made their way toward the hospital. "Pretty night, huh?"

"Yes, it is." She added no further comment.

They drove along in silence for a while. "Should be a fun evening."

"Yes, it should." Silence again settled over the inside of the truck. Except for the whine of his tires against the pavement, the cab of the pickup was completely quiet.

Should he ask if she was feeling okay, or would that set her off? The last thing he wanted or needed to do was start the night off on a bad foot. After another minute or two, he could take the silence no longer. "You okay?"

"Yes, why?" She turned her pretty profile to face him.

"You seem a little quiet."

A soft sigh escaped from her parted lips and she directed her gaze to her lap, only her fingertips exposed beneath the too-long-for-her sleeves of his tux jacket. "I'm a little nervous."

"Why?"

She shrugged. "I'm not used to fancy Cinderella balls and fancy Cinderella clothes and fancy Cinderella sho--"

Chance laughed. "I get the picture." He paused a moment, gathering words. "I know this isn't your typical style or get up, Dakota, but I don't want you to feel nervous or uncomfortable. Truth is, as beautiful as you look tonight, I like you just as well in blue jeans and a t-shirt. I hope you can relax and just enjoy the evening. You deserve it."

The curve of her cheek glowed in the reflection of the dashboard lights as she once more looked his way. For some reason her eyes seemed especially large tonight, glowing with a light that both drew him in and scared the daylights out of him. A slight smile curved her lips. "Thank you. I just hope I don't do something to embarrass you."

A frown creased his brow. Embarrass him? Is that how she saw herself in relation to him? And just how far back did this tendency of hers go? "You don't embarrass me, Dakota."

Her gaze returned to her lap. "I'm not cut from the same cloth as most people that will be there tonight. I haven't had the sort of social training one needs to shine at this kind of function."

The tug on his heart increased seven-fold. She'd spent what little money she had on a dress that made her uncomfortable to go to an event that made her feel equally uncomfortable. And her greatest concern was somehow embarrassing him. He reached across the cab and lightly touched her shoulder. "Just be yourself. There's plenty there to like and nothing that will embarrass me. Okay?"

She smiled, the same slight smile on her lips, and nodded.

They drove the last few miles in complete silence, Chance's mind bouncing between memories of the past and thoughts of the woman at his side. The sudden realization of his attraction to her on every level--not just physically, but mentally, emotionally, and spiritually--mortified him beyond explanation. How could that be? Especially with everything that had happened between them in the past? This was supposed to be a fun night out for both of them, not a constant battle to control his emotions.

A few minutes later, Chance pulled under the hospital's day entrance awning where high school seniors served as valet parkers. He handed off his keys to one of the youth he remembered seeing at church, then moved around to the passenger side to help Dakota.

She'd already removed his coat and handed it to him as she stepped from the truck, her golden sandal-style heels peeking from beneath the bottom of her dress.

How he wished he'd thought to rent a limo for the night and some jewelry to make her feel like a princess. Chance clamped his lips together as he shrugged on his jacket and adjusted the collar. Okay, these rampant thoughts had to stop now. There was still way too much to talk through with Dakota before there would ever be that sort of relationship between them again.

She sent a timid, closed-mouth smile.

But here she was putting herself out in the public eye for no other reason than to make him happy. Chance smiled back and took her hand in his. Together they walked into the large rotunda-shaped foyer, the Thanksgiving Fundraiser Ball already underway. Soft music played in the background, combined with the conversation and laughter of guests garbed in all their finery.

Beside him, Dakota pressed her other hand to her stomach.

He smiled down at her. "Butterflies?"

She laughed, a gentle, pleasing sound that fit her perfectly. "A little, but I'm okay."

Chance pointed to their left. "There's Mama Beth and the rest of that crew. Want to join them?"

"Sure."

He tucked her hand around his elbow and moved through the crowd toward his friends.

"Well, look who else is all dressed up." Mama Beth beamed, her round face radiant.

"Oh, Dakota, you look stunning." Dani, very pregnant with baby number two, was all smiles as she fingered the fabric of Dakota's evening gown. "Did you find this at the consignment shop I told you about?"

She nodded. "Yes. Thank you."

"And your hair is absolutely gorgeous," added Trish, who raised a hand to fix another one of Dakota's escaped curls. "Did you have it done?"

"Nope. Just used a can of hairspray until I made it look halfway decent."

Chance chuckled, both fascinated and amused by Dakota's choice of words. She didn't put on airs like some girls he'd dated. Didn't pretend to be someone she wasn't.

Matt elbowed him, but spoke loud enough for everyone to hear. "Have you noticed that not one comment has been made about how great we guys look in our penguin suits?"

Andy and Steve both nodded.

Chance laughed, then peered down at Dakota. "Probably because we've been a little out-classed by these beautiful ladies." He sent a reassuring wink.

"Hear, hear." Andy spoke the words in his typical dry tone of voice. "But I'm not complaining."

Gracie, dressed in a bright red dress that complimented her dark complexion, sidled up next to Dakota. "I'm going after something to drink and nibble on. Want to come with me?"

Dakota brightened. "I'd love to." She faced Chance, her green eyes shining with joy. "I won't be gone long."

Good, 'cause suddenly the idea of being there without her was more than he could bear. He watched them walk away, arm in arm, chatting away like they'd known each other a lifetime. His heart lightened. So far she was having a good time.

Chance turned to join the conversation with the others. The two women returned a few minutes later, and Dakota handed him a Dr Pepper. "Here you go. I thought you might want something to drink."

"Thanks." Chance took the proffered cup of carbonated drink, and swigged down a refreshing mouthful, all the while chastising himself inwardly. Why hadn't he thought to go get drinks for the both of them? He swallowed the fizzy liquid and smiled. "Having a good time?"

She nodded excitedly. "Thanks for bringing me. It's much more fun than I expected."

At that moment Chance's boss sauntered over. His eyes latched on Dakota as he took her hand in both of his. "I'm Jeremy Gains, the new hospital administrator. And you are?"

Dakota lowered her head and took a step back. "Dakota." She tugged her hand away, obviously uncomfortable, and gestured to Chance. "I'm here with Chance."

Gains barely acknowledged him, but instead stepped even closer to Dakota.

The country-and-western band from Morganville began to play. One of the guys stepped to the microphone, his voice booming from a nearby speaker. "Let's get this party in full swing."

The crowd applauded, and the band launched into a rollicking country swing song that sent people scurrying to the dance floor.

Gains leaned toward Dakota. "May I have this dance?"

Discomfort showed on her face with a pasted-on half-smile. She leaned closer to Chance. "Thank you, but I think I'll sit this one out."

"Oh, c'mon. A pretty little thing like you should be out on the dance floor."

Chance's right hand balled into a fist. "She said no." He kept his voice under control. The last thing he needed was a confrontation with his boss. Already the man disliked him for whatever reason.

Gains persisted. This time he put a hand around Dakota's waist and started toward the dance floor, pulling her along with him.

Dakota dug in her heels and shook her head from side to side, her face flushed. She glanced back over her shoulder at Chance, her eyes panicked and pleading.

Anger erupted inside him. How should he handle this? If he got all macho on Gains, the guy would make his life miserable at the hospital for a long time to come. He handed his cup to Matt. "I've gotta do something."

Matt leaned in close. "Just don't hit him. He's your boss, remember?"

A thought popped into Chance's head as Gains made his way closer to the dance floor. Chance stepped to the stage and motioned to a guy on guitar.

Still playing, the man stooped down. "Yeah, buddy. What can I help you with?"

"I have a request for a special lady."

The guy grinned. "Just give me the name of the song, and we'll play it as soon as this number ends."

Chance named the song, then stepped in front Gains and Dakota just as the other song ended. "Sorry to have to do this, sir."

"We've had a special request. A song for Dakota and Chance. Let's see how many of you know this one."

An electric guitar launched into the familiar opening to *Sweet Home Alabama*. Chance swept a surprised Dakota into his arms--a mesmerizing smile on her lips--then glanced back at Jeremy Gains. "Sorry, but they're playing our song."

Dakota laughed all the way to the dance floor. "I can't believe you just pulled that off. Smooth move."

He smiled into her happy face. "Think you can still remember how to two-step?"

"Sorta like riding a bike, isn't it?"

On the dance floor, everything and everyone else seemed to melt away, as though the last few years had been nothing but a bad dream, and they were back to that summer after high school. The dance was easy. Not getting lost in her was the hard part.

When the song ended a few minutes later, the gathered crow all cheered and applauded, while Dakota's cheeks flushed the prettiest shade of pink.

Matt made his way toward them. "Good job, you two. Just so you know, Mr. Pushy's on his way."

Already Gains shoved his way through the crowd surrounding the stage.

Chance thought fast. Their best chance of escape was the silent auction. He grabbed Dakota's hand. "Follow me."

They made their way through the crowd, but the determined Gains still followed. Coot stood a few steps ahead, and a plan formed in Chance's mind.

"Hey, Coot. The guy coming up behind us is the new administrator and won't leave Dakota alone. Would you mind--"

"You betcha." Coot grinned. "This is right up my alley. Step aside and watch an expert at work."

Chance and Dakota moved behind Coot just as the persistent administrator stepped up.

"Say, ain't you the new doctor?" Coot's words thundered across the whole rotunda.

"Actually, I'm the new hospital administrator."

Ignoring the comment, Coot pulled open his jacket to reveal his familiar orange suspenders, then lifted his white shirt, too. "Would you mind taking a look at this spot on my side?"

The crowd roared with laughter and moved in closer, which gave Chance and Dakota the perfect opportunity to slip into the silent auction room unnoticed.

Chapter Seventeen

Breathless with laughter, Dakota swiped at tears of amusement. "That was the funniest thing I've ever seen in my life."

Chance grinned and shook his head. "Leave it to Coot to steal the show." He motioned to the tables loaded with donated items. "Wanna look around?"

"I guess. What does one do at a silent auction, anyway?"

He started toward the first table. "These are all donated items, and beside each one is a sheet where you write your name, contact information, and bid. At the end of the night the person with the highest bid wins. It's a great way to help raise funds for the new hospital wing."

Not really her cup of tea, but Chance seemed eager to browse. "I don't have money to spend, but it'll be fun to look."

They browsed about three tables when Chance's face lit with a brilliant smile. "Hey, look. Wonder who donated these?"

Dakota smiled at his boyish excitement and glanced down at the table. A frown immediately replaced her smile, and her heart took off in a sprint as though someone had just fired a starting pistol. A complete set of A.K. Aston books. From the looks of them, they were brand new. She peered back up at Chance. "Did you donate these?"

He shook his head back and forth. "Nope, but I'm sure gonna bid on them." He leaned forward, picked up the pen, and wrote, the pen scratching against the paper.

She raised fingers to her lips and peered around the empty room. Had Kane discovered her books? Even worse, had he found her?

"Who donated them?" She did her best to keep the fear from her voice, but it held a tremor in spite of her efforts.

Chance examined the bid sheet. "Says here anonymous donor." He looked at her quizzically, his head twisted to one side. "You okay?"

She mustered her best pasted-on smile. "Of course, why do you ask?"

"'Cause your face is as white as a sheet." His eyes were barely visible under his wrinkled brows.

Her eyes latched on to his, and she swallowed. "Do you mind if we leave?"

"Not at all."

Dakota clutched his muscled arm tightly as they made their way down a darkened corridor to avoid the party in the rotunda. Her imagination took flight, and she trembled.

"Cold?"

"A little."

Chance removed his jacket and draped it over her shoulders, then maneuvered to a side exit. A minute later, he helped Dakota into the passenger side, then moved around the front of the truck and crawled in. He started the truck and peered over at Dakota. "The night's still young. Anything else you want to do?"

She thought through his question. This night had been so important to him, and she'd all but ruined it for him. "I hate to ruin your evening. If you want to take me home and then come back to the party, I understand."

"Doesn't make much sense to waste that pretty dress of yours."

She smiled. How long had it been since a man treated her like a real lady the way Chance just had? Had it ever happened? "Well, I am hungry."

"Oh, you are?"

"I just had a little snack before you picked me up and some finger food at the party." Hopefully, Chance wouldn't fall back into his judgmental practice of criticizing her eating habits.

"Any place in particular you want to go?"

"I really want pancakes."

He leaned his head back and laughed out loud. "Then pancakes it is."

Several minutes later they arrived at an all-night diner in Morganville and took a seat in a booth by the front door. The waitress brought them menus and water. "Well, aren't you two all fancied up?" After ordering her short stack and his Caesar's salad, Chance leaned back against the faux leather seat of the booth and peered over at her, a gentle smile on his lips and his eyes questioning.

"You have question marks in your eyes, Chance. What is it you want to ask me?"

He smiled at her a minute more, as though as fearful as she was of breaking this magic spell that had settled over the both of them. "What all happened to you since the last time you lived in Miller's Creek?"

A wave of sorrow crashed over her, though she managed to keep her smile pasted in place. *Keep it general, Dakota.* It just wouldn't do to be overcome by his kindness and incredible good looks. Boundaries were a must to keep the secret where it belonged. In the past. "I won't go into all the details, but life's been rough. Thankfully I was able to pull myself together and get back on my feet."

"Must've been difficult."

She nodded slowly. "In some ways, but in other ways it was wonderful."

"How so?"

"I met some of the nicest people at the shelter where I landed. People with nothing but the clothes on their back, yet possessing everything." How could mere words do her sentiment justice? "A friend taught me about true riches, and that's when I gave my life to Christ. Jesus helped me out of a very difficult a time, a time when I wondered if life was even worth it."

His forehead scrunched up tight. "You were thinking about...?"

"Yes."

His eyes closed as though the thought brought pain. "What happened to make you even consider that as an option?"

"I can't go there. Let's just say I was far from a saint. I've done many things I'm not proud of. Things I'd change in a heartbeat if I could." Tears sprung to her eyes. But the past couldn't be undone. There was no such thing as a do-over in real life. "What about you? What happened to you after I left?" Her gaze landed on the jagged scars on the left side of his face.

At first he didn't respond. Just stared at her. Then he brought a hand up and touched his scars as though to see if they were still in place. "I was on my way out to the farm that night after I saw you at the baseball game."

She stiffened, fearful of what he might say next. No, this couldn't be. Her stomach roiled.

"Drove a little too fast going around that big curve. Veered over in the other lane and hit a truck."

She gasped and lifted her hands to cover her mouth, her eyes wide and tear-filled.

"Mom and Dad were in the car with me. Both of them were killed."

Tears slid down her cheeks. Something else that was all her fault. Something else she couldn't undo. No wonder he couldn't forgive her.

"I would've died, too, if there hadn't been a woman in the car right behind me who saved my life. That's why I decided to become a nurse."

Unrelenting pain closed her eyes, and more tears slipped from beneath her eyelids. It took every ounce of strength she had to open her eyes and look him in the face. "I'm so sorry, Chance. I never meant to hurt you or your family. After I saw you at the ballgame with that other girl, something just snapped, and I had to leave. Please forgive me."

He reached across the table and took her hand. "I already have. But you should know that girl was my cousin. She'd come down for a family reunion. At one point I did blame you for everything that happened, but I don't anymore. God used it for good."

Pure grace, but would that same gracious spirit be extended to her if he knew the rest of the story? Her gaze returned to the scars. "Are they painful?"

"Not physically." He hesitated. "I'm just afraid no one will ever want me this way."

Her heart pounded, partly because he felt that way and partly because she was powerless to do anything about it. "That's a lie straight from the enemy. If someone truly loves you, it won't matter."

He went quiet again, his probing gaze delving deep.

Just when she thought she couldn't take another second of his perusal, the waitress stepped up with their food, then left to take care of a large group that entered.

Dakota brought finger tips to her face to wipe away tears. "Hope I can eat these now."

He smiled. "Let me bless the food, and then we'll talk about happier times."

True to his word, throughout the rest of the meal, Chance regaled her with happy memories of their time together that summer, bringing forth laughter from both of them.

Just as they checked out a half hour later, her new neighbor entered the diner and moved straight to them. "Well, isn't this a coincidence?" He shook hands with Chance, but his gaze rested on her.

Spider legs crept down her back. What was it about this guy that gave her the creeps? He seemed nice enough.

"You two are sure dressed up." His beady eyes focused on the neckline of her dress.

Instinctively, Dakota brought a hand to her chest.

Chance must have noticed her discomfort, because as soon as he put away his wallet, he placed his hand on her back and faced Vincent. "Yeah, we went to the hospital party and then decided we needed some real food. Good to see you." Without giving the man a chance to respond, he led Dakota outside to the truck, his hand still on her back. After helping her in, he moved around the front of the truck and crawled in the cab.

"Something about that man gives me the heebie-jeebies."

"So you've mentioned before. What is it about him that bothers you so much?"

"A lot of things actually. It's like he's not who he's pretending to be."

Chance started the truck. "I don't think you really have much to worry about. He seems pretty harmless to me."

Thoughts rolled in her head. Was this nothing more than her overactive imagination at play? Definitely possible. She inhaled a deep breath to relax and focused on the topic of work still to be done to the house and property. In what seemed like just a few seconds, they arrived at the farmhouse.

A current of disappointment tugged at her heart as Chance walked her to the door. How nice it would be if their relationship were different. If instead of telling him goodnight and giving back the jacket she still clutched around her for warmth, he would enter the house with her as her husband.

Blood rushed to her head. *No, Dakota! You know better.* A slow breath whooshed from her lungs. Things worked out the way they did for a reason, and she wouldn't go back on her decision to be anything but his friend.

With fumbling fingers, she unlocked the door, then faced him. "In spite of everything, I really enjoyed the evening. I..." Her words trailed off momentarily, and she fidgeted with her hands. "I really enjoyed spending time with you."

Before she even realized what was happening, he leaned in and kissed her.

And for one heartbreaking moment, she allowed it. Even kissed him back. Alarms rang in her head. No. This had to stop. She raised her hands to his chest and pushed him away.

His eyes held raw anguish.

She yanked her gaze away, and without a word, let his jacket slip to the porch floor, entered the house, and slammed the door behind her. Her back to the door, she slid to the ground, her green dress pooled about her, and released the heart-breaking sobs that refused to be contained any longer.

Chapter Eighteen

"Chance, may I speak with you a minute?" Dakota blurted out the words and half-ran to catch up with Chance as he headed down the steps of the church building. If only there were an easier way to handle issues other than talking through things.

He continued down the steps and into the grass, then spun around to face her, his expression dark and unsmiling. "I came to the farm to work yesterday. You weren't there."

She melted beneath his laser-like glare. "Sorry. I needed time to think."

Chance didn't respond at first, but kept his eyes averted to the ground where he dug up the sod with the toe of his boot. "I thought you'd baled on me again."

Yes, he would naturally come to that conclusion after the way things ended before. "I understand why you'd think that, but as you can see, I'm still here." She released a heavy sigh. "Look, can we at least talk about what happened Friday night?"

His head cocked to one side, his eyes once more delving into the depths of her being. "Well, that's progress, I suppose. At least you're attempting to work things out."

"I hate confrontation worse than a root canal, but it's not going to get any better unless we work through it."

He nodded, apparently satisfied with her answer. His expression had lost at least some of the animosity, but he still didn't smile. "Okay. I'll pick up a bucket of chicken and meet you at the farm."

"Sounds good."

Without another word, he turned his back and strode away, his head lowered and steps purposeful, keys dangling from one hand.

Her heart ached. If only there was someway to make this work. His kiss the other night had resurrected a myriad of powerful feelings inside her, the familiar pain and fear crippling. But it had stirred up more. Emotions she didn't want to admit. Emotions that had driven her to leave town yesterday in an attempt to escape.

Dakota traipsed to her truck. The trip through downtown Miller's Creek on her way out to the farm unleashed the typical nostalgia. With its quaint city square and people milling about, the placed oozed home and deep-seated roots, two things she wanted more than air to breathe.

The ache in her heart intensified as she turned onto the farm-to-market road that led back to the farm. More than likely she'd soon be on her way to somewhere else. How many somewhere else's did she have to endure? With a shake of her head and clamped lips she pressed the gas pedal. *Get over it, Dakota. That's just your life.* She'd just have to make this work until the house renovation was finished and figure out the rest later.

She pulled up outside the farmhouse and climbed the steps slowly. Oh, the plans she had for this place. But even after hundreds of hours of work, it still felt like she'd never see the project's completion. She stopped at the front door and closed her eyes. *Oh, Lord, give me the right attitude and the words to say to Chance so we can move forward.*

Dakota moved into the house with a promise to herself to go for a walk to the bridge later and enjoy this unusually mild November day. She'd just finished changing into her jeans and a sweater she'd picked up for a quarter at a garage sale, when the motor noise of Chance's truck sounded outside. With nimble feet she descended the worn steps and made it to the door just as he knocked. She swung open the door with a smile, hoping to somehow soften his earlier sullen demeanor. "Come on in. Boy, that chicken smells good."

Instead, he barely acknowledged her presence and stepped over the threshold with the aromatic bucket and bags without smiling. "Coffee table okay?"

She nodded and followed him to the living room. "Want a bottle of water?"

He sat down the food and produced a can of soft drink from his inside jacket pocket. "No thanks. I picked up a DP." Chance popped the top of the can of Dr Pepper and took a swig.

Dakota nodded and moved to the kitchen to get herself a bottle of water, his atypical choice of drink not lost on her. A bona fide health nut, Chance wasn't one to drink carbonated drinks unless he was stressed and at his limits. This should prove to be a fun conversation.

Her resolve diminishing more by the minute, she returned to the living room and took a seat on a chair, rather than sit beside him on the couch.

"Too good to sit next to me?"

She shook her head. "No. I can just tell you're in a foul mood, and I'd like to keep my head today, thank you." Dakota chomped into the juicy chicken breast, the crispy outer layer crumbling in her mouth.

Once more he chose not to answer, but the dark look on his face spoke volumes. With brusque movements, he tore into the sack and produced two small containers of mashed potatoes smothered with brown gravy and two spoons. Not bothering to hand her one, he removed the lid of one and plowed into the potatoes.

Dakota scratched the itch right above her eyebrow. Okay, she needed to figure out how to turn this around fast. If not, one or the other of them was bound to blow their cool. She'd much rather turn the day around now than pick up the pieces later. "I enjoyed the other night, Chance. You made me feel very protected at the party. I couldn't have asked for a better evening."

He didn't look up, but continued to eat.

Well, at least she'd tried. Once more she put her mind to work on a solution and took another bite of the tasty chicken.

He leaned back against the couch, arms crossed. "So you enjoyed everything but kissing me? Am I that repulsive?"

The vulnerable words he'd spoken at the diner about his fears scrambled into the forefront of her brain. She shook her head. "I don't find you repulsive at all." In fact, just the opposite. But she couldn't tell him and stay true to her promise. Now was the best time to let him know that she could only be his friend. She laid the remainder of the chicken piece on a napkin in her lap, then used another one to wipe her greasy fingers and lips. "I know I should've mentioned this earlier, but I don't intend on ever being a part of another romantic relationship." Dakota glanced up to gauge his reaction.

"Why?"

"Things that happened in my past. Things I'm not prepared to discuss."

He didn't move, and his forehead creased into an even deeper frown. "I don't think you're being completely truthful."

"You're passing judgment on my decision?"

Chance leaned forward, his elbows at rest on his lanky legs. "No, but I think you're afraid."

"Afraid?" She released a derisive snort, more than a little bothered that he knew her so well. "Afraid of what?"

"Of having feelings for me again." His voice was velvety low. "You can deny it if you want, Dakota, but I saw it in your eyes Friday night. Felt it in the way you kissed me back."

She picked up the chicken and chomped into it again, deliberately keeping her gaze lowered. No way she would confirm the truth of his observation. "Think what you want."

The rest of the meal was eaten in silence. No matter how hard she tried to think of something to change the subject and bring things back in the direction she wanted to go, nothing came to mind.

After lunch was cleaned up, Chance moved to the door, then paused to look back over his shoulder. "Pretty day outside. Feel like taking a walk to the bridge?"

Hadn't she already had that thought? But she hadn't planned on walking there with him. So much of their history had taken place at that very spot, the bridge inexorably tied to their relationship. And she wasn't prepared to confront its dilapidated condition after the last storm, yet another symbol of her fractured ties with Chance.

He sighed impatiently. "Come on, Dakota. You're the one who wanted to talk. Maybe it will be easier for both of us if we're out enjoying the fresh air and sunshine."

Reluctantly she dragged herself from the chair and followed him out the door, Daisy scooting past both of them in total abandon and joy. If only she could feel the same way. Instead, she was confined and trapped in a jail of her own making, with bars that were impossible to remove.

Chance grabbed at a piece of the tall dried grass and broke off a piece, twining it through his fingers. "You know, I tried very hard the other night to be open and honest with you, even though it was uncomfortable."

"If it was so uncomfortable then why'd you do it?" She squinted against the brightness of the mid-afternoon sun.

His gaze focused far in the distance. "Hoped it would make you want to reciprocate. Can't exactly get past those castle walls of yours on my own. It's a two-way street and I need your help."

Yeah, well, it was help she couldn't give. If the truth be known, she'd love to be completely upfront and honest with him, but she knew beyond a doubt that it would only drive him away in the end, leaving her without a place to live, without the resources to relocate, and with a Texas-sized hole in her heart. No, that was a risk she just couldn't take. At least not yet. Not until after she'd exhausted every option. She walked beside him in silence, refusing to respond.

"What's wrong? You afraid something from your past is so bad I couldn't accept it?"

How did he do that? How could he guess so accurately? "What do you think I've done, Chance? Imagine the worst."

"Drugs and alcohol?"

"Done it."

"Lived with someone without being married?"

"That, too."

He grew quiet and pensive. "I can get past both those things."

They reached the bridge, its bleached boards leaning and covered with debris from the recent flood. A very muddy Miller's Creek rushed just a few inches below. Sudden tears pricked her eyes, but she blinked them back and stared into the muddy depths of the creek. There was no going back, no fixing what had been broken. There was no use in even trying, the water too deep and murky and the trip too dangerous.

She faced him. "Have you ever stopped to consider that maybe I can't get past it? That maybe I don't ever want to go there again?"

His blue-gray eyes challenged her, but she refused to look away. Somehow she had to get the message across to him. Finally he lowered his head. "Okay, but before we go back, do you mind if I pray?"

Her mouth sagged open. He wasn't backing down, just momentarily retreating, and calling prayer into the process. She somehow managed to nod.

Man, how could he find the words to pray with his heart ripped to shreds and bleeding? Chance filled his lungs with the fresh air, immediately comforted. "Lord Jesus, thank You for loving us and for Your forgiveness. Help me move past my fears, bitterness, and judgmental attitudes. I also pray that You'll help Dakota as she tries to deal with her own stuff from the past. Show me how I can help her. Help us find a way to move on from here and finish the work You've given us to do. We ask this all in Jesus' name, Amen."

Big crocodile tears pooled in Dakota's eyes as she stared at the bridge.

His heart picked up its pace. Was he somehow getting through to her? Was God? Instinctively he pulled her into his arms and hugged her close.

Her tears multiplied, but he didn't try to stop them. She'd never been one for displays of emotion, had always been one who refused to cry. Memories pulled him to the day she'd sliced her hand open on a piece of flashing. Tears had glistened that day, but she'd practically bitten a hole through her bottom lip to keep them from coursing down her cheeks. Maybe a good cry was exactly what she needed.

Finally she pulled away and immediately turned her back to him, wiping tears away.

This was twice in three days for her. Progress.

When she faced him again, her walls were up, just as he'd expected. "So about the bridge. Do you think it's worth repairing?"

With weathered boards and a leaning structure, it would require time, materials, and effort. "Definitely." He took hold of her chin and turned her face toward him. "What about you? You think it's worth the effort?"

She pulled away from his touch. "Not sure actually. It's not like we use it that often anyway. Not sure it's worth the cost involved." Dakota peered over the side at the deep water. "Or the risk."

"The water won't always be so deep and fast."

"Yeah, but the distance to the bottom is the same. And it's a lot of hard work. Maybe we should just concentrate on getting the house finished."

A smile worked onto his face. Her and her tendency toward fear and running away. "The house will get finished, Dakota. I know it might not seem like it right now, but it will. And we'll have time to rebuild the bridge, too. Besides part of Grampa's request was making the property viable as a farm, remember?"

She nodded reluctantly, but didn't speak.

"So what do you think? Can we continue to work together?"

Her green eyes held doubt. "I want us to, but I can't offer you anything but friendship."

He studied her face, committing its every detail to memory. Her perfect nose with just a small sprinkling of freckles. Her pointy chin. Her soulful eyes. Friendship was enough, at least for now. The only way he could get her to open up to him was spend time with her. The only way he could spend time with her was working on the farm and house. Rebuilding the bridge was just a way of extending that time, another opportunity for coaxing her into giving him a second chance. "I can accept that."

She nodded, her chin lifted higher than normal. "I guess it won't hurt to rebuild this old bridge then."

A ray of sun beamed between two trees, sending a shaft of light to rest on them. Chance smiled, his gaze focused on Dakota as she inspected the old bridge. No, it wouldn't hurt a thing to rebuild the bridge.

Chapter Nineteen

Dakota's heart rose to her throat as she stared down at the fresh footprints. Not again. She knelt to examine the prints more closely, and her gaze followed them until they disappeared into the grass. Definitely a man's shoe, most likely left overnight. The thought only served to make her heart race faster. Who'd been so close in the middle of the night without her knowing?

Her mind immediately jumped to Kane.

She pulled herself to a standing position and peered around the area. No other evidence she could see. Of course, whoever had left the prints could still be hiding in the vicinity, watching her every move.

Fear clawed its way to her brain. She hurried into the house and locked the deadbolt, then leaned against the door.

Daisy moved to her feet and sat, her head cocked to one side, questioning.

Dakota reached down to pet her friend. Never would she have believed she'd grow to love Daisy so much since Chance dropped her off for protection. "No more going outside without you, Daisy." So much for crossing the paint-scraping off her to-do list. And such a pretty day, too.

She moved to the list on the table to see what other chore she could tackle. Hmm, maybe finish the kitchen. Chance had helped install the cabinets last week, and the countertops would hopefully be in before Thanksgiving. All that left was painting and installing the backsplash and flooring, all materials she already had on hand. That should keep her busy.

Within a few minutes, she'd gathered her tiling supplies--trowel, mastic, grout, and sponge--and set to work, her mind on Chance as usual. Last week he'd kept to his promise of keeping their relationship strictly platonic. Instead, her own thoughts and emotions had betrayed her as she imagined a lifetime with him. How much longer could she withstand the temptation to let him in completely, sharing even her darkest secret?

Beside her, Daisy thumped her tail against the floor.

"No. I just can't do it." But at what cost?

Daisy's tail stopped wagging and a frown creased the space between her pointy ears.

"It's okay, girl. I just have to remember that things will work out the way they're supposed to." She returned to her work with added fervor and by noon used up her last tile. One corner of her mouth turned downward. How had she miscalculated so badly? It would take at least one more box of the pale blue glass subway tiles to finish the job.

She moved to the sink to clean her sponge and trowel. "Guess this means a trip to town." Daisy, who'd been lying in her usual C position, roused to a sitting position as if she understood.

Dakota laughed. "Yeah, you can go too, but let me get us both some lunch first."

After she fed the dog and downed a cold slice of pizza, Dakota put Daisy on her leash and flipped off the kitchen switch as she passed. Pop! The sound crackled from the ceiling, followed by the distinct smell of smoke. Okay, not good. She grabbed her cell phone to call Chance.

He picked up on the first ring. "Hey, Dakota. Everything okay?"

"Not exactly. I just cut off the kitchen light and something popped. It smells kind of smoky now." She flipped the switch to on position. Nothing. "And when I flip the switch on, nothing happens."

"First things first. Go outside and wait while I call the fire department. I'll call you back in a sec."

Uh, based on the footprints she'd seen this morning she might not be so safe outside, but she couldn't tell Chance. Already he worried about her far too much. "Okay." She led Daisy outdoors, her brain churning for a way to continue to work on the house. Maybe she could hold the leash with one hand and scrape paint with the other. If there were anyone outside watching her, surely they wouldn't attack as long as she had a German Shepherd in tow.

An uneasy feeling churned in her stomach, as though someone watched her every move. She peered around, but saw nothing. *Shake it off, Dakota. You're just being paranoid.* With a shake of her head, Dakota made her way to the oversized tool box Chance had left in the barn and dug through the contents. Strange. There'd been a paint scraper in the old red metal box that once belonged to J.C. just yesterday, but now it was nowhere to be found.

Her phone rang. Chance. "Hey."

"Fire department's on the way. You outside?"

"Yep, I'm being a good girl. But don't you think I should go inside, so if a fire does start, I can at least try to put it ou--"

"No!" His voice exploded through the phone. "Do not go back in that house. Understand?"

"Yes, sir."

"Sorry." He controlled his voice this time. "Didn't mean to bark orders."

Dakota stared down at the tool box. "While I've got you on the phone, wasn't there a paint scraper in J.C.'s tool box?"

"Yeah, I knew we'd need it when we tackled the outside of the house."

"Well, it's not there now." Where could it be?

"Hmm. Listen, I gotta run, but call me after they've been there and checked everything out. Okay?"

"Okay."

Without bothering to say goodbye, she closed the phone and made a mental note to pick up a paint scraper in town. "C'mon, Daisy, let's go wait for the fire truck."

A few minutes later the fire trucks approached, their sirens sounding for miles down the road. Daisy's ears pricked up, and she barked and howled.

"It's okay, girl. They're friendlies." Dakota moved out to meet them as the large red truck careened around the corner and came to an abrupt halt.

Matt Tyler was the first one out of the truck. He strode toward her, his face awash with concern. "You okay?"

"I'm fine, but what are you doing here?"

"Just another hat I wear. Volunteer fireman. What happened?"

Dakota repeated the story again, then stood back while several men scurried to the house arrayed in full gear. A few minutes later they returned, and Matt, a good-natured grin on his face, stepped toward her and Daisy. He reached down to scratch Daisy's ears and peered up at Dakota. "Nothing to worry about. No fire detected. But you need to call an electrician. Based on what we just saw, this house is dangerous with the current wiring. A fire waiting to happen."

Alarms went off in her head. Chance would throw a conniption fit at the added cost. "Will do, Matt. Thanks."

"No problemo. See you around." He waved back at her as he moved to join the other guys as they loaded into the truck.

Dakota stepped toward the house, Daisy right behind. Before she called Chance, she'd phone the electrician to get a price. Might as well kill two birds with one stone.

The phone call to Mr. Downey took just a few minutes, but Dakota hung up the phone with her mind spinning. Five thousand dollars. At this rate, she'd never be able to pay Chance back and have enough money to start over somewhere else. In addition the electrician indicated the work would take at least a week. A week of having someone else under her feet all day?

She pulled up Chance's number on her cell phone.

"What'd they find?" No hello, just straight to the matter as hand. Typical mode of operation for Chance.

"No fire." She gritted her teeth to garner the courage to tell him the bad news.

"I hear a 'but' in your voice. What else?"

She swallowed hard. "Um, the whole house needs to be rewired. Matt said it was a fire waiting to happen."

"Okay. When you hang up, call Mr. Downey and get him out there ASAP. I'll call around and see if I can find you somewhere else to stay."

"First of all, I already called Downey. It's gonna be around five thousand dollars and a week to get it fixed."

"So? What's your point?"

Her eyebrows raised. She had certainly missed the mark with guessing his response.

"Are you sure we can afford that?"

He sighed. "We don't have a choice. Yeah, it's an added cost we hadn't counted on, but we'll just have to cut back somewhere else. I won't have you staying in a house that's unsafe."

Her heart melted at his concern, and she closed her eyes against the ensuing pain. All his thoughts were for her and her safety. If only she could reciprocate. She could, but only by leaving Miller's Creek so he could get on with his life.

"You still there?"

"Yeah."

"Pack your bags and find something else to do this afternoon. Go to town. Do some shopping. Whatever. I'll call you later."

"Okay."

The line went dead.

Dakota traipsed up the stairs to gather her clothes, essentials, and computer. At least she'd have some writing time and safety away from whoever left the footprints, even if it did delay the completion of the house.

A few minutes later they sped down the road toward Morganville. She spent the early afternoon hours picking up supplies, and then headed to the thrift stores to pick up a few more clothes, a newfound spring to her step. How long had it been since she'd just had a fun day? Way too long. Would there come a time in her life where she could take more days like this? Not likely. Especially with the house renovation and a flailing writing career to resuscitate.

Her phone rang, and she answered. "Hey, Chance."

"Just got through talking to Matt. He and Gracie have a place for you to stay and a fenced-in back yard for Daisy."

Warmth spread throughout her at the mention of Matt and Gracie. It would be fun to spend time with her new friends. Yes, time away from the house and with new friends might just give her the fresh perspective she sorely needed.

"Awesome. I'm looking forward to spending time with them. Mr. Downey can start tomorrow. I'll go out there during the day to work on the house as long as he's there."

"Sounds like a plan." Again his voice was laced with concern. "I'll be off work early today. Why don't you meet me at the farm, say around five? We'll get some more work done, then I'll go with you to Matt and Gracie's house to make sure you feel comfortable."

He'd thought of everything. "Okay. See you then."

The rest of the afternoon proved to be both fun and relaxing. Dakota snagged two pair of jeans, a dress, three shirts, and a pair of tennis shoes that looked as though they'd never been worn for under ten dollars. Clutching her bag of bargains, she climbed in the truck and headed back to the farm.

Once at the house, she parked and exited the truck, Daisy still on her leash. She'd just had time to grab her packages as Chance made the bend in the road. She waited by her truck as he parked and strode toward her.

"You two are a sight for sore eyes." He squatted to pat Daisy. "Had me scared earlier today." His weary face gave credence to his words.

"Sorry. I didn't mean to scare you."

He rose to his feet, his eyes on her face and his arms twitching restlessly, but didn't step toward her or give her a hug.

Unexpected disappointment flooded her heart. *Quit it, Dakota.* She couldn't very well complain when he complied with her wishes to keep things on a platonic level, now could she? She started for the house.

Chance followed. "How was your afternoon?"

"Actually fun. I got a good deal on a few clothes at the thrift store." Dakota spoke the words over her shoulder as they climbed the steps.

Suddenly his face darkened, and he stopped in mid step, his gaze trained on something beyond her.

She turned in the direction of his gaze.

A gigantic hunting knife pierced through a fluttering sheet of paper and into the door. Large computer-printed letters covered the note. "Glad I found you, Amy. We'll meet again...soon."

In what seemed like slow motion, Dakota crumpled to the floor of the porch as everything went black.

Chapter Twenty

Chance's pulse exploded into high gear. He quickly fell to his knees beside Dakota. Breathing? Check. He moved her head to his lap, and patted her cheeks. "Come on, Dakota. Wake up, honey."

Her eyes flitted open, her face deathly pale. "What happened?"

"You passed out on me."

At his words her entire body shook furiously, as though reminded of the note and knife. She moved to a sitting position, head in her hands, still trembling from head to toe.

He brought her chin up so he could see her eyes. "Hey, this could just be a prank by some kid. Don't be afraid." Her trembling moved into his body as well. No, this wasn't a prank. It was serious, and her entire body bore witness to the fact. He reached for his phone and quickly dialed 911.

"911. Can I help you?"

"Yeah, I need you to dispatch the county Sherriff's Department and the Miller's Creek Police to 9612 Cedar Bend Road. The police will know it as the Levi Kelly farm."

Dakota placed a hand on his arm, her eyes pleading. "No, Chance. Don't call the police. Please." Her trembling moved to a 7.0 on the Richter scale.

Part of him wanted to give in to her request based on the fear that darkened her green eyes. But he couldn't. She might not like it, and most assuredly wouldn't like him for doing it, but this was the right move.

"And your name?"

"Chance Johnson."

"The reason for your call?"

"Someone left a threatening letter attached to a single woman's door with a hunting knife."

"Do you feel safe now?"

Chance scanned the area, already darkened by approaching nightfall. "As far as I can tell."

"Do you have a safe place to wait until the police arrive?"

"Yes." They could move indoors to wait with Daisy and Levi's old shotgun.

"I can stay on the line."

"That won't be necessary, thanks." He clicked the phone off. With a hand on both of Dakota's shoulders, he helped her to a standing position. "Come on, sweetheart. We're gonna wait this out inside."

She wrenched from his grasp, visibly angry, and hurried inside.

He followed, made sure the door was shut securely behind them, and faced her.

Stiff-armed and with both hands clenched into fists, she lit into him with both barrels blazing. "How dare you call the police! Especially after I asked you not to." She paced like a caged animal, raking fingers through her long red curls. "You don't know what they're capable of. What this might mean." Dakota stopped, planted both palms over her face, and began to wail hysterically.

His chest tightened at her anguish, and in two steps he was by her side and took her in his arms. "Shh, it's okay. I won't let anyone hurt you."

"You don't understand." Dakota sobbed softly for a moment, her palms hot and sweaty against his shirt, then yanked herself from his arms, her hands swatting at tears, her breaths coming in short, shallow bursts. "Okay, think

Dakota." She began to pace again, talking to herself under her breath.

His own panic escalated. Never had he seen her like this, like a wild animal on full alert. "Why are you acting this way?"

She shot him a look that told him exactly what she thought of him and his question and finished it off with a derisive laugh. "Trust me, you don't want to know. Besides, don't you realize that whatever I say to you puts you in danger?"

Danger? He frowned and cast his gaze to the floor in deep contemplation. What had she endured? What kind of trouble had she gotten herself into during the past few years? And if he'd been on time that night of the wreck, could he have prevented her from leaving? In some dark, twisted way, her dangerous situation was all his fault. Would she ever forgive him? "So you know who left the note?"

Across the room, Dakota nodded, then doubled over, hands on knees, gasping for air.

Chance hurried to her and laid an arm across her back. "You okay?"

"Just...a little...dizzy...can't...catch a...breath."

He knelt in front of her to force her to look at him and to check the color of her face. Pale and sweaty. Her eyes cloudy. "Listen to me, Dakota. I want you to concentrate on taking deep, slow breaths."

She nodded, her lips tinged in blue. Following his instructions, she opened her mouth wide like a fish and sucked in a deep breath.

"Okay, hold it, and let it out slowly."

Once more she complied.

"Good girl. Keep up the deep breathing."

After a couple of minutes she raised to a standing position, her color much better.

Chance guided her to the couch. "C'mon. You need to sit." He swallowed hard, knowing she wouldn't take kindly to what he was about to ask. "What all have you had to eat today?'

"A bowl of cereal and a slice of pizza."

Now it was his turn to take a deep breath and release it slowly, not because he felt faint, but in an effort to control his anger and ensuing censure. Best to approach this topic with gloves on. "And the other day at B&B Hardware? Had you eaten anything?"

She twisted her head slowly from side to side.

He sent a soft smile, praying she'd see his concern rather than a scolding. "That explains these dizzy spells you're having. Your blood sugar plummets without food, and in a stressful situation it'll be worse."

Dakota nodded, but didn't reply, completely zoned out, her gaze locked on nothing but thin air.

Had she heard one word he'd said, or was she back in the stress zone, her thoughts on the note? "Did you hear me?"

"Oh. Yeah. Sorry."

"Promise me you'll take time away from working to eat?" Somehow he had to find a way to break her junk food habit, before those artcrics of hers turned to baling wire.

She nodded, a close-lipped smile on her still-pale face. "I'll try."

"Good."

Sirens pierced the silence. Chance stepped out onto the porch as Ernie's car followed by a Sherriff's car plowed up a cloud of dust down the driveway.

Carter climbed from the car first and made quick strides toward him. "Everyone okay?"

Chance nodded. "Just a little shaken up."

"What happened?" Ernie strode toward him, his enormous moustache twitching, two Sherriff's deputies right on his heels.

"We got out here a few minutes after five and found this on the door." He stepped out of the way to reveal the note and knife.

All four guys quickly scaled the steps and gathered around the knife-penned note.

"Man, that is one serious knife." One of the Sherriff's deputies moved in closer, careful not to touch anything. "And brand new by the looks of it."

Carter nodded, his face grim. "And expensive. This is a military knife with DLC coating. About three hundred and fifty bucks."

Chance frowned. "DLC?"

"Diamond-like carbon. Practically indestructible. Razor sharp. Will cut through metal like it's paper."

A slow shudder traveled down Chance's spine, suddenly thankful for the electrical problems that had kept Dakota away from the farm all day. What if she'd been here?

Ernie's bushy eyebrows matched his pinched moustache. "Whoever did this means business."

Chance's heart rate went on a rapid-rise climb. No wonder Dakota had gotten so panicky. She, better than anyone, realized the danger, because she knew the person responsible.

"I'll go get gloves and bags," offered one of the deputies. He clomped down the steps toward the parked car.

Chance turned to Ernie. "How long before we hear back on possible evidence?"

Ernie shook his balding head. "This is technically out of our jurisdiction. We came because of you and Dakota. But it can take awhile." He released a short puff of air, condensation curling into the cold night air. "I'm guessing they won't turn up much." He looked back at the knife. "This guy knows what he's doing."

The other deputy caught Chance's attention. "So there's a young lady involved?"

"Yeah. This is her house." Funny how easily the words slipped from his lips when it was technically his house, too. "She's inside."

"I'm going to need to question her."

"Yeah? Well good luck with that." Chance entered the house, Carter, Ernie, and one of the deputies right behind him. "Dakota?" The living room was empty. Maybe she'd gone to the bathroom. He hurried down the hall, still calling her name.

Long claws raked across his heart at the empty bathroom. Where was she? Upstairs, maybe? He took the steps two at a time. "Dakota?" Daisy's whimper sounded from the far bedroom. He hurried to the door and knocked. "Dakota? Are you in there?" No sound other than Daisy's whine and scratching on the door. He turned the knob. Daisy immediately rushed past him and down the stairs, then rounded the corner toward the kitchen and the back door, her claws slipping against the newly-finished floors. Chance followed at full speed, the others with him.

Daisy whined and scratched her feet against the kitchen floor directly in front of the back door in an effort to dig her way out if need be to get to Dakota.

Chance's heart fell to his feet. Had she run away again? Or even worse, had the person who left the note nabbed her?

Shivering, partly from cold and partly from the fear that snaked throughout her entire being, Dakota half-ran, half-walked away from the farmhouse, the moonless night making it difficult to see even her lily-white hand in front of her face. A darkness she welcomed, since it also provided much-needed cover.

It'd be just a matter of time before they came after her, hopefully on foot. If they were on foot that would buy her more time. But eventually, their pursuit could involve highly-trained search and rescue teams on horseback, K-9 units, and possibly even air surveillance.

Her thoughts raced as she mentally zoomed through the hours of online videos she'd watched on escaping and disappearing. At some point she needed to locate mud--and lots of it--for the purpose of covering her scent and providing at least some protection from possible infrared thermal imaging cameras now used by police as well as the military.

Another shiver ravaged her body at the thought of rolling in wet mud with these near-freezing temps. The creeks and stock tanks around here were used to water cattle and horses. And wherever there was a livestock watering hole, there was also manure.

She forced her mind from the unpleasant prospect and back to the matter at hand. Because of her sprint away from the farmhouse, her breath came in short, painful bursts, and deposited wisps of white smoke in front of her face. At some point she'd hopefully find a place to hole up and lay low for a few days. A place where no one could find her. A place of safety.

She shook her red mane in the darkness. This chance at escape was slim to none, but what choice did she have? A sudden sense of hopelessness and discouragement filtered through her veins, sagging both her shoulders and their heavy load. Had she made it to the safe haven of Miller's Creek only to be returned to Kane's evil hands?

Oh, God, help me. I had to take this route to protect them, but I can't do this without You.

The resulting silence was deafening, the only sounds were her boots against the ground, her erratic breaths, and the pounding of her heartbeat in her ears. Everything in her wanted to turn around and run back to the safety of the farmhouse, but she stumbled on. Hopefully, this would remove potential danger for Chance and her other friends.

After what seemed like hours, Dakota reached a dirt road several miles south of the farmhouse, one she'd seen many times on her way to Morganville. The lights of a farmhouse winked at her from the right, so she crossed the road far to the left. She'd barely made it across the road and into the underbrush before a police car passed slowly, shining a big light into the field where she'd just stood.

Her heart pounded as she knelt behind a cedar bush, its powerful scent pungent in the cool night. Her skin itched from the bush's burrs. Thankfully, the spotlight traveled past where she hid and moved on down the road. She breathed a sigh of relief. Close call.

A few minutes later she stumbled upon the dreaded stock tank. Time to do the unthinkable. She grabbed handfuls of the cold mud and manure combo from the banks of the water and coated her backpack with the mixture, careful to protect the bag's contents. Her nose wrinkled at the gosh-awful smell.

Once the backpack was completely coated, she followed suit with her clothing, starting at her feet and working her way up to her hair and face. Twice she gagged and heaved, but somehow managed to keep the meager contents of her stomach in place. Well, at least K-9 unit dogs wouldn't be able to detect her scent beneath the stench that now surrounded her.

With a quick swig of water from her bottle, she hoisted the backpack back onto her aching spine. Now to find a place to hide.

Minutes drug into hours, her feet heavier by the second, partly from fatigue, partly from cold numbness invading her bones. At least the shivering had stopped. Maybe her body had finally adjusted to the cold.

Her eyelids grew even heavier than her mud-laden boots. Sleep. She needed sleep. Still she trudged on.

Two tiny lights appeared, and in her weariness, seemed to bounce in tandem. Her eyes widened. Those weren't lights. They were eyes. The shivering returned, but not from cold. She moved away from the lights, but they followed no matter which way she turned. A coyote? Or possibly a big cat of some kind?

A wildfire unleashed inside, propelling her legs to a stumbling run, her lungs exploding from exertion and freezing air. *Come on, Dakota.* She forced her weary, unwilling muscles past their limit, and they screamed in protest.

Steps. She heard footsteps. Dakota dared not stop to uncover their source, but continued to stumble forward. Then, out of nowhere, she ran headlong into something big and wide and hard. Or was it someone?

Exhausted, she fell in a heap on the ground, unable to move.

Two big hands reached out of the darkness and grabbed her by the shoulders.

Her feet drug the ground, and as even the dark night faded away, her last despairing thought was that Kane had finally caught up to her.

Chapter Twenty-One

How dare the sun to shine. Chance squinted against its brilliance as he moved eastward toward the bridge, still questioning his decision to spend the day at the farm. While part of him wanted a distraction from his constant worried thoughts over Dakota's whereabouts, another part longed to be near her. At the moment, with her still missing, his best way to keep her close had been the farm, in spite of the memories it brought to mind.

"C'mon, Daisy." He jammed his fingers in his jeans' front pockets and whistled over his shoulder.

Daisy just ambled, head to the ground, sniffing for clues. She'd moped around ever since Dakota's disappearance, barely eating anything and constantly whimpering or whining. For someone who hated dogs, Dakota had done a good job with her, teaching Daisy to sit patiently by the door before an outing in order to easily secure the leash.

An unexpected smile came to his face as he remembered Dakota's initial response to the dog.

Oh, Lord, keep her safe, and bring her home soon.

The ache in his chest returned. The prayer had become his constant mantra. Very few minutes slipped by without the words throbbing in his heart, mind, and soul. How had she managed to vanish without a trace, and where had the week gone? Now it was Thursday. Thanksgiving Day. A day of gratitude to God. A day to spend with those you loved.

In his right pocket, his phone vibrated. He pulled it out and checked the screen. Matt. "Hey, bud."

"How you doing, my friend?" The voice held the familiar sincerity Matt was known for.

Chance froze in place, unwilling to glimpse the bridge while on the phone, uncertain of his ability to maintain control of his emotions. "Been better, actually."

"Still no word?"

"Nope." The word pretty much summarized the hopelessness swirling in his gut.

Silence sounded on the other end for a brief moment. "You still think she ran away?"

"Yeah, and as crazy as it sounds, that's what I'm hoping for." Compared to the alternative, anyway.

"Don't give up believing, Chance."

"Trying." But with each passing day, the trying was harder to do.

"Someone will find her."

A scared laugh fell from him. Yeah, but who would find her first?

"Listen. I don't think it's a good idea for you to be alone today. We're all headed over to Mama Beth's mid-afternoon. I know there'll be plenty of food, and I know she wouldn't mind you being there."

No. He couldn't. For one thing, his current disposition would just bring everyone else down. Besides that, seeing everyone with their mates was more than he could bear at the moment. "Thanks for the invite, Matt, but I'm going to try to get some more work done around the farm while I'm off work."

Silence again. "Well, if you change your mind, you know where we'll be."

"Thanks."

Once the phone was re-deposited in his pocket, Chance resumed his walk to the creek, Daisy still lagging behind.

Not long afterwards, they arrived at the broken-down bridge, memories of the past and the present mingling together.

He blinked back sudden tears and raked both hands through his hair, air whooshing from his lungs. *Please let me have another chance.*

A twig snapped to his right, and he jerked his head around to see the new neighbor standing nearby. How had the guy managed to get so close without giving away his presence?

"Sorry. Didn't mean to startle you." The man smiled, an open friendly smile.

"It's okay. My mind was elsewhere."

A frown knitted the guy's eyebrows into a wiggly line above his hooded eyes. "Don't mean to pry, but I noticed all kinds of sirens and lights at your house earlier this week. Everyone okay?"

Dakota's suspicions of the man rose like bubbles in water. How much should he reveal? "Yeah, just a minor incident."

"And your lady friend? She okay?"

Every muscle in Chance's body stiffened and forced his spine into a tense upright position. He stared at the man--what was his name again?--through narrowed eyes. "Why do you ask?"

The guy shrugged. "Just curious." He took a step backward. "Well, I best be going."

Chance acknowledged his words with a head nod, suspicions weighing heavy in his chest. Did the guy know something? And why had he asked specifically about Dakota?

Once the man disappeared from view behind a clump of bare-branched trees, Chance scratched Daisy behind the ears. "Let's go back home, girl."

Not too many steps from the creek, his phone vibrated again. The screen revealed the caller as Mama Beth. He released an exasperated sigh. Sometimes his friends just didn't know how to take no for an answer. "Hi, Mama Beth. What's up?"

"My ire, for one thing."

Chance raised his eyes to the sky and gave his head a shake, an immediate close-mouthed smile on his lips. Typical response. "Oh?"

"I understand Matt invited you to our Thanksgiving dinner, and you refused."

"Well, that's putting it a little harshly."

"I know you're missing Dakota and worried about her. We all are. That's exactly why you need to come over." He could almost picture her finger wagging in the air.

"Don't much feel like celebrating right now."

"Which means it's exactly the time you need to celebrate. Remember the story of Paul in prison? He was locked up, but singing praises to God. That's what set him free." She rattled off the words in machine-gun fashion.

She did have a point, but he just couldn't. Not today. Not without Dakota. "Well, thanks, but I'm still gonna decline." Without giving her a chance to argue any further, he clicked the off button and shoved the phone back in his pocket.

A few minutes later, he and the dog stood just inside the front door of the old farmhouse. Daisy resumed her whimpering whine.

If the truth be told, he felt like joining her in her lament. Everywhere he looked he saw Dakota. In the new crown molding that lined the ceiling, the fresh paint, the gleaming woodwork and floors. Not one room in the house had she left untouched. Once the kitchen was completed, the inside portion of their joint project would be finished, leaving only the mending of fences, plowing of fields, and the restoration of the bridge and outbuildings.

Then what? A sick feeling landed in the pit of his stomach at the realization of their almost-completed work. Would Dakota want to stay around? And even if she did, would she want him in her life?

With a sudden vigor that surprised him, Chance bolted out the front door and slammed it behind him. Enough of this. If and when Dakota did come back, he wanted her to see how committed to this project he was through what he accomplished in her absence. Wanted her to understand that the commitment extended to her, in spite of the hurt and betrayal and resentment that had kept them both bound in chains for far too long.

For the rest of the morning and into the sunny afternoon, Chance scraped paint from the house's exterior. Though the constant back-and-forth movement made his arm muscles protest, it worked wonders for his disposition.

A little before two, his stomach grumbled. He climbed down from the extension ladder and moved up the steps to find something to eat, but the sound of approaching cars caught his attention. Chance clomped down the steps and out into the driveway, his hand over his eyes to shield them from the mid-afternoon sun. A whole passel of vehicles paraded down the drive. Only when they came to a halt and the passengers disembarked carrying dishes laden with food did he understand.

He hadn't joined their Thanksgiving Day celebration, so they'd brought the celebration to him.

For the first time all day, in spite of his concern for Dakota, gratitude swelled in his heart and fully worked its way to his face.

❖ ❖ ❖

A shaft of sunlight fell across Dakota's closed eyes. She grimaced and groaned, then rolled onto her left side. Her eyes slowly opened, dry and gritty from too much sleep, her tongue stuck to the roof of her mouth. Gradually her surroundings came into focus, dark, menacing, and unfamiliar. Where was she? And how did she get here?

She attempted to push herself up on one arm, but her head swam to the point that her stomach joined in. Instead she rolled onto her back once more, her gaze immediately focused on the only window in the room. The wallpaper, which displayed gigantic roses and swans, made her feel as though she'd taken a step back in time--maybe to the 30's or 40's? Her ears honed in to detect any sound, but only a deathly quiet pervaded the room.

Dakota weakly brought a hand to her hair. Though tangled, it was devoid of the mud she'd caked on it earlier. The mud. More memories of recent events filtered through her mind. The note. The knife. The overwhelming need to run.

Chance. Was he okay? Did he miss her as much as she missed him? Was the farm still okay? The house nearing completion? Were her new friends in Miller's Creek safe from the monster who pursued her?

Her things. Where were they? For the first time she noticed the strange clothes she wore. Clean, but strange nonetheless. Her eyes scanned the room for her backpack, boots, and clothing. Nowhere in sight.

God, help me.

I am with you.

The reassuring and still, small voice brought immediate comfort. Whoever had found her might be able to confine her physically, but never again would she be held hostage in any other way. Christ had bought her freedom, and it was a freedom no man could take away.

Newfound resolve steeled her backbone, and once more she tried to sit. The room spun in circles, her arms like wet noodles, but she managed to scoot her weight against the rusty metal bed frame. She sat for a moment, her head leaned back until the wooziness passed.

From somewhere beyond the closed door another door opened and shut, followed by the sound of shuffling--or was it something being dragged?--across the floor.

Dakota trained her ears on the slightest of sounds. The dragging sound continued, followed by thumps and bumps.

In a single motion, she threw off the ragged quilt and sheet under which she'd slept. Bare feet on the floor, she stood, holding the head rail for support until her weakened leg muscles at least partially responded to her brain's demands. As quietly as possible, she took the few steps to the door and laid her ear against the dusty bare wood, hoping for any clue. Nothing. Dakota grasped hold of the antique metal doorknob, and turned, but it didn't budge. Locked.

Panic galloped inside. She pounded the door and yelled at the top of her lungs. "Let me out of here!" A rustle of movement outside the door, followed by hushed whispers, caught her attention. "Hello? Is anyone there?"

More hushed whispers, indecipherable through the wooden door. Finally a man's gruff voice sounded. "Step away from the door, and don't try nothing funny."

Dakota did as the voice commanded, backing as far as the bed, but she chose not to sit. "Okay, I'm away from the door."

A click, then the door swung open to reveal an elderly man and woman, their faces weathered and frozen. The man clutched a shotgun.

"Who are you?" Dakota tried to keep the tremor from her voice, but to no avail.

Neither answered, but continued to stare with hard, cold eyes. Great, she'd evaded Kane only to end up with an unfriendly version of Ma and Pa Kettle.

"Where am I?"

"At our house, on our property," replied the woman, with an emphasis on the word 'our.' "Who are you?"

Rather than give out too much information, Dakota countered the woman's question with one of her own. "How long have I been here?"

"Since about midnight Monday, when I caught you trespassin'." The old man growled and raised the drooping shotgun a little higher.

The missing pieces of her puzzled memory fell slowly into place. She'd run into something or someone on her escape. "What day is it?"

"Thursday. Thanksgiving."

Her eyes widened. She'd been asleep for three whole days? No wonder her mouth felt as though she'd tried to ingest the beige-colored sands of Monahans. No wonder she was so weak. No wonder she really needed to go to the bathroom.

Dakota grimaced. "I--uh--is there a restroom nearby?"

At this the old woman grinned and released a high-pitched cackle. "Well, it ain't exactly nearby, but we do have facilities." The witchy laugh continued, and she pointed to a pair of men's slippers at the foot of the bed. "Put those on and follow me."

"And I'll follow both of you with the gun, just in case she decides to try sump'n' funny."

A few seconds later Dakota found herself escorted outdoors to a little hut several feet away from the main house. "You still use an outhouse?"

The old woman's eyes twinkled. "More cost-effective than modern-day plumbin', if you ask me."

But not as convenient. Or sanitary. Dakota stepped into the tin-covered building. Her eyes adjusted quickly to the darkness, but not her nose to the horrendous smell. She held her breath, one hand over her nose, emptied her bladder, then quickly exited the building.

The old woman's grin revealed a few missing teeth, but the man's piercing and unyielding gaze never wavered.

In tandem, they moved back inside the house. The man brought his gun down and closed the door behind them. "You remind me of someone I used to know. A man by the name of Levi Kelly."

Elation mixed with surprise, and her mouth popped open in response. "You're kidding. Levi Kelly was my grandfather."

From that point on, it was as though they'd all known each other forever. Over a delicious Thanksgiving meal of venison, mashed potatoes, and fried okra, they swapped stories of her grandfather. Finally, unable to eat more, Dakota leaned back in the rickety old chair, both hands on her stomach, and groaned. "I haven't had a meal like that since I don't know when."

The woman, who'd identified herself as Emma, stood and gathered plates. "And thin as a rail, you are. Looks like I need to fatten you up." She cackled again.

Dakota moved to help her clean the small kitchen, really just a small corner of the entire living space, but

Emma waved her off. "No, you been sick. Just sit there and talk to us."

"How sick was I?"

"With that fever of yers, I's afraid you just might not make it." Hank hurried the words, then looked at her from the bottom of his bifocals, bearded chin in air. "Didn't your grandparents teach you not to roll around in muddy water when it's freezing outside?"

Dakota shrunk a little lower. They knew nothing, but did she dare tell them? Not since her grandparents were alive had she felt so safe and cared for. Maybe God had provided the listening ears. "Yes sir."

"Then why in tarnation did you do it?"

One word followed another as the story spilled from her mouth. She stopped only when they asked a question. At last, the whole story told, Dakota leaned forward, both hands in her palms.

"How long you been holding that in fer?" Emma's face held astonishment and weariness.

Dakota laughed, a laugh like she hadn't enjoyed in such a long time. "Too long. Thanks for listening. I really needed to get that off my chest."

Hank turned sideways in the chair and rested his elbow along the chair's back, his head leaned on one fist. "Boy, I'll say." The room grew quiet, and he turned to look at her, a quizzical air about him. "So all that time on the run, and you finally ended back on Levi's farm with J.C.'s grandson helpin' ya. Well, don't that beat all?" A brief laugh sounded from his white-bearded face, then he returned his head to his fist, deep in thought.

Emma disappeared from the room, then returned, Dakota's cleaned clothes folded in her hands. "Here are yer clothes. Liked to a' never got those things clean."

"Thank you, Emma." Knowing that the woman had most likely cleaned her soiled clothes by hand humbled her. Dakota glanced over at Hank, his eyes now closed. "Is Hank okay?"

Emma waved a hand. "Aah, he's either sleepin' or prayin'. I try not to interrupt either one."

"I heard that, old woman."

"Good, old man." Emma cackled as she walked away from the table to clean the dishes.

Hank faced her once more. "Just so you both know, I's a-prayin'."

"And?" came Emma's voice from the sink.

He looked Dakota square in the face. "You may not much like this, missy, but I hafta treat you as though you were my own. Tomorrow I'll be takin' you back to Miller's Creek and all the good people worried about cha. There comes a point when you hafta stop runnin' and start trustin'. Don't much think it was an accident that you ended back on the farm workin' with that young man. Now ya gotta wait on the Lord and see what He has for ya."

Her heart felt like he'd filled it full of buckshot. "But the sheriff's department will most likely arrest me on trumped-up charges."

Hank stood wearily, bending toward her. "Then you gotta pray that the Almighty will deliver ya." He tottered away from the table, but turned as he reached his rocking chair, wagging a finger in the air. "And then you need to get things worked out between you and this young man. Sounds like he's willing to rebuild a bridge, and you gotta meet him halfway, no matter what happened in the past."

Without another word, he parked himself in the chair and rocked, eyes closed.

As though to let her know it was time to think and not talk, Emma hummed loud enough to bring in all the bees from surrounding counties.

Chapter Twenty-Two

I'm on my way." Tension mounted, tightening his shoulder muscles. With a quick glance at Daisy who sat in the seat beside him, Chance punched the gas pedal. As if it weren't bad enough that he'd been thrown off schedule by the lack of checkers at the hardware store, now the electrician had beat him out to the farm. He'd sounded none-too-happy on the phone, and even threatened to leave if Chance didn't arrive pronto.

His thoughts turned to the previous day. As much as he'd loved spending time with his friends yesterday at the surprise Thanksgiving dinner at the farm, his goal to finish some projects had not been met. Though his friends had held an impromptu prayer meeting for Dakota, there was still no word.

The familiar prayer floated from his heart once more as he sped down the dirt road, a cloud of dust and gravel in his wake. *Lord, keep her safe and bring her home soon.*

Two minutes later he came to a quick stop next to Dakota's pickup. Jake Downey leaned against his truck, arms crossed and sour-faced.

"Sorry I'm late, Jake." Chance grabbed hold of Daisy's leash as she jumped from the front seat of his pickup.

"Your dime, not mine."

Chance clamped his lips together and took the front steps two at a time to unlock the old wooden door that would soon be replaced with the metal door he'd just purchased. He swung it open and stepped aside so Downey could enter with his tools.

"Let me show you what I got done on Wednesday." Downey's tone demanded rather than asked.

Chance resisted the urge to tell him that he'd already inspected the work and followed him into the kitchen instead. Hopefully, the man wouldn't take too long, which would only make him even further behind than he already was.

Downey unscrewed the electrical panel cover to reveal the new board. "Almost got through the other day, but didn't wanna leave you without power over Thanksgiving. Just a few more connections to make."

"Looks good." Chance made a move toward the front door to get started on his own work.

"Y'all have done a lot of work to this old place. Have it looking mighty nice."

Yeah, and if he wanted it to look even nicer, he needed to get busy. He faced Downey, more than a little impatient. "Thanks. Dakota did most of it."

The man's eyebrows raised. "Well, she's good at what she does. Might could even make a living at it."

"I'll tell her you said so." If he ever got the chance. "I'll be out front if you need me." Once outside, Chance penned Daisy up, then located the screwdriver he needed and set to work on the front door, the gash in the center of the old door yet another reminder of Dakota. In a matter of minutes, he'd removed the hinges from the frame. How had this thing even opened and closed properly? And what had kept a good stiff wind from blowing it down? The new door would definitely provide more safety. Especially after the special treatment he had in mind.

He hoisted the old door onto his back and started toward the barn. Knowing Dakota, she'd find another use for the door as a table or headboard. While at the barn,

Chance fed the chickens Coot had bestowed on Dakota and picked up another round of fresh eggs.

As he strode back toward the house cradling the eggs in the hem of his t-shirt, Ernie's car pulled around the corner down the driveway and then came to a stop next to the truck. Both Ernie and Carter climbed from the police car. Neither one looked hopeful.

Chance met them in the driveway. "Hey, guys. What's going on?"

Ernie shook his head. "Not much. Wish I had some good news for you."

The air caught in his lungs. Bad news instead?

"The forensic report on the knife and note didn't turn up anything. Pretty much what we expected."

Chance nodded, still waiting. The other men exchanged glances, seemingly reticent to say more. "And Dakota? Any news on her?"

Carter looked his way. "Haven't found her."

Chance's chin dropped to his chest. If only they could hear something. Some little snippet of information on her whereabouts.

"But I do have some other news."

His head snapped up, eyes wide. "What?"

Ernie's mouth twisted, and he shifted his weight from one leg to the other. "There's an APB out for her arrest under the name of Amy Barnes."

The words knifed into him. No wonder she'd changed her name. No wonder she'd run away at the prospect of talking to the police. "What for?"

"Theft."

She'd mentioned her past experience with drugs. Had she stolen to buy them? "So if she's found, what happens?"

"She'll be taken into custody and returned to the location of the crime for arraignment."

The news knifed through his heart, and he closed his eyes. So even if Dakota did come back, it wouldn't be for long.

Carter stepped closer and laid a hand on his shoulder. "You okay?"

Still in a daze, Chance shrugged. "Don't know. A lot of stuff in my head right now." And his heart.

"Just 'cause there's an APB doesn't mean she's guilty."

Carter's comment rained soothing balm on his soul. He sent the tall policeman a half-smile.

"We'll keep you posted." Carter patted his arm and headed back to the car, Ernie right behind him.

Downey was replacing the cover on the electrical panel when Chance entered the kitchen to put the eggs away. "Just finished the panel."

"Good." Once the electrician was gone, he'd be able to finish his work without further interruption. A few minutes later, Chance hauled the new door up the front porch, just as Matt's Suburban rounded the driveway corner. His friend hopped from the vehicle, the typical laid-back smile on his face.

"Weren't you just here?"

Matt sauntered up the steps, his hand extended. "Trying to get rid of me already?"

"No, but I might just put you to work."

Matt stepped back, both hands in the air. "Just remembered an appointment."

The two laughed, then Matt's face sobered. "Actually, I came out to see how you're doing."

"Been better, but I'm okay." Chance leaned against the house and crossed his arms.

"Glad to hear it. Still no word?"

"They still haven't found her, but I do have some news." He relayed what Carter and Ernie had told him earlier.

"I can't tell you what Dakota told me about her past, Chance, but I can tell you this. She's a good person with powerful enemies."

The words both encouraged and disturbed him. Encouraged him because they offered hope that she wasn't guilty, but disturbed him because of whoever was out to destroy her. He searched for words, but nothing came.

Matt turned the conversation to other topics for a while. Then his friend engulfed him in a bear hug. "Wish I could stay longer and give you a hand."

Chance managed a smile. "Yeah, right."

"You have my number if you need me."

"Thanks, pal."

Chance returned to his work with renewed gusto, the day now warm and sunny. In no time at all, the door was in place and shimmed to level and plumb. He reached for the package of four-inch screws he'd bought that morning. The stronger the frame the better, and he'd make sure to repeat the process when it came to the hinges and lock plate. If Dakota did come back, at least she'd have secure doors.

Chance worked straight through lunch and into the afternoon, his thoughts never far from Dakota, but happy for the work that kept him somewhat distracted. His concern for her spurred him on to finish the tasks in record time. First he finished the installation of the front door and trim and moved to the back to repeat the process. Then he added security lights to the front and back, tying them into the lights already in place. Once that project was finished, he tackled the chore he'd been itching to do after finishing up the paint scraping yesterday--building shutters.

What was there about shutters that made a house feel homey? Maybe the shutters would make Dakota feel at home. Make her want to stay. Forever. With him.

The ache in his heart returned and lingered, as he took measurements, used the noisy chop saw to cut the boards to length, and installed the first two shutters. Chance stepped back to view his work, pleased with the results.

A vehicle with no muffler growled in the distance and grew closer. Then a truck in worse shape than Dakota's pulled into view. Chance raised a hand to shield his eyes from the sinking sun, still unable to make out faces inside the noisy truck.

The pickup stopped, and the engine went silent. An old man he didn't recognize climbed slowly from the cab and tottered toward him.

Chance stepped toward him. "Can I help you?"

The man's long white beard reached to his chest. "You might not remember me, son, but I was a friend of J.C.'s."

Chance offered his hand. "Any friend of Grampa's is a friend of mine."

"I'm Hank, and I have something for you."

A frown cinched his brows. This man he didn't know had something for him?

"But before I hand it over, I need to tell you something." Hank raised long wrinkled fingers in the air and peered directly at Chance. "Sometimes things happen we have a hard time gettin' around. After it's all said and done, we wish we could go back and do things differently, but we can't."

Where was he going with this line of conversation?

"That don't make us bad people. It makes us like everyone else in the world. Sinners in need of grace." Hank's voice held a gruffness that bordered on scolding.

"Part of forgiving someone means lettin' the past go and movin' ahead without all that garbage holdin' you back. You get what I'm saying, young man?"

"Yes sir." But not why he was saying it.

"Sump'n' else I want you to know."

The sun sunk lower and lower behind the old man. Chance turned sideways to keep the sun from his eyes. Just how much longer was this gonna take?

"It ain't always easy for people to talk about the past. When I came back from the war, I vowed to never mention it, even if people asked. Didn't mean I had sump'n' to hide. It meant it hurt too much to talk about." He paused. "Whatever you do, don't let her shut you out."

Chance's pulse quickened. Who? Don't let who shut him out?

"She needs to get this settled, and she needs your help to do it."

Behind them both, soft footsteps sounded.

Chest pounding, Chance whirled around.

A familiar figure stood in front of him, silhouetted by the sun, her red hair gleaming like that of an angel. In two steps he had her in his arms, whispering against her hair. "I thought I'd lost you forever." His voice broke, and he struggled to keep his emotions under control.

Dakota pushed away gently. She peered into his eyes, her face full of both sorrow and questions. Then she turned and walked over to Hank. "Thank you for everything, Hank. Words just can't expre--"

The old man pulled her into an embrace. "Hush now, 'fore you go and make me cry." Hank moved her to arm's length, tears shining in his ancient eyes. "You do things right this time around, girlie. No more running away, no matter what. Trust the Lord to take care of you. And don't be a stranger."

Dakota hugged him again. "I won't. Give Emma my love."

Hank waved his bony fingers again, tottered to his pickup, and drove away.

Dakota faced Chance. "We have lots to talk about."

He breathed a silent prayer of thanksgiving for her safe return, then pulled her into his arms once more. "We certainly do."

Chapter Twenty-Three

Dakota's heart did that strange little flip-flop thing in her chest, and it was all because of the love and relief shining in Chance's clear blue-gray eyes. She pressed her lips together and lowered her gaze. So much for her determination to tell him everything. How could she tell him the truth and risk changing his tender expression to one of anger?

Daisy began to bark and whine from the barn. A grin she couldn't control spread across Dakota's face as she hurried to her old friend. The dog practically jumped into her arms as she unlocked the gate, eliciting a laugh from both her and Chance. "Down, Daisy. You're a German Shepherd, not a Chihuahua." She glanced over at Chance and moved outside. "I think she missed me."

"She's not the only one." He placed one arm around her shoulder as they strolled toward the house, Daisy on their heels. "Glad to have you back." His handsome grin set off a swarm of butterflies that made their way to her queasy stomach. "Why'd you stay gone so long? In fact, why'd you leave in the first place?"

Good. This Chance she could handle. She pulled away from his embrace and raised both hands. "Look, don't push me. This isn't easy."

An apology crept into his eyes, mingling with the love and relief.

Oh no, not that again. Dakota snatched up her backpack from off the ground and then stopped in her tracks, for the first time noticing the work Chance had done on the house in her absence. This place would look phenomenal once they added a few coats of paint. "You've been busy." That he would use his holiday and evenings to work on the old house even without her there touched her in a way she didn't expect.

Chance ambled up beside her. "Looks good, huh?"

Gross understatement. "It looks wonderful. New doors, old paint scraped off, and I love the shutters. It's a perfect touch."

"Wanna help me finish?" Chance peered back at the setting sun, eyes squinted. "Should have time to get a few more shutters done."

"Sure." Dakota dropped her bag on the front porch and followed him to where he had the sawhorses and chop saw set up.

He handed her a tape measure and pencil. "You mark the boards in four-foot sections, and I'll cut them. If we create an assembly line, we'll be able to whip these out in no time at all."

They soon fell into an easy rhythm and managed to churn out enough shutters to finish the windows on the front of the house before dark. As they moved to clean up the debris and tools, Chance smiled over at her. "We make a pretty good team you know."

Her thoughts exactly, and it troubled her to no end. No matter how sweet and kind he was, no matter how good-looking, no matter what he said or did, she had to find a way to fight the incredible waves of attraction that kept washing over her, yanking her below the surface, and leaving her gasping for breath.

He leaned against the barn door, one lanky leg across the other, those vivid eyes of his highlighted by his blue plaid shirt. "For someone who said we need to talk, you're not doing much."

Dakota finished putting the tools away, struggling for words. What was this sudden inability to make a coherent sentence? "Guess I'm having a hard time figuring out how to start."

A lazy smile curved his lips. Chance uncrossed his legs and stepped toward her. He stopped just inches from where she stood, his eyes searching her face.

Dakota struggled to maintain aloofness, praying that she wasn't sending off any unspoken signals.

He reached up and fingered one of her curls. "I like your hair this color."

"You do?" Why did her voice suddenly resemble Minnie Mouse?

"Mmm-hmmm." He continued to wind it around his long fingers as though mesmerized. "Let me take you out to a nice dinner, Dakota. A place where we can both relax. Maybe that'll make it easier to talk."

"Okay." The traitorous agreement escaped her lips before she could stop it. What was she thinking? It would be much easier to handle this conversation in a less intimate setting.

After locking Daisy inside, they set out for the lake, Chance insistent on seafood. Once they arrived, they were immediately seated at a table in the back, overlooking the lake. Dakota pursed her lips as she scanned the room. At least they were the only customers in this part of the restaurant, which might or might not make it easier to talk.

Chance helped her remove her jacket, his breath warm against her cold cheek. "We'll have privacy here. I work with the wife of the owner, and called in a favor."

Thoughts tangled in her brain. Privacy. Good for conversation, if it weren't for the romantic setting. Apparently this room was used for special occasions, because the decor was much less casual than the noisy front room they'd passed through on their way in. In addition, soft music played in the background. With the lights low, the flame from the flicker of the candle on their table danced about in sync with the flames from a nearby stone fireplace. But the best part was the view.

Their intimate booth for two sat beside a large plate glass window overlooking the lake, where the sun melted into the horizon, leaving pink, orange, and gold streaks on the underbelly of the fluffy clouds.

Chance motioned for her to have a seat.

Warding off the romance as best she could, Dakota scooted into the booth.

He took a seat beside her, his smile wreaking havoc with her insides. "You look like you're on pins and needles, Dakota. Relax. Enjoy the evening. Take in the view."

After they placed their order, Chance filled the time with talk about his week and had her laughing at stories of Daisy's antics. By the time their food arrived, the atmosphere had worked its magic on her, her tense muscles unwinding in spite of her earlier resolution to stay on her guard.

Chance took her hand to bless the food. But once the prayer was over, he maintained his grip, his gaze still searching hers.

Dakota sent a tight-lipped smile, pulled her hand away, and busied herself with her napkin and food. For the next few minutes she focused on devouring the meal in front of her. Never had she had such delicious shrimp scampi.

Chance chuckled softly. "What's wrong? Did Hank and his wife not feed you?"

"Well actually, I was out for a few days."

His eyebrows rose, but he didn't speak.

"They said I was running a fever and delirious, I guess from my hike in freezing temps." She downed a bite of the fluffy baked potato, loaded with butter, sour cream, cheese, chives, and bacon.

Chance laid his fork on his plate, his forehead creased, his eyes dark and troubled. "Why did you do it?"

Eyes down. No more eye contact. Her nerves couldn't take it. "Do what?"

"Leave the other night."

She closed her eyes, focused on the memory of all Hank and Emma had encouraged her to do. "I don't trust policemen." Dakota took a sip of her water, gathering courage and words. Might as well just get it out there. "Just so you know, I was in an abusive relationship for several years."

"The guy you lived with?" The words were low and full of emotion.

She nodded, but kept her eyes down.

"Why didn't you just leave?"

"I did. He had a lot of power and influence. The kind of person others would never suspect. The first time I left him, he had the police take me straight back to him."

A hushed gasp fell from his lips, but still she stayed true to her vow to avoid eye contact. "And then what happened?"

"He almost killed me." There. She'd said it. Let him know the hell she'd endured.

His groan captured her gaze. He rested his forehead against his fist. "I'm so sorry, Dakota. To think of someone hurting you..."

She blinked back tears. His compassion on top of her weakened emotional state just might be her undoing. With slow steady breaths, she willed herself back to a place of control.

Silence ensued. Chance took small nibbles of food, lost in thought. Finally he laid down his fork, his eyes once more boring a hole through her head. "Had a lot of time to think over the past few days, and I have some questions."

Uh oh. Was she ready for this?

"I know you mentioned seeing me with my cousin and thinking the worst, but something else must've played into your decision to leave." He worked his lips back and forth a minute, before he looked back her way. "Was it because of the way I acted?"

How could she answer truthfully without hurting him? She couldn't. "Partly."

He grimaced and lowered his head. "I'm so sorry. Any other reason?"

She couldn't answer. Couldn't force the words past her clenched teeth. But why? Wasn't this part of the story that she most needed and wanted to tell him?

"You might have spared both of us a lot of hurt."

A tinge of condemnation colored his comment, slicing through her heart. So he still blamed all this on her?

Without warning, he reached over and lifted her chin, his face a hair's-breadth from her own, his eyes once more toying with her emotions. "Tell me the truth, Dakota, no matter how painful. I can't help you if you don't trust me." His lips claimed hers.

Though a struggle ensued within, in the end she allowed the kiss. Kissed him back, her heart aching for him to know the truth and understand why she'd done the unthinkable.

No! This wasn't fair to either one of them. Dakota pulled away, once more refusing eye contact.

The tension between them was palpable.

"What is it, Dakota? What is it that you have locked up inside you?" Hurt and pain oozed from his voice, as though she'd dealt a lethal blow.

In a heartbeat, sudden understanding dawned within, and she shut her eyes against the pain it produced. She loved him. Had never really stopped loving him. But if he knew the truth, this brief respite from the wounds of the past would vanish like yesterday's blossoms. He would hate her, a thought she just couldn't bear. "I can't." The sentence fell from her mouth in a hushed whisper, full of anguish. "Maybe one day, but right now..." The monstrous knot in her throat gobbled up the rest of her words. *If only...*

For the rest of the evening Chance remained silent, not a word slipping from his lips. The silence forced Dakota from her self-promise to avoid looking at him. His lowered head, slumped shoulders, and especially the sorrowful expression on his face all combined to reveal his troubled hurt.

Dakota shivered against the cold as they left the restaurant a half hour later. She crawled into the pickup cab through the door Chance held open for her.

Chance closed the door and made his way to the driver's side, his sullen features lit softly from the parking lot lights.

Dakota released a slow breath. His unusual silent treatment was wearing her down and fast. Okay. Maybe she should tell him and get it out. Let the chips fall wherever it was that chips fell. Just as she opened her mouth to release the final bit of truth, Chance turned left on the farm-to-market road, headed toward Miller's Creek rather than the farm. "Where are we going?"

His troubled sigh flowed through the darkness toward her. "I don't want to do this, but I have to. Hopefully, you can trust me to do what's best." He hesitated briefly. "And forgive me."

The contents of her stomach curdled instantly. Forgive him? For what? "You're scaring me, Chance." Her voice trembled as proof of her fear. "What are you talking about?"

"I have to turn you in to the police."

Chapter Twenty-Four

A sick feeling landed in the pit of his stomach, but Chance clenched his jaw and pressed on in the same direction. This was absolutely the right thing to do, but inside it killed him. Not only would Dakota never trust him, she'd never forgive him. Never give him the second chance he'd hoped for.

Dakota slouched beside him in the pickup seat, one hand on the door handle as though waiting for an opportunity to escape. Angry tears brimmed in her eyes, her lips pinched and taut.

"Please trust me, Dakota. I know y--"

"You know nothing!" She glared at him, her lovely green eyes glistening with tears. A sarcastic laugh fell from her parted lips as she shook her head from side to side. "All this time I thought you'd changed. Thought you might actually be a nice guy after all. You've just been waiting for your chance to betray me, haven't you?"

Anger roared up inside him at the injustice of her accusations. "That's not true!" His fury subsided with the realization that hurt and anger fueled her comment. He inhaled a slow breath to steady his emotions and nerves. "I'm doing this because it's the right thing to do."

"The right thing to do? Don't you realize the danger this puts me in? What will happen if..." She burst into tears and buried her face in her hands, the gut-wrenching sobs clawing at his heart.

Fear clamored into his chest and shoulders, tightening them like a rubber band about to snap. Was he endangering her life? He gnawed the inside of his lip. Or had her former boyfriend done such a number on her that she was frightened and upset for no reason? "Please don't cry, Dakota." Chance reached a hand across the seat and caressed her arm.

She jerked away, plastering herself to the door to get away from him.

Lord, give me the words to help her understand.

"I have a plan, if you'll hear me out. This former boyfriend of yours has another APB out for your arrest."

Dakota didn't seem surprised by the news, but at least she stopped crying long enough to listen.

"That's why I'm taking you to the Miller's Creek police rather than the Sheriff's Department. They'll be a little more lenient. I'm also gonna speak with Andy, to get his advice and hopefully his representation."

She still didn't speak or look at him, still balled up in an unyielding, defensive posture.

Chance reached in his pocket and grabbed his cell phone to call Carter.

His friend answered quickly. "Hey, Chance, what's up?"

"I have Dakota with me. Would you mind calling Ernie, Andy, and Matt, and have them meet us at the police station?"

"Will do, buddy. See you there."

Dakota, still stone silent, now wore a look of weary resignation.

A few minutes later they pulled up outside the police department. Ernie and Carter met them at the door. "Hey, Chance. Dakota." Ernie nodded to both of them and held the front door as he pointed to the end of the hallway. "Why don't we meet down here? There's a little more room to spread out."

Dakota walked down the hallway sullenly, arms crossed, looking very much like a cornered criminal. Once inside the room, she plopped into a chair. Chance took a seat across the table.

Clamor outside the room let them know that Andy and Matt had arrived. The two brothers entered the room together. Andy took a seat on Dakota's right, while Matt chose the chair to her left. The younger Tyler brother leaned close to Dakota and patted her arm. "You okay?"

She shrugged. "That remains to be seen."

"We'll do all we can for you, Dakota." Andy attempted to reassure her, then turned his attention to Chance and Ernie. "Okay, guys, fill me in."

Ernie related the details of Dakota being wanted for theft. Chance filled in the rest of the details with the story of her abusive ex.

Andy peered at Dakota, and she made eye contact. "All that true?"

She nodded. "He'll kill me this time."

The softly-spoken words cast a deathly pall over the entire room.

Chance leaned forward, for the first time able to capture her gaze. "I'm not gonna let that happen. But you've got to trust me."

Something flickered in her green eyes. A spark of hope, maybe? She turned her head to Ernie. "Am I going to be arrested?"

He nodded, his moustache firm. "I don't have a choice."

Chance's heart wrenched at the pitiful expression on her face. He swiveled his chair in the direction of Ernie and Carter, who stood at the far end of the table. "I don't feel comfortable with her staying here overnight, especially with that note stabbed to her front door Monday night.

Aren't there other options, like an ankle bracelet or house arrest or something?"

Ernie considered the question, his lips and moustache puckered into a small 'o.' He shook his head briefly. "Wish I had another answer for you, but no. I'll do what I can to get the judge to grant her a bond hearing first thing in the morning."

Chance grimaced. He obviously hadn't thought this through well, and now Dakota would be forced to spend the night in the holding cell. And to make matters worse, someone out there still had it in for her. "I'm still worried for her safety."

Carter shifted his weight and leaned against the wall. "I think Ernie and I can handle it. This is really the safest place for her to be."

The police chief nodded his agreement.

Dakota shifted in her seat, her face especially pale. "Will I have to go back to Houston for the arraignment?"

Clearly the thought terrified her.

"Depends." Andy scribbled something on a legal pad, then faced Dakota. "I'm going to do everything in my power to get the charges dismissed, but I need to know what all you took when you ran away from your boyfriend."

Dakota shifted uncomfortably. "Only his car and a little cash, but I left the car at a bus station. I'm sure he got it back."

Andy nodded and wrote some more. "That's enough for now, but sometime early next week I'll need to ask you a few more questions."

The flicker of hope Chance previously glimpsed in her eyes now sparked to a full-blown flame as she smiled timidly at Andy. A flare of jealousy shot through his system as two questions rose to the forefront of his mind. Would she ever look at him with that same hope and admiration? And would she ever forgive him for putting her through this?

Familiar feelings of shame washed over Dakota, her head and shoulders headed south as Ernie read the Miranda rights and then stepped from the room to prepare the holding cell. When she gathered the nerve to lift her gaze, Matt sent an encouraging smile.

In spite of her predicament, Dakota smiled back. "Matt, thanks for coming down here tonight. Please send Gracie my appreciation for sharing you."

"My pleasure. Just so you know, you and Gracie have more in common than either of you realize. I'm sure when she learns what has happened, she'll be down here in a heartbeat."

The policemen and Tyler brothers owed her nothing, but here they were doing all they could to help. And Chance, too, in his own bumbling way. But still the truth remained. She wouldn't even be in this situation if it weren't for him.

Chance closed the distance between them, his expression one of sorrow, fear, and pleading. He engulfed her in a hug.

Dakota let her arms dangle, her neck and back stiff.

He pulled away, both hands on her shoulders. "Please don't do this, Dakota. I had no choice."

She didn't answer, but instead turned her head toward Matt.

A frown darkened Matt's expression as he stepped around her and took hold of Chance's arm. "Give us a sec,

Dakota." They moved to a far corner and talked for several minutes, too far away for her to hear. A few minutes later Chance left the room without looking her way.

Matt ambled back around the table to where she stood. "He really cares about you, you know."

A snort escaped her nostrils. "Yeah. So much that he turned me in."

"You do realize he could've been charged with aiding and abetting if he hadn't? Besides that, he truly believes this will help resolve your situation so you can stop running."

The words gored a hole in her heart. She hadn't seen it from that perspective. "Guess I'm still a little angry."

Matt sent a close-lipped smile. "Hurt does that to you, making it hard to understand someone's actions and making it hard to forgive."

Forgive. That word again. How many times had she forgiven Chance? And this felt like just another one of those times, resurrecting old hurts and memories, making her hurt as badly as they had the day they'd happened. She released a sigh. "Why is it so hard?"

"Maybe it's just easier to hold onto resentment and bitterness. But when you hold on to them, you're imprisoning yourself, not the other person. Not forgiving is pretty heavy baggage to carry around."

The profound words echoed in her brain, rolling around like a tasty morsel on her tongue. It was true. Heavier than even her stuffed backpack on a long walk, holding on to past hurts and grudges locked her behind bars that prevented escape, imprisoned her for someone else's behavior. A double whammy or even more. Not just the original offense, but the weight of the painful memories which replayed themselves in her mind.

Matt patted her shoulder. "Chance has gone to get Daisy and a few things you might need. He said to tell you he'd be back as soon as possible."

The hole in her heart enlarged. Here she was blaming him for the situation, and all while he did what he could to take care of her. It was her who needed his forgiveness, not the other way around.

Ernie entered the room and motioned to her.

She moved to the door.

"The holding cell isn't the Hilton, but it's not Alcatraz either." His moustache bobbed up and down as he talked.

Dakota followed him down the narrow hallway. Though the cell was small and somewhat dark, at least it was clean. Fresh sheets, a pillow, and a blanket lay on the end of the cot. She moved inside, flashbacks of her previous experience with the police assaulting her memory.

Ernie smiled apologetically as he locked the door. "Either Carter or I or both of us will be in the office. Just call if you need anything."

After he left the room, Dakota turned to make the bed, then laid down and peered up at the ceiling, one arm across her forehead to block the light's glare. Still too early to go to sleep, but nothing else to do.

A wave of fear rumbled through her like a pre-earthquake tremor. How long before she was back in Kane's clutches? And what if her bail was set higher than the measly amount she had in the bank?

A knock sounded on the door. Dakota sat up as Ernie held open the door for Chance.

"You already have a visitor."

The strain from the situation visible in the lines around his eyes, Chance stepped into the room and handed her a cardboard box. "I wasn't sure what all you'd need, but I picked up a few things for you."

The box held a baggie with her toothbrush and toothpaste, her makeup bag, brush, deodorant, Bible, a pair of sweats, and the laptop. He'd anticipated what she needed with perfect accuracy. Now her time here would be more like a mini-writing retreat, and not the imprisonment she'd expected. All because of Chance.

She set the box on the bed, gave him a hug, and planted a soft kiss on his scarred cheek. "Thanks. Sorry for the way I acted earlier." She pulled away quickly.

Chance's mouth hung open for a moment, but then snapped shut. He gave his head a shake as a chuckle erupted from his throat. "You're gonna get whiplash bouncing around like that." His cheeks took on a tinge of red as he rubbed the back of his neck. "And take me with you." Chance moved his gaze to the floor, the tip of his right boot moving some imaginary object across the concrete floor.

Why was he suddenly so shy? "Chance, I promise to make this all up to you someday."

A weary smile appeared, and he caught her fingertips in his own. "I'm gonna hold you to that." He planted a kiss on the top of her head. "Sweet dreams, Princess. I'll see you in the morning." Chance stepped past Ernie and exited the room. The police chief nodded briefly, then clicked the lock.

A few minutes later, still trying to overcome the effect of Chance's lips planted in her hair, Dakota arranged the lumpy pillow so she could sit up in bed and type. She'd barely had time to boot the computer when another knock sounded at the door.

"Most popular prisoner we've had in a while," explained Ernie, a sheepish grin on his face.

Gracie hurried into the cell with a grocery bag. "Up for some girl talk?" She retrieved a carton of Blue Bell Dutch Chocolate ice cream and two spoons from the sack.

Dakota laughed. "Only if you bribe me with Blue Bell."

In a matter of seconds, Gracie sat on the opposite end of the bed, handed Dakota a spoon, then opened the carton between them and scooped out large dark chunks of chocolate ice cream. "I saw Chance on the way in. I take it things have improved between you two?" She sent a sideways glance and gorgeous smile.

Dakota gave her head a slight shake as she let a spoonful of ice cream melt in her mouth. Yes, but where was this leading except to certain heartbreak? And how could she backtrack with Chance so he didn't expect more than what she could give? "I don't see how it can work."

Gracie's pretty face darkened. "Why not? I think you make a good couple."

Yes, they were a good couple. They worked well together, able to anticipate the other's needs in advance. But was that enough to make a relationship work? Especially with so much excess baggage from the past? "There are some things I don't think he'll be able accept." Things she hadn't even been able to tell Matt.

"Such as?"

Gracie's abrupt question took her by surprise, and she floundered. "Uh..."

"It's okay, you don't have to tell me. But if it involves Chance, and you have such obvious feelings for him..."

Obvious? Her feelings for Chance were obvious? Not good. "I care about him as a friend, Gracie, but it doesn't go any deeper than that."

Her friend's chocolate-drop eyes rounded. "You sure could've fooled me." Her dark brows drew inward. "And I think Chance thinks there's more. That's not being fair to him."

Dakota took another bite of the rich ice cream. True. It wasn't fair to let Chance think there was more to their relationship than what she could offer. More than likely she'd gone a little overboard in her display of gratitude a few minutes ago and inadvertently sent the wrong message. "I'll explain it to him." Again.

Gracie's eyes turned to slits, one corner of her mouth twisted to one side. "I think you have feelings for him. But for whatever reason, you think he can't forgive you for something. So you hold him at arm's length and hide how you really feel."

The truthful words sunk in deep. Dakota lowered her head.

Across from her, Gracie's weight shifted, bouncing the mattress in the process. "I'm not trying to pry, but if you care about him, be honest about your feelings and the past. If he can't get past it, then you have your answer. But if he can, it just might make your life better than you could ever imagine. That's how it was for me and Matt."

Dakota considered the comment. Though the prospect of telling Chance everything still frightened her, there was wisdom in Gracie's words. The problem was finding the courage to follow through.

"Matt filled me in on a few details, but what can you tell me about your ex? He sounds..." Gracie's dark eyes glazed over momentarily. "...eerily familiar." Her lips flattened into a straight line.

"That depends. Are you here as my friend or Andy Tyler's law partner?"

Gracie giggled, then her amused look vanished. "Both actually. I'm your friend first and foremost, but I intend to help him on your case."

At first her words came haltingly, but soon spilled out, as though weary of their confinement. "Kane was so charming when I first met him, and he treated me so well. I was flattered, you know? That someone like him was interested in someone like me."

Gracie's eyes took on a moist sheen, but she didn't speak.

"But once I moved in, he changed. Not all at once, but little by little. At first it was just little verbal jabs when we were out in public. Then the verbal attacks happened more often and got worse. He undermined my friendships so no one wanted to be around me. Told lies to my family." Her thoughts splintered as memories replayed in her mind.

"And he beat you?" Gracie's question yanked her from the past.

"Yeah."

"I'm so sorry for what he did to you and can't even imagine how hard it must've been. My experience was similar, but never made it to the point of physical abuse."

"I'm just relieved it's over..." Her words trailed to a whisper. Or was it? What if it happened all over again?

"You don't have to worry, Dakota. We're all determined to take care of you and to keep you safe." Her friend's eyes held conviction.

But what if he got to them as well? A man with his power and influence could make it happen. Her heart raced at the though.

"So why'd you stay as long as you did?" The spoon disappeared in Gracie's mouth.

"First of all, he told me he'd kill me if I left. I guess I started to believe it. And there was a part of me that wanted to help him. I thought if I tried hard enough I could make him change. Thought if I could please him, he'd be happy."

Two vertical lines instantly appeared between Gracie's eyebrows. "Sometimes I think those kinds of guys must take a special class on manipulating women."

Though her heart agreed, Dakota didn't answer. Instead her mind returned to very real possibility that her friends' involvement had endangered all their lives. And the worst part? There was absolutely nothing she could do to protect any of them.

Chapter Twenty-Five

Chance ran a palm down his neck as he left the police station and ambled across the street to his parked truck. Everything in him longed to run back inside and plead for permission to sleep on the floor outside the holding cell. So many things could go wrong. Possible scenarios raced through his mind. What if whoever was after Dakota shot the policeman on duty and took her hostage in the middle of the night? He gave his head a shake. Okay, time to bring his rampant thoughts under control.

He climbed in his pickup and inserted the key in the ignition, but stopped short of actually turning it. There was no way he could leave. Besides, even if he went home, he'd be up all night worried for her safety.

Frustration pushed air from his lungs. Spending the night in his pickup was the best option to ensure her safety. Then in the morning, he'd go home for a quick shower and shave before returning to the police station to accompany her to the bond hearing.

His thoughts turned to the panic on her face at the mention of bond money. Something told him she wouldn't have the resources to post bail, which meant digging deeper into the quickly-receding pockets of his inheritance. His dreams for the drugstore would just have to wait. Dakota took priority.

He popped in his ear buds and turned on the iPod, the comforting sounds of his favorite guitar instrumentals twanging away in his ears. A few minutes before ten,

Gracie exited the building and made a bee-line for his pickup.

His face flashing hot red, Chance rolled down the pickup window. Good thing it was too dark for her to see his face. "Hi, Gracie."

"What are you still doing here? I've probably been in there a good hour. I figured you'd be home by now."

"Just wanna make sure she's okay."

She didn't respond for the longest time, and Chance could almost imagine the compassionate gleam in those big brown eyes of hers.

"Chance." She spoke his name softly and with a hint of pleading. "Ernie's there. Both the outside door and the holding cell door are locked. And this is Miller's Creek, remember? She'll be okay. Really, she will. Why don't you go home and get a good night's sleep?"

"Not tired right now, but I might head home later."

Silence again. "Mm-hmm. Yeah, right." She headed away from the car. "Don't catch cold."

He rolled up the window as Gracie climbed in her car and drove away, already preparing himself for Matt's impending phone call. His phone never rang, but a few minutes later a car pulled up behind him and shut off the headlights. A second later Matt crawled in the passenger side door and threw a folded blanket across the cab.

A laugh fell from Chance's mouth as he caught the fuzzy warm blanket and covered himself. "What are you doing back up here?"

"Well, when my beautiful wife told me my best friend had lost his mind and was spending the night in his pickup outside the police station, I felt it was my professional and personal responsibility to come administer a psychological evaluation."

The pickup cab filled with both their laughter. Chance finally brought his laughter under control. "So, have I completely lost my mind?"

"Naah." Matt reached in his jacket pocket and procured a napkin, which he unrolled to reveal four home-made chocolate chip cookies. He handed two to Chance. "But I do have a diagnosis for your condition."

This ought to be good. "Do tell."

His best friend chomped down on one of the cookies and spoke with a garbled mouthful, typical Matt-style. "You're in love, man."

A piece of the cookie he'd been chewing lodged in Chance's throat, and he coughed.

"You okay?" Matt pounded on his back.

Chance reached for his water bottle in the cup holder, took a swig, and twisted the cap back on. Matt's words were true, and he'd known it for a while now. He just hadn't expected anyone else to notice. "So you think I'm in love?"

Through another mouthful of cookie, Matt exclaimed, "Oh, man, you have it bad. Cupid hit you with at least four or five of those poisoned arrows."

Chance couldn't help but chuckle. "I'm sure your wife would love to hear the use of your word 'poison' when describing love."

"Hey, don't break bro-rule number one."

"Yeah, what's that?"

"What's said in the pickup stays in the pickup." Matt laughed and placed the last few cookie crumbs in his mouth. "So you're staying here all night, aren't you?"

"Yep."

"Even though you lied and told my wife you might go home later."

"Yep." Chance glanced across the street. Still no unusual activity.

"You are aware that Miller's Creek gets pretty dead by eleven o'clock on a Friday night? You won't miss much excitement by heading on home." Across the seat, Matt chuckled. "Just wasting my breath, huh?"

"Yep."

His best friend punched him on the arm, then opened the passenger-side door. "Okay. Well, try to stay warm, bud. I'll call you some time tomorrow to see if you enjoyed your little camping trip."

"Tell Gracie thanks for the cookies and blanket."

"Will do."

"And thanks for coming to check on me. And for understanding." What would he do without Matt?

"Yeah, well, I've been where you are. Crazy out of my mind with worry one minute, filled with fear that she'd never want me the next."

Yeah, that pretty well described his emotional state at the moment.

"Good night." Matt slammed the pickup door, and a few seconds later, drove off into the dark night.

Okay, enough visitors for the night. At some point Carter would come to relieve Ernie. Chance looked around for a good location--one that would allow him to see without being seen. His gaze landed on the Ford dealership up the street. Perfect. He cranked the engine. Within a minute, he was parked next to other Ford trucks on the lot with a clear view of the front door of the police station.

The night wore on. Chance passed the time by playing Sudoku on his cell phone, raising his head every few minutes to make sure everything looked all right. A few minutes before midnight, just as he'd predicted, Carter pulled into the police department parking area, his tall frame impossible to miss. Shortly afterward, Ernie exited the building and drove away.

One o'clock came and went. At almost two a.m. on the dot, another pickup, dark-colored, pulled into the lot and parked just a few spaces down from him.

His forehead tightened. Obviously, whoever sat in the dark pickup had something similar in mind. Should he go see who it was and what they were up to? He gave his head a slight shake. Not a wise move. First, it would give away his location. Secondly, he had nothing to defend himself with should he need it. Best to just stay put and see what happened.

The time approached three in the morning. Chance leaned his head back and stared at the ceiling of the cab, trying to untangle the knots that had built in his shoulder muscles. As he leaned his neck to one side and then the other, movement caught his eye. Down the street sauntered a lone figure. Definitely a man, based on his size and the way he moved, but beyond that Chance couldn't make out any details, due to the dark street and the man's black hooded sweatshirt.

The guy stopped outside of the police department, mostly hidden from view by shadow of a nearby tree. He faced the station as though studying the possibilities. Then he continued his walk, white puffs of steam drifting from his mouth in the cool night air.

Chance slouched down in the seat to avoid being seen, but peered over the dashboard as the man ambled past and disappeared from view.

Once more, Chance considered leaving his post, but in the end opted to stay and keep watch over the building where Dakota slept in a lonely, small, and confining jail cell, all because of him.

The next thing Chance knew, sun streamed in the side window and struck his face. He groaned and reached for a pillow that wasn't there. His eyes cracked open and his surroundings came into focus. Dakota. Was she okay?

He sprang to a sitting and checked his watch. Already after 9 a.m. Carter's car was gone, and Ernie's car had returned. Chance scratched the itchy stubble on his chin. He wanted to see Dakota as soon as possible to assure himself that she was okay, but it wouldn't hurt to take a peace offering.

He started the truck and sped down the highway to the donut shop to get the chocolate cake donuts Dakota loved more than Daisy loved dog biscuits.

Ernie grinned expectantly when Chance walked in the door five minutes later. He eyed the donut bag. "You don't eat donuts. So I'm assuming those are for me?"

"You can have one." Chance held out the bag.

Ernie fished out a donut. "Thanks."

"Dakota awake?"

"Yeah, you wanna see her?"

"Please."

As they walked to the rear of the building, Ernie turned his head and called back over his shoulder, "So how was it?"

"How was what?"

"Camping out in your truck all night." The police chief grinned and knocked on the door.

Matt and his big mouth. He'd pay for this. "Ha ha. Guess I've been the butt of a few jokes between you and Carter?"

"Just a few." Ernie winked and pushed open the door.

Dakota sat on her bed, reading her Bible. She glanced up as they entered, the dark circles beneath her eyes testifying to her own lack of sleep. A tiny smile turned up the corners of her lips.

Chance held up the bag of donuts. "Hungry?"

Her smile widened. "Chocolate cake?"

"Your favorite."

She climbed from the bed and nabbed a donut from the bag, then glanced up at him. "You look awful."

"Gee, thanks."

"No, I mean, did you sleep okay?"

Better that she not know the depth of his concern. He shrugged. "Just okay. What about you?"

She returned to the bed, the donut half gone already, and plopped down. "Very little, but I did get a lot of writing done for the first time in forever. Nothing like personal angst to bring out the writer's muse."

He laughed, not only at her words, but her sardonic tone. Then he sobered. This whole experience must be hard. Harder than she was letting on. "You okay?"

"I guess so. Staying awake most of the night gave me a lot of time to think, you know? I can't undo what's already been done. While I wish I could go back and do things differently, I can't. No sense wasting time worrying about it. I've prayed through it and given it over to God. It's in His more-than-capable hands. Whatever happens, it's all under His control and timing and to suit His purposes."

"Even if you end up having to confront Kane?"

A determined tilt raised her small chin, but fear still clouded her eyes. "Even then."

Ernie, who'd stood right outside the door to give them privacy, knocked again. "Dakota, you ready to head to the bond hearing?"

"As ready as I'll ever be."

"Mind if I tag along?"

Ernie's lips sagged at the corners, like a bull-dog. "Okay with me if it's okay with Dakota."

She nodded with a shrug. "The more the merrier. Right?"

Chapter Twenty-Six

More calmly than she'd ever thought possible, Dakota entered the magistrate's office. The only possible explanation was hours of prayer--not only her own, but her friends' as well. Now if she could just get through this and enjoy the rest of her day. In the very sterile and unassuming room, unbefitting the term magistrate, a man sat behind a desk dressed in camouflage clothing, his reading glasses perched at the end of his short, plump nose as he thumbed through a stack of papers.

He glanced up as they approached. "Hey, Ernie. Is this young lady the accused?"

"Yes sir. You look ready for a hunting trip."

"Just got back actually. Didn't see a thing. And who are you?" His gruff voice resounded in the large empty room as he addressed Chance.

"Chance Johnson."

"Aren't you J.C.'s grandson?"

"Yes sir."

"Mighty fine man. Sorry for your loss." Now his eagle eyes honed in on Dakota. "You, young lady, are in serious trouble." He cranked the volume of his words, accenting each one.

Her neck and shoulder muscles tensed. "Yes sir."

"Have you been informed of your rights?"

"Yes."

"Have an attorney?"

"Two, actually. Andy and Grace Tyler."

The man's eyebrows arched. "You're fortunate to have such good friends. They're two of the best in the state." His gaze moved briefly to Chance then back to her. "Your bail's been set at five thousand dollars."

An uncontrollable gasp fell from her lips.

"I know that's high, but you have a history of running. It's my job to see that you don't."

She swallowed hard, unsure of the proper protocol in this situation. "I don't have five thousand dollars."

Chance stepped forward and pulled his checkbook from the back pocket of his jeans. "I'd like to pay her bail, if that's okay."

The magistrate nodded. "Okay by me, but are you sure? You might not ever see that money again."

Chance sent Dakota a reassuring smile. "I'm sure."

A few minutes later, the details from the bond hearing behind them, they escaped into the bright sunlight of a beautiful fall day. Dakota's spirit soared in spite of her fatigue. Time to rest and relax and take her mind off her worries by working on the house.

Ernie stopped to shake both their hands before heading to the police car.

As he drove away, Dakota turned to Chance. "Thanks, Chance. I'll pay back every cent. I promise."

He nodded. "Right now let's just enjoy this beautiful day."

"My sentiments exactly."

After they stopped by the hardware store for supplies, the Pig Pit for barbecue, and Chance's house to pick up Daisy, the two headed out to the farm, both windows down, country music streaming from the radio.

Dakota leaned her head back against the seat and closed her eyes. Yes. This was just what she needed. The warmth of the sun on her right shoulder spread across her back and chest, melting her tense muscles into soft wax.

"Tired?" Chance's voice interrupted the golden silence.

She didn't open her eyes. "Beyond description. But also relieved."

"I want this to be a good day for you. You deserve it."

His thoughtful words seeped into her soul. Deserve it? Not a chance. But she'd take it nonetheless.

A few minutes later they passed the farmhouse and drove straight to the creek and dilapidated bridge. The warmer-than-normal temps and southern breezes had dried out the fields so there was no chance of getting the truck stuck. After they unloaded the lumber and gathered necessary tools, they set to work repairing the bridge. First they worked on the structure and used braces to shore up the bridge. Broken and rotten planks which spanned the bridge were then yanked from their place and replaced with new boards. Rusty nails, heads popped up from the dry boards, were pounded back down.

They worked through the morning and past noon, the sun climbing high in the sky.

Chance rubbed the sweat from his forehead with his forearm and turned his attention to her. "Ready to break for some barbecue?"

"Yeah." Dakota licked her dry lips. "But let's go to the house to eat. I need some sweet tea."

"Now you're speaking my language."

Once at the house, Dakota made the tea and carried two full mason jars to the front porch, the ice clinking against the sides. Chance reclined his head and back against the house, the bucket of ribs and a roll of paper towels at his side. He reached for the glass the minute she stepped outside and quickly guzzled it down.

She laughed. "Guess I should've brought the whole jar. Be back in a sec." Once back outside, she and Chance enjoyed the tasty barbecue spare ribs and the ice-cold sweet tea without conversation. Dakota's thoughts returned to the 'what if's' that lay ahead of her like a long dark tunnel with no end in sight. And when she did catch what might be the end, it involved Kane, and the end of her. A sigh escaped.

"Stop it." Chance's gruff words were softened by the tender expression in his eyes, a look that reminded her so much of J.C. "Don't let yourself dwell on what might happen. God's got it under control."

"Okay how do you do that?"

"Do what?'

"Read my mind."

A boyish grin curled his lips, and his blue-gray eyes teased. "I just know you better that you'd like to believe. But seriously, don't worry about stuff. It's okay."

It's hard not to worry, but you're right." Especially when fear had a death grip on her throat.

"What are you afraid of?"

Good question, but where did she start? "So many things." She sunk her teeth into the tender meat of the rib. It pulled away from the bone and practically melted in her mouth.

"Such as?"

"Afraid I'll end up where I started." And of everything that would come with it.

Understanding shone from his face. "You know I'll do everything in my power to keep that from happening."

She nodded and peered out across the front pasture, the tall wheat-colored grass rippling in the breeze. "I'm also afraid to tell you the real reason I left Miller's Creek the first time."

His eyes searched hers. "Why are you afraid?"

"I'm not sure you can forgive me."

"Try me."

No, she'd said enough for the moment. "I know I need to, and trust me, I want to tell you. But I--I can't right now, Chance. Not with everything else that's going on."

His shoulders heaved in apparent disappointment, but he nodded. "Fair enough, but once all this is over..."

"Okay." A shiver rippled through her. *God, give me strength.* "What about you? What are you afraid of?"

His eyes took on distance as though reminded of memories long past. "Like I said last night. These stupid scars."

Compassion seized her heart. "Oh, Chance. When I look at you, I don't see scars. I see you."

Their gazes locked with an intensity that shook her to the core. She needed him. Needed to feel the comfort of his embrace.

In a heartbeat, they were in each other's arms, his soft lips claiming hers. She clung to him like a baby, her knuckles white from gripping his shirt. When the kiss finally ended, she rested her head against his chest.

His rapid pulse pounded in her ears, and he snuggled her close, his cheek against her hair, as though he'd never let her go. How long had it been since she'd felt so loved? So comforted? So protected? And did she have the strength to pull away from it when she needed his embrace so badly? How would she ever recover when the truth was out and he no longer wanted anything to do with her?

Tears sprang to her eyes. She blinked rapidly to bring them under control, but it was no use. Fatigue had proved her undoing. Dakota lifted a shaky hand to her face to swipe away tears before he could see.

Chance shifted, and one finger tilted her chin upward toward his microscopic perusal. "Hey, what's wrong?"

The perfect opportunity to pull away and escape his piercing gaze. She sat upright and sniffled. "I'm just tired, and it's turning me into a weepy mess."

He pulled her back into his comforting embrace, and planted a kiss in her hair. "Oh, sweetheart, it's okay."

No, it wasn't okay, but she felt powerless to do anything about any of it.

"You're under a lot of stress and strain right now. I was the same way after they put the steel plate in the left side of my head."

Dakota pulled back to look him in the face. "Steel plate?"

Chance lifted a finger to trace the general location. "Had to have some way to keep my brains from falling out." He smiled and winked.

"That's not funny." That steel plate in his head was her fault, for running away from him in the first place. Would the consequences of her sin never stop rearing their ugly heads?

"Sorry, just trying to lighten the mood." He kissed her head once more, then made a move to stand. "Ready to get back to work?"

Yes. That was exactly what she needed. Anything to ground her in the here-and-now.

Chance helped her to her feet. Once the food was put away, they headed back to the creek to finish the job of rebuilding the bridge.

As the afternoon wore on and fatigue set in deeper, Dakota's heart grew heavy and more confused. Finishing the bridge was one more thing to cross off the lengthy to-do list. One more step that moved them closer to the end. Though she longed to stay on the farm, to put down roots, to explore the possibility of a life with Chance, he deserved to have his dream of re-opening the drugstore come true. The only way that would happen was if she could pay him back. And the only way to do that involved selling the farm. Though hard to even consider, he'd be better off once she was out of the picture.

As the sun sank in the western sky, Dakota nabbed her water bottle from the bridge railing and stepped back to enjoy the fruits of their labor. Crack! Without warning, the board beneath her feet gave way and a gaping hole appeared. The world went upside-down for a split second. Then she landed, her right ankle between her and the rocky soil, the underside of the bridge shielding her eyes from the sun.

"Dakota!" Chance scrambled down the steep embankment, his face panic-lined. "You okay?"

She groaned. "Give me a second." Dakota moved her neck slightly. No problem there. Next she moved her arms and fingers. All good. Left leg? Yep. It worked. Then she tried to move her right leg from beneath her. Pain shot white-hot flares. "Ayyy! Something's wrong with my right leg."

Chance knelt over her, his face near hers. "This might hurt, Dakota, but I've got to get you up this embankment to level ground so I can check your leg. And just so you're prepared, this is probably going to require a trip to the hospital."

Hospital bill on top of everything else? Not if she could help it. She gritted her teeth as Chance scooped her in his arms and looked for sure footing to make it up the slope.

Once on level ground, he sat her down gently and checked her leg. "Any pain here?" His fingers probed around her knee.

"No. Lower." As in throbbing lower. "I think it's the ankle."

He lifted her pant leg, and sucked in a deep breath. "Here?"

Throbbing waves crashed, starting at her ankle and exploding through her body, bringing forth a throaty scream. "Yes. Is it broken or just a sprain?" The words made their way from behind her clenched teeth.

"Can't make that call without an x-ray."

She moaned and covered her face with her forearm. Why this? Why now? "Let me just lie here a second. Then I'll try standing."

His face appeared in front of hers. "Not advisable, Red. Based on what I just saw, the sooner we get you to the hospital the better."

She pounded the ground on either side of her with both fists. "Oh, all right."

Though Chance placed her sideways in the pickup seat and rolled up a blanket to elevate the ankle even further, the throbbing pain continued all the way to the hospital. Once in a room, Chance hovered over her. "How you doing?"

"Just great. I can't seem to catch a break for anything."

A deadpan expression coated his face. "Wouldn't be too sure about that. A break might be exactly what you caught."

She backhanded his arm. "That's not what I mean, and you know it."

A lazy grin stretched his lips outward. "Least I made you smile."

A doctor entered the room, iPad in hand. "Hey, Chance." He shook hands with Chance, then moved to the bed and stood above her. "Hi Dakota, I'm Dr. Phillips. What happened?"

The nurse in Chance took over. He explained all that had happened and her pain level.

Dr. Phillips nodded and tapped his tablet with a stylus. He set the small computer on a nearby counter and donned a pair of plastic gloves. "This won't be fun, but I have to determine if further tests are needed." He moved to the end of the bed and began his probe.

Fireworks exploded in her head as he manipulated her ankle. Dakota clutched the sides of the bed and practically ground her teeth to nubs to keep from crying out. With every brief break from the pain, she caught a quick breath for the next round.

Finally, he stopped, removed the gloves, and tossed them in the trash. "You already have considerable swelling and bruising. Based on your pain level, I'm going to order several images to figure out exactly what we're dealing with."

"Several?" How much would that cost? "Won't a simple x-ray show what's wrong?"

"Not necessarily. That's why I'm adding an MRI to the x-rays of the foot and lower leg, just to make sure there's not more damage than we're aware of."

Dakota stared at the ceiling, unsure of what hurt worse, her ankle or her almost-nonexistent cash resources. Why hadn't her book sale deposits showed up in her account yet? She made a mental note to check when she got back home.

Chance patted her arm, his way of saying that he'd handle it if need be. At this rate, she'd be indebted to him for the rest of her life.

Two hours later, after the x-rays and endless waiting, the results were in. Not broken, but a level-two sprain. A representative from the accounting department handed her the bill as Dr Phillips strode into the room. "You're fortunate it wasn't broken."

Her heart climbed into her throat as she eyed the bill. Yeah, fortunate, and more destitute than ever, to the tune of about fifteen hundred dollars. She glanced over at Chance. "Get me out of here, before they start draining my plasma to pay the bill."

Once in the lobby via a wheelchair which Chance graciously pushed, Dakota unzipped her wallet and removed her debit card. This would all but zap her savings, but once her book royalties landed in the bank all would be well. She slid the card through the scanner.

The receptionist, who multi-tasked on paperwork while she manned the checkout, glanced at her computer screen. "Hmm, it says payment was denied. Try again."

Once more Dakota scanned her card.

The other woman shook her head. "No go. Do you have another way to pay?"

Heat crept into Dakota's cheeks.

Chance stepped to the side of the wheelchair. "Here, let me--"

"No, I've got it." Dakota pulled out her one and only credit card, one she kept for emergencies like this, one she hated to use. She located the strip and ran it through the scanner.

A line of people backed up behind them, their growing aggravation evident in the glares, comments, and huffy sighs.

The receptionist shook her head. "That one's not working either."

The heat in Dakota's cheeks zipped to the top of her head.

Chance knelt beside her, his eyes kind and gentle. "Please let me help."

A few minutes later they were on their way back out to the farm. Dakota rested her elbow against the door of the pickup and laid her cheek against her fist. Chance must think her a complete idiot. "I'm sorry, Chance. I don't know what's going on. I'll call the bank and credit card company as soon as we get home." Why had both cards been denied when she rarely used them? Something was definitely amiss, one more thing in a long line of misses.

Back home, Chance helped her to the couch. "I'll give you some privacy while you make your calls. Be back in a little bit to check on you."

She nodded, grateful for the reprieve. As soon as he stepped out the door, Dakota dialed the bank. "This is Dakota Kelly. My debit card was denied earlier today and I need to know why. According to my checkbook, I have enough money in my account to cover the bill I tried to pay."

The voice on the other end took the necessary information. "Miss Kelly, according to our records, you withdrew all your funds last night and closed out your account."

Her breath caught in her throat. "That's not possible." She almost added the fact that she was in jail last night, but that couldn't help matters.

"Well, according to our computers, you closed the account at seven fifteen p.m."

While she was out to dinner with Chance?

"Look, I don't know what's going on, but I did not withdraw funds or close the account. What do I need to do to get this resolved?"

"Just a moment please." Several agonizing minutes of blaring phone music later the woman's voice came back on the line. "My supervisor suggests that you report the incident to the authorities. It may be that your account has been compromised. We'll check into things from our end as well"

That's all they had to say? Contact the authorities? As in the ones who'd locked her up last night? A heavy sigh whooshed from her lungs.

"Was there anything else I could help you with?"

Dakota scratched her head. What she wouldn't give to be able to pace right now. "Yeah. I normally have an electronic deposit in the middle of the month. Would you check to see if that made it to my account?"

"No ma'am. The last electronic deposit was last month."

The blood drained from her head, and she brought fingertips to her forehead to rub away a blossoming headache. This was getting weirder and weirder. Okay, now add contacting her publisher to her quickly-growing list of financial to-do's.

Once the call ended, Dakota flipped the credit card over to the back to locate the number for the billing department. She punched in the number, then listened to fifteen minutes of crackly music until someone answered. She gave the person on the other end of the line the necessary security information.

"How can I help you?"

"I tried to use my credit card earlier today, but it was denied."

"Yes. You're over your credit limit."

Her heart pounded against her ribs. "I don't use this card often. Just for emergencies. And then I pay it off each month."

The guy on the other end had the nerve to snort. "Our records show several large online charges over the past two weeks."

Dakota flipped her cell phone shut and stared into space. Phrases like closed account, fraudulent activity, and wracked-up charges played in her mind, and grew louder and more insistent by the minute. Someone out there not only wanted her dead, but completely destroyed.

Chapter Twenty-Seven

Chance stepped off the porch and took off in a full sprint to the bridge. A thought had lodged in his brain during Dakota's time at the hospital. He'd kept his mouth shut, not wanting to concern her without reason. But now that they were back at the farm, with Dakota securely locked inside and Daisy and the shotgun nearby, he could wait no longer about checking out his suspicions.

Out of breath, he came to stop just shy of the bridge, his lungs pleading for mercy. The place where she'd fallen through was an area of the bridge they'd repaired earlier that morning. He'd gone over every board in that bridge to make sure they could cross over safely to the farm's far pasture. No way the accident should've happened, unless someone had intentionally sabotaged their work while they'd eaten lunch.

With careful steps, Chance eased onto the bridge, checking each plank with one foot before placing his full weight on it. When he reached the place she'd fallen through, he knelt to inspect the area more carefully. Yeah, he remembered this spot. Several smaller pieces created one section across two or three rows, with jack studs underneath for support. But somehow or another the old pieces of lumber had worked their way loose in the short time they'd left the bridge to eat lunch. And not just one or two. All of them.

Chance stood and peered around, searching for any unusual motion or a sign that someone had been here, or was still here. Nothing. He pulled out his cell phone and dialed Carter as he retraced his steps toward the farmhouse.

"Hey, Chance."

"Hey."

His friend laughed. "Well, you sound glum. What's going on?"

Chance explained the situation.

"Tell you what. I'll call Ernie, and we'll come out to take a look." Carter's tone took on a tone of authority.

"Don't come to the house. Just drive down to the bridge. Dakota's had a rough few days and I don't want to upset her. Just shoot me a text when you get here."

"Got it. See you in a few."

Chance sprinted back to the farmhouse.

Dakota looked up from her place on the couch as he entered the house with the spare key. Her face was red and splotchy, and she sniffled.

He hurried over to her and pulled her into his arms. "Hey, what's wrong?"

"As if my life weren't messed up enough, someone has managed to access all my financial accounts online."

Chance leaned back to better view her facial expression. "What?"

"My bank account, my credit card, even electronic deposits I receive for my writing. They've all been tampered with." An uneasy look took up residence in her eyes. "Which reminds me of something else I need to tell you."

"What's that?"

She inhaled deeply. "I'm A.K. Aston."

Had she hit her head when she'd fallen from the bridge? "You are not. He's a guy."

Dakota shook her head. "No. He's me. I'm him. A.K. Aston is my pen name."

He fell back against the couch. Aston was an independently-published fantasy author, one he and the rest of the world assumed was a guy. But in light of Dakota's history of living in hiding away from Kane, it made sense. "Don't know what to say, except that I'm very impressed."

"Don't be. Besides, it looks like even that has been washed down the tubes."

"What're you gonna do?"

"I've reported it. Now it's just a matter of getting all my account numbers changed and new cards issued. But it's not likely that I'll get back what I've lost."

His phone ding-a-dinged to let him know he had a text. Carter and Ernie were here. "I've got to step out for a bit. We'll talk more when I get back."

She didn't respond, but stared blankly into nothing, her lips pinched tight and her eyes troubled.

Back at the bridge, he showed Ernie and Carter where Dakota had fallen through, and explained how they'd worked to secure the bridge earlier that day.

Both Ernie and Carter stooped low to examine the loose boards. Finally Ernie stood. "Don't see a bit of evidence that the boards were tampered with, Chance. I'm not saying it didn't happen, but these boards could be loose for several reasons, not the least of which is the age and condition of the wood."

"Yeah, but we just repaired it this morning."

Ernie shrugged and shook his head. "Still no definite proof."

A few minutes later, Carter and Ernie drove away from the bridge as Chance made his way back to the farmhouse. Regardless of what Ernie said and without any doubt in his mind, the bridge had been tampered with. Someone definitely had it in for Dakota. Had figured out a way to drain her financial resources and had even stooped to the extent of loosening boards on the bridge. Evil and sabotage seemed to be the new kids on the block in Miller's Creek, and whatever it took, he had to protect her.

Dakota still sat on the couch, sullen and staring out the window.

His heart melted as a sudden wave of exhaustion swept over him. Shoving past it, he made his way to her side. "I don't want you worrying about all this, Dakota."

Her gaze moved to her hands, hands like that of a pianist, with long, thin fingers. "I'm trying not to, but between the case and the probability of seeing Kane, then the money problem..." Her words trailed off.

"We'll get through it together."

Dakota faced him, her thick red waves of hair flowing over one shoulder. "I can't ask you to do more than you've already done."

"God's with us. We just have to leave it all in His hands." Even if it meant spending the money he'd saved for the drugstore. "I want to pack you a bag."

"What for?"

"You're spending the night at Matt and Gracie's. I'll feel better knowing you're safe."

At first she looked ready to protest, then weary resignation landed on her face. "Whatever. I'm too tired to argue."

The sun sank behind the horizon, painting the sky a vivid orange as they made the drive into town, both silent. Chance tried to wrap his brain around all that had transpired in such a short time, but fatigue cut him short. Chance made sure Dakota was situated at Matt and Gracie's house then headed home for a quick shower, shave, and meal. Whoever had it in for her was still out there, stepping up his attacks. No matter how difficult, he would stay at his post and do everything in his power to protect her. Even if it meant spending every night in his pickup.

Breakfast smells wafted upstairs to Dakota's nose as she finished putting on her makeup.

"Dakota, breakfast is ready." Gracie's words drifted up the staircase.

"Coming." Dakota zipped her makeup bag and hobbled down the hallway, still fearful of putting too much weight on her ankle. She held on to the banister and hopped down the stairs on one foot.

Matt, coffee cup in hand, beamed up at her. "Hey, that's a pretty nifty trick. Maybe I should try that."

"Uh, no." Gracie eyed him from the stove. "With your klutziness, you'd end up in a pile at the bottom of the stairs."

Dakota laughed as Matt rolled his eyes. Her love and appreciation for the both of them had skyrocketed over her past few days of staying at their house.

Gracie smiled. "You look pretty. Do you and Chance have plans for the day?"

"No." Dakota limped to the cabinets to help set the table. "But I'm determined to get the farmhouse finished."

Matt's eyebrows shot up to his hairline. "By yourself? Chance know about this?"

"Not yet." She sat a plate and fork at each of their places. "I'll call him right after breakfast."

The couple exchanged glances, which Dakota opted to ignore. She'd been here five days already. At first it had been fun to spend the time with Matt and Gracie, to get to know them better. And while they were at work, her writing had flowed as it hadn't in months. But something inside still pressed her to finish the house as soon as possible.

Dakota clamped her lips as she set glasses, milk, and juice on the table. Was fear to blame for the compulsion inside her? Fear of seeing Kane again and being delivered right back into his abusive hands? Fear of the upcoming court case and how that would play out? Fear of her finances never being the same after fraudulent activity had emptied her accounts and made her debit and credit card unusable? Fear of whoever was after her--of whoever had left the note knifed to the door--catching up with her? Or worse yet, catching up with the new friends she'd grown to love. Fear of feeling too much for Chance?

As the questions rolled in her mind, she pulled out a chair at the dining room table and sat. After breakfast, she'd pull out the Bible verse cards Matt had suggested for dealing with the fear.

Matt bowed his head to offer the blessing.

Lord, I know all my fears aren't from You. Help me to trust You more.

After the amen, Dakota placed a paper napkin in her lap and spooned scrambled eggs on her plate. "I appreciate what y'all have done for me over the past few days."

Gracie eyed her suspiciously. "You're not planning on moving your things back out to the farmhouse, are you?"

"Actually, I am."

"You know it's okay with us if you stay here while we're out of town." Matt frowned.

"I know, and I'm grateful. But my ankle is better, and there's work to be done." Plus the only way to get past all these fears was to confront them head on. And the sooner the better.

"And, let me guess, Chance doesn't know this either." A wry grin spread across Matt's face. "After breakfast." He spoke the words in unison with her.

Once breakfast was over, the kitchen cleaned, and Matt and Gracie gone for the day, Dakota pulled out her cell phone and plopped down on the couch, peering out the front window at the abnormally beautiful day. A great forecast for getting the outside of the house painted.

Chance answered on the first ring. "Hey, Red." His voice held an odd combination of warmth and weariness.

She frowned. Was he not sleeping well? He'd been leaving Matt and Gracie's every night around nine. "You sound tired."

"Just a bit." He didn't elaborate. "You need something?"

Dakota steadied her nerves with a deep breath before she delivered the news that he was sure to protest. "Um, just wanted to let you know I'm going back to the farm today. Matt and Gr--."

"No." The warmth vanished from his tone.

No? Since when did he give her orders? And did he really expect she would heed his command, especially when spoken in that tone of voice?

"As I was saying before you so rudely interrupted, Matt and Gracie are headed out of town, so now's a good time to go back to the farm."

"I'll call Mama Beth and see if you can stay with her."

A sigh of frustration escaped. He could be so obtuse. "I'll be fine. My ankle's better, and there's work to be done. I want the house finished before I go to court." Before Kane found yet another way to make her life miserable.

"You stay put until I get off work. Understand?" His tone grew more cranky and demanding, and she envisioned the thunderstorm in his eyes.

A fire sparked within. "Why are you so cranky? I'll do what I want, thank you very much. You're not my boss." Without giving him a chance to answer, she flipped her phone shut just as Gracie entered the front door, a serious expression on her face.

"Something tells me Chance didn't like the idea of you going back to the farm." Her friend spoke the words as she stepped to a nearby console table to pick up a file.

"That's the understatement of the year. I just don't get why he's so cranky." She stood and faced her friend. "It's almost like he hasn't had any sleep."

"He hasn't."

Dakota's head cocked to one side.

"In case you haven't noticed, Chance is very concerned for your safety. When he leaves here every night, he doesn't stay gone."

"What do you mean?"

"He drives down the street, turns around and parks his truck so he can keep an eye out for anyone who might try to hurt you."

Her lips parted. The growing fatigue she'd seen on his face every night. The worried expressions she'd glimpsed on his face when he didn't notice her studying him. "How do you know?"

"I first saw him the night you were in jail. Matt and I both tried to talk him out of it." Gracie's dark eyes flashed. "He wouldn't hear of it. Then a few nights ago, when Matt took Daisy for a walk? He saw him camped out in his truck again."

The familiar ache took up residence in Dakota's heart, as his current concern and future unforgiveness waged war inside.

"And those are just the nights we know about." Gracie's lips flat-lined momentarily. "Well, I just came back to pick up this file. Talk to you later." Without another word, Gracie let herself out the front door.

Dakota let the news sink in. Yeah, it was flattering that Chance was so concerned, but she couldn't let it stand in the way of all she had to do. With each passing day, Chance grew more attached, something she couldn't let continue any longer than necessary. Not to mention the peril her own heart faced.

Her backbone stiffened, and she headed for the stairs. Time to pack up her things and follow through with her plans. Plans, that no matter how difficult, were best for everyone involved.

Chapter Twenty-Eight

Dakota sped down the dirt road to the farmhouse later that morning, her newly-purchased paint sprayer and exterior-grade paint in the truck beside her. Thank goodness B&B Hardware--thanks to Chance--allowed her to put the items on a tab. She pulled up outside the farmhouse and threw the gearshift into park. Daisy bounded from the back of the pickup, obviously as glad to be back on the farm as she was.

A smile flew to Dakota's lips as the sunny day warmed her skin and the slight southerly breeze tossed her hair. A high pressure front had stalled over the area, bringing uncharacteristic warmth to the Texas winter. And though the weatherman had announced the possibility of a major winter storm, nothing about this beautiful day gave any credence to his report.

A few minutes later, Dakota limped to the barn for the extension ladder, Daisy on her heels. A sudden uneasiness deposited chill bumps down Dakota's back and arms. She peered around for signs of someone watching. Nothing. Still uneasy, she rejoined her trek to the barn, hoisted the aluminum ladder over one shoulder, and moved back to the house.

The uneasiness stuck with her throughout the rest of the day. Several times she turned around, half-expecting someone to be standing beneath her as she covered the windows, shutters and trim with plastic to protect them from the paint.

"What time I am afraid, I will trust in you." Dakota spoke the verse out loud, mainly to hear something besides the sounds her paranoid brain heard with every gust of wind or creak of the old house. The verse did the trick, and familiar peace settled over her like a blanket of bluebonnets in spring.

Careful not to put too much weight on her bum ankle, Dakota descended the ladder one step at a time, always leading with her left foot. Once at the bottom, she read the instructions for the paint sprayer and set up the bucket of paint to accept the plastic tubing from the sprayer. Dakota lightly sprayed a swash of the tan paint against the weathered gray siding of the house. Immediately the house took on a hint of newness, like a woman with a new spring dress.

She climbed the ladder once more to start at the top and work her way down, careful to keep the tubing in the paint bucket. Just a minute after she arrived at the top of the ladder and sprayed the first section, a sporty-looking car pulled around the tree-lined curve of the road leading to the farmhouse.

A burst of fear tensed her legs, as one name drilled through her head. Kane. It was just the sort of car he would drive. Just the sort of image he wanted to project to all his friends and acquaintances who worshipped the ground he walked on, unaware of the monster that lurked within.

As quickly as possible with her sore ankle, she scooted down the ladder, every muscle in her body tensing in preparation for a possible fight.

But as car doors opened, and the people inside climbed out, Dakota relaxed. Andy Tyler and Gracie. A relieved smile spread across her face. "Hi, y'all."

Gracie's eyes held censure, but she didn't speak.

"Hey, Dakota." Andy Tyler took off his suit jacket and tossed it into the back seat. "We have some news for you."

Her throat tightened, and the smile slid off her face. Words wouldn't come.

"Your ex has dropped the charges. No court case."

Dakota's knees attempted to buckle at the news, but she caught herself, hurried toward Andy and Gracie, and hugged them both. "Thank you so much. I needed some good news." How was it possible that Kane had let her off so easy?

Andy grinned, his dimples pronounced and his blond curls whipped about by the wind. "Happy for you. We stopped by Gracie's house first, but when we couldn't find you there, she though you might be out here." He peered down at her foot, still encased in the lovely boot Chance had provided and insisted she wear. "Sure it's a good idea for you to be up on that ladder?" His eyes shifted to the top of the ladder, which rested against the second story of the house.

"I'm fine." Dakota's gaze flitted to Gracie, whose lips were pressed into a pencil-thin line. She still hadn't spoken a word. "Gracie, what do you think of the new house color?"

"Very pretty." Gracie faced Andy. "I know you need to get back into town, Andy, but do we have time for me to talk to Dakota for a quick second?"

"Oh, sure. I'll wait in the car. See you around, Dakota."

Once Andy was back in the car, Gracie turned back to her. "Does Chance know you're out here by yourself?"

"I called him earlier."

"And?"

"And I told him."

Gracie's stiff body language relaxed a bit. "Okay. Just wanted to make sure, even though I do not like the thought of you up on that ladder with no one else here. Especially with your hurt ankle."

"It's okay, Gracie. I'm a big girl."

Her friend didn't look convinced. "Okay, but please promise to be careful."

"I will."

Dakota watched them drive away, then climbed the ladder again, her heart happy and light. Never in a million years had she expected this outcome. She sprayed the next section, the house quickly morphing from tired gray to a warm tan color, a perfect metaphor of the new lease on life Kane's change of heart had provided.

Suddenly a rogue thought almost pushed her from the ladder, and she released the trigger to bring a hand to her cheek. Of course. How had she not figured this out at Andy's first mention? Kane didn't want her prosecuted. He just wanted to know where she was. He had no reason to spend the money on a court case when his objective had already been met.

Heart pounding uncontrollably, Dakota fumbled in her back pocket until her fingers latched onto the verse cards. She yanked them free. *"For God has not given us a spirit of fear; but of power, and of love, and a sound mind."* She read the words out loud several times, gaining strength with each repetition.

Fear didn't come from God, which meant it came from the enemy. Instead, God granted power, love, and a sound mind, all things she needed to battle fear and the objects of her fear. She inhaled deeply, willing her fast-paced pulse to slow its stampede.

Finally the panic attack subsided. Determined to finish in spite of her fears, Dakota tackled the upper section of the house and then moved down and sprayed the lower floor. She finished the front of the house and started toward the ground when Chance's pickup sped around the corner, throwing up a cloud of dust and gravel.

The truck came to a screeching halt. Chance killed the engine and flew from the pickup, his face dark and foreboding. Never had she seen him so angry. He strode toward her in long, furious steps, his fists clenched.

Dakota flinched out of habit born at the punishing hands of Kane. Her left shoulder rose in defense, and she turned away to ward off a coming blow.

The movement stopped Chance in his tracks, and the anger immediately dissolved from his face. He stood there several seconds, his eyes soft and apologetic. "I'm sorry, Dakota. I hope you know I'd never hit you." He advanced slowly and held out his right hand. "Please forgive me."

She gave her head a shake. "It's okay. I'm sorry for making you so angry." In an effort to diffuse the tense situation, Dakota motioned toward the house. "What do you think?"

He faced the house, both hands on his hips. "Not sure you want to hear what I think."

How was she supposed to respond to that comment?

"The house looks beautiful, but the thought of you out here by yourself on that rickety old ladder with a bad ankle terrifies me." His weary words accentuated the fatigue on his face. Then in the blink of an eye, he side-stepped to where she stood and took her in his arms.

Chance breathed a prayer of gratitude as he pulled Dakota close, comforted by simply being able to put an arm around her shoulders and feel her next to him. His fear had exploded in shards that embedded themselves into every part of his body when he'd arrived at Matt and Gracie's to find her not there. He'd broken every speed limit between here and town to make sure she was okay.

A sudden round of deep weariness threatened to pull him under, and he clung to her more tightly.

"Gracie told me."

Her soft voice trickled through him, bringing forth another round of gratitude. He opened his eyes to Dakota's beautiful upturned face. "Told you what?"

"That you've been camping out in your pickup to make sure I'm okay." She placed a hand on his upper arm. "I appreciate your concern, but you don't have to go that far."

Yes, he did. "Someone has to look out for you." His voice had gone all mellow on him. Obviously his lack of sleep over the past week was affecting him in ways he hadn't expected.

"I'm a big girl, Chance. I hereby relieve you of your duties." Dakota wriggled free from his grasp and hobbled toward the front door. She grabbed a paint sprayer as she passed and hauled them up the porch and into the house.

The front door slammed shut. Chance raked a hand across the top of his head and down the back of his neck. How could he explain his feelings of protectiveness to her? Would any of his reasons make sense to her? Cause they sure didn't make sense to him.

Chance marched into the house. He found her at the kitchen sink cleaning the sprayer. "You buy that today?"

"Yep." She didn't look up from her work.

"The house looks great, inside and out."

"Thanks, but when I look at it, I see at least one project in every room, not to mention the one million plus projects outdoors." Her voice held despondency.

Must be her writer's attention to detail, because everywhere he looked he saw perfection, from the crown molding to the floors. He crossed his arms and feet and leaned back against the newly-installed quartz countertop. "How is Matt's suggestion about the Bible verse cards going? You doing okay today?" She'd opened up to him a lot the past couple of days as they'd sat next to a crackling fire at Matt and Gracie's outdoor fireplace, though he still got the impression there was much she kept locked inside.

"Seems to me that you're the one with fears. I'm not spending my nights in the cab of a pickup."

Touché.

"But since you asked, I have moments when I do just fine, followed by overwhelming panic attacks."

He frowned. "About what?"

She continued to scour the various pieces of the paint sprayer. "Well, here's an example. Andy and Gracie came out with good news. Kane's not pressing charges, so the judge dropped the case."

Her voice held an unidentifiable quality. Like she was happy about the news, but still unsure. "That's wonderful news, but you don't look so happy about it."

In a flurry of movement, she cut off the water and tossed the last part down to dry, then faced him. "I was until I realized why Kane dropped the charges. He's not after my incarceration. He's after me. Now he knows where I am. I have to finish this house and sell it so I can move on." Her voice cracked.

Chance latched onto her as she whizzed past, then ᵗood her in front of him, his hands on her shoulders. "It's Dakota. You don't have to run anymore. I'm here. I'll
of you."

drifted from his face to his shirt, practically ᴊle through him as she considered the words.

Something had her troubled, but in typical fashion, she wasn't about to clue him in.

"Besides, it's been three years since you've seen Kane. Maybe he's changed. People do that you know. Just look at you and me if you don't believe me."

Her troubled expression remained, her eyes dark and stormy.

Obviously she didn't believe him, and that set off a wave of fear in his own heart. The way she'd flinched earlier and the troubled expression she now wore all bore testimony to past suffering. This Kane guy must be some piece of work.

As the evening wore on, Dakota morphed into a crazed woman, working from one room to the next, completing a host of little projects. In his fatigue, it was all Chance could do to keep up with her. They secured and caulked baseboards, repaired a few places in the floor, hung curtains, cleaned, and touched up paint.

Chance managed to get Dakota to stop for a little food, but she said very little, finished the meal quickly, and set straight back to work. By the time he left at nine o'clock, Dakota had him convinced more than ever that Kane was indeed a threat to watch out for.

Though tired beyond description, Chance decided not to return to Miller's Creek. Instead, he drove down the road a little ways and turned into a pull-out. He stepped from his truck in the darkness, fumbled with the gate latch, then moved the pickup into the pasture, through the wild grass that had sprung up from years of no plowing, planting, or harvesting, and didn't stop until he saw the lights from the farmhouse.

It was well past one in the morning when the last light in the house went off, leaving Chance with the part of the long, sleepless nights he dreaded most. He grimaced as he swallowed, suddenly aware of a dry tickle and ache in his throat, immediately followed by a sneeze that rattled his brain.

This wasn't good at all. In fact, he couldn't think of a worse time for him to get sick.

Chapter Twenty-Nine

A ray of morning sunlight made its way through the lace curtains and scattered a lovely pattern across the bed as Dakota yawned, stretched, and glanced at the clock. Already eight a.m.? How long had it been since she'd slept so late?

Though she'd had a little trouble falling asleep, it hadn't been as bad as she'd suspected after her fears yesterday had burgeoned to elephantine proportions. Poor Chance. He'd tried to assuage her fears last night, but to no avail. Instead of listening, of trying to let things go, she'd gone on a rampage, like a she-version of the Tasmanian Devil, working on various projects until past midnight when she'd stopped to do a little writing.

A smile lit her face, and she blinked drowsily. At least her rampage had resulted in most of the small inside projects being completed. Today she'd do better about not letting her fears take over, even if she had to read through her scripture cards a million times.

She stumbled downstairs for breakfast and Bible study, then traipsed back upstairs to don some work clothes. With just one step out the front door, the familiar nagging sensation returned. *Okay, Dakota, that's enough. Just get on with your work, and quit being so paranoid.*

Dakota quickened her step, Daisy at her side, and made her way to the barn. Mid-morning she stepped back to view her work with a feeling of satisfaction. She'd managed to clean up all the debris for a trip to the garbage dump. Once Chance arrived after his last-minute half-day shift, they could get one more thing crossed off the list.

A frown wrinkled her brow. Where was Daisy?

She inserted her thumb and index finger in the corners of her mouth and gave a shrill whistle, but with no results. That was odd. The dog always came when called. Maybe she'd gone to the creek.

Dakota set off through the overgrown pasture toward the bridge, the warmth of the sun on her head and back. She breathed in deep, suddenly happy and secure. "Daisy!"

Nothing. No happy bark. No pounding through the grass.

She reached the bridge. Still no sign of Daisy. Dakota walked onto the planks and leaned against the railing to search the creek banks. "Daisy!" The tall grass rustled behind her, and she whirled around. "There you are, D--"

It wasn't Daisy who stood before her, but her new neighbor. What was his name? The guy with really clean hands for a backwoods Texan.

"Sorry. Didn't mean to startle you." He smiled and stepped toward her.

Her pulse exploded in her throat and moved to her ears and temples. Out here in the middle of nowhere with nothing to protect herself. No weapon. No Daisy. *Keep cool, Dakota. Use your brain.*

"I see y'all finished the bridge."

"Yes." She backed away slightly, to keep a distance between them. "I'm sorry. I don't remember your name." Her gaze strayed to his hands. Still clean in spite of his scruffy face, a fact that still didn't compute.

"Vincent. Your boyfriend at work?" He moved a bit closer, so she backed up again.

"No." Where was he going with this? "But he should be here soon." Would the ploy work?

He nodded. "Y'all have been doing quite a bit of work on that old house."

"Yes sir."

"I'm surprised a young woman like you would want to live way out here."

Okay, this guy was giving her the heebie-jeebies. "Not at all. I have my dog and my work."

"Pretty dog. Real friendly. Didn't I hear you calling her earlier?"

No way she would answer that question in this situation. "Well, it was nice seeing you again, Vincent, but I've got to go get lunch ready before Chance gets off work. Bye." She waved over her shoulder as she stepped away.

One step. Two. Three.

"Bye."

Dakota turned back to smile at him. Thankfully, he'd stayed in place, though it was more than a little creepy that he just stood there, staring.

Four. Five. Six.

When she reached ten steps and still didn't hear footsteps behind her, she inhaled a deep breath and released it through pursed lips. But it was still all she could do not to turn around to see if he was following or staring or had left in the other direction. She nonchalantly lengthened her stride, but as she neared the farmhouse, she broke into a sprint, bounded up the porch steps and into the house, and locked the door behind her.

She leaned against the door and tried to slow her racing pulse. Was Vincent the reason she'd felt on edge this morning and yesterday? Had he been watching her? And where in the world was Daisy?

As if on cue, scratching sounded from upstairs, followed by whimpering.

Dakota froze, her mind racing. Daisy had been outside with her earlier. How had she gotten back in the house?

There you go again, Dakota, making mountains out of molehills. She gave her head a shake. Obviously, Daisy had followed her inside when she'd come back to the house to use the restroom. Then she'd gone upstairs and somehow pushed the door shut so she couldn't get out.

A relieved laugh sounded from her throat. "Daisy? Is that you?"

A happy bark sounded, followed by more scratching and whining.

Dakota hobbled up the stairs. "It's okay, girl. I'm coming. I've been looking for you, you silly dog."

Daisy's sounds came from her bedroom, the last one on the left. She started down the hall, still talking to Daisy, but as she passed the second doorway, the hairs on the back of her neck stood on end.

Footsteps sounded behind her, and someone stepped from the darkened doorway she'd just passed. "Well, well, we meet again."

Icy fingers tingled down her spine. Kane had caught up to her at last.

Chance leaned his elbow on the counter at the nurse's station and lowered his head to his fist. He attempted to breathe through his nose, but couldn't. It was as though a drain inside his head was clogged.

"You look awful." Chelsea rounded the corner and entered the nurse's station.

"My head feels like it weights twenty pounds."

"Last time I checked, that's about fourteen too many." She smiled.

Chance didn't.

"You really shouldn't be around the patients with a cold. Why don't you go home? It's a light day anyway."

"Gains will have my head on a silver platter if I miss any more work."

"It's Friday. He's long gone. Take off. We've got you covered."

Yeah, it made sense. He had to get well in order to protect Dakota. "Thanks, Chels. I owe you one."

A few minutes later he dragged himself to the pickup, feeling worse by the minute, his whole body achy. He shivered in spite of the warm day. Must have a fever.

Everything in him wanted nothing more than to head for the house, dose up with medicine, and sleep for the entire weekend. But he couldn't. Not yet anyway. He'd tried to call Dakota all morning with no luck. His lips flattened. She'd probably turned her phone off to keep him from interrupting her every five minutes. It didn't matter. He couldn't rest until he knew she was okay.

Fifteen minutes later he parked his pickup behind hers and slowly made his way to the front porch, his feet dragging as though loaded with lead. He leaned against the house with one fore-arm and rapped on the door. "Dakota?"

From inside muffled voices sounded, then multiple footsteps headed for the door. What was going on? Chance frowned. Maybe it just sounded that way because of her limp.

The door opened. Dakota peered up at him, her face unusually pale. "Hi."

She didn't budge from her location. "You gonna let me in?"

"Sorry, I'm busy right now. Call me later."

His ire spiraled upward driven on by fatigue. If she only knew how sick he felt, she wouldn't be playing these games. "I've been trying to call you all day."

Up and to his left, a scratch sounded from a bedroom window, followed by a bark and whimper. "You have Daisy locked up?"

"I told you. I'm busy. I'm also tired. I spent all morning cleaning out the barn. Now can you please just leave?"

Chill bumps rose on his back, and his eyes narrowed. Something was up, but what?

"C'mon, Chance. If you won't leave, I'll be forced to slam the door in your face."

He stood his ground, mind whirling as he tried to get a grip on what was happening.

Her frightened green eyes took on a brief flash of apology, and then the door slammed.

Footsteps sounded across the floor again, but no talking. Up above, Daisy whined and whimpered, her nails clicking against the window pane as she clawed. Okay, sick or not, something just didn't feel right about this whole scenario.

Chance moved slowly down the steps, not allowing himself to look back. Instead he climbed in the pickup, backed up and headed down the driveway and out onto the main dirt road. Once he reached the pull-in for the gate he'd entered last night, he parked the truck, then hurried back to the farmhouse. He hurried to the north side, ignoring more shivers brought on by his rising fever. Crouching, he made his way to the living room window.

From within an unknown male voice railed down curses while Dakota pleaded for him to stop.

Warning bells rang in his head and sent shockwaves throughout his body. No time to waste. Chance hurried to the back door, quickly dialing the police station. Ernie answered.

"Hey, Ernie, this is Chance. I'm outside the farmhouse. I think Dakota's ex might be inside and hurting her. I'm about to go in and see if I can help." He kept his voice intentionally low.

"We're on our way, but I advise not going in. Wait 'til we get there."

Chance hit the 'end call' button and let himself in the back door. Yeah, it would be better if he could wait until they arrived, but he couldn't take the chance of the guy in the house hurting Dakota. Hopefully, the element of surprise would work in his favor. He moved noiselessly to the pantry where she stored the shotgun, then tiptoed to the living room door and raised the gun at the man who could only be Kane. Dakota cowered on the couch beneath his raised fist.

A volcano erupted inside Chance, spewing frantic words from his mouth. "Stop it!"

The man turned, his fist still raised.

Dakota faced him, teary-eyed and pleading. "Chance, please leave. I'll be okay. Please."

Gut churning, he forced his gaze away from her. "Kane, I presume?"

An evil grin spread across the man's grizzled face as he lowered his fist. "So she's told you all about me, eh?" A spiteful laugh sounded from his throat. "Chance, huh?" He grabbed a handful of Dakota's hair and yanked her head back. "This the guy responsible for the shape you were in when I first met you?"

"Kane, don't. Please don't do this. I'll go with you. I'll do whatever you say, but please don't." Her voice lowered to a whisper.

What was she doing? A sweat broke out on his forehead and his vision blurred as he struggled to keep Kane in the gun sights.

"Well, since she's told you all about me, let's see if she told you the really good news." Kane's face held pure hatred.

Dakota lowered her head, red curls obscuring her face, but not concealing her heaving shoulders or her gut-wrenching sobs.

Kane raised her chin to meet his gaze. "You mean you didn't tell him that you gave his baby girl up for adoption?"

In slow motion, the room began to spin, whether from the blow of Kane's words or the fever, Chance couldn't tell. He spread his legs wide to steady his body weight, which seemed intent on giving in to gravity. With the gun still miraculously raised, he blinked. Baby? She'd been pregnant when she'd left Miller's Creek? Puzzle pieces fell neatly into place. It all made sense now. He had a baby girl. A baby he hadn't known about. A baby she'd given up for adoption without consulting him.

Focus, Chance. You can deal with it later. Right now he had to get Dakota--and himself--out of the house alive.

Dakota released a guttural groan and drew his fuzzy attention. Her face creased, and her words sounded between sobs and sniffles. "I'm so sorry, Chance. I wanted to tell you, but I didn't think you'd forgive me. I'm so sorry."

In one swift movement, Kane was on the couch beside her. He yanked her head back once more to peer into her tear-stained face. "You never talked that nice to me, and after all I did for you." He looked up at Chance, a sneer on his face, then turned his attention back to Dakota. "I should've known you'd run right back to your lover boy. Or maybe I should call him Scar Face." Kane laughed, a maniacal laugh that further revealed his twisted personality.

Dakota's sobs returned in earnest.

Out of nowhere, Kane's demeanor changed, like a chameleon in new surroundings. Tears coursed down his cheeks as he took Dakota in his arms and wiped away her tears with his fingertips. "Oh, pretty baby, I'm sorry to hurt you. But if you hadn't run away I wouldn't have done this. You made this happen."

His finger tightened on the trigger. Yeah, blame it on her, you disgusting... Chance brought the thought under control.

Kane pulled Dakota's head to his chest and stroked her red curls. "Don't you know you belong to me?"

Dakota shivered uncontrollably.

In the next instant, Ernie and Carter stood beside him, revolvers drawn and trained on the mad man who cradled Dakota in his evil embrace. Carter spoke in a slow and soothing voice. "Stand up and put your hands above your head, and no one will get hurt."

Kane rose to his feet, but pulled Dakota in front of him, effectively blocking his body with hers. A shot sounded, and Kane slumped to the floor, left hand on his right shoulder and a dazed expression on his face.

Dakota, no longer confined by Kane's clutches, raced across the room toward Chance, placed both arms around his waist and her head against his chest, sobbing.

Chance let the gun slip to the floor and leaned it against the wall, the reality of all that had just taken place coming into focus once more. He gripped Dakota's shoulders and pushed her away.

She stared up into his eyes, horrified. "Please don't do this, Chance. At least give me the opportunity to explain."

He turned to Carter. "Y'all got this?"

His friend frowned and nodded.

Numb, Chance stumbled out the door, relieved that the battle was over, but too dazed and too sick to consider anything else.

Chapter Thirty

Clouds hung low and dark as Dakota finished up feeding the chickens, proof that a winter storm was on the way. Two weeks had passed with no call, no visit, no nothing from Chance.

The stabbing pain in her chest returned. She closed her eyes against the pain and leaned against the old weathered wood of the barn. She'd been right all along. Chance would never forgive her for giving their baby up for adoption. But being right didn't lessen the pain, nor did it bring satisfaction. And it was her own fault. Hadn't she sworn off ever falling in love again? And bit by bloody bit, she'd allowed herself to fall in love with the one she could never have.

Lord, I'm not asking for you to bring him back to me. That's the last thing I deserve. But I do pray for his sake that he'll someday forgive me, so he won't be locked behind bars for as long as I was.

The pain intensified, and she brought a hand to her chest to rub it away. On the deepest of levels she understood his hurt. Even after all these years, whenever she saw a dark-haired little girl with the same blue-gray eyes as his, her heart ripped open just a little bit more. Tears dripped from her chin and plopped to the dusty ground. Already she'd cried bucket loads, enough to fill the dry creek bed in a July drought. But crying wouldn't change anything. Wouldn't bring him back. Wouldn't change the past. Wouldn't undo what had already been done.

She straightened and moved toward the house, Daisy right behind. The best thing for her to do right now was to get so involved in the story-world of her new book that everything else faded away. Surprisingly enough, since the day Chance walked away without looking back, her words seemed to flow as generously as her tears. Almost as though the pain of losing him forever served as a catalyst to transfer her emotions to the page.

Her phone jingled in her pocket. She pulled it out and examined the screen. Gracie. A big part of her was tempted not to answer. After all it wouldn't be long until she'd have to leave that relationship behind as well. But answering it was the right thing to do. Gracie and Matt had been so kind and generous. "Hello?"

A relieved sigh sounded through the phone. "Glad I finally got a hold of you. Why haven't you returned my calls?"

Dakota kicked at the dry dirt with the toe of her boot. "Sorry. I just wasn't in a place where I could talk." At least not without breaking down.

"I understand, trust me, I do. But it's not good for you to lock yourself away from everyone. Can I come out to see you?"

Everything in her wanted to say no, but she couldn't. It might be painful, especially when it came time to say goodbye, but the last thing she wanted was to hurt her friend. "I guess so."

"I'll be there in a few minutes."

Dakota flipped her phone shut, climbed the porch steps, and entered through the front door of the farmhouse that no longer resembled the shell of a house she'd found just a few months earlier. It had taken a while to feel safe here after the incident with Kane, but for now he was behind bars, and the police and Sheriff's Department made regular visits to check on her.

A cynical laugh fell from her mouth as she slouched to the couch and stared at the ceiling. Finally safe after all these years, but the running away wasn't over. Tomorrow she'd visit with the new realtor in town. Once the house sold, she'd pay Chance what she owed him. Hopefully it would be enough to jumpstart his dream of opening the drugstore. As for her, she'd do what she'd done continuously her entire life.

Cut her losses and move on.

"You sure you can live with that decision?" Matt lobbed the words and fell back against the sofa in his and Gracie's beautiful home.

Chance took in his best friend's tight-lipped frown. Maybe trying to talk to Matt about the matter wasn't wise. He and Gracie had both grown fond of Dakota during her stay with them. But could he live with the decision to sever all ties with the woman who'd once more captured his heart only to break it?

The familiar ache returned. But with expertise gained over the past couple of weeks, he conjured up a mental image of what she'd done. His heart turned to stone.

"Maybe you just need more time."

Chance shook his head forcefully. "Nope. My mind's made up. I won't pretend that nothing happened, and I won't excuse what she did."

"No one's asking you to." Matt leaned forward and made eye contact. "But you need to forgive her because it's the right thing to do."

Frustration built until he thought he'd explode. Chance raked a hand across the top of his head. "And just how am I supposed to do that?" His voice broke, and he lowered his head to his hands. That's what hurt most of all. Yes, he'd been angry at her. Had blamed her for the entire incident. But had his attitude and treatment of her been the catalyst for her running away? He balled up a hand and slammed it against his knee.

Matt leaned back and released a slow breath. "What is it Chance? There's something you're not saying."

He swallowed against the lump in his throat. "I just feel so guilty." Where had that come from?

His friend's light brown eyes softened. "Good. You had me worried there for a sec."

Chance snapped to attention, his back stiff. Good that he felt guilty?

Matt chuckled. "Sorry. That's just my version of shock treatment."

Well, between Matt's version and the real version, he'd gotten off pretty easy.

"Why do you feel guilty?"

Discomfort crawled up Chance's spine as he considered the question. Okay, this wouldn't be easy, but if Matt could help him get past all the twisted emotions inside, it would be well worth it. "For a long time, I blamed Dakota for what happened that night. In some ways I still do."

"That's projection, my friend." Matt certainly had no qualms about laying it all out on the table. "It happens when we can't handle our own poor behavior and move all the blame to someone else's shoulder."

Was he projecting his blame on her? Is that why he felt so bad?

"So after that night so many years ago, what happened between you two?"

"I quit going to the farm. Just kind of shut down and pretended she didn't even exist. I didn't see her for several weeks, but then she showed up at a baseball game the weekend of the Watson family reunion. My parents were down, along with aunts and uncles and cousins." Chance allowed the scenes to replay in his memory. "We'd all gone to the ballpark, and I was hanging out with my cousin Brittany when I saw Dakota coming toward us, looking through crowds of people as though searching for someone."

"You."

"Yeah." He closed his eyes, briefly transported back to that muggy autumn evening. "She saw me and smiled." Then her smile had disappeared, like the sun going behind a cloud. For an eternity. "She saw my cousin and assumed the worst. I tried to run after her, but there were too many people. I told my parents I was leaving. They saw how upset I was and wanted to come with me."

His friend's face held compassion, as though he had already guessed the final outcome. "And then?"

Chance clamped his jaw tight and ran a hand across his equally taut lips. Never had he' discussed this with anyone other than and Dakota. "We headed toward the farm. I was driving too fast, but I was scared because she had a thing about running away when life got too hard to handle. Something just clicked inside me. I knew I didn't want to lose her."

The knot in his throat made it impossible to squeeze out another word. Even after all these years, the memories were crystal clear and vivid. His mother's screams. The headlights bearing down on them. The sickening crunch of metal against metal and the sound of shattering glass. His head snapping against the glass, and the world going black.

"It was weeks before I could function, and then I learned about Mom and Dad." He paused to regain control of his emotions.

"And you blamed Dakota for the wreck?"

"Yeah." Blamed her for something that was his fault.

"You think Dakota realized how much you blamed her when she came back a few months ago?"

He nodded shamefully. Hadn't he made sure she'd known it?

"Chance, why do you think the Bible's so explicit about forgiveness?"

Chance opened his mouth to answer, but Matt kept going, unrelenting.

"Is there anything you've ever done that God hasn't forgiven? Did you have to somehow earn His forgiveness? When Christ forgave you from the cross, did He wait for you to apologize, ask for forgiveness, or change?"

He jumped in before Matt had a chance to turn the screws any tighter. "Okay, okay, I get your point, but I'm not Jesus. I can't do this. At least not right now. Besides, there's no guarantee that even if I could forgive her, anything would change in our relationship. There's just too much garbage from the past."

Matt nodded. "Agreed on the last point. Both of you have to be willing to bring about reconciliation, and I'm not sure you're there."

The blow to his gut doubled him over, elbows on knees, head in his hands. He'd worked so hard to show Dakota he was willing to reconcile as they'd worked on the house and bridge. In spite of her reluctance, slowly her heart had opened like a rose bud waiting for the sun's warmth to unfurl its blossoms. Now here he was on the opposite side of the fence, unwilling to take even a step in that direction. A sigh escaped. "Part of me wants it to work, but then..."

"...then you feel like there's a boulder in the way you just can't crawl over?"

Exactly.

"I can't make this decision for you, Bud, but you know how I feel. She's had a rough life and needs you more than she'll ever let on." Matt patted his back. "And you may not be Jesus, but His power's in you. He can give you the strength to blast that boulder to smithereens."

His friend's choice of words elicited a smile. *Thank You, God, for Matt. Help me to forgive Dakota as You've so graciously forgiven me.* "Thanks. Keep us both in your prayers."

"You know it."

Chance stood and made his way across the room. At the door he grabbed hold of the knob, then turned toward Matt. "If I don't see you between now and then, y'all have a Merry Christmas."

"You, too. You got plans?"

Chance shook his head. The first Christmas without Grampa. Without anyone, for that matter.

"The whole gang will be at Mama Beth's. You know you're welcome."

"I'll think about it. Give Gracie my love. Where is she anyway?"

"Gone to see Dakota."

Meddlers, the both of them, but how could he protest? They loved him and Dakota and weren't the kind of people to not intervene. Chance sent Matt a goodbye smile, then exited the house.

He climbed into his truck, his mind on all he needed to say and do to get past this. Sometime tomorrow, he'd make a trip to check on Dakota, to see where they stood, to see if there was a chance at reconciliation. But for now, his time would be better spent at home. On his knees.

Chapter Thirty-One

A gentle knock sounded at the front door. Had Chance finally come to his senses? Dakota flew down the stairs and yanked open the door.

Her spirit deflated. She'd half-hoped to see Chance standing there. Instead it was his new boss, dressed in nice blue jeans and a sweater. What was he doing all the way out here? And what was his name again? She quickly searched her memory for their introduction the night of the hospital benefit, but nothing came to mind. "Hi. Can I help you?"

He smiled, a disarming kind of smile that immediately put her at ease. "Hi, Dakota. You might not remember me. I'm Jeremy Gains, the new hospital administrator." He stretched out a hand.

Dakota took his hand, her stomach in knots. Was Chance okay? Had he come to deliver bad news? She forced the frown from her face and took his hand, her lips closed in a polite smile. "Yes, Jeremy, I remember you. Is Chance okay?"

"As far as I know Chance is okay. That's not why I'm here." His cheeks reddened, and he lowered his head. A sudden gust of winter wind tossed his dark curls. "I--uh--wanted to apologize for my behavior the night of the party. It's this weird habit I have of becoming slightly obnoxious when trying to impress a pretty woman."

Dakota smiled. "No need to apologize."

"Yes, there is. I was wrong. Please forgive me." His face held humility.

Her heart pinged at his plea for forgiveness. It hurt not to be forgiven, something she knew all too well. "No worries. It's over and done."

Relief blanketed his features. "Thank you so much."

"Would you--uh--like to come in?"

A smile blossomed on his face and revealed perfect teeth, brilliant white against his ruddy cheeks. "I'd love to." He stepped in the doorway as she moved back to let him enter. "Being the new guy in town has been kind of rough. And since I'm new to the job I don't have vacation time built up to go visit my family over the holidays."

"Where's your family from?" She moved to the living room and motioned for him to sit on the new-to-her chair she'd found at a thrift store in Morganville, while she took the couch. Daisy moved close to her side and plopped down to the floor, her head between her paws.

Jeremy eyed the dog. "East Coast. What about yours?"

Dakota shook her head. "No family." At least none that wanted anything to do with her.

"Sounds like we have a lot in common. Maybe we should make a holiday plans of our own."

She didn't respond, though his words held a certain appeal. Was there anything worse than being alone during the holidays?

Without warning, Jeremy sneezed, then sneezed again. He blinked rapidly, then released yet another sneeze.

"Bless you." Dakota passed him a box of tissues.

"Sorry about that. I'm allergic to dogs."

Her mouth fell open. "I'm so sorry. You should've said something." She stood, and Daisy did the same. "Let me take Daisy to her kennel."

He held up one hand and shook his head. "That's not necessary, but thanks anyway."

"It most certainly is. Besides, it won't hurt her to get some fresh air. I'll be right back."

A few minutes later, she re-entered the room.

Jeremy's eyes flitted to her momentarily and then returned to the thick crown molding she'd installed to accentuate the home's high ceilings. "Your home is beautiful."

"Thank you. If you could've seen it a few months ago, you wouldn't have thought so."

"Ah, so you're into renovation."

She laughed. "In some respects." A stray thought wiped the smile from her face. If only she could renovate her relationship with Chance.

"Would you mind giving me the grand tour? I'm a bit of a history buff, and I find places like this fascinating."

"Sure. I'd be honored."

Dakota showed him each room and discussed all that had been done to fix it up. Jeremy let her do most of the talking, but interjected comments or questions from time to time. Fifteen minutes later, they made their way downstairs, Dakota marveling at how comfortable she felt in his presence after such a short time, especially since their first encounter had been so strange.

Rather than the expected comment about time to leave, he moved toward the chair. A little odd, but maybe he was lonely. "Jeremy, would you like something to drink?"

"Sure. What do you have?"

"A few different kinds of coke--root beer, Big Red, and of course, Dr Pepper."

"I'll have a Dr Pepper, please."

She returned a short time later, two iced drinks in hand.

"So this place belonged to your grandparents, huh?" He took the drink she offered and sipped, his gaze on her over the top of the glass.

Melancholy squeezed her heart as she eyed the place she loved so much. "Yeah. I enjoyed spending time on the farm when my grandparents were alive. It's very special to me."

He cocked his head to one side. "You seem sad. Why?"

"I'm probably gonna have to sell the place soon."

Jeremy frowned. "Why?"

She shrugged. No way would she give him all the horrendous details. "Just time to move on."

"I was under the impression you moved back to Miller's Creek not too long ago."

"Yeah, but only to work on the house."

He peered at her with a sideways glance through narrowed eyes. "So you and Chance aren't an item anymore?"

"No." Nothing more to add. Just no.

He didn't speak for a long minute, and for the life of her, Dakota could think of nothing to say. She shifted in her seat, the air in the room growing thick, almost ominous.

Jeremy still said nothing, but just studied her, as though finding some weird enjoyment in her discomfort.

The hair on the back of her neck did that stand-on-end thing. What was with him anyway? "The weather was nice earlier in the month, wasn't it? It's just been in the last week or so that it's turned chilly." Her words seemed to bounce off him.

Still he said nothing.

Enough of whatever game it was he was playing. Dakota rose to her feet and moved toward the front door, praying he'd follow her cue. "Thanks so much for coming to visit, Jeremy. I hate to be a party pooper, but I have work to do."

He didn't move.

Now the hair on the back of her neck moved to full alert. Dakota frowned and cleared her throat.

With a creepy smile on his face, Jeremy stood and moved toward her.

Finally. Dakota released a quiet, but relieved breath. She reached for the doorknob, but his hand closed over hers and remained there.

Heart pounding furiously, her gaze jumped to his.

Gone was the earlier warmth, replaced now with a sadistic gleam. "You writing a new book, Amy? Or is it A.K. Aston?"

Sheer terror ripped through her insides, but she struggled to control it. Best not let him see her fear at this point.

"How'd you know?"

He studied her, like a scientist might study growth in a Petri dish. "You mask your fear right now, Dakota, but I promise that won't last."

Intimidation. She'd seen it enough in Kane to know the tactic. Dakota sent up rapid prayers to heaven for strength and wisdom.

"Impressive. I like a woman who can keep her wits about her in an impossible situation." He uncurled her fingers from the doorknob and locked the door.

Her heart zoomed to race car speed, her brain grasping for a solution to her predicament. She was here all alone, and he knew it. And with it being the weekend before Christmas, many had already left town to spend the holidays elsewhere. Who would remember her, especially now that everyone assumed she was safe, with Kane locked up? She swallowed involuntarily, a move not unnoticed under the careful scrutiny of Jeremy Gains.

"Ah, the facade slips with the realization of your predicament." His lips curled into a wicked grin. "I like that." He brought fingertips to stroke her cheek.

She pulled away from his caress.

His face hardened as he lowered his hand. "Pack anything you might want or need in that backpack of yours."

Time. She had to buy some time. "Where are we going?"

"Does it matter?"

"I have to know what to take."

He laughed and placed a hand on her shoulder. "Quit stalling, but I do admire you for trying. You have five minutes. If you're not down here in that time...well, let's just say it won't be pleasant." His grip tightened.

Pain exploded in her shoulder and moved to her ribs beneath his eagle-like grip.

Just as quickly he released her, and she used her opposite hand to rub away the remnants of pain. "As you can see, I've mastered certain techniques in pain. Unless you want more--and worse--you'll do what you're told."

Thoughts racing, Dakota hurried upstairs, her eye on her wristwatch. Man, what she wouldn't give for her cell phone, but it lay on the coffee table downstairs. She had to do something in the off chance that someone came here looking for her. Dakota moved to her desk and scribbled a hasty note, then shrugged on her jacket and stuffed her laptop into the backpack. Time was ticking. What next?

Down the road, a truck engine sounded. She peered out the window to see Chance's pickup make the bend.

An electrical shock rampaged through her veins. Though relieved to see him, her fear escalated. Next to

Jeremy Gains, Kane looked like Mother Theresa. Where Kane had been cruel, Gains was obviously both intelligent and cruel, a deadly combination. Chance would be in danger. Somehow she had to convince him to leave.

Backpack slung over one shoulder, she hurried down the hallway to the stairs. Below, she could hear Jeremy letting Chance in the front door with words of friendly greeting. Her gaze met Chance's as she descended the steps, and she forced the biggest smile she could muster. "Hi, Chance. Jeremy, honey, close that door before it gets cold in here." She gave a pretend shiver and dropped her backpack to the floor beside the coffee table.

Chance frowned and looked from her to Jeremy. Then his gaze landed on her backpack. "Going somewhere?"

"Yeah." Dakota kept her plastered-on smile carefully in place. "We're going to visit Jeremy's parents." She somehow found the strength to glance pseudo-lovingly at Gains, his eyes narrowed at her charade, before she turned back to Chance. "My first time to the East Coast." Dakota paused just long enough to hopefully sound convincing. "Did you need something, Chance?"

His gaze lowered to the floor, his forehead drawn up tight. "I--uh, just was--that is, I wanted to see how you were doing."

She used both index fingers to point to her smiling face. "I'm doing pretty well, wouldn't you say?" Time for the final blow. *Lord, let it work..* Dakota ran to Jeremy's side and leaned against him with a one-armed hug. "And it's all 'cause of this sweet guy." She planted a kiss on the cheek of her deadly enemy.

Face still creased in a frown, Chance didn't speak or move. His gaze flitted from her to Jeremy as though trying to make sense of everything.

Jeremy moved toward the front door with a cynical laugh. "Nice try, Amy, but I don't think your attempt to save Chance's life is working well, do you? He's obviously not buying it."

Dakota exchanged a hurried glance with Chance and at the same time grabbed her cell phone and tucked it in the pocket of her jacket.

Gains locked the door, including the deadbolt, and then reached for the shotgun, which sat in a nearby corner.

"Sorry to have to do this." He leveled the gun at Chance. In what seemed like slow motion, his finger tightened on the trigger.

Fireworks exploded inside her. "No!" Dakota rushed toward Jeremy while Chance dove for his knees.

The gun exploded and tore a gaping hole in the wall where Chance had stood just a minute earlier. Jeremy slung her to the floor, and in one swift move, brought the butt of the rifle down against the side of Chance's head with a sickening crunch.

Chance slumped to the floor in a lifeless heap.

"Chance!" Dakota screamed his name and crawled to where he lay, cradling his head in her lap. Blood oozed from the scarred side of his face. The steel plate in his head. Had Jeremy done more damage than even he realized?

The monster knelt beside her and checked the wound. "Hmm. Too soon to tell. I was hoping to get past that steel plate in his head."

A gasp fell from her open mouth.

"What?" He released a soft laugh. "Surprised that I know that about him? Hospital records, my dear. They're all on the internet and easy enough to access if you know computers."

Her mouth went dry, as sudden understanding trickled through her. "You're the one who hacked my bank account."

"Of course. And your book payments and your credit card. I do it all the time. How else can I afford to live the way I do?" Jeremy once more raised the back of his fingers to caress her cheek. "It's how I found you." He rose and yanked her to her feet as Chance's head slid to the floor. "Get your things. We're leaving."

She stiffened, the Irish blood inside her starting to boil. *Easy, Dakota. Bring it under control.*

One of Jeremy's eyebrow raised ever so slightly. "Are you sure you want to fight me?" He gripped her chin so hard that her lips popped open, his face close to enough to feel his hot breath. "Tell you what, I'll make you a deal. Come with me without a fuss and I might let him live." The threatening words were edged with ice.

In a heartbeat, she knew her course. She moved to the coffee table, hoisted the backpack, and pushed her arms through the straps. "I'm ready when you are."

One corner of his mouth lifted in a sneer. "How touching. Maybe some day I'll teach you to love me that way." He latched onto her elbow and yanked her through the open door and down the steps.

Never! Every fiber of her being screamed the word in unison. Never would she love any man the way she loved Chance.

Chapter Thirty-Two

Chance groaned, rolled to one side, and used his arms to push himself to a sitting position. His head throbbed. Where was he? He gazed around the empty room of the farmhouse, his memory slowly returning. Dakota!

Adrenaline surged through him and pushed him to his feet, followed immediately by intense pain and nausea. He brought a hand to the left side of his face and the familiar scars then checked his now-sticky fingers. Blood. Gains had hit hard enough in one blow to bring blood and render him unconscious. But where had he taken Dakota?

Chance moved out to the porch. Already the sun drooped near the horizon. Not much daylight left for a search. But where did he start?

Directly ahead of him, something bright fluttered in the breeze at the edge of the pasture's tall grass. Dakota's hair ribbon. Had she left it as a clue of where to find her? He descended the front steps as quickly as his head would allow and dialed the police at the same time. Carter answered.

"Carter, you're not gonna believe this, but there was someone else besides Kane after Dakota. Jeremy Gains."

"As in the new hospital administrator?"

"Yeah. And this guy's worse. He knocked me out with the butt of a shotgun and took off with her. I'm outside now. Just found her hair ribbon." From the barn, Daisy's frantic whimper and whine sounded. Good. Her nose would hopefully lead him right to Gains. He headed that direction.

"You're kidding."

"Wish I were."

"Stay put 'til Ernie and I get there."

"Normally, I'd refuse, but the way my head's feeling, I don't have much choice. But hurry."

Carter and Ernie pulled up ten minutes later, just as Chance stepped from the barn with the frantic Daisy. She tugged against her leash in the direction of the creek.

Carter eyed the swollen left side of his face. "Man, he got you good. You sure you're up to this?"

"Yep." Well, not really, but there was no way he would stay here with Dakota's life in danger. "Ready for me to let Daisy go?"

Both men nodded and readied themselves to run behind the German Shepherd. Chance knelt in front of her and scratched her ears. "Go find her, girl." He unsnapped the leash's clasp.

Daisy kept her nose to the ground, which slowed her down considerably. Keeping up with her turned out to be much easier than he'd anticipated, in spite of his pounding headache. They reached the bridge and crossed just as the new neighbor stepped out from the brush.

"I think you guys had better follow me." He pulled a wallet from the camouflage pants he wore and flashed a badge. "Jack Hanson, FBI. We've been after this guy a long time, and we finally have him surrounded."

"And Dakota?"

The guy's face was grim. "He still has her, which makes this whole scenario more serious. They're holed up underground."

Within a few minutes, they all stood behind an unmarked dark truck, parked not far from a densely-wooded area. The only thing that looked out of place was a ventilation pipe that stuck out of the ground, painted to blend into the surroundings.

Jack Hanson pointed toward the pipe. "The entire area is surrounded. If he tries to escape with or without her, we'll have him."

"What exactly is he wanted for?"

"Fraud and forgery to name just a couple. This guy's a technological wizard."

"Dakota's bank account and credit card." The words popped from Chance's mouth without permission.

"Yeah, and she's one of many. Slippery little devil, too. We've nicknamed him the chameleon for his ability to blend into his surroundings."

"Let me guess. He doesn't have hospital administration experience."

"Nope."

Chance scratched the top of his head. Well, that explained a few things. "How long have you been watching Dakota?"

"We found out he had a thing for her a couple of years ago when we stumbled onto his headquarters. He had pictures of her hanging all over the place."

A shudder tingled down Chance's spine.

"Unfortunately, he found out we were there and disappeared again. I don't mean to sound callous, but we had no choice but to tail Dakota. She was the only bait we had to catch this guy. We had a feeling he'd make a move for her at some point and time."

Chance swallowed. That was all well and good if Dakota weren't in danger. "Is she safe?"

The grim face returned. "We don't think he'll hurt her if that's what you mean, but you never really know. Guys like him are unpredictable."

Chance's pulse ratcheted up a notch, his mind spinning with all the info it had gathered about Gains over the past couple of months. Yeah. Just one problem. Unpredictable wasn't a strong enough word.

"You guys might as well make yourselves comfortable. This could take a while. I'll be back later." Hanson moved off into the woods.

Minutes passed. And then hours. More than once either Carter or Ernie offered to take him to the hospital to have the side of his face looked after. More than once he turned them down. He was here to the very end, no matter the outcome.

Chance wrapped his jacket tighter around him, looked up at the cloudy sky, and prayed once more for Dakota's safety.

Dakota slept fitfully, unable to fully relax, though Gains--if that was his real name--had given her a private room. It wasn't so much that she expected him to barge in on her or try anything. It was just an uneasiness over all she'd seen in her few short hours underground.

Upon entering his hideaway, the first thing she'd noticed were the pictures. Scattered all around the room were snapshots of her, some from the internet, others candid, as though he'd dogged her every step for the past few years.

Next were the knives, displayed in a case like some would display stamps or spoons. One empty spot especially caught her attention. The perfect spot to display the knife left in her front door.

After that, he'd shown her around the bunker, including the stash of food that would last months if necessary. In the same room sat several tall file cabinets, the contents of which remained a secret.

The main room was a giant circle of a room, housed with enough electronics to put Ft. Knox to shame. Proudly he'd boasted of all he had--multiple computers, night-vision surveillance cameras, the best and most expensive the digital age had to offer. He'd even set up a writing station for her, complete with a dictionary, thesaurus, and library of writing books.

How long did he intend to keep her here? And what was it about the space that seemed vaguely familiar? A sound outside her bedroom door caught her attention. Quietly she stood and tiptoed in her bare feet to the door. She cracked it open and peered out.

Jeremy Gains sat behind a span of small monitors, casually observing the activity from all directions. He turned as though sensing her presence. "You're up early."

"I...uh, needed a drink of water."

"I'll get it for you."

He reached into a mini-fridge beneath his desk, then stood and brought the bottle to her. "Here you go."

"Thanks." She removed the lid and swigged the cool liquid.

"Just so you know, we have visitors."

"Visitors?" She struggled to keep excitement from her voice and face.

"Come over here and I'll show you." He moved to the array of screens.

She followed. Each screen held a green tint, with human bodies as visible as though in noon-day sun. "Who is it?"

"My guess is people looking for you. But you don't have to worry. We're safe." A particularly wicked grin appeared on his face. "If they try to get in, they'll get a taste of what modern technology can do."

He pointed to one screen in the middle. "Recognize that guy?"

She leaned in closer. Chance sat beside a truck, his hands beneath his arms for warmth.

Her heart leapt in her chest. *Thank You, Lord.* Knowing he was alive brought relief and encouragement that she could endure this underground imprisonment. A soft sigh fell from her lips as her eyes honed in on him, afraid to even blink for fear of not seeing him again.

Jeremy wheeled around in his chair, his eyes intense. "He means a lot to you."

She nodded, suddenly aware of her vulnerability. No use in denying it. "Yes."

"Because you gave his baby girl up for adoption?"

Dakota quickly lowered her head to hide her surprise. He knew? But how? The answer came immediately. He knew about the baby just like he knew everything else about her--stalking. She lifted her gaze. "No. In spite of it. I'm going back to bed."

Gains didn't answer, but she sensed his eyes on her all the way.

Once back in the room with the door shut, Dakota sat on the edge of the bed and sipped her water. How could she get out of this place alive, especially if he had the place rigged with who knew what?

A sudden realization hit with alarming clarity. She sprung back to a sitting position, her spine rigid. The reason the bunker seemed so familiar was because it perfectly mimicked a setting in her very first book, appropriately titled *No Escape*. Though definitely in the creepy category, at least the new-found knowledge gave her a chance.

Noiselessly she tiptoed to her backpack and removed her laptop. Within a few seconds the PDF file of the book showed on her computer screen. She scanned the material, searching for spots in the storyline where the fictional bunker was described. The clock beside her bed read almost six a.m. by the time she finished her research and closed the laptop.

Dakota stowed the computer in her backpack and crawled back under the covers with a yawn. Now she could rest for a few hours, but at some point she had to find a way to locate the secret back door through which the heroine in her book had finally escaped.

Chapter Thirty-Three

Chance gulped down the coffee, its warmth slowly spreading through his body. He looked up at Carter. "Thanks, man." To his right, the sky lightened on the eastern horizon.

"You're welcome. Want something to eat to go with that?"

He shook his head. There was no way he could eat with his stomach all tied in knots.

A fresh round of grief squeezed his heart. Why had he let his foolish pride and anger--his inability to forgive--keep him from her these past few weeks?

Lord, I'm so sorry.

He blinked back tears, brought on by exhaustion and worry. Not forgiving only locked everyone involved in prison, then robbed them of life's most precious commodity. Time.

Chance swigged another gulp of coffee. Not knowing what was happening to her was killing him. If only he had some indication of how she was, a way to communicate with her. A sudden memory flooded his brain. Her cell phone. She'd picked it up from the coffee table and stuffed it in her jacket right before Gains had tried to beat his brains out with the shotgun. Did she still have it, or had Gains confiscated it?

"What is it?"

Carter's words shook him from his thoughts. "Hmm?"

"Your wheels are turning. You have an idea, don't you?"

"Yeah, but I haven't thought it all the way through yet."

His friend's eyebrows raised. "Well, what is it?"

"She might have her cell phone. I could send her a text, but if Gains has confiscated it, it could put her in danger."

"C'mon. Let's go talk to Jack."

Jack listened carefully to all they said, all the while scratching his chin in contemplation. "It's worth a shot."

Within a few minutes, all permissions were secured. With shaky fingers, Chance typed the burning question in his text to her. "You okay?"

A long minute passed, then his phone dinged.

"Y."

An excited grin blossomed on Chance's face. He glanced up at the others standing nearby. "She's okay. What should I ask next?"

"Make sure it's safe for her to talk."

Chance nodded and quickly thumbed in the next question. They waited again, but this time longer. His heart sank. Had Gains found the phone? The phone dinged again.

"Y. Came to BR to answer."

"BR?" Carter's face held questions.

"Bedroom." She'd used the same abbreviation in her plans for the farmhouse.

Another text came through. "Will look for back door as I can. JG says place is rigged. Be careful."

Back door? The place had a back door? He read off the text. Several FBI agents immediately scrambled for their gear and headed back into the dark woods to search for a back exit.

His phone screen lit up in the semi-darkness of the frigid morning. "No Escape book. No more texts for now."

He puzzled over the cryptic words. Was she trying to tell him there was no escape? But why would she include the word book? He moved back to the truck and poured another cup of coffee, his thoughts whirring. Book. What book?

Swifter and harder than even the butt of the shotgun that knocked him unconscious, the answer hit. Dakota's first book. He hurried back to where Carter stood. "I'm going to the farmhouse for a few minutes."

Carter frowned, but nodded. "Okay. Everything all right?"

"Yeah. Be back soon."

His head pounded more furiously with every step--partly from the blow he'd endured, partly from the lack of food and sleep. Chance raced back to the farmhouse. Within five minutes he arrived at the front door, breathless. He pushed through the fatigue and entered the house. A few minutes later he exited, book in hand, and made his way back to the underground bunker.

Carter waited by the pickup. "Just about to send out a search team. Glad you're back."

"Thanks." Chance sucked in a deep breath of air from a bent-over position. "I think we might have something here." He held up the book.

His friend's eyebrows wrinkled. "What's that?"

"First book Dakota wrote." The words came in spurts, his lungs still screaming for oxygen. "It tells the story of a woman held captive by a maniac in an underground bunker. She referenced it in her last text. Based on what Jack said earlier, I think this guy has been stalking her and may have built his bunker to mimic the one described in the book."

"Whoa." Carter's expression changed to one of incredulity.

"You have something to write on?" Chance palmed his pockets and produced a pen. "I'm going through all the descriptions of the bunker in this book and attempt to draw a map of the place."

"Good thinking. I'll find you something to write on." A minute later Carter returned with a legal pad. "Jack says to see him when you're through."

"Will do." Chance opened the book and began the tedious process of skimming through the book for descriptions of the bunker, all the while comforted by one thought.

This might very well save Dakota's life.

Dakota buried her cell phone in her backpack, away from the ever-searching eyes of Jeremy Gains. She hurried out the bedroom door and to her computer station. Perhaps if she pretended to be writing a new novel, her captor would ease up on his eagle-eyed watch.

Her mind whizzed at lightning speed as the computer booted. If Jeremy had indeed copied this place from the descriptions in her first book, it was a distinct possibility that he had physical copies of the books here. Typical of the stalker type. She should know. She'd researched plenty of them. If she could get him away from his desk, it would give her the opportunity to search for clues as to where the back door might be.

Swallowing her fear, she stood and moved to the center of the circular room, where Gains monitored everything going on outside from his array of computer screens. He looked up, unsmiling, as she approached. "What is it?" His voice held a touch of anger and impatience, previously missing when he'd spoken earlier, and his eyes were lined with fatigue from his all-night stint behind the monitors.

"I...uh, just wanted to know if you have copies of my books here. I like to reference details from previous books in my new stories."

"Yeah. Wait here." Gains strode to a door on the far side of the room--one not on the personal tour--and unlocked it. He disappeared long enough to allow her a glimpse at the screens.

Chance sat near the same pickup, pouring over a paperback, a pen and legal pad in hand. Good. He was already at work on the same puzzle she'd tackled in the wee hours of the morning.

Her heart lightened with overwhelming love. *Oh, Lord, bring us back together.* She stepped away from the center station as Jeremy exited the door on the far side of the room, a stack of paperbacks in his hands.

He strode across the room in tense, angry strides, dumped the books in her waiting arms, and repositioned himself behind the screens. "Our visitors are persistent, though foolish."

Her stomach lurched, her nerves instantly on high alert. What did that mean? "How so?"

Gains peered up, a sneer on his face. "I've made this place impenetrable. The ultimate fortress, if you will. Our water and food supply can far outlast them, and if necessary, I have the means of obliterating them." A flicker of doubt passed briefly through his eyes, quickly replaced with cold confidence. A derisive laugh sounded in his throat as he turned his focus back to the computers.

Dakota made her way to her writing station, her thoughts on Jeremy Gains. Though at cursory glance he appeared to have no chinks in his armor, she knew better. Every villainous character--whether real or imagined--had a fatal flaw. And in most cases it was their proud belief that they were invincible. Somehow she'd use that to her advantage.

But the danger? The longer he stayed awake, intent on watching her every move and every move of the men outside, the more of a loose cannon he'd become. In addition to locating her escape, she had to do it all in a way that didn't draw his suspicion or his anger.

Either one could prove deadly.

Chapter Thirty-Four

Jack Hanson plopped down to a cross-legged position across from Chance just as he finished skimming the last page of the book.

His heart brimming with fresh hope, Chance smiled over at him. "I think we might have something here." He handed Jack the legal pad with the map he'd drawn. "Based on the book, that's a pretty accurate rendering of what the inside of this place should look like."

The other man studied the drawing. "How sure are you? If we're wrong, even in the least little way, it could cost people their lives. Including Dakota."

Chance's pulse roared in his ears. The thought had occurred to him more than once. But did they have any other option other than this incessant waiting? And wouldn't Gains--or the Chameleon, or whatever his name really was--wouldn't he become more and more agitated and dangerous the longer they waited? Animals could get more than a little testy, especially when they felt cornered.

He sent a silent prayer heavenward, immediately comforted by the presence and peace of the One who'd both forgiven him and given him the capacity to forgive. "If the place fits the book descriptions, that map's correct."

Hanson picked up the paperback and looked at the foreboding cover, one that eerily matched their current surroundings. "Never read her books. Are her descriptions that good?"

"She's got a knack for placing the reader firmly in the story world without their knowing it. That's why I think the drawing is accurate." His cell phone jangled in his pocket.

He hurriedly fished it out. "It's her. She says she's in a round room." Chance pointed to the map. "Just like the book." His phone dinged again. He read the message out loud. "Far room locked. Could be escape hatch or tunnel. Kitchen to right. BRs & bath to left."

Chance waited for more, but nothing came. He raised his gaze to Jack's. "It matches what we have on paper."

"Yeah, but yesterday she said the place was rigged."

True. He ran a palm across his lips. "So what do we do?"

Hanson scratched his head, lost in thought temporarily. "One of the guys found a buried power cable earlier. If we coordinate cutting the power with Dakota getting away, she might stand a chance."

Chance positioned his thumbs over the keypad of his phone. "Just tell me what to say. I'm ready to get her out of there." More than ready.

Jack looked away and released a breath through puffed-out cheeks. "Let me take it to the boss. No guarantees."

Chance watched him walk away, the yellow notepad dangling at his side, pages a-flutter in the brisk and cold wind of the late December day.

Oh, Lord, help us get this right.

Dakota glanced at the clock. One minute till. She leaned back in her chair and stretched both arms upward, doing all she could to appear convincing. A huge yawn flowed from her mouth, more real than even she expected.

Gains looked her direction. "Tired?"

She nodded and rolled the chair away from the desk. "Exhausted."

"You've been at it all day. Is that pretty typical when you write?"

So he didn't know everything about her. That one thought alone brought immeasurable comfort. "Not all the time. But there's not much else to do down here, is there?" Maybe planting little seeds of doubt in his mind would work to her benefit. She stood and moved toward the bathroom, his hawkish eyes boring a hole in her back.

Dakota clicked the bathroom door in place and locked it just as a loud pop sounded and everything went black.

"Amy!" Gains shouted. "Get out here now!" Shuffling footsteps sounded outside, and he pounded on the door. The lock wouldn't hold long with that kind of punishment. With a crash, the door gave way and strong hands latched hold of her in the dark. He wrapped both arms around her neck in a firm grip, his breath hot on her cheek. "If you so much as breathe the wrong way, I'll snap your pretty little neck like a toothpick. Got it?"

Fear spiraled throughout her. *Jesus, help me.*

Gains prodded her outside the tiny bathroom and hugged the circular wall as they moved to the far side of the room, headed straight for where she suspected the escape hatch to be. But where were the agents she'd expected to enter as soon as the power was cut? Had Jeremy's traps worked even without electrical power?

They reached the locked door. Jeremy shone a flashlight on the lock and fumbled with his jangling keys, cursing under his breath as he attempted to fit the right key in the lock. After what seemed like an eternity, the door opened. Up the stairs he dragged her, closer and closer to the exit. Once more he struggled to unlock the escape hatch in the dark, one elbow crooked tightly around her neck.

She gasped for air and clawed at his arm. He relaxed his grip, and air flooded her lungs.

With one final shove, the hatch gave way, and both of them tumbled through the darkness in piles of musty decaying leaves.

"Let her go, Krater! You're surrounded." The voice called out from the darkness of the forest.

In a last ditch effort, Dakota struggled to free herself from the grasp of her captor, praying for a good end to all of this. A shot rang out in the darkness, and Gains went down. From every direction men ran toward his writhing figure and quickly subdued him. He railed a string of cusswords, obviously in much pain as he clutched his right knee.

Arms from above reached down and pulled her to her feet. "You okay?"

"Yeah." The word came with great effort. She peered around. Shafts of light flickered on as more rescuers advanced. Dakota faced the one who'd helped her stand, shocked to see her new neighbor's face. A frown tightened her forehead. "I don't understand."

"Jack Hanson. FBI. I'll explain it all later. Right now there's someone pretty desperate to see you."

Within five minutes, they exited the dark interior of the wooded area into the soft dusk of a day she thought she might not ever see again. In spite of many happenings around her, Dakota's eyes latched onto only one. Tears streaming down her cheeks, she emerged from the darkness of her captor into the wide-open arms of forgiveness and love, the unforgiving past a quickly-fading memory.

Chapter Thirty-Five

Chance looked up from his open Bible and stared out the plate-glass window to the boys across the street playing basketball. Without warning, the friendly game escalated into a scuffle and shouts. One boy, probably around ten years of age, catapulted to his feet, screaming at the others. "This is basketball. You can't tackle in basketball."

An involuntary smile moved to Chance's lips as he watched the boys from the confines of his house. In a matter of minutes the boys were back at play as though nothing had happened. If only adults could forgive as quickly. He frowned. But then grown-up actions were a little more hurtful and far-reaching than a minor childhood scuffle, weren't they?

His mind traveled to the distant past, a time when he'd let his lack of good judgment take over. A time when he'd blamed Dakota for his own sins because he couldn't confront them in himself. He closed his eyes and rested his head against the back of the chair. Personal sin created ripples--like raindrops on a body of water--which touched everyone else around you. And in this case, he'd hurt Dakota, wounding her deeper than even he'd realized.

In the two weeks since her escape, she seemed happy enough to see him on his daily visits, but still a barrier existed, one he couldn't quite figure out how to tear down. Chance turned to the inside cover of his Bible and removed Grampa's last letter.

"Dear Chance, The money and earthly possessions I'm leaving to you are yours to use as you choose. But I do have a suggestion. Remember others. As an only child, I know it was easy to focus only upon yourself, but there are others that truly need what I'm giving to you. I pray and trust that you'll use your inheritance wisely. All my love, Grampa."

He let the letter fall to his lap and peered out the window again, his thoughts once more on Dakota. Though she hadn't given any indication that she'd forgiven him, in his heart he felt like she had. But was there more there? That was the question that had hounded him ever since that cold December evening when she'd flown out of the woods and into his arms. Next his mind flitted to his plans for the Watson family drugstore, plans that would never be realized without the capital from his inheritance.

It didn't matter. Chance laid his Bible on the nearby end table, stood, and made his way to the phone. He searched through the phone book, found the listing he wanted, and punched in the number.

"Mara Hedwig Realty."

"Yeah, Mara, this is Chance Johnson. Have you--uh--heard from Dakota by any chance?"

"As a matter of fact I have. She called a little while ago and asked to meet with me this afternoon."

Pain ripped through his heart, and Chance closed his eyes against the pain. So she'd decided to leave after all.

"Chance? You still there?"

"Yeah, I'm here." The words came out in a hoarse whisper.

"Can I help you with anything else?"

It was the right thing to do. "Actually, there is one more thing." He gave Mara the details of his plan, then hung up the phone.

Now Dakota would at last be free and able to start anew, even if it meant losing her forever.

❖ ❖ ❖

Dakota finished her last bit of cleaning and called Daisy. Her unexpected friend trotted over obediently and stared up at her, unconditional love shining from her big brown eyes.

"Oh, Daisy, I love you so much." She scratched Daisy's ears, then attached the leash and led her outside to her kennel. "I need to run to town to meet with the realtor, but I'll be back soon."

She clipped the leash to the outside of the kennel fence and retraced her steps to grab her purse and keys. Why did her heart ache so? The answer came immediately. Over the past two weeks, Chance had been to visit everyday, but hadn't verbally said the words, "I forgive you for what you did."

Her eyes moistened, and she blinked back tears. If he couldn't forgive her, then there was no chance of any sort of meaningful relationship between them. Yes, he'd been kind and supportive, but that wasn't enough. Not anymore. Instead, she'd follow through on her plan to sell the place, give Chance what she owed him and then move on to another place. Hopefully her broken heart would heal with time.

She locked the front door behind her, still amazed at the final results of the farmhouse renovation. Never in a million years could she have anticipated this outcome, especially after seeing the house's condition when she'd arrived a few months ago. Like a lady with a new dress and new attitude, the old farmhouse had a spring to her step and a gleam in her eyes. She looked loved and in love. Okay, so maybe that wasn't the best use of words, especially in light of her aching heart.

Dakota climbed into her old truck and took off down the road, suddenly anxious to escape the memories that pursued her. Would she ever be able to rid her heart of Chance Johnson? Her only comfort was the fact that by selling the farm, Chance would at last have the resources to fund his dream of restoring Watson Drugstore. That one fact alone gave wings to her plan.

A few minutes later she pulled up in front of Mara Hedwig Realty on the square of Miller's Creek downtown area. Mara, although fairly new to Miller's Creek, had come highly recommended by several people at church. Dakota let her bodyweight carry her feet to the ground, slammed the pickup door, and hurried inside, eager to get this over with before she chickened out and changed her mind.

"You must be Dakota." The woman exited a doorway with a heavily-bejeweled hand extended.

Dakota smiled and shook her hand. "Yes, and you're Mara?"

"That's me." The woman's smile didn't quite reach her eyes, as though fearful of letting others too close.

A fear Dakota knew all too well. She sent up a quick prayer for the woman.

"So you want to put your property on the market?"

Her lips pressed together, Dakota inhaled a deep breath through her nose. Better get this over and done with. "Yes."

"Okay. Let's draw up the paperwork." Mara moved to a nearby table and motioned for Dakota to take a seat. "By the way, I had a call from a gentleman earlier today who might be interested. Said he'd heard through the grapevine that the place was for sale and wanted to know if he could see it later today."

The news sent a shock clear to her bones and deposited an unpleasant taste on her tongue. So soon? Part of her had hoped for at least a few weeks at the farmhouse she'd labored over in the hopes of making it her home for a lifetime. Obviously God had other plans. "Uh...sure. What time?"

"He asked for a four-thirty showing. I told him I already had an appointment at that time, but he was persistent. So you'll have to show the property. Would that be okay with you?"

"But I don't know how."

Mara waved a hand through the air. "You know the property much better than I do. Just let your love for the place shine through." The pretty realtor shoved a stack of papers across the table. "Oh, and one more thing before we get started on all this, he asked to meet you at the bridge."

The bridge? Definitely had to be someone local to know the bridge even existed. "Okay."

Fifteen minutes later, Dakota signed the last of the papers, said her 'good-bye' to Mara, and sped to the farm, one eye on the clock. This was definitely cutting it close. What if the potential buyer beat her to the farm? Would he leave if she weren't there?

Relief washed over her as she made the bend in the long driveway. No other cars, thank goodness. She gathered Daisy from her pen and headed toward the creek, the sun parting the clouds as she traipsed through the tall grass. How she would miss this old place so laden with fond memories.

Melancholy and nostalgia tore into the flesh of her heart as she arrived at the bridge. In spite of years of neglect, the old bridge had stood its ground, not yielding to the pressure of wind or weather, but constantly providing safe journey from one place to the other.

"You belong here."

Dakota's hand flew to her chest at the unexpected voice, and her head whipped around. "Oh, Chance, you startled me. I was expecting someone else."

"Sorry. Forgive me?"

The simple words latched hooks into her heart. "Always."

In quick strides, he moved closer until he stood inches away, the blue-gray eyes she loved so much searching hers. "Do you mean that?"

"Of course."

"But how can you forgive me for how I treated you? For blaming my mistakes on you?"

"It's a two-way street, Chance. How can you forgive me for not telling you about your beautiful baby girl? Forgiveness is something you do to free everyone involved."

He stepped even closer.

She sucked in a deep breath. It was now or never. Even if she left, she'd leave knowing she'd laid it all on the table and left nothing unsaid. "Basically, I forgive you because I love you." The words rolled off her tongue as though in a dream. "That's the only way any of us can forgive."

His eyes took on a smoky darkness, and she backed away and leaned her arms on the rails of the bridge, her heartbeat pounding in her ears. Had she gone too far? And why? The words she'd spoken so hastily a minute before had never been part of the plan. Where had they come from?

Chance moved in beside her and mimicked her position.

Best to let him know the truth now. Maybe that would lessen the shock of her previous words. "Just so you know, I'm meeting with a potential buyer for the farm."

He didn't say anything for a long minute. Nor did he look her direction. "So you've decided to leave?"

She nodded. "It's for the best." Wasn't it?

"If love forgives, then why doesn't it also stay and try to make a go of things?"

The blood rushed from her head, and she faced him. "What do you mean?"

A small smile touched the corners of his lips. His eyes took on a look she hadn't seen in such a long time. He pulled her into his arms, bringing his lips down to touch hers.

Just as quickly he pulled away, his arms still encircling her waist. "I mean that I love you, too, and all that implies."

Her mouth gaped open. Did she dare hope that he'd forgiven her? "You mean...?"

"I've forgiven you, and I don't want you to go. I came out here prepared to set you free, and I still will if that's what you want."

Set her free? What? "I'm not sure I understand."

A soft chuckle escaped, and he tilted his head toward the blue sky above. "I'm your buyer."

Her jaw dropped even further. "You'd do that for me?"

His face sobered, his eyes suddenly sad. "If that's what you want."

"But the drugstore..."

"Oh, Red, I want so much for you." He tenderly tucked an escaped curl behind her ear. "I want rainbows and laughter and a home. If buying the farm will give that to you, then yes, I'll do it."

A single tear slipped down one cheek, and she shook her head. "You buying the farm won't give me those things at all. It would only give me one more reason to run away to another lifetime of loneliness. But I can't stay if..."

He silenced her with a sudden and thorough kiss. "No more ifs, Dakota. I'm here to stay, no matter what."

A burdensome weight immediately lifted from her heart and shoulders. After all these years, she was free at last.

Together they walked, hand in hand, toward the newly made-over farmhouse, Daisy bounding ahead of them.

Chapter Thirty-Six

With a final sweep of the rag, Chance cleared the last bit of dust from the drugstore counter and stepped back to view the results. He and Matt had worked late last night to finish cleaning up the last bit of construction debris for the store's grand opening in a couple of weeks. Now the place shone like the jewel he'd known it could be, and a sense of satisfaction trickled through him.

Matt pushed through the old wooden swinging doors that led from the back. "Wow. This looks great." He moved to stand beside Chance and bumped knuckles with him. "We do good work, bro, even if I do say so myself."

Chance grinned at his best friend. "Agreed. Thanks for helping me get it finished. Don't know what I would've done without you, especially since I'm gonna be out of pocket all week."

His friend lightly punched Chance's upper arm. "Quit rubbing it in. Just 'cause you're gonna be in a tropical location with the woman of your dreams while we're enduring the unpredictable weather of springtime in Texas."

A laugh erupted from Chance's throat. It still felt like a "pinch-me" kind of moment. Somehow he and Dakota had made it through the worst, and in a few hours she'd become his wife forever and ever.

Matt eyed him. "You're so giddy it's not even funny. Now, based on the text my beautiful wife just sent, I'd better get you out to the farm for the wedding before she takes me to court. You ready?"

Silly question. He'd been waiting for this day for so long. The woman he'd thought would never be his loved him with her entire being, even in spite of his scars. "More than ready."

"You look absolutely stunning, Dakota." Gracie, already dressed in her pale blue bridesmaid dress and her hair piled into immaculate curls on top of her pretty head, smiled at her through the full-length mirror in front of them.

Dakota released a shaky breath, moved a hand to her tummy to still the butterflies, and took in her appearance. Never had she dared dream that life would turn out like this for her. Now here she stood, in a dress that perfectly captured who she was, simple and understated, but somehow still a fairytale princess in white about to marry Chance.

Prince Charming? Well, he could be, though he'd always have his moments just like she would. But the past few months had proved that they had what it took to stick together in spite of their human tendency toward sin. Simply put, they'd both learned to forgive.

The door to her bedroom swung open and Dani, Trish, and Mama Beth entered. Dani, already back to her normal petite size after the birth of little Andrew Steven back in January, smiled broadly. "I just knew that was the dress for you when we spotted it in the bridal shop in Dallas. It's perfect."

Mama Beth bustled over to her and gave her a squeeze. "You look radiant, my dear." She planted a soft kiss on Dakota's cheek. "Chance Johnson is one blessed man."

Dakota shook her head. "I'm the one who's blessed."

"You both are," added Trish, her dark eyes sparkling. "By the way, we finished decorating the bridge. It looks amazing."

"I can't wait to see it." Dakota smiled. In truth, as much fun as this wedding had been to plan, there was only one thing she truly longed to see--Chance's face as she walked across the bridge to become his wife. She glanced at the clock. Time to get moving.

A few minutes later, she and the other ladies arrived at the bridge and made their way from Trish and Andy's SUV to the screen Trish had crafted from white lattice, ivy, and daisies. On both sides of the creek, as far as one could see, bluebonnets danced in the sunny spring day, last winter's flood their catalyst. Beyond that the pasture furrows boasted new sprigs of corn and sorghum, which would be used to feed their growing herd of livestock. Already their little barnyard boasted Coot's chickens, a few goats and rabbits, and a beautiful mare named Nelly. Hopefully during the summer they'd be able to add a couple of calves as well.

The comforting sound of Matt's guitar began, the signal for the wedding to begin.

Gracie straightened the train of Dakota's dress, then stood, excitement shining in her eyes. "I don't have to ask if you're ready. Your face is the definition of contentment."

One by one, the ladies left to walk down the carpeting between the rows of white folding chairs. Within a matter of minutes, Dakota stepped out in front of the lattice, her eyes firmly latched on the man she loved with every fiber of her being.

His handsome grin and steady gaze drew her down the aisle where he stood waiting, Daisy at his side, their wedding rings dangling from a blue ribbon around her neck. He reached out a hand toward her as she neared, then leaned his head toward hers, his lips touching the top of her head. "You look beautiful."

"So do you."

He laughed and tucked her hand in the crook of his elbow. "Let's do this."

Together they stepped onto the bridge and toward the pastor. The rest was a blur, except for the vows, a part of the ceremony she and Chance had decided to write themselves.

Chance faced her completely, his right hand cupping her face. "Amy, Dakota, A.K...."

Dakota couldn't help but laugh, and many others joined in.

"I don't care what your name is or what color your hair is," continued Chance. "I don't care about what has happened in the past. At the moment, I don't even care about what the future holds, as long as I get to spend it with you."

She blinked back tears, her heart crying out prayers of gratitude to God for all He'd done for her, but especially for giving her this man.

"I promise to love you, to protect you, and to do all I can to make your life wonderful for the rest of forever."

Then came her turn, and she took a deep breath to still her racing heart. Though part of her rebelled at the idea of being so vulnerable in front of so many, another part of her wanted the world to know how she felt. Dakota smiled into the eyes of the man her heart had always loved. "Sometimes I think I've loved you forever, Chance Johnson. Our past has been rocky and sin-stained, but God, in His incredible love, grace, and mercy, has used it for our good. On our own, we never could've reached the place of forgiving each other. His ultimate example of forgiveness on the cross--the bridge He built to close the gap between Holy God and sinful man--enabled us to let go of old hurts and wounds. Now, together with Him, we have the privilege of living our lives together." A tear of gratitude trickled down her cheek.

Chance's eyes also flooded with tears as he brought a hand to her face to whisk away the tear.

Dakota swallowed against the lump in her throat. "I promise to love and care for you, with no running away, for the rest of my life. And I thank God that He, and you, have forgiven me."

The crowd erupted into applause and everyone jumped to their feet. Chance engulfed her in a hug and swung her up in the air, his lips near her ear. "Thank you for forgiving me, too." The husky words belied the tears on his own face.

A few minutes later, Matt and Gracie moved to one side of the bridge and began to sing the song they'd written especially for the occasion, while Chance and Dakota, both with smiles on their faces and hearts, together picked up a hammer and nail and knelt on the bridge.

The guitar strummed the opening bars while Dakota and Chance together landed the first blow to the nail.

Their voices in perfect harmony, Matt and Gracie began to sing:

> "The ugly scars from a dark and painful past.
> Broken promises, the hurt, so vast.
> Forgiveness doesn't come because you're holding on, but
> You must let go to build a bridge."

Tears flowed freely down Dakota's face and plopped to the weathered wood.

Chance clutched the hammer with one hand atop hers and reached up once more to wipe away her tears, just as his own tears began to flow.

Tentatively, she reached up to his scarred cheek--the scars she'd caused--and caressed his face. "I love you."

"And I love you." He smiled, and together they landed another blow to the nail.

> *"There's a bridge that beckons you and me,*
> *Made from rusty nails and an old rugged tree.*
> *A bridge to cross from death unto life,*
> *Where Jesus died for you and me."*

The song ended just as they delivered the last strike to the nail.

The moment profound and sacred, everyone bowed their heads as the pastor delivered a final prayer. Other than his words, the only sounds were the gentle breeze rippling through the leaves of nearby trees and an occasional sniffle.

Just moments later, Chance and Dakota faced these people who had chosen to spend this day with them, and were introduced as Mr. and Mrs. Chance Johnson.

The party commenced moments later up at the farmhouse. Once the cake had been cut, with Daisy taking her bite before schedule, the band from Morganville kicked off the music with *Sweet Home Alabama*.

Chance swept her into his arms with a handsome grin. "Think you can two-step in a wedding dress?"

Dakota smiled back, her heart full. "I dare you or anybody else to stop me."

He leaned his head back and laughed, before twirling her around the floor of the barn. "That's my Irish girl.

About the Author

Although a native daughter of Texas, Cathy currently resides in the lovely Sangre de Cristo mountains of northern New Mexico with her husband of over thirty years. She loves to spend time with her family, romp around in the great outdoors, and weave heart-stirring stories about God's life-changing grace.

In addition to penning the Miller's Creek novels, Cathy also has written devotional articles for The Upper Room magazine and collaborated with other authors on two devotional books. Her website blog includes devotional posts and interviews with everyday heroes.

To learn more about Cathy and her books, visit her website at www.CatBryant.com. Besides her website, Cathy also loves to connect with readers in the following places.

 Cathy.Bryant.Author

 Cathy_Bryant

 cathyjbryant

Dear reader friends,

I hope you enjoyed Chance and Dakota's story as much as I did. As is usually the case, this story was birthed through my own spiritual journey. After going through a particularly difficult time, I struggled with forgiving others the way Christ commands.

I searched the scriptures, hoping for an exception, but found none. As I researched the topic of forgiveness for the story, I especially became convicted by the fact that when I pray the Lord's prayer, I'm asking God to forgive me the same way I forgive others. Perish the thought! That's all it took for me relinquish the death grip I had on my current resentment and bitterness.

I wish I could say that I no longer struggle with forgiving, but I'm human. The enemy knows the chinks in my armor and directs his fiery darts likewise. Especially during the writing of this book, Satan seemed determined to trip me up with an unforgiving spirit.

Forgiveness is one of the most difficult things we'll ever be called to do, because it's so personal and often so devastating. But the truth is that we imprison ourselves and not our offender when we choose not to forgive.

C. S. Lewis put forgiveness in perspective when he said: "To be a Christian means to excuse the inexcusable because God has forgiven the inexcusable in you."

We live because He forgives,
Cathy

BOOK CLUB DISCUSSION QUESTIONS

1. Forgiveness seems to be one of the least understood concepts in Christianity, yet it is central to our faith. Why do you think forgiveness is such a difficult concept to grasp?

2. Why do we sometimes feel we've forgiven someone, only to come face-to-face with the truth that we haven't?

3. What are some ways in which Chance and Dakota are holding on to unforgiveness in the first part of the story?

4. What are some of the other concepts tied closely to forgiveness? How are they related, and why are they important?

5. What are some of your favorite scriptures concerning forgiveness? Least favorite? Why?

6. What analogy can you think of for the idea of letting it go? What does it say about our relationship with God when we're able to let an offense go?

7. How do we know when we've truly forgiven someone? What brought Chance and Dakota to the place of forgiveness?

8. What steps are necessary to forgive someone? Why is it so difficult to actually do? What sin is at the root of an unforgiving spirit?

Coming Next in the Miller's Creek Novels

Crossroads

A bitter prodigal denies God's existence until faced with her own mortality. Can a struggling veteran, with his own demons to overcome, help her find the road back home?

Other Miller's Creek Novels
Available in Print and Digital Format at Amazon.com

Texas Roads

A hurting seeker longs for home in a back roads country town until malicious rumors propel her down a road she never expected to travel.

A Path Less Traveled

A widow with shaken faith is determined to blaze a trail for herself and her traumatized son, but must regain her faith to take a path less traveled.

The Way of Grace

Can a fallen perfectionist--especially in the face of life-altering circumstances--bestow on others the grace God has lavished on her?

Pilgrimage of Promise

A dusty stack of unopened love letters forces a betrayed woman to revisit a part of her past she'd rather leave buried—especially when confronted with her husband's impending death.

CPSIA information can be obtained at www.ICGtesting.com
Printed in the USA
LVOW06s1611161015
458582LV00001B/214/P